DATE DUE 6/02

JUL 24 02			
AUG 2 02			
OCT 7 02			
OCT 25 02			
NOV 26 02			
11/08/04			
JUL 27 05			
MAR 10 06 L M			
GAYLORD			PRINTED IN U.S.A.

THE JERUSALEM SCROLLS

BODIE AND BROCK THOENE

*J*THE
ERUSALEM
SCROLLS

THE ZION LEGACY

Book IV

WHEELER
PUBLISHING, INC.
ROCKLAND, MA

★ AN AMERICAN COMPANY ★

Published in large print by arrangement with Viking, a member of
Penguin Putnam Inc., in the United States and Canada.

Wheeler Large Print Book Series.

Set in 16 pt Plantin.

Map illustration by James Sinclair
   Excerpts from *The Poems by Propertius*, translated by W. G. Shepherd
(Penguin Classics, 1985). Copyright © W. G. Shepherd, 1985. Reprinted by
permission of Penguin Books Ltd.
   Excerpts from *The Holy Bible, New International Version*. Copyright ©
1973, 1978, 1984 by International Bible Society. Used by permission of
Zondervan Publishing House. All rights reserved.
   Excerpts from *Complete Jewish Bible*, translated by David H. Stern.
Copyright © 1998 by David H. Stern. Used by permission of Jewish New
Testament Publications, Inc., Clarksville, Maryland.

Library of Congress Cataloging-in-Publication Data

Thoene, Bodie, 1951-
   The Jerusalem scrolls / Bodie and Brock Thoene.
      p. (large print) cm.(Wheeler large print book series)
   ISBN 1-58724-229-X (hardcover)
   1. Israel-Arab War, 1948–1949—Fiction. 2. Jews—Palestine—Fiction.
3. Scrolls—Fiction. 4. Large type books. I. Thoene, Brock, 1952- II. Title.
III. Series

[PS3570.H46 J494   2002]
813'.54—dc21
                                                                  2002024977
                                                                          CIP

*With love and joy we dedicate this story
to our dear son, Jake,
our beloved daughter, Wendi,
and to their tribe of
precious sons.*

Isaiah 54:13 and Isaiah 55:10–13

ACKNOWLEDGMENTS

The authors wish to gratefully acknowledge the invaluable insights provided by the *Complete Jewish Bible* and the *Jewish New Testament Commentary*, both by David H. Stern (Jewish New Testament Publications, Inc., Clarksville, MD, 1998).

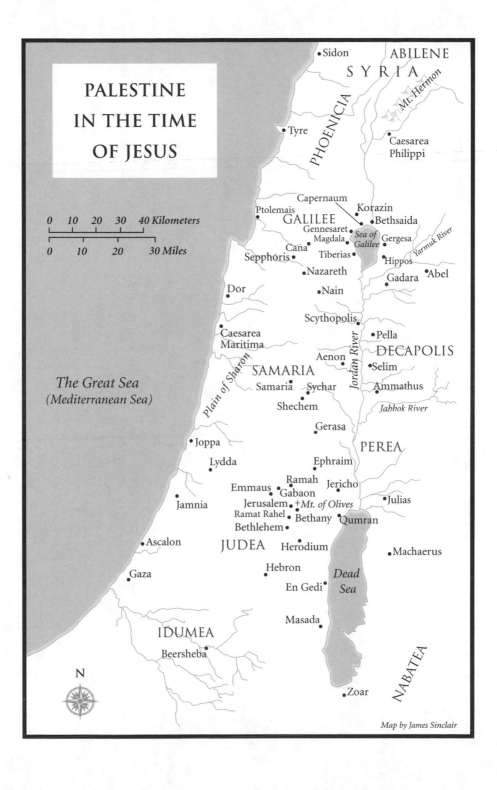

PALESTINE
IN THE TIME
OF JESUS

0   10   20   30   40 Kilometers

0   10   20   30 Miles

The Great Sea
(Mediterranean Sea)

Sidon

ABILENE

SYRIA

Mt. Hermon

PHOENICIA

Tyre

Caesarea
Philippi

Capernaum

Korazin

Ptolemais

GALILEE

Bethsaida

Gennesaret

Sea of
Galilee

Gergesa

Yarmuk River

Cana

Magdala

Sepphoris

Tiberias

Hippos

Nazareth

Gadara

Abel

Dor

Nain

Scythopolis

Caesarea
Maritima

Pella

DECAPOLIS

Jordan River

Aenon

Selim

Plain of Sharon

SAMARIA

Samaria

Sychar

Ammathus

Shechem

Jabbok River

Gerasa

Joppa

PEREA

Lydda

Ephraim

Emmaus

Ramah

Jericho

Gabaon

Jamnia

Jerusalem

Julias

Ramat Rahel

+Mt. of Olives

Bethany

Bethlehem

Qumran

Ascalon

JUDEA

Herodium

Machaerus

Gaza

Hebron

Dead
Sea

En Gedi

IDUMEA

Masada

Beersheba

NABATEA

N

Zoar

Map by James Sinclair

PROLOGUE

Friday, May 28, 1948

The night sky glowed orange by the light of the flames that consumed the Great Hurva Synagogue.

It was over.

The food and ammunition carried from Tel Aviv to the besieged Jews of Jerusalem arrived too late. The secret mountain path, bustling with men and mules, might save the New City, but not those within the Old City's walls.

After months of privation the Jewish district of the Old City had fallen. One thousand three hundred Jewish civilians passed through Zion Gate for the last time. The Jewish defenders, reduced to a meager handful, were now prisoners of war on their way to internment in Amman, Jordan.

The grief of Jewish defeat was palpable. As the flames licked the sky some spoke of the burning of the Warsaw Ghetto. Others remembered the furnaces of Auschwitz. Still others whispered of the destruction of Jerusalem, when the Roman general Titus led the Jewish populace away in chains and torched the temple and the city.

Where was God in all of this? they questioned. Would Messiah ever come?

But for the troops of Jordan's Arab Legion

and the mercenary soldiers of the Islamic Jihad who had come from across the Muslim world to fight for the Holy City, this was a night of great celebration.

Jewish homes, shops, and places of worship were looted. Sacred Hebrew scrolls carried from the synagogue libraries lay heaped in the streets. The consecrated texts fueled the bonfires of the jubilant Muslim Holy Strugglers. Torches lit from these pyres were tossed into Jewish structures until, at last, the entire Quarter was ablaze.

Three thousand years of Jewish presence in the shadow of the Temple Mount had come to an end.

Today the vows of the Muslim leadership and Muhammed Said Haj Amin el-Husseini, Grand Mufti of Jerusalem, were partially fulfilled. The Mufti had promised his followers that for the sake of Allah and his prophet the Muslim world would finish what Hitler began. The Jews who survived the Holocaust would be driven forever from Jerusalem and drowned in the sea.

Rachel Sachar, twenty-two-year-old wife of Moshe Sachar, Haganah commander of the Jewish Old City defense, crouched on the stone steps of the New City Russian compound hospital. She stared numbly at the distant conflagration. The pungent smoke masked the smell of death that had permeated the city for days. The eerie glow reflected in her blue eyes and bleached all color from her complexion. Rachel's ten-year-old brother,

Yacov, hugged the neck of his mongrel dog, Shaul, and huddled miserably beside her. Their grandfather, Rabbi Schlomo Lebowitz, lay dead in the compound's crowded morgue.

"Where will we go?" Yacov wiped his tears with the back of his grimy hand and stroked the dog's muzzle.

Rachel did not reply for a time. How could she? The answer had always been, "Next year in Jerusalem!"

From her childhood in Warsaw her prayers had always ended with Jerusalem.

When the Nazis came in 1939, the Jewish cry had been for Jerusalem.

When the enemy had gassed Mama, Papa, and slaughtered all her brothers but Yacov, her heart had longed for Jerusalem.

When she was taken to the camp brothel and used for the pleasure of the SS officers, she had dreamed of Jerusalem. Of grandfather. Of the redemption of a homeland where Jewish suffering would end!

Jerusalem meant life to her! A dream of freedom!

Tonight the destruction of the Jewish Quarter seemed to end their hope. Where would they go? How could she answer that question?

Moshe was gone. In the last moments before surrender he had vanished at Grandfather's command into the secret tunnels beneath the Old City. Would she ever see him again?

She knew why Moshe had not taken her with him. She was pregnant, and they had an

3

adopted baby girl safely cared for in Tel Aviv. Rachel must be a mother first, a wife second. And then there was Yacov. All these depended on her, needed her alive. She could not leave them to follow Moshe no matter how much she longed to be with him.

But now that their home was in ashes, where would they go? What would they do? She could not say. She could not even answer whether the infant state of Israel would survive.

"Rachel?" Yacov rested his cheek wearily on the ruff of the dog's neck. "What will we do now?"

She swallowed hard, her tongue swollen with days of unquenched thirst. It had begun with such hope and promise. And now to end like this! "We will live. For the sake of The Name," she replied.

Yacov rambled. "Daoud says we are building a road through the wilderness all the way from Tel Aviv." The boy referred to his Arab friend from the Old City souks who had helped to find the ancient Roman highway through the Judean wilderness. "Daoud says we will make a road and bring food for the Jews of the New City to survive. But what good is it since the Legion has destroyed the Old City? Look! The synagogues are burning. The Torah scrolls! There is no one of us left to bear witness, Rachel. Grandfather always said as long as Israel had two witnesses left to pray beside the stones of Solomon's Temple then the Shekinah would descend and hear the prayers of the Jews. Like Jeremiah and Baruch after the first destruction, Grandfather said. God's glory would still come to Zion on *Shabbat* for the sake of the remnant. This is why the Muslims fear Jewish presence within the Old City so near the Temple Mount...why they drove us out and will not let us back. Not ever! No witnesses left for Israel! Rachel? Will God forget us then? The Legion drove everyone out."

Her head throbbed. She lifted her chin and narrowed her eyes in defiance as she thought of Moshe and Alfie somewhere beneath the Temple Mount. "Not everyone."

■ ■ ■ ■

The secret passage from the Eliyahu Hanavi Synagogue led Moshe Sachar and Alfie Halder beneath the Temple Mount.

What was this place? From childhood Moshe had heard the legend that told of the tunnel used by the high priest. Through this passage the *Gadol Hacohen* had entered Solomon's Temple.

No myth, this forgotten route wound away from sunlight and life into a long-forgotten world.

Darkness was absolute, pressing ponderously on the two men's senses. *Like swimming through black ink,* Moshe thought as they inched forward.

The hush of their subterranean path was profound. They could not hear the thousands of

Islamic Jihad voices raised in joyous triumph over the surrender of the Jewish defenders inside Old City Jerusalem.

As explosives tore the Jewish Quarter of Jerusalem apart, Muslims offered prayers at the Dome of the Rock to thank Allah. Leaders of the Arab nations received the news: "Not one living Jew remains within the walls of Jerusalem!"

Bonfires consumed Jewish scrolls and synagogue walls. Yeshiva schools and Jewish homes collapsed.

But the conquerors could not know two defenders of the Jewish Quarter remained behind. The Jihad could not imagine the oldest and most sacred Jewish texts safely hidden beneath the earth of the Holy City. These unharmed documents stood as mute witness to Israel's continuous presence in Jerusalem for three millennia.

The narrow way Moshe and Alfie traveled had been hewn thousands of years before by Jewish stonecutters instructed by the High Priest of Israel according to the blueprint God had given to King Solomon. The foundation stones beneath the earth endured intact, an eternal testimony of the existence of Solomon's Temple.

Those whose hatred now consumed and destroyed the outward evidence of Jewish life in Jerusalem could never eradicate the archaeological evidence of Israel's claim to Jerusalem. To destroy this proof, the Muslim army would first have to tear down the mosques built on the foundations of Solomon's Temple.

Moshe was confident that the Arab nations feared the truth of history, that they secretly trembled at what lay beneath the paving stones of their plaza. The God of Israel had not forgotten His promises to Abraham, Isaac, and Jacob. The Lord had spoken through the prophets and in the psalms of Israel's shepherd-king, David. The Hosts of Heaven remembered the great temple of Solomon, and one day the Messiah would claim this holy site for His throne.

So it is written....

But for the present Israel's historic right to exist in this violent land seemed forgotten by all nations. Moshe knew that, in the constricted streets of the Old City, evil rejoiced in its victory over the Jews. Arab leaders crowed to the world that Islam would finish what Hitler began. Jews would be driven from Jerusalem and the land of Eretz-Israel forever. There would be no Jewish homeland! The call for Jihad would be renewed! The annihilation of Jews would be accomplished!

Meanwhile the people of Israel would grieve once more. "How long will it be, O Lord, before we can again pray at the Western Wall?"

Moshe, the remnant of Israel who stayed behind, heard merely the shuffle of his own feet, his breath, and the pounding of his heart as they moved cautiously downward.

One raised finger fit into the guiding slot on the roof of the tunnel. Alfie Halder clung to Moshe's belt like a blind man holding the

7

tail of a horse moving down a dangerous slope.

Unlike the first path through which Rabbi Lubetkin had led Moshe to the cavernous underground library almost two weeks ago, this passage followed a more direct route. Sometimes curving, sometimes straight, the stone beneath their feet was worn smooth. Moshe sensed, by changes in temperature, that they were passing many side tunnels and chambers. Would the hour ever come when these secret rooms might be explored?

For the moment Moshe followed the instruction of the old rabbi. "Raise one finger, fit it into the groove. This will guide you along the one path you must take to the chamber of scrolls. Take no other way, or you will surely find death."

Alfie did not speak as they progressed inch by inch through the blackness. He did not ask Moshe where they were going or why.

Rabbi Lubetkin had told Moshe, "Alfie is one of the Thirty-six Righteous. For the sake of such innocent hearts, the judgment of the Lord upon the earth is held back."

Strange how the old man's words replayed in Moshe's mind. He found the company of Alfie a comfort. Together they would be guardians of this holy place. If the tunnel was discovered by the Arabs, Moshe would have to seal the entrance to the chamber. Perhaps their task beneath the earth would stretch into a lifetime. Years without sunlight. Without news of the outside world.

8

Alfie, childlike in his acceptance, was undaunted. The thought of long life beneath the ground did not trouble him. Time was an eternal present to him.

A useful gift in a world without day or night.

Moshe also considered that they might die protecting the incomparable treasure of Jewish thought and history. It was good to face such a possibility with a companion who was utterly unafraid of death. How often had he seen the large-framed Alfie fearlessly heft a wounded man and carry him through a fusillade of hostile fire? "He goes out as if Arab bullets are raindrops," Ehud Schiff had exclaimed from the barricades.

In the front lines of the Old City siege, Moshe had not expected Alfie to survive for long. But he had walked through the fire unharmed, as though someone guided his steps. Could it be, Moshe wondered, that this one, who had the mind of a child in the body of a man, somehow heard the whisper of God's voice?

At last Alfie spoke. "Almost home."

An instant later the guiding groove on the ceiling came to an abrupt end against a wall. Moshe extended his hand and slid it down the stone face until, waist high, he found the arch of a low entrance.

"From here we kneel to pass through," he instructed Alfie.

"Like pilgrims." Alfie dropped down.

This entrance into the library was not the

same as the door Grandfather had showed Moshe earlier, yet the dimensions were the same.

Moshe prayed the *Shema*. "Hear O Israel, the Lord our God is one Lord..."

Alfie stammered through the creed he had learned as a boy in Sunday school in Germany, "I believe in one God, the Father, the Almighty, Maker of heaven and earth, of all that is seen and unseen...."

So much was yet unseen and unknown! Yet the totality of truth and knowledge confirmed the testimony revealed through the Scriptures.

Alfie murmured, "They have been waiting a long time."

A chill coursed through Moshe. He did not ask who had been waiting. Ducking his head, he crept forward on his knees through the cramped tunnel. The top of his head brushed the roof.

He stopped, seemingly at a dead end. Sliding his finger over the cool facade, he found the indentation in the stone. He pushed inward as Grandfather had instructed.

With a *whoosh* the hard wall groaned and yielded. Unhurriedly it slid away. Moshe squeezed his eyes shut.

For an instant, in the rush of wind, he thought he heard faint music, the bells of a carillon echoing from a distant place.

Could it be?

They entered. Alfie sighed with relief, then whistled softly.

Shoulder to shoulder, they remained crouched on the paving stones of the floor. Stillness embraced them.

Moshe sensed space opening above them.

The soft scent of lavender hung in the air, like a summer garden on a moonless night.

"Look! So many! *Sehr schön!*" Alfie exulted. "Just like Mama showed me on the mountain when I was a kid!"

Aware they were in a confined chamber, Moshe opened his eyes. The foyer was perfectly round. The door behind them slid shut. Instinctively Moshe glanced up and drew his breath in sharply as he realized he could see familiar pinpoints of light across the arched dome.

Luminescent stars, re-created with painstaking accuracy, cast a glow across the pavement of the entry.

Moshe knew he must have passed this antechamber on one of his earlier visits. But why had he not seen the stars? It came to him that he had not dared to open his eyes until the old man had lit the lantern and given him permission to survey the space. The artificial glare of the lamp had overwhelmed the skyscape just as true daylight overpowers the splendors of night.

Moshe sat back on his heels and gazed upward at the heavens as he had done as a child sitting out on the roof of his Jerusalem home. And what he saw left him breathless.

This was a map of Jerusalem's sky!

Early summer. Accurate in every detail.

There was Polaris, the North Star, fixed

like a jewel in the handle of the Little Dipper. The star by which travelers found their way. And so even here, far beneath the ground, Moshe knew what compass direction he faced.

Set within myriad lesser lights were spirals of galaxies, faint pastel hues of nebulas, open clusters of stars and double stars balanced in perfect orbit with one another. The summer triangle of Deneb, Altair, and Vega were the brightest gems in the east. Antares beamed from the south. Regulus marked the paw of Leo the Lion in the west. Directly overhead was Arcturus.

Woven into this miracle of artificial night were Hebrew letters proclaiming, "In the beginning God created the heavens and the earth." Seventy-two names of God were inscribed on the sky with a fine thread of gold connecting one star to the next.

Adonai... Elohim... El Shaddai... YHWH... King of Kings... Lord of Lords... Wonderful... Counselor... Savior...

The glory of the heavens and their message provided light enough for Moshe and Alfie to see by.

A round stone altar, in the center of the room, was crowned with a seven-branched candlestick and a clay jar used for storing wine.

"We'll need a lamp." Moshe rose to his feet.

"I'm not afraid of the dark," Alfie replied in a good-natured tone.

Beside the entrance Moshe found a niche containing an antique, English-made army lantern and a box of ordinary strike-anywhere kitchen matches.

"Shield your eyes," Moshe warned, striking the match.

The hiss of the flame and the glare of the lantern was intrusive, out of place. Stars vanished. The walls and ceiling now appeared to be unadorned stone.

Moshe carried the lamp to the altar. There, propped against the wine jug, was an envelope with his name written in neat Hebrew letters: a sheaf of instructions from Grandfather.

FOR MY SON, MOSHE SACHAR.
THE ORDER OF STUDY.
INVENTORY OF SUPPLIES.
FOOD FOR YOUR JOURNEY.

Beneath that was a brief notation:

SCROLL CHOSEN FOR YOUR FIRST STUDY

So the old rabbi had thought of everything. Even reading material.

Pressed into a lead seal tied around the neck of the wine jug were the Latin letters spelling MARCUS AND MIRYAM.

The man's name was Roman. The woman's, Jewish.

Deep red pottery was from the second half of the first century. Surprising.

"From Rabbi Lubetkin?" Alfie asked.

Moshe, certain somehow that the old man

13

had died, nodded and tucked the bulky envelope into his shirt pocket. Passing the lantern to Alfie, he hefted the jar, cradling it in the crook of his arm. It was surprisingly light.

A west-facing doorway led to a balcony overlooking the huge main hall of the library. Alfie followed Moshe to the banister where the two men stared down in awe at the true treasure hidden in Jerusalem's heart.

All around them were shelves containing thousands of scrolls. In the center of the cavernous space were three study tables where Moshe and Grandfather sat during their first visits. From where they stood Moshe counted twelve doors from the main chamber leading into other rooms.

Letters of three languages—Hebrew, Greek, and Latin—ringed the parapet.

WHAT WAS—WHAT IS—WHAT WILL BE

"We will be here a long time." Alfie lifted his chin and scanned the vast dome of the main hall. "Maybe forever."

For a time Moshe gazed solemnly at the study tables. "Maybe." He thought of Rachel. Of the child she carried within her. Of Tikvah, their baby girl in Tel Aviv.

Forever was a long time.

In quiet contemplation they descended the steps and placed the lamp and the jar on the scarred wood of the center table.

Alfie lit a taper and explored the chamber. He peered into every alcove and opened doors as Moshe reviewed Grandfather's instructions.

It was clear the old man had been preparing for the worst for years.

First an inventory listed categories of scrolls and documents and the order in which they should be read.

Long pages of supplies followed. Army K rations. Canned peaches. Bottles of condensed lime juice. Thousands of tins of matzo bread. Hundreds of jars of jam. Tea for a lifetime. And on and on. Food enough to last two men for many years.

Attached to these lists with a hairpin were directions to a water closet, a cistern for bathing, and two cells for sleeping. Further information was provided about blankets, clothing, a cistern for drinking water, and a chest containing candles, lantern wicks, and lamp oil.

These were the practical matters dealing with long-term survival. After that came twenty-six pages written in Hebrew code headed by these words: "*Yisrael, kudsha berikh hu veoraita had hu*... Israel, God, and Torah are one."

This was followed by six words:

SEKEL—Understanding
TORAH—The Word
KEVER—grave
HAYYIM—life
KETER—crown
SOD—secrets

Moshe hastily thumbed through the old rabbi's letter. At first glance the message made no sense. Grandfather had conveyed perhaps the most important facts in a cryptic code of his own creation. The message would take days, possibly weeks, to unravel.

Rabbi Lubetkin had assumed Moshe could and would break the cipher. The old man's first command, however, was for Moshe to read the scroll of Marcus and Miryam.

Moshe examined the jar. Alfie plopped down and grinned at him from across the table.

"We have nothing but time." Moshe rapped his knuckles on the clay that encased the scroll.

Alfie jerked his thumb toward a wood-paneled door. "At least, you know... There's lots to eat. Behind that wall. I found it through the little door. Rooms and rooms of stuff. One after the other."

How long had it been since Alfie had tasted food? Moshe wondered.

"Hungry?"

"The first room. Peaches in glass jars. Shelves and shelves of peaches. A room stacked with biscuit tins. Two whole rooms of army rations like we had sometimes in the DP camp. Lots of other stuff."

Moshe's stomach felt as though his backbone were trying to break through. "I fancy some peaches."

"Sure." Beaming, Alfie produced two quart-sized Ball canning jars from behind his back.

"Rabbi Lubetkin...he thought of everything. Except forks."

It did not matter. Savoring every bite, they plucked the peach halves out with their fingers and broke the fast imposed on them by weeks of the siege. Finally they drank deeply of the nectar.

It was a meager meal after so many days of hunger and yet Moshe felt full.

Alfie patted his stomach and stretched. "I found a toilet. Just a hole in the floor, but that's what it is all right. I heard water running down below. And there are two little rooms...not much bigger than closets...with cots in there. Places to sleep. Behind the room of biscuit tins. You care which one is mine? I ain't slept in a long time."

It occurred to Moshe that he had never seen Alfie Halder sleep. Or eat. Or drink. Until now.

The battle for Old City Jerusalem had been lost. Only now would Alfie allow himself the luxury of food and rest.

"No one has followed us," Moshe said.

"They won't find the way. Not now, anyway."

Did Alfie mean they were safe for a day? A week? Ten years? Long enough to sleep soundly anyway.

"Go on then." Moshe reached for the scroll. "I'll be along later. We'll rest first, then get our bearings. There is a world to explore beneath the Temple Mount."

Alfie rose, stood at attention, and saluted. Moshe returned the gesture.

Alfie retrieved his candle and hesitated. "There are stars in the sky. Everywhere. Even in the room with peaches, you know."

Moshe nodded, wondering how soon they would regret the absence of the real sky. Sunrise. Moonrise. The heavens spinning in a measured arc above the earth. Involuntarily the image of Rachel came to mind. The night they lay in one another's arms and gazed out the window at a patch of star-frosted heaven. The moon had risen, and her skin had glowed in its light.

Did Alfie see the pain in Moshe's eyes?

With an uneasy shrug Alfie excused himself. Moshe turned his attention to his first assignment.

The canister was sealed with wax. Moshe opened it with a penknife and carefully removed the tightly rolled scroll. Locked within an airtight environment for centuries, the document appeared in perfect condition. Tied with a purple thread, the papyrus was fresh and supple. The lettering was in bold Latin script, with ink as vivid as though it had been written yesterday.

Two names were inscribed along the exterior edge of the papyrus:

MIRYAM M.
MARCUS LONGINUS
PENETRALIA MENTIS...*heart of hearts*...

Moshe was acutely aware these were not merely names, but lives.

18

A woman and a man.

Long since dust, they remained alive through this fragile scrap of paper and ink. The Latin inscription meant literally that their innermost thoughts were recorded in the document. This was their story, the record of their existence and, perhaps, of Jerusalem as it had been.

Why had the old rabbi chosen this story as a place of beginning?

Beneath the names were these words: *"Ad perpetuam rei memorium..."*

For perpetual remembrance.

Moshe untied the thread and rolled back the first sheaf. The smell of ink was distinct. A thumbprint of the scribe marked the top of the page.

Above him and all around him, the vaulted chamber was infused with a sound like waves gently lapping the shore....

ALEF

While her lover slept to the gentle rhythm of the waves, Miryam left the bedchamber and emerged onto the balcony that overlooked the Sea of Galilee.

The half-moon illuminated a highway of liquid silver on the water, urging her to come.

Stripping off her clothes, she descended the steps and waded in until she was waist deep.

Nervously brushing the surface with her fingertips, she hesitated.

A few steps forward and the slope of the shoreline would drop away into the gaping depths.

She could swim toward the moon.

Somewhere in the center of light, Mother would meet her.

Embrace her.

Comfort her.

They would drift away together into peace, eternal sleep, and everything would be finished.

Why not?

She had heard the voices calling her a thousand times. Each night the desire to leave was stronger than the last. Still she did not obey.

Was it Marcus who kept her so tenuously moored to life? There was no one else, nothing of consequence, to keep her from taking her life as her own mother had done so many years before.

Yet Marcus meant no more to Miryam than her other lovers. He was only a diversion from the desperate hollowness of her existence. An opiate to dull the pain of living.

Why then did she stand rooted there, digging her toes into the sand? Why cling to life when consciousness brought a burden of dread and loneliness?

Yet it was not love of living that held her back, but fear of what dying might bring. Suppose the sleep she longed for was only a door into another dream? Suppose that dream was more horrifying than this existence?

Unlike her brother and sister, she could not believe in a personal God. The course of all life, she had decided, simply followed a series of accidental twists and turns, arriving, inevitably, at the open mouth of the grave. Better to enjoy the journey than be burdened by the laws of an empty religion.

Yet somewhere along the path of pleasure she had lost her way. There was no lamp to light her steps. No absolute truth. No life but what the moment offered her. She had truly loved a man only once in her life and even now dreamed of what she might do to possess him once again.

After an hour on the brink, the stars began to fade and with them the voices she had heard calling her name through the long night. Morning was near. Returning to bed, she was grateful to have Marcus close.

Anticipation of his passion and pleasure quieted the fears that haunted her.

Pulling on a yellow linen shift to cover her slender body, she braided her thick, dark hair.

The air was perfectly still. Through the open door she saw the surface of the lake, a mirror reflecting the sky and hills of Galilee. A thin lustrous line on the far shore separated heaven from earth.

The cold winds of winter were past; so too were the rains. Spring was more than a promise. It was a reality. The fields northward looked no different than they had one day earlier: verdant stands of wheat still months from harvest. Nor did the leaves appearing on the grapevines along the terraced lower slopes show any visible change.

But on the barren hills and rocky ledges beyond the reach of cultivation acres of red anemones and blue lupines blended with thousands of golden flowers to perfume every breath. At the first touch of sunlight they splashed the hills with vibrant color. Yet Miryam found no joy in the change of seasons.

It was the twentieth day of the month of Ayyar in the fifteenth year of the emperor Tiberius. What had been the kingdom of Israel was now carved up into diminutive provinces of the glorious Roman empire.

Herod Antipas, son of Herod the Great, governed Galilee as Rome's puppet. His brother Philip ruled Trachonitus east of the Jordan River.

The new Roman governor, Pontius Pilate, controlled Samaria, Judea, and Jerusalem. The Jewish high priest, Caiaphas, had been appointed and remained in power by the will of Caesar.

An uneasy peace existed between the Jews and their Roman overlords.

But at Miryam's lakeside villa, Rome and Israel united in the perfect harmony of a secret pact.

Marcus Longinus, a Roman citizen and centurion, was stationed at Tiberias, the Galilean capital of Herod Antipas. Living only four and a half miles from Magdala, Marcus was Miryam's frequent guest.

Miryam was the wealthy, twenty-six-year-old widow of old Yosef ben Reu.

Her centurion lover was discreet, arriving after dark and leaving before light. After all, Miryam's husband had died only four months earlier. But rumor of the liaison was whispered in every village in Galilee.

Miryam knelt at Marcus' head and studied his features. It was true he was merely one in a long line of suitors. So what was it she saw in him? At thirty, he was the battle-hardened *Primus Pilus* of the First Cohort. Senior officer of five hundred mercenaries in the pay of Rome, he was known to his men as *First Javelin*.

Stocky, muscled, and strong as a bull's, his sun-bronzed body was scarred from a dozen old wounds. The son of a British slave and a Roman officer of the equestrian order, he was not handsome. His nose had been broken. His clean-shaven cheeks were pocked. Russet hair was short and just beginning to show a touch of gray. Dark, brooding eyes and a hot temper betrayed the ancestry of conquered Britannia.

Marcus often quoted the poetry of Propertius, which Miryam accused him of memorizing for the sake of seducing women. He did not deny it. And she did not resist it. Marcus was as passionate and hungry for Miryam as her aged husband had been cold and without appetite throughout their loveless marriage.

Miryam stroked Marcus' brow lightly with her fingertips and whispered his name.

He exhaled, opened his eyes, then grasped her wrist, pulling her down beside him.

"Where were you?"

"Swimming."

"You're chilled."

"Warm me then."

He kissed her.

" '*He watches, a vigilant guard, and once you're captured, He never lets you lift your eyes from the ground...*' "

"Poetry again?" she teased.

"Don't interrupt. Where was I?"

"I am captured."

"Ah yes...something, something... *'But then, if you sin, he is a placable god, Provided only he sees your prayers are heartfelt...'* "

She struggled weakly. "Let me up, I pray."

"Why are you dressed?" He kissed her drowsily and then more fiercely as he tugged at her shift. "Sacrilege to cover such a shank of lamb as this in a sheet of yellow mustard. Take it off."

She pulled away from him and leapt to her feet. "Not now."

"I'm ready for battle or for breakfast." He grinned and sat up. "It's up to you. Either will do."

"I will neither serve you...nor serve under you...this morning." She inclined her head toward the east. "It is morning, you see. And we have a bargain about you being here in daylight."

"Tonight then." He shrugged and reached for his tunic.

"Strength and courage, Marcus," she mocked. "I'll be in Cana three days."

"Then I'll have you now or die." He lunged and grasped her ankle, toppling her onto the pallet.

"The servants! They'll see." She laughed as he pinned her shoulders and straddled her.

His eyes hardened with desire as he quoted Propertius gruffly:

> "'Stern old men may denounce
> those carousals of yours:
> Only let us, my life, wear out our
> purposed way.
> This is the spot where you, skilled
> flute, shall sound...'"

"Is it music you want from me?" she said softly, suddenly wanting him. "Then you'll have a song for breakfast."

"Miryam. Miryam. Should I be ashamed to live content with one girl?"

"And a Jewish girl at that. What would Sejanus say if he knew?"

He blinked down at her as the stern face of Caesar's most trusted advisor, commander of the Praetorian Guard, came to mind. It was well known that Sejanus detested Hebrews.

Marcus smiled. "I would tell him you are fair to all the gods. You worship each equally. You worship nothing."

"I worship only one," Miryam corrected. "You are the god of my idolatry, Marcus Longinus. My morning sun."

"May I rise to your expectations," he whispered as he pressed his lips against hers.

"Let them see," she said fiercely. "If this is guilt, the guilty party is love."

■ ■ ■ ■

Marcus stayed late.

Morning had already drenched the hills when the centurion and his young servant slipped from the villa through the orchard gate.

Fishermen sorted their catch on the beach. Farmers and merchants sold their wares in the market square. It was hopeless to imagine that the people of the Magdala would not notice a Roman officer and his servant riding along the road from Miryam's estate.

Miryam closed the curtains, then lay in bed and told herself it did not matter. Her reputation had already been carved up, chewed, and digested by the town gossips. So what if Marcus was seen? It simply confirmed what everyone already knew.

Miryam's aged nurse, Tavita, shuffled, scowling, into the bedroom.

Her face turned to the wall, Miryam pretended to sleep.

Tavita slammed a heaping tray of hot bread, hummus, figs, boiled eggs, and a pitcher of milk onto a low table. She flung the curtain open, flooding the room with unwelcome glare.

"I have a headache," Miryam said with a sigh.

"She has a headache," the old woman mocked.

"The light hurts my eyes."

"Ah. It would. And your good name."

Miryam rolled over and sat up with a look meant to shush the toothless old woman. "Leave the tray," she instructed coolly.

Her sun-weathered face a mask of contempt, Tavita made no attempt to obey. She filled a cup from the pitcher and in stony silence held it out to Miryam. The aged woman would not be moved.

Exhaling loudly, Miryam sat up and took the cup in resignation. "Get it over with."

Tavita savored her victory. "The little boy, Taddi, delivered the milk to the kitchen this morning. You know the one."

"With the crooked spine?"

"He brought the milk and gave the news straight. No. Not news. With a question. He would not give me the milk jug unless I answered."

"And?"

"Who were those Roman fellows coming out of the orchard gate? he asked. Who was the centurion on the black horse and the red-haired youth who ran along before the horse?"

"What did you tell him?"

"That they had come early to inspect the orchard. That they had bought the next harvest of figs and pomegranates for the soldiers stationed at the palace of Herod Antipas in Tiberias."

"Clever Tavita." Miryam smiled into the cup and took a sip. "Produce from my orchards to be savored by Rome? The nuance of it is food for gossip. The boy's question has already been expanded into a feast by now."

"I won't lie for you again. All these lies on my soul. You lie where you will, lie with whom you will, but I will not lie for you again!" Tavita clucked her tongue. "And your poor husband not even cold in his grave these four months."

"My husband was cold for a lifetime before I married him. And he was cold in our bed for the ten years I was married to him after."

"He's not been dead long enough."

"You're right about that. I would have buried him sooner if he had cooperated. He was dead enough before he stopped breathing. Three childless marriages before he wed me is proof enough of his deadness. Our bed was a tomb."

"A kind old gentleman. Deserving of your honor."

"He, at sixty-nine, took my honor when I was sixteen."

"Barak had it before that."

"Enough! For the holy estate of marriage I endured, I deserve the estate I inherited. I will enjoy my freedom."

"You knew no one in Judea could take you or your brother or your sister in marriage." Tavita cracked the shell of an egg and peeled it.

"The sin of my mother branded us. El'azar and Marta accept loneliness, but I won't live by their rules. You may think that my orchard satisfies the appetite of the centurion, but I'm the one with the appetite to be satisfied."

Tavita raised her hand as if she did not want to hear any more about it. "When old ben Reu made his offer for your hand, your brother counted it as a great opportunity."

"To be rid of me. He knew I was in love with...someone...else." Her words trailed away at the memory of what she had wanted for her life. How differently everything had turned out.

The old woman's face puckered in disapproval as she straightened the bed. "Your brother was wise. You could not have married Barak bar Halfi. His father would not be convinced."

Miryam shrugged and drained the cup. "It doesn't matter. The one I loved has wife and children, debt and care. He is indebted to me. I am his landlord, even though not his mistress. I hope his father is pleased with the outcome of his life. I know I'm better off. From now on I'll only attend weddings that aren't mine."

"Just so." Tavita was pleased by this.

Miryam arched an eyebrow and sprung the news. "So. I am going to Cana."

Tavita drew in her breath sharply. "No! You can't!"

"I can and I will."

"You won't be welcome," Tavita protested.

"I'm invited."

"You're invited because your husband owned their orchard!"

"Now I own it. I'm cousin to the groom by marriage. My late husband would not have me neglect a duty to his kin."

29

"His kin hate you with real pleasure. They cherish the hating of you."

"My mind's set. Wait until they see my gifts."

"I nursed you! Cradled you in my arms! Miryam! It was I who heard your first word, which was NO! And nearly every defiant word after! You always were a stubborn, willful, wicked girl! Going to show poor Barak how well things are with you! Rich and fine and beautiful you! You will flaunt yourself in front of Barak's wife."

"I have business to discuss with him. And my brother and sister will be there," Miryam argued.

"You said yesterday you wouldn't go."

"I've changed my mind. I want to see El'azar and Marta."

"They will not want to see you. After this latest fellow...the centurion. The gossip will be there ahead of you."

"Then I'll catch up with it. I wouldn't miss it. Everyone will be there. A reunion."

"And you're going to see Barak! Miryam! Send the gifts and stay home!"

"An ounce of saffron and one of cinnamon for the bride and groom. Two jugs of the purest olive oil. They won't refuse. I'm going. I'll wear the thing Yosef brought me from Alexandria. Gold embroidered...you know the one...pack it. Tell the Freeman to get everything ready."

■ ■ ■ ■

Sweat beaded Marcus' brow as he rode south-ward along the lakeshore toward Tiberias. Though it was springtime, the heat of approaching noonday was already unpleasant. Looming ahead was another blistering summer's duty eating Judean dust to maintain order among the ungrateful and arrogant Jews.

Yet despite what experience had taught him to expect, on this morning the centurion viewed the immediate future cheerfully. How-ever, he knew he must be careful. Marcus quickly corrected his public visage to one more suitably stern for a senior Roman officer.

He glanced down to see if his young servant had noticed anything amiss. Matching stride for stride with the prancing horse, Carta-mandus ran easily alongside, his gaze fixed on the stony, uneven ground. Though the thirteen-year-old was on the shady side of the stallion, his light auburn locks had dulled into dark ringlets. Staining the boy's gray tunic from his shoulders to his trim waist was a dagger-shaped triangle of perspiration.

Reining up, Marcus turned round in the saddle. There was no one in sight either direction, and Tiberias lay three miles ahead. Extending his right arm to the boy, Marcus ordered, "Come."

Unquestioningly Carta obeyed, and at the slightest tug from the centurion, the slave vaulted into place behind his master. Such kind-ness was infrequent but not unique. Marcus

31

was often humane when in a good mood, but dangerous to cross when foul-tempered.

Urging the horse into resuming his trot, Marcus did not spur the animal to greater effort. Tiberias would appear soon enough and with the city his return to official duties and official headaches.

The centurion's thoughts vaulted back to Miryam. The recently banished smile crept across his face at the memory of the previous night. Three days! How could he tolerate the separation from the excitement of that passion? Unlike any woman Marcus had ever known, Miryam was fierce in her lovemaking, as though intent on eliminating everything else from her thoughts.

There were very few possessions Marcus valued: this horse named Pavor, meaning "terror," and the boy, Carta, for two. His hard-earned rank for another. There was not much else about which he cared, other than the crown of honor and his short sword, or *gladius*. He let no one borrow, abuse, or presume upon any of them.

Miryam was close to joining the brief list of treasures. Marcus was irritated at her absence, then snorted at the paradox. He was annoyed that she, the possession, was taking herself away.

He could suggest a more definite, long-term arrangement. Many of the men took mates from the local populace. The empire encouraged the practice among legionaries, hoping thereby to settle retired soldiers on the frontiers as a kind of permanent reserve force.

Elsewhere in the empire native women enjoyed receiving the attentions of a Roman soldier. Such connections improved a family's livelihood and standing in society. Tribal elders often supported the relationships as a way to curry favor with Rome.

Almost everywhere except in the land of the Jews.

Though Miryam seemed not to care about her reputation, Marcus knew that living with him openly would heap derision on her head.

He could invite her to move to Tiberias, a place pious Jews avoided as corrupt and defiled. She would face no scorn there.

But what if she refused him? Then he would be the one open to humiliation and ridicule. Intolerable!

Another snatch of Propertius came to mind.

> What wonder that a woman
> steers my life,
> And drags a man enslaved
> beneath her laws:
> Why trump up the nasty charge
> of cowardice
> Because I can't smash my yoke
> and burst my chains?

Marcus would never allow himself to be ruled by a woman in that way. Desire, yes. Passion certainly. But never enslavement to a female, or to anything that spoke of weakness or frailty.

He owed allegiance only to a source of

demonstrated power and unchallengeable dominance. Rome ruled the world because it was mighty enough and capable of destroying any and all opposition. The force of the state was therefore the one thing worthy of submission.

Distant white dots representing fellow travelers appeared on the road ahead. Without waiting for instruction, Carta slipped over the haunch of the horse, churned his feet in midair to match the pace of the animal, then dropped lightly to the ground. His legs already moved in perfect jogging rhythm.

Customary scowl firmly in place, Marcus ignored the first pair of rudely dressed, coarse-featured Jews. The centurion pretended not to notice as they turned their heads and spat when his shadow fell across them.

The next man Marcus encountered was more sumptuously dressed in linen robe and turban. The fellow bowed deeply at the centurion's approach and stayed that way. The man's forehead almost touched the earth in his fawning. Marcus knew that one: Levi Mattityahu, the toll collector from Capernaum. Obsequious, as well he should be. A publican who harvested taxes for Rome from his fellow Jews was even more despised than Miryam.

As he anticipated, Marcus' good mood had soured by his arrival at the First Cohort's barracks. Nor did the appearance of Decimus Vara, the cohort's second-highest-ranking centurion, do anything to improve his outlook.

Vara was a brutish, bitter, habitually angry man, who felt slighted that he was not *Primus Pilus* instead of Marcus. Vara made no secret of his imagined superiority. He lost no opportunity to criticize Marcus for any error in judgment. He cultivated political connections to advance his career. He bullied subordinates and civilians while catering to superiors able to assist him. Vara flogged troopers at the slightest provocation, enjoying inflicting pain.

Vara's century hated him for his cruel ways, but even more for the way he kept favorites. He was praised by those who feared him. He despised, abused, and attempted to discredit the rest.

Moreover Vara took his pleasure from those...male or female...too young or too weak to resist him. He had once beaten a slave to death for refusing his sexual demands.

Marcus, revolted by Vara, chose to ignore him. The present issue was not a military emergency. If it were really significant, Flavius Salop, the camp prefect, would be there also. Anything else could wait.

"Cool him out before you water him," Marcus instructed, passing the horse's bridle to Carta. Vara stepped forward. "Not yet," Marcus ordered. "Wine to cool me out before you founder me with news."

■■■■

Marcus made Vara wait while he downed a goblet of Galilean wine. The centurion hid his

35

enjoyment at watching Vara chafe under enforced patience. No virtue came easily to the bald, coarse-featured, thirty-five-year-old officer. Since both were centurions of the same cohort, the two were equal in rank. But as the *Primus Pilus* Marcus was superior to all other centurions. It was a matter of degree, but an important one.

It was also one that could be lost if Vara found the right connection.

Vara had an abysmal record as a professional soldier. Unlike Marcus, who had risen from the ranks, Vara was a political appointee. The Varii clan were equestrian-class, Roman-born, and distant kin to the head of the Praetorian Guard, Lucius Sejanus. Poor relations, Marcus guessed. Otherwise Vara would have received more than a second-rate office in a second-rate post like Judea. According to rumor, the brutal way Vara achieved satisfaction was even too much for Rome. It was the vicious rape of a merchant's daughter that had banished Vara to the provinces.

"Now what is this news which is near to bursting your seams?" Marcus demanded.

"We are summoned to an audience at the palace of Herod Antipas. The meeting is to be at the ninth hour."

Romans, unlike the Hebrews whose days perversely began at nightfall, reckoned the passing of time from noon. The ninth hour was well after sunset and still many hours away.

So far Marcus had heard no cause for excitement. Herod Antipas, the half-Samaritan, half-Idumean, tetrarch of Galilee, held his appointment at the will and pleasure of the emperor. Roman soldiers and mercenaries in the pay of Rome protected Herod's domain against lawlessness, but they were not directly accountable to him. What else did Vara know that he was holding back?

Looking smug, Vara supplied the answer before being asked. "The prefect, Governor Pontius Pilate, will be there as well."

That piece of information explained much. Half of the Roman empire's provinces were under the authority of the Roman Senate. The others, including Judea, were directly administered by the Emperor Tiberius through his prefects. Pilate, as Caesar's chief representative, had already made an official tour of Galilee. This return visit came unannounced and unexpected.

Pilate, whose headquarters in Caesarea Maritima was on the cool and pleasant seacoast, had not been in Judea long. He was, Marcus remembered, also the specific appointee of Vara's patron, Sejanus. More and more of late, Emperor Tiberius reportedly withdrew from the affairs of state, leaving key issues to be handled by his chief advisor. It was whispered that Sejanus was maneuvering toward an even higher role.

Marcus glanced at the crown of bronzed holly leaves hanging over the plank table. He recalled the dramatic events of a decade earlier, when Sejanus had shown himself to be ruthlessly ambitious. Pilate had been on the edges of

Sejanus' crowd even then. The new governor's presence in Caesarea was one reason Marcus did not object to being stationed farther away, in the Galilee.

No wonder Vara acted so pleased with himself. No doubt he expected particular favor at the hands of a governor sharing the same political connections. Such preference might come at the expense of others. Marcus, whose loathing for Vara was returned a hundredfold, would have to be more on his guard.

"All right," Marcus said dismissively. "Alert the other centurions and send Camp Prefect Salop to me." Ever since the departure of Tribune Lentulus, there had been no overall commander of the Galilee, leaving Marcus as the highest military authority in the region.

Vara vaguely waved his arm across his chest. The caricature of a proper salute was insolent, and Marcus' temper blossomed.

He timed his parting remark to catch the bulky Vara in midturn and make the arrogant ass look clumsy. "And Vara," Marcus said coldly, "as long as I am *Primus Pilus, I* assign the duties here. If I ever discover you had advance word of this meeting and did not mention it, you will find your century guarding tar caravans to Asphaltites for the rest of your tour of duty."

"Not I," Vara protested, his bushy eyebrows raised in mocking denial. Then scornfully he said, "Lately the *Primus Pilus* has often been away from Tiberias. Perhaps a message miscarried because of it. But big changes *are* coming," he added. "Depend on it."

Vara bowed his way out of Marcus' quarters, leaving Marcus to ponder the exact nature of the threat.

BET

Past the twin peaks known locally as *The Horns,* Miryam of Magdala's Freeman led a pair of donkeys bearing his mistress and old Tavita. Their route wandered upward, westward into the hills. Behind and now below Miryam's view, the Sea of Galilee took on the shape from which it drew one of its many names: *Chinnereth,* Harp Lake.

Cana was a village of less than one thousand souls ten miles west of Magdala. Named for the abundant reeds growing nearby, Cana nestled in a marshy swale below orchards and terraced slopes. Now sleepy and unimportant, Cana had once been a military headquarters for Herod the Great. His army bivouacked there during his successful war to liberate Judea from the Parthians and deliver it into the hands of the Romans.

Miryam's excitement rose as they approached the walled settlement.

Mouth-watering aromas drifted up from a beef roasting in a pit in preparation for the wedding feast. The joyful music of pipes and drums swirled in the air. Families dressed in their finest crowded the single lane leading to Cana. Miryam knew that somewhere among the throng was Barak bar Halfi, the lone man she had fully loved.

She glanced indifferently around, expecting to see her brother and sister, who had come from Bethany. She recognized many faces. Among them was Barak's father, a Levite who had been a vinedresser for Miryam's brother in Bethany ten years earlier. When Barak and Miryam had been discovered in the barn together one night, the vinedresser had chosen to move to Cana rather than allow his son to marry Miryam. The old man called her a harlot and forbade Barak ever to go to her again. Such was her reputation even then.

But she had never stopped wanting him. And she knew he could not forget those hot summer nights when they lay together beneath the stars. Every other man Miryam had been with was merely a substitute for him.

And now? Barak had grown handsome with black hair, rich brown eyes, and a body of bronze. As a tenant farmer, he had contracted to work the poorest Cana land of Miryam's husband.

Since the death of her husband, *her* fields. She was Barak's landlord. What did he think about that after remaining aloof from her for so many years?

From the day Miryam arrived in Magdala, she had taken every opportunity to travel with old ben Reu into the hill country to examine his rocky farmland and the orchards he rented to his relatives.

Always Barak addressed her with downcast eyes, as if she were a lady worthy of his respect. As if they had never exchanged secret notes. Or met at midnight in the barn. As if he had never seen her smooth skin glowing in the moonlight. Or felt her breath hot on his cheek.

He could not have forgotten. She willed him to remember, to awaken in the night and long for her.

Miryam had done what she could to catch his eye, but he would not look at her. Poor Barak. Handsome Barak, married to the fat, jolly woman who had given him three plump daughters. Had he ever told her that their master's new wife had been his lover in Bethany?

For years Miryam had reasoned that Barak could not really love such an uninteresting creature. Was it fear that kept him from coming to Miryam? He must have believed he would surely lose his house and fields if he let Miryam know how he felt.

However, with old ben Reu dead, perhaps she could persuade Barak to bring his crops personally to Magdala. No more secret notes. It was her house. Her room. Her bed....

But where was Barak?

He would be walking with his wife and daughters.

The air, which had hummed with conversation, fell silent when Miryam and Tavita appeared.

Was there even one person in the entire

population who did not loathe Miryam of Magdala? Not likely.

Miryam endured the hostile glare of the guests as they surged toward the gates of Cana. She kept her chin raised, eyes straight ahead, a steely smile on her lips.

Tavita whispered, "If you expected a warm welcome, forget it. We'll not be houseguests in any home tonight."

Miryam ignored her and instructed the Freeman, "You will pitch the tent at the edge of my walnut grove. The fig orchard has a spoiled smell this time of year, I think."

Behind her a woman's voice muttered, "Rotten figs aren't the only smell in her orchard." Derisive laughter from several others approved the sentiment.

Miryam tossed her head and pretended not to hear. After all, what did it matter? She was the one riding while they were on foot. She would dress in the finest silk while they wore nothing but coarse wool.

Tavita whirled round and cast an evil look at twenty walkers entering the gate of the wall surrounding Cana's whitewashed houses.

Tonight the wedding would take place outdoors near the common well in the village square. Then everyone would go in to the banquet. The celebration would be illuminated by tiny clay oil lamps held aloft by every guest. Cana would shine as though the stars had come down from heaven for the occasion. Miryam had always loved weddings. That is, every wedding except her own.

The Freeman, his brown, leathery face fixed like weathered stone, turned off from the crowd and tugged the mules toward a stand of towering walnut trees.

There were already two dozen tents in the orchard to accommodate an overflow of servants and guests. Donkeys were tethered to the trees. Herds of children squealed and played tag around the thick tree trunks.

"Your orchard is crowded," Tavita commented. "Your husband's relatives must not have expected you to show up."

"It's my orchard. If they don't like our company, they can leave," she replied.

What did it matter if she was not liked? She was a businesswoman. The people of Cana were laborers. She had the brains and the money. So let them have their piety and poverty.

Cana was the center of production for Galilean flax, figs, and walnuts. Miryam owned an orchard of figs and another stand of walnuts, both of which were rented to her late husband's poor relations. To the west of the village lay the field Barak farmed and beyond that were twelve acres of rocky, fallow ground. It was worthless by many accounts, but she had big plans for its cultivation. She carried the plan with her to Cana to share with Barak.

Though not as profitable pound for pound as olive oil or wine, the fig trees produced fruit ten months a year. The walnuts were famous for plump, meaty perfection. In combination, walnuts and figs provided a delicate dessert for the richest households of Rome.

Since taking over management of her husband's businesses, Miryam had raised the rents of her Cana orchards to a share of 40 percent of the crop. It was always a poor crop, but she used Roman connections to sell her produce well under market price. This drastically undercut the fig and walnut growers in Cana, leaving them with a surplus on their hands and no ready buyers. When farmers became desperate, Miryam stepped in. She offered to help sell Cana's surplus crop to the Romans but at a greatly reduced charge. Her reward? A hefty 15 percent fee. As for the farmers, what choice did they have but to cooperate?

Even with these tactics she had not yet amassed the kind of wealth she dreamed of. One day she hoped to have the sort of fortune Marcus called "I-make-the-rules-money." By his definition it meant that with enough money, anyone could tell the rest of the world where to go and get away with it. Miryam was working toward that goal.

It was no wonder that she was both feared and hated in the hills of Galilee.

But now she had much to offer Barak. Not only her passion, but the promise of wealth and property. Tonight she intended to offer him the use of her unused fields for the cultivation of a crop more valuable than gold. If she could just find him, talk to him alone, present her offer. And later she would hold him as she used to. She was certain she could win him back.

Freeman studied the boughs of an enormous tree at the edge of the stand. "Here, lady?" he asked his mistress.

She nodded curtly as she spotted her tall, studious brother, El'azar, and squat, plain-faced sister, Marta, conversing with Barak's father at the side of the road. El'azar's angular features stiffened as he saw Miryam. Then he pivoted away.

"Your brother is eager to embrace you," Tavita remarked caustically as she slid from her mount.

"As always." Miryam shrugged as if it did not matter. But an old anger welled up in her. She had always suspected that El'azar had paid Barak's father to leave Bethany and keep the affair quiet. She had never stopped hating her self-righteous brother.

Marta, her thin lips turned down in a pout, did not bother to conceal her disgust at the sight of Miryam. Marta's hair, streaked with gray, made her appear older than her years. The bitter middle-aged woman was envious of Miryam's beauty, envious that in spite of every bad fortune, Miryam had gone on to build a life for herself. Of course it was a life outside the moral walls of Judaism.

El'azar and Marta had imprisoned themselves in the cage of religion. The two lived a miserable life among the vineyards of their fine Bethany estate. Bachelor and spinster, they were young enough to enjoy life. Yet they chose the sober and lonely existence that law and tradition demanded of them. In their eyes Miryam was no better than a common prostitute. Her money was tainted. Her reputation was unredeemable.

Miryam smiled and waved at Marta. Marta, teeth clenched, returned her greeting insincerely. No matter how intensely Marta disapproved of Miryam in private, she always managed a controlled civility in public.

Little hypocrite! Miryam inwardly fumed. Pleasantries and smiles were simply to hide the family shame. Marta deceived herself into believing that no one else knew Miryam took on an occasional lover.

"I have already ruined the feast for my brother and sister." Miryam stepped down beside Tavita. "Look at Marta. What a cow she is. How she hates me. So, I'll be her shadow all evening. I'll stand by her during the ceremony, eh Tavita? Sit beside her at the supper."

"She'll choke if you do."

"Join in her conversations with the other women."

"You are enjoying this far too much." Tavita began to help Freeman unload the packs from the donkey. "You have come here to amuse yourself by tormenting them, I think." She inclined her head slightly toward the village gate. "Or maybe to steal away with a husband for yourself?"

Miryam followed the old woman's amused gaze.

There was Barak at the head of a delegation between the grizzled rabbi and the freshly scrubbed groom. Laughing, greeting old friends, patting children on their heads— today Barak was governor of his best friend's wedding feast. It was a high honor, and he was loving every minute of it.

Her stomach churned with the rush of seeing him again. Her pulse quickened, and color rose to her cheeks.

What would he feel when he saw her? she wondered. Would his expression of joy evaporate when he saw she had come?

As the Freeman erected her tent, she stood apart, watching Barak interacting with the people who called him friend and neighbor. A pang of loneliness stabbed her. How long had it been since a neighbor embraced her and called her friend?

For an instant she almost envied his ordinary wife and the tedious life they led in this out-of-the-way village.

She thought again of swimming into the waters of Galilee. Deep and peaceful. A place to find rest from longing and disappointment...

A familiar voice interrupted her reverie.

It was her brother, El'azar. "Miryam." His whole expression, from wrinkled brow to clenched jaw, was set in a disgusted frown. Even his shock of brown curls vibrated with anger. No friendly greeting. No pleasure at the meeting. Just her name spoken in the same tone he might have used to describe the arrival of a storm.

She fixed a smile on her lips and turned to him. "*Shalom*, El'azar."

"I'm surprised you're here." He exhaled as if to say he was also sorry to see her. He led her away from the hearing of others, as if embarrassed to be talking to her.

"The wedding. My husband's relations. My tenants. How could I stay away?"

"It would have been better if you had." His clear green eyes would not meet hers. He scratched his wiry reddish beard and lowered his voice.

"Thank you for that, El'azar. Lovely to see you. I too have brought the couple gifts...to make up for the fact that they must breathe the same air as me for a while."

"People are...uncomfortable around you."

"And how have you and Marta been? Are the vineyards healthy?"

"Your Roman friend. He's the latest gossip."

"I have many Roman friends."

"An officer, this one. A centurion?"

She shrugged. "I suppose no one in Cana has anything better to do than to gossip."

"Four months a widow, Miryam. Can't you at least make some pretense for the sake of propriety?"

"That's the difference between you and me, El'azar. I never could pretend." She glanced toward Barak. He still was unaware of her presence.

El'azar followed her look. He scowled. "So that's what's on your mind. Forget it. He's happily married."

"But not to me. You saw to that, didn't you, dear brother?"

He grasped her arm, digging his fingers into her flesh as he led her to the trunk of a great tree. His words fell to a murmur. "Look. Miryam... Here it is, plainly. You and your money are not welcome. They loved your husband. But you? You cannot buy the friendship of these people."

"I haven't tried."

"They won't tolerate you here. Not today."

"I'm here. They'll have to get used to it."

"Everyone knows what sort of person you are. You, at a wedding? It's a mockery. Why don't you pack up, turn around, and go back to Magdala and your Roman lover before you make a fool of yourself?" He put his mouth close to her ear. "The bride and groom will not accept your gifts. They have been forbidden. There are those at this gathering who will shame you publicly for the harlot you are if you go through those gates. You will be driven out. It is already agreed to by the elders. I've been warned. Don't do this to yourself. Don't do it to..."

"To you and Marta?" Tears of rage brimmed in her eyes.

"You are still my sister. You know what it means to be driven out."

"So. I suppose I should thank you for sparing me the humiliation?"

"Yes, Miryam. Thank me. Thank me by not entering Cana tonight. Stay here in your tent until everyone else is at the wedding. Slip away before dawn. In the future, if you have any business in the village at all, send your steward to tend to it."

They had decided to make an example of her. Because of Marcus? Or Barak? Because of a thousand things. No matter what the reason, she was to be the first item of entertainment before the wedding began.

Did everyone know? Even strangers stared openly at her!

Miryam's gaze was drawn to a tall, strongly built man of about her age there, at the far side of the road. His dark, sad eyes studied her and El'azar. It was as though he knew what was being said by El'azar and what had been planned by the elders of Cana. *Run, Miryam! Run, or today they will destroy you!* For a timeless instant he held her captive with the sorrow in his eyes. Then he turned away as an older woman approached and spoke quietly to him. Miryam glanced down, and when she raised her head again he was gone.

If he had stayed she might have gone to him, begged him to help her. But help her now? Perhaps it was enough that this one glance of kindness and pity crumbled her resolve. She would not stay to torment her tormentors. There was no winning when the rules of the game were already written by her opponents.

She could not let El'azar see her pain. Tossing her head defiantly, she could barely form a sentence. "Word...word...has come from...Magdala. Urgent...business calls me...calls...me to the shores of Galilee..."

El'azar's face flooded with relief. "Good. Yes. Now live your life as you wish. But don't expect to be welcomed or accepted by your own people. You've done this to yourself, Miryam. But still I'm sorry for you."

"Save your pity," she snapped. "You're right. I came here to scorn them. To mock them and their boring lives. They are nothing to me. I'll go."

■ ■ ■ ■

"What did El'azar want?" Tavita held the tent flap back as Miryam took refuge inside. The old woman clasped Miryam's hands in alarm. "Your fingers are cold as ice. You're trembling all over! Each time you see your brother it's always something, something, something... Never peace! Can't he leave it alone? Let you lead your life?"

Miryam fought back tears as she groped for the cushions and buried her face. How could she explain to the old woman what the citizens of Cana had planned for her? She turned over and lay staring dumbly at the wall as the shadows lengthened.

"Tell me, lamb! What did he say to put you in such a state?" The old woman's faded eyes flashed with fury. "I'll give him what he deserves."

Miryam shook her head from side to side and put a finger to her lips, silently pleading with Tavita to say no more. The fabric of the shelter was thin. What if someone heard Miryam, the whore of Magdala, break and sob? The news would be carried into the village elders. Like a pack of dogs with a cornered fox, they would see her weakness and tear her to pieces. She wanted only to hide. To escape back to Magdala under cover of darkness!

"Leave me," Miryam instructed Tavita. "Don't let them see anything is wrong."

The old woman put a hand to her chin as a glimmer of understanding came to her. "So. That's it. You are not welcome." She stood abruptly and left Miryam alone.

For twenty minutes Miryam listened as Tavita and the Freeman chatted and joked amiably with other servants in the orchard. As though nothing was wrong. As though their mistress was inside readying herself for the wedding.

"Well done, Tavita," Miryam managed to whisper. Loneliness nearly choked her. There was no defense against it, no anger or disdain. What good was her money if she had no true friend? No real family to love her?

■ ■ ■ ■

Twilight descended at last. Three long blasts of the shofar called guests to the wedding. The babble of voices moved from the orchard and the road into the town until all Miryam could hear was the chirping of crickets in the grass.

Soon the wedding would be under way. The lamps lit. The procession of the bride: her eyes covered as she was led through the street by her mother...her mother!

Miryam closed her eyes as she thought of

her own mother. What might have been if she had not given up! Mama! If she had only found the courage to live! If only she had loved Miryam enough not to die!

The first tears escaped. Did everyone else hate her so much then? El'azar? Marta? The rest of them? And could Barak be a part of their plan to shame her? No! He would not do such a thing! He could not know!

After a time she heard a distant cheer. Music began again. The wedding ceremony was over. The feast had begun.

As melody filled the night, a plan formed in Miryam's mind.

Tavita entered the dark tent. "Are you sleeping?"

"Are they gone?" Miryam asked softly.

"They've gathered for the supper, if that's what you mean. All full of wine soon enough."

Burning with anger and new resolve, Miryam wiped away her tears and sat up. "I will need to borrow your cloak. Your veil."

Tavita clutched Miryam's arm and scowled into her face. "What demon is whispering in your ear? You mean to go into Cana? As a servant? Unwelcome as you are?"

Miryam leapt to her feet and asserted, "I'm going! I won't be kept out like a common slut. They hate me. Except...for Barak. I will find him. And...take this to him." She plunged her hand into a tapestry bag and withdrew a box with a scrap of parchment tied to it.

"I won't give you my clothes." Tavita pulled away.

"You will! Or I swear I'll put you out on the road!"

Tavita's eyes narrowed. "When will you learn?"

"This is business."

"Can't it wait until daylight? In a public place?"

"A public place? There is no place public enough for me to speak with Barak bar Halfi, and you know it."

"Wicked girl. Headstrong! What can you give him that won't be considered a gift from an ex-lover?"

"A crocus bulb. Karkom...for growing saffron."

"Saffron! Why not give him gold?"

Miryam sighed and began her deception. "If it is any of your business, saffron is the only reason I came to this shabby place. To make a bargain with Barak." She had captured Tavita's interest. Saffron was the most expensive spice on earth. Each crocus blossom yielded a meager three strands of saffron. An acre of crocus produced a mere two and a half pounds of the spice. But it could be sold for the equivalent of ten years' wages. It was an authentic business proposition. It would also give Miryam the opportunity she wanted to spend time with Barak.

"What do you mean?" Tavita puckered her face in doubt.

"I have Persian bulbs coming. Enough to plant my twelve acres. It's been fallow for ten years. Barak bar Halfi is a good tenant. I think he might be the man for the job. It's all there in the note. I wrote it before we left this morning, so put away whatever evil thoughts you have."

Reluctantly the old woman peered into the box. "Take it to him then. But the Freeman and I are packing. And in the morning I'm taking you home from this place."

Tavita grudgingly exchanged her clothes with Miryam.

Miryam emerged into the fragrant night air. Inhaling, she felt the pain in her head release a bit. She was grateful to be wearing the disguise of a servant. The clamor of the celebration increased. A glow illuminated the north quarter of the village where the feast was being held. She decided she would not carry a lamp for fear that someone might recognize her.

Covering her face with the veil, she made her way through the gate of Cana, entering the village. She heard the voices of the groom's relatives, raised in endless toasts to the newly-weds.

Soon enough they would be so full of wine that no one would notice her. It was a good plan, and yet she hung back, afraid to join the festivities. Wishing she had not come, she clutched the box of bulbs more tightly. What if Barak publicly scorned her?

She decided to wait a while longer.

Suddenly she was thirsty. Making her way back to the well in the town market square, she sat on the stone rim and tossed a pebble in. Seconds passed before she heard it splash.

How deep was it?

One hundred feet straight down?

If she simply leaned back, let herself fall, everything would be over. She might die from the fall itself. And then El'azar and Marta would carry her back to Bethany. They would be sorry for treating her like an outcast. Sorry they were the reason she was dead. They would place her bones in the tomb beside Mama and Papa...to rest. Sleep.

The urge to jump increased. The voices called for her, promised her peace.

But what about Barak? What if she perished just when she might win Barak back again? Find happiness in his love again?

She covered her ears and moved away from the well. Leaning against the rough stone of a squalid house, she willed herself to think of fields of saffron, purple crocus blossoms, and the gratitude Barak would have at being part of such an enterprise.

And then she spotted a man leaving the courtyard of the feast. He was coming to the well!

The light was behind him, his face lost in shadow.

Tall and slender, he carried himself with an air of confidence. She concealed herself behind a shelf of large stone jars, which had been used that morning to carry water to the *mikveh* for the ceremonial cleansing of the bride.

He seemed to consider the containers for a long moment. Then he looked away. Did he sense she was hiding there? Had he blocked her route up the street and into the banquet on purpose? Had he seen her at the well's edge as she had contemplated suicide?

Yet, strangely enough, this man's presence drove away thoughts of drowning herself.

Twenty feet separated them. He too sat on the rim of the well. Perhaps he planned to meet someone here? Or had the noise of the crowd become too much for him?

She wished she could see his expression, know what he was thinking.

Then fear surged through her as voices echoed from the courtyard entrance. Six lamps bobbed through the darkness.

Miryam crouched behind the rank of jars.

Were the elders coming for her? Had someone spotted her? Was the word out that Miryam of Magdala was here?

Pressing herself between the stone wall of the house and the rear rank of jugs, she watched and listened. A group of twelve females followed an older woman with a round, pleasant face and pear-shaped figure.

"There's my son!" The woman spotted the man at the well and scolded, "Yeshua! I've been looking all over for you!"

"Here I am." He rose and greeted his mother with a kiss on her cheek.

The women stood to one side, heads bobbing in urgent conversation. Something had gone wrong at the wedding supper. The wine was already all gone.

With this man's mother leading the foraging party the serving women had come in search of someone who could fix the problem.

Linking her arm with her son's, the woman tugged him closer to Miryam's hiding place. "They've run out of wine. Absolutely drunk the last drop. And the blessing has not been recited." Then she addressed her son. "'Blessed art thou, Adonai, King of the universe, who creates for us the fruit of the vine and gives us wine to drink...'"

Had the woman really called her son *Adonai*, Miryam wondered in amazement?

The woman clasped her son's fingers, imploring him to help. "Yeshua, can it be when you are here? No wine to offer to bless the marriage?"

His strong hand cupped his mother's face. He chided playfully, "Woman, what am I going to do with you? It's not yet my time."

Time for what?

Yeshua's mother arched a questioning eyebrow at her son as if to say, *Will you do this because I ask?*

He laughed and the music of it bounced off the jars of Miryam's hiding place.

Was this Yeshua the owner of a local vineyard? she wondered. Would he send the twelve servants to his cellars to fetch back wine?

His mother, satisfied with his reply, whirled around and said confidently to the delegation, "Do whatever he tells you to do." Then she scuttled up the street and back to the celebration.

The twelve waited expectantly for instruction.

Where would Yeshua get wine?

With the arrival of the lamps, Miryam could now see the man clearly. Dark hair and a thick black beard framed his angular face. He had a prominent nose, wide-set brown eyes, and his sensitive mouth curved in a slight smile.

Miryam squirmed uncomfortably beneath the gaze that pierced the dark shadows where she hid. Could he see her somehow?

He inclined his head toward six jars that would hold about thirty gallons each.

He instructed, "Fill them with water."

Miryam held her breath as teams of servers took up one jar at a time. Layer by layer her hiding place was nearly stripped away. She burrowed further into the gloom as the containers were filled to the brim with water drawn from the village well.

His back to Miryam, Yeshua told them, "Now draw some out and take it to the master of the feast."

With that he left them and strode away through the village gate and into the orchard.

The women gawked at one another in horror at his joke.

"Take water to the master of the banquet and tell him what?" asked one of the servants. She mocked, "Mary's son sends water to bless the wedding? It's an insult that won't be forgotten."

"A scandal."

"Mary's mad. Always has been."

An older woman shook her head. "So? Mary said to do what he tells us. She volunteered to find wine. Promised there would be enough for everyone. He's Mary's son. Though heaven knows who his father is! Oh well. It's her reputation at stake, not ours."

Another teenaged girl chimed in derisively, "And everyone from Cana to Nazareth knows Mary's reputation."

The others in the group sniggered and nudged one another. It was true—Mary's past was questionable, her life tarnished by disgrace.

None of this mattered to Miryam.

The master of the banquet was Barak bar Halfi!

Here was Miryam's chance to attend the feast unnoticed—a servant among other servants. This was her one opportunity to get near to Barak. Perhaps she could speak to him alone. She would give him the box of saffron bulbs and the note inviting him to come to Magdala!

She waited until the women, carrying their burdens, were several paces ahead of her. Then, lowering her eyes and concealing her face with the veil, she joined them.

Her heart was pounding. She was in hostile territory. Would her brother El'azar notice when she came with the servants? Would Barak recognize her by the look in her eyes or the way she moved?

The grounds were crowded with well-wishers.

Guests, unaware of the shortage of drink, milled around talking and laughing. Miryam trailed discreetly behind the twelve servants as they made their way toward Barak at the head table.

Her heart quickened when she saw Barak, his black hair and beard shining in the torchlight. His handsome face was intent as he carried on an earnest conversation with the village elders and the bridegroom about the Roman threat to the sanctity of the temple.

These were the very men who had warned El'azar they would drive Miryam from the village if she entered. What a risk she was taking! What if they discovered her? Shamed her in front of everyone? She knew at once that she had made a mistake. Trembling, she remained at the rear of the servers and waited for an opportunity to escape.

A miniature drama unfolded as she watched.

With a flourish, the eldest serving woman dipped a cup into her jar. Winking at her companions, she approached Barak. He gave a cursory nod, acknowledging that wine had been brought. As was customary, he intoned the blessing: "Blessed art thou, O Adonai, King of the Universe, who creates this fruit of the vine and gives us wine to drink..."

Raising the glass to his lips, he tasted the liquid, closed his eyes to savor the flavor. Then he exclaimed to the bridegroom, "Incredible! Everyone else brings out the choice wine first and then, after the guests have had too much to drink, they bring out the cheap wine. But you've saved the best for now. Well done!"

With a broad, befuddled grin, the bridegroom thanked him.

Barak waved a hand at the tribe of stunned servants. "What are you waiting for? Pour the wine!"

The women, disbelieving, dipped fingers into the large stone jars and tasted the miracle for themselves.

Wine drawn from the well at Cana? Wine of a choice quality? Could it be?

Miryam blinked at the scene in disbelief. How had Yeshua managed?

The hum of wonder rippled through the servants. Yeshua's mother merely beamed.

When Barak raised his glass for another toast, Miryam gazed longingly at him. She knew now that there could be no words between them, no sweet moment of recognition, no rekindling of his desire for her. Worse, she had taken too big a chance attending the feast!

As she averted her eyes and turned to go, she noticed someone glaring at her from across the gathering. El'azar! He had recognized her! Expression furious, he pushed through the guests.

Miryam tucked her head and fled the joyous celebration, escaping into the starry night beyond Cana. She did not stop until she was at the encampment in the orchard.

El'azar had not followed, yet. But it was just a matter of time.

In her hour's absence Freeman and Tavita had taken down the tent and loaded everything onto the donkey for an immediate retreat back down the mountain to Magdala.

Miryam arrived breathless, terrified. She

wanted to run from this place, to be safe in her own bed. "El'azar saw me. We have to get home."

Tavita, hands on her hips, declared, "This is what your stubbornness brings. Twelve miles home in the dark. We should make it by morning."

GIMEL

Bathed, dressed in a fresh dark-red tunic and parade armor, Marcus was ready for the evening's appointment well before the announced time. Accompanied by Vara, Camp Prefect Salop, and the other officers of First Cohort, Marcus and his comrades rode away from the barracks. Their course followed the curve of the Sea of Galilee toward the southeast.

Herod Antipas' palace was built on a promontory, offering sweeping views up and down the length of the lake. As he did each time he observed it, Marcus analyzed its columned porticos and lavish gardens with a view toward battle tactics. Again he concluded that the place would require a legion to successfully defend against half that many attackers. A bold assault by a band of determined assassins could easily storm the place.

Clearly Antipas did not live in fear of such an attack. Such was the contrast between the founder of the dynasty, Herod the Great, and his pleasure-loving son.

Herod the Great had likewise built lavish palaces, but he also had an eye to warfare. The senior Herod had been friend to Marc Antony and the divine Augustus, and the architect of citadels like Masada and Herodium. He had ruled a state stretching from Egypt to Syria.

His son technically ruled Galilee, a tetrarchy he visited as seldom as possible.

Of course, Marcus reflected, Herod Antipas should be credited with one talent: he *was* a survivor. His father had ruthlessly murdered friends, wives, and sons for their roles in suspected plots. Yet since the death of Herod the Great, Herod Antipas had successfully wooed succeeding Roman overlords, enabling him to hang on to his land and title for three decades.

A trio of slaves met the Roman officers in the mosaic-tiled anteroom, offering basins of perfumed water for washing hands and faces. Next the slaves washed the men's feet.

It was while Marcus was unlacing his caligae boots that Kuza, Herod's steward, appeared. The overseer of Herod Antipas' palace and Galilean farmland was also Idumean, a short man with a round face and harried look about him.

"Greetings, honored sirs." Kuza's words leapt from his mouth. "My master bids you welcome and asks you to come and take refreshment. He also asks me to tell you that Governor Pilate is still at the bath but will join us shortly."

Kuza ushered the soldiers into the banqueting hall. On its vaulted dark-blue ceiling was a realistic presentation of the night sky as seen from Galilee. The stars gleamed with gold leaf. It was early springtime, Marcus noticed. Orion's jeweled belt and shining sword hung directly overhead.

Underfoot was a mosaic-tiled floor, laid out in a circle. The animals, humans, and imaginary beasts of the zodiac chased each other around the central marble roundel. Images of leering satyrs and voluptuous nymphs cavorting through a grape vineyard covered the walls. Some of the characters were drawn to be holding torches, and from each uplifted arm a real lighted brass sconce protruded. Below each light fixture hung a portrait of Emperor Tiberius. The room was an almost exact copy of wall art Marcus had seen in the Italian city of Pompeii.

Jewish law forbade the representation of graven images. Yet here in his home Herod Antipas clearly felt no compunction about his decidedly un-Jewish tastes.

Three tables, arranged around the outside edge of the mosaic, formed a U-shape. Posted about the room were mute servants and motionless guards.

The host, Herod Antipas, reclined on a sofa behind the middle of the center table. Just like a fat spider at the center of a web, Marcus noted.

Though Herod Antipas dressed Roman-style in a white robe bordered with a seashell pattern woven of gold thread, no amount of attention to fashion could make him handsome to look at. Still in his forties, he was a portrait of dissipation. Sallow, stubbled jowls hung from rouged cheekbones like half-empty money pouches. His eyes bulged as if to protest their proximity to a bulbous, veined nose. His hair, though bleached and tinted with saffron, was not blond but a sickly yellow.

"Hail, worthy Romans." Herod Antipas saluted without rising from his couch. A smile flitted across his thick lips but never reached his eyes, which remained wary. Waving hands thickly clustered with rings, the ruler of Galilee gestured for Kuza to show the officers to their places.

Instead of complying, the soldiers formed three ranks facing Herod Antipas, seniormost to the fore. Kuza bustled around them. The steward wrung his hands, imploring the guests not to antagonize his master.

"Respectfully, tetrarch," Marcus explained for the Romans, "we wish to stand until Governor Pilate has entered."

Herod Antipas waved away the response as if of no consequence, then proceeded to drain a silver goblet. Drips of red wine glistened on his chin. Unbidden, two servants leapt noiselessly forward. One refilled Herod Antipas' chalice while the other wiped his face.

A tall, haughty woman entered the room, accompanied by a swarm of servants holding mirrors, brushes, and pots of makeup. Her copper-colored hair was pulled back and arranged in tight curls above her forehead. Her demeanor suggested her superiority to everyone present, including Herod Antipas. *A woman harsh, vain, and used to getting her own way,* Marcus thought. *A dangerous combination, and not at all attractive.*

Marcus heard one of the junior officers whisper the name *Herodias.* He recognized it as the name of Herod Antipas' mistress, but nothing more.

Clearly Herod Antipas wanted his woman to join the company at dinner. Just as clearly, she refused, and she and her entourage swept away.

Thankfully for Marcus, Pilate was not long in coming. He arrived accompanied by young tribunes and a brace of legionaries in elegant uniforms. Their appearance made Marcus feel shabby. The real authority in the land of the Jews had entered the room. Making no apology for his tardiness, Pilate accepted as his due the seat at Herod Antipas' right hand.

Marcus and the other officers reached their assigned places but stood until Marcus gave a brief nod. All sat as one.

Although Galilee was one of the most remote areas in one of the least consequential provinces in the empire, still Marcus demanded his men show proper bearing and drill. He would not allow the governor any cause to complain of slackness, or anything else.

■ ■ ■ ■

Though they had met before, Marcus used his place at the end of one wing of the dining table to study Pilate. The governor was tall, thin, erect of bearing, and keen-eyed. Indeed, Marcus recognized that the given name *Pilatus* meant "javelin thrower." Clean-shaven with high forehead and graying curls, Pontius Pilate appeared every inch the aristocratic Roman. But he really was of the equestrian class, the same as Marcus.

A slave extended a platter of *gustatio,* then plied silver tongs to furnish Marcus' plate with the appetizers he indicated. Boiled eggs and a bit of cheese were all he took.

A junior member of Pilate's military staff, Tribune Dio Felix, reclined on the couch at Marcus' right. The young officer remarked on the perfection of the mussels wrapped in pastry and the whole thrushes stuffed with pine nuts. He asked if Marcus was unwell.

"I've lived too long as a plain soldier to enjoy much beyond the fare of a plain soldier," Marcus replied. Marcus disapproved of gluttony and soft-living for soldiers in the field. With someone so close to the governor, however, it was wise to give civil responses that could not be reinterpreted as criticism.

Felix shrugged and helped himself to a lobster. "Judea seems to have precious little to offer in the way of luxuries," he noted, "so I plan to make the most of this opportunity."

Marcus returned to his contemplation of Pilate.

The family Pontii were Samnites, residents of central Italy whose ascendancy there predated the Romans. Perhaps Pilate's clan had been of the nobility in those bygone days.

Here the governor was the biggest fish in a very small pond. Judea did not even rate the presence of actual Roman legionaries, apart from the member of the governor's personal troop. The forces at Pilate's disposal were mercenaries organized into auxiliary units like the one Marcus commanded. There were about three thousand soldiers total. Five cohorts of infantry and one of cavalry represented the might of Rome in Israel.

There were Roman legions, four of them in fact, stationed just over the border in Syria. But to call on them would mean admitting to the Syrian prefect that a situation had gotten beyond Pilate's control. This was not something any bureaucrat with an eye toward future advancement would ever do lightly.

Pouring honeyed wine from a golden pitcher, another slave refilled the soldier's goblets. The second course was a haunch of wild boar with preserved figs.

"I thought Jews did not eat pork." Felix nodded toward Herod Antipas, whose cheeks were streaked with grease. The tetrarch and the governor were in conversation. Herod Antipas gestured with both hands, animatedly making a point. Pilate was cool, reserved, noncommittal.

Marcus thought before replying. Felix was young, an amateur, an aristocrat filling a political appointment. In looks, no more than twenty. He seemed eager but without the obsequious quality that Marcus found so obnoxious. Marcus decided he could be trusted with genuine opinions so long as the subject was not another Roman. "What the Jews eat is just one of many paradoxes in this confusing place. Herod Antipas is not Jewish. With us he will act more Roman than a whore on Viminal Hill." Marcus referred to the notorious brothel area of Rome closest to the Praetorian Guards' barracks. "But if you saw him with a crowd of Pharisees? You know, they call themselves 'the equals.' What they mean is, 'we're better than everyone else.' Well, then you would see Herod Antipas in a different light...."

"Pigeon with dates for Centurion Longinus," ordered Steward Kuza. Herod's chief servant directed the substitution of a clean plate and a serving of the third course. Marcus rinsed his fingers in a bowl of rose water.

"Marcus Longinus," Felix said, repeating the name. "There was a famous soldier named Marcus Longinus in the army of Germanicus in Gaul. Are you related to him?"

Marcus did not have a chance to answer, for Herod Antipas' voice rose above the din, interrupting other conversations. "Yochanan the Baptizer is a danger, I tell you. He is raising dissension and must be stopped!" The tetrarch's bejeweled fingers beat a tattoo against his wineglass.

Perhaps Herod Antipas was no longer as free from anxiety about rebels as he had previously maintained.

"So far," Marcus heard Pilate reply, "all you have told me is that this Yochanan the Baptizer preaches that men should mend their ways. Where is the harm...the sedition in that? Anyway, you said the man is not operating in your tetrarchy, but down in Judea proper. Given the amount of corruption among your tax collectors, perhaps you should hire him to preach around here."

A splotchy flush rose on Herod Antipas' liverish cheeks. Clearly Pilate's barbed words had angered the tetrarch, but Herod Antipas mastered his rage.

"It is bad enough that crowds of rabble are going to see him. Now even reputable people are standing in the river and letting him dunk them in muddy water!"

"How they must love that!" Pilate said with sarcasm. "And are they being initiated into a secret army?"

Herod Antipas' eyes took on a vicious, animal-like quality, and his lower lip trembled as he spoke. "He says he is a voice shouting in the desert! He says he is making the roads straight for one who will come after him!"

To Marcus, Herod Antipas appeared very near the edge of the madness that had reportedly swallowed his father.

"Well, Jove knows this country needs better highways and cleaner water too, for that matter!" Pilate's sally brought a laugh from the guests, if not the host. "In fact those are two of the things in the brief given me by Tiberius Caesar, so perhaps this Baptizer is doing my job for me."

At the mention of the emperor's name, Herod Antipas' demeanor altered again. The aggressive hostility folded in on itself and disappeared. "Of course the governor knows how to maintain order," he said with a wheedling tone. "No doubt you will do what is required."

Pilate seemed tired. "I'll look into it. But I will not make a martyr out of a self-proclaimed holy man."

Throughout the rest of the meal Herod Antipas merely looked sullen, darting glances at the Romans from under drooping eyelids.

Clearly there was no love lost between the tetrarch of the Galilee and the governor of Judea. Marcus knew that each man would be sending secret reports to the emperor. Each would offer complaints about the other, hoping to take over the government of the entire area.

Dinner concluded with pears and pastries. Marcus was offered another cup of wine, but he diluted it by two-thirds with water and drank sparingly.

Felix was not as temperate, nor were many of the others. "You didn't answer me...my question, that is," Felix said, slurring his words. "Are you related to that other Longinus?"

"I'll explain some other time," Marcus replied. The events in his legendary past happened ten years earlier, but they could still be a political danger to him. Young Felix might appear to be trustworthy, but it was too soon to reveal that he was indeed the famous Marcus Longinus, hero of the battle of Idistaviso.

DALET

Since her return from Cana two mornings ago Miryam had not slept more than an hour at a time. Disembodied voices haunted her waking hours, urging her to end her life. When she lay down to sleep, familiar faces, twisted with hatred, appeared in her dreams. Old friends, family, lovers, and servants harvested baskets of fist-sized rocks from the barren acres where she had hoped to plant a crop of saffron. They encircled her, shrieking accusations as they hurled stones. Always she awoke cowering and weeping, pleading for mercy.

Exhausted from the nightmares, Miryam stared at the placid pre-dawn waters of Galilee. She could not see the sunrise. Blocking out reality, her thoughts took her back to images of Cana...to Barak. Reviving his love was her one hope, the lone reason she had not obeyed the voices and ended her pitiful existence.

She must see him somehow, speak to him face-to-face!

The parcel of bulbs remained on the table beside her bed.

Passover holiday was approaching. Barak would be traveling to Jerusalem, no doubt. Miryam decided she would dispatch the package to him. She would ask him and his family to stop at Magdala along the way to discuss her business proposal.

Even Miryam's most suspicious detractor could not accuse her if Barak's wife and daughters were along. Miryam would find a way to get him alone even if it was for a brief time. Then she would see in his eyes that he had never stopped loving her, wanting her. They would find some way to begin again.

This morning she paced the length of her balcony. Her resolve strengthened. Carefully she penned the invitation to Barak and his wife. At last she called for Freeman to saddle the donkey and carry her hopes to Cana.

■■■■

On the second day after the banquet at Antipas' palace, Marcus rose early. At sunup he was already on the parade ground, practicing with the six-foot-long pilum. The pilum's spearhead was attached to a wooden pole by a slender metal rod. At the juncture of the two shafts a brass weight added force to the cast and served as a handgrip.

This form of javelin was the primary missile weapon employed by the Romans. Developed and refined, it had been in use for over four hundred years.

Most of Marcus' soldiers were Syrians

trained to be archers. Nevertheless he kept himself in constant drill with the pilum.

A trio of targets, wooden shields propped against sheaves of straw, stretched out in front of him down the length of the practice ground. The nearest was twenty yards away, the farthest close to forty.

Carta stood behind Marcus. Three javelins lay on the ground at his feet, and his master held a fourth. Two spears already transfixed the nearest vaguely human form.

Despite the heft of the weapons, Marcus' next pair of throws, made at the middle target, were almost flat trajectories. The centurion's strength of back, shoulders, and arms was such that he took no notice of the weight.

Part of the satisfaction connected to each successful throw came from imagining Vara as the mark.

Though the physical effort was demanding, Marcus found his early-morning drills gave him valuable time for reflection. This morning, the second in a row, his mind was occupied with thoughts about Governor Pilate.

Pilate had barely acknowledged Marcus, though the two men had known each other years earlier. Nor did Marcus believe Pilate had forgotten him. Was he being ignored as an expression of displeasure? Was it something more sinister? But to what end? Pilate had the power to have Marcus arrested by snapping his fingers. There was no need to lull Marcus into complacency first.

For the final two throws, Marcus bent his

body backward and angled the javelin toward the sky with a tremendous toss. The weapon arced into the morning sunlight, flashed across the intervening distance, and plunged downward into the top half of the shield. After hanging there an instant, the shaft holding the barb sagged under the drag of the bronze grip. As the rod bent, the shield was tugged away from the straw man.

"Well cast, centurion," a voice called.

Marcus turned, squinting into the sun.

Pontius Pilate stepped from behind a palisade fence that encircled the drill field. With him was Dio Felix, the young tribune of the governor's guard.

Carta backed up a pace, holding the final pilum upright with the butt resting on the ground.

"Well done, Marcus Longinus," Pilate repeated. "You have lost none of the ability you needed at the battle of Idistaviso."

From the wary look in the eyes of Dio Felix, plainly Pilate had repeated at least a portion of Marcus' history.

Marcus saluted and then shrugged. "Fortune smiled on me that day."

"But you spurned Fortune's hand in response," Pilate continued. "Prefect Sejanus has never forgiven you for refusing his offer to make you part of the Praetorian Guard."

"I'm sorry to hear that, Governor." Marcus replied with the proper response, but his tone carried no regret.

"You must have your reasons," Pilate suggested, "to remain forever stuck here. Some would say that disloyalty to Sejanus is the same as disloyalty to Caesar."

Disloyalty to Caesar! And Vara was ideally placed to be one of those who would reinforce that notion!

Marcus' spine stiffened at the accusation. He mentally cursed himself when he saw that Pilate observed the reaction.

The politician continued smoothly, "Your reputation as a courageous and resourceful man makes you a valuable asset to my province. Serve me well, and you will not find me ungrateful. I am returning to Caesarea today, but I have an assignment for you."

"Command me," Marcus said, saluting again.

"I suspect there is nothing to this prophet business...Yochanan the Baptizer, you remember? The man sounds harmless enough. But Antipas could be right. You have heard of the rebel leader, Judas the Galilean?"

"I have," Marcus acknowledged. "About twenty years ago he led an uprising here."

Pilate nodded. "Just because his Zealots were put down then does not mean the sentiment was eradicated. Things are quiet at the moment, but this race of Jews is not as docile as the emperor wishes. We do not want a new leader spouting resistance as a holy cause. So, Centurion, this is your charge: Take a file of picked men and young Felix here."

"Leaving Second Centurion Vara in command of First Cohort?"

Pilate's speech became more guarded. "There are other matters involving Centurion Vara. No, the camp prefect will remain in charge here. But your concern is to seek out this Yochanan."

"And arrest him?"

"Not immediately, no. Merely observe, then come to me with a report and your assessment."

"It shall be done at once, Governor," Marcus replied, gesturing for Carta to retrieve the spears from the targets.

"Wait," Pilate commanded. "The mission is not so urgent that you must skip your last throw."

Though his back was to the field Marcus did not stop to aim. Grabbing the javelin from Carta, he whirled, coiled his body, and released in one smooth motion. Flashing across the expanse the spear plummeted into the mark, striking the dummy full in the body behind the drooping shield and scattering the straw to the wind.

If only an enemy like Vara could be eliminated so easily!

■ ■ ■ ■

With misgivings about what mischief Vara was about to create, Marcus prepared for his assignment. Marcus told Camp Prefect Salop that he did not intend to be away more than a week, including the trip to Caesarea.

One last thing he did before mounting his

horse was to dispatch a hasty note to Miryam. As a pretext for the message he apologized for being unable to sign the contract for the produce of her orchard. In it he offered to conclude their business when he returned.

Accompanying Marcus and Felix on the assignment to investigate the Baptizer were ten old campaigners. Veterans of skirmishes with Parthians and Judean bandits, they were solid men who would not shrink from a fight. But they would not rush headlong into one either.

As the two officers rode and the soldiers tramped along behind, Felix queried Marcus about the size of the group. Why not go with a hundred, or even the entire cohort, so as to be ready for any hostile encounter?

Marcus replied by jerking his thumb over his shoulder. "Take a look at Quintus there." He indicated a grim-faced, square-jawed trooper marching at the head of the right-hand column. The man looked like a common soldier, as coarse as the sandstone outcropping snaking along beside them. His only adornment was shining brass studs on the cheek pieces of his helmet. These marks identified him as the *tesserarius* or guard sergeant of the detail. "Quintus is old enough to be my father. He was at Idistaviso, then came east, as I did, with Germanicus." Marcus frowned. He had not intended to bring up the history that concerned himself so closely. He hurried on with his recital of the guard sergeant's experience. "Fought in Dacia, Pontus, Syria. Thirty years' service, almost that many campaigns."

Felix raised his eyebrows at the résumé and appeared about to ask a question. It might be innocent, but it might be uncomfortable. Marcus was not ready to be deflected toward a discussion of his own life. "Now look at the other nine," he instructed. "Younger, perhaps, but everyone seasoned and steady. More than enough force to deal with bandits and rebels. A lesson, Tribune Felix: a few battle-hardened veterans are better than many untried recruits." With that he reined his horse to the side, indicating that he needed a word with Carta, who was trudging at the rear of the files of soldiers. Carta led a donkey loaded with Marcus' and Felix's personal gear and supplies. The other legionaries toted their equipment on their own backs. Each carried shield, mess kit, long cloak that doubled as a bedroll, rations for three days, and either pick-axe or shovel. When added to the chain mail and helmet, the short sword and a pair of javelins, each trooper marched with eighty-five pounds of kit.

This situation did not last long. Outside the first village they passed, a Jewish man plucking figs from a tree was pressed into service. Knowing protest was futile, he accepted the pack from Quintus' back and set off on the road. The farmer's head was down as he muttered to himself, counting off the obligatory two thousand paces. When the mile of his duty was over, he sat down. Without speaking, he waited until the weight was removed, then retraced his steps without looking back.

Before the squad covered three miles of their journey, every legionary had dragooned an onlooker into being his pack animal. Since their route lay within the fertile and well-watered Jordan valley, there was no shortage of porters for the taking.

Some of those pressed into service grumbled and cursed for the whole of their terms, but only once did anything unusual result.

Their path traced the river's flow. The stream passed from the Galilee into the region known as the *Decapolis*. This league of ten cities was founded by Greek colonists following in the wake of the conquests of Alexander the Great.

Near the Greek city of Pella the detail surprised a pair of Jews, brothers by their looks, laboring over a grinding stone. The two men, with their matching bright red hair, were engaged in putting a keener edge on a bronze sickle. The grating noise of the sharpener kept the pair from hearing the soldiers' approach.

When Quintus laid his leathery hand on the younger man's shoulder the fifteen-year-old cast a startled glance backward. Then he jerked free and attempted to run. The guard sergeant spun his javelin like a quarterstaff, the wooden shaft knocking the boy flat with a blow to the head.

The incident would have gone no further if the elder brother had not shouted a protest and swung the reaping knife. The swipe of the blade missed Quintus, and an instant later the

Jew was pinioned on his back by three legionaries. The point of the sergeant's short sword rested in the hollow of the twenty-year-old man's neck. Quintus looked at his centurion for instructions.

It was, Marcus thought, a good opportunity to test Tribune Felix's judgment. "What would you do?" he asked.

Felix swallowed, set his jaw, and said, "Kill him."

The teenager, just coming round from the blow he received, cried out for mercy. He appeared not much older than Carta. Held at spearpoint himself, he begged on his knees for his brother's life. "The man might have maimed Quintus or killed him," Felix said. "It cannot be excused."

Marcus frowned. "But you admit that they acted more out of being startled than intentional malice. They weren't lying in wait to ambush us. This fellow is fortunate to have missed his aim, or we would have no choice. Under the circumstances we can be lenient."

The boy slumped back to the ground. His brother stopped struggling and sagged in the arms of his captors.

Then Marcus added, "But a lesson is in order. Flog him."

Guard Sergeant Quintus uncoiled the whip called a *corax* or *raven* from around his waist. As the target of the sickle, he was not disposed to show mercy. The name *corax* was also applied to the grappling hooks used in naval warfare. For both purposes the comparison to a bird's talons was apt: they were designed to dig in and hold.

Twenty strokes of the knotted leather cords left the victim in a pool of blood.

The man collapsed into unconsciousness while his dazed sibling was prodded into motion as a porter. Sullen faces regarded their passing from every stone wall and shadowed doorway, but no one resisted.

When darkness fell, the squad was on the outskirts of the village of Aenon. As Carta pitched the tent which Marcus and the tribune would share, Marcus rode into the village. He greeted the headman, who was a Samaritan and not hostile to Romans. Marcus asked for any information about the Jewish preacher known as *the Baptizer*.

When he returned to camp Carta was preparing supper. Marcus invited Felix to share lentil stew and news. "We're in luck," he said. "The so-called prophet has moved northward from his last reported location. He is dunking people in the river near Selim, not a mile from here. We'll see him in the morning."

"Why don't we go there now?" Felix suggested.

"He doesn't preach in the dark," Marcus said wryly. "Even if we could locate his lair, what then? He's not a fugitive. We're not here to arrest him but merely to observe and report. Tomorrow will be soon enough."

After the lentils and dried meat had boiled long enough to be edible, the two officers ate their fill. Marcus instructed Guard Sergeant Quintus to post a rotating watch of two men, even though he knew Quintus had already attended to every detail.

"I asked simply to let him know *I* have not gone slack," he explained to Felix. "Not because I think *he* has."

As the fires of dried acacia branches burned low, the off-watch men of the detail wrapped themselves in their long red cloaks and fell asleep. Marcus and Felix talked in low voices about Rome...the capital Marcus had not seen in a dozen years, though he had served it faithfully through that time.

Then Felix diverted the discussion.

"The emperor has turned over the everyday business to Sejanus," Felix said. "It is said that Tiberius is unwell and that he has gone to Capri to die. Some believe Sejanus will be the next ruler."

"I know nothing about such matters," Marcus said flatly.

"You know more than you say," Felix said. "For instance, Idistaviso. The governor told me. You *are* that Longinus who saved the army from the German tribe. Why hide such an achievement...such an honor?"

After a pause Marcus said tersely, "It was a long time ago. Germanicus is dead these eight years, and I am a centurion carrying out my duties in Judea."

"But I don't understand."

"Tribune," Marcus replied frankly, "you outrank me and can make whatever demand on my sworn allegiance that you will. Moreover, I like you and have no wish to be rude, but hear this: just as the Jews do not lay out cities above ancient graves, so it is with me. There are things best left dead and buried and not trespassed upon. If you will pardon me, my duties call."

Marcus turned away from the fire. His new position allowed the flickering light to shine over his shoulder onto a wax tablet enclosed in a leather-covered wooden frame. With a stylus he made brief observations about the day's march and the countryside through which they had passed. Later he would expand his notes into a journal, noting water holes, trails, and wadis that might hide rebel encampments.

When he folded the tablet's cover and handed it to Carta before retiring to sleep, he noticed Felix remained awake. Though reclining within their tent, the tribune regarded Marcus with a curious stare.

Marcus sighed. Perhaps a bare recital of the facts and then the matter could rest.

"You already know I was at Idistaviso," he began. "The Cherusci had us outnumbered and trapped between dense forest and the river. We were being cut to pieces. I was able to rally some men."

"It is said you went berserk, charging a hundred of the enemy and waving a spear in one hand and an axe in the other! The Cherusci fled as if you were the god Mars himself!"

Marcus shrugged. "We held long enough that

the army's flank was not turned. Eventually the cavalry came up, the Cherusci panicked, and we routed them."

"I looked into your quarters in Tiberias," Felix admitted, "and saw the crown of holly. That *is* the *corona obsidionalis,* isn't it? A crown made from leaves or vines growing on the spot where an army was saved from certain destruction? The highest distinction a Roman soldier can receive!"

"A battlefield honor given me by Germanicus," Marcus allowed. "It also explains why I am here in Judea."

Felix waited for further details.

"There was bad blood between Sejanus and Germanicus. Some blamed Sejanus for getting the army into the trap in the first place. After the fight he tried to cover himself with glory, even though he had no hand in the victory. He offered to make me a Praetorian...and I refused, preferring to stay with Germanicus."

"But that was right and honorable," Felix asserted indignantly.

Marcus grimaced. "Much good it did me," he said. "Germanicus was sent east into more wars, while honors were heaped on Sejanus in Rome. Then in a couple years, Germanicus was dead of poison." Marcus stopped to let the implications of that sink in. "So," he resumed, "I remain here, carrying out my duties."

Marcus flipped his dagger at a chunk of wood on the ground. Its point buried itself in a coin-sized discoloration in the grain.

"What about the boy?" Felix asked.

"So you heard that the two stories go together?" Marcus asked, brightening. "All right, here's the rest: I am half British. My mother was a princess of the Catuvellani. After Idistaviso I was offered my pick of the spoils of the Cherusci camp." He shrugged. "I found Carta...he was only three...tied to a tent pole. He had been captured during a Gaulish raid in Britannia and sold to the Cherusci. Something about him reminded me..."

It was enough. Time to stop himself.

"I chose him as my share," Marcus concluded. "He has been with me ever since. Now we should both get some sleep."

■ ■ ■ ■

In the morning Marcus was up early, reviewing his orders with Guard Sergeant Quintus. "Carta and I, and you also if you want, will go along the riverbank," he explained to Felix, "wrapped in these." Marcus produced a brace of dirty brown homespun robes he had obtained the previous evening from the Samaritan village. "Romans would put Yochanan on his guard. To hear him preach we mustn't alarm him."

"We're clean-shaven," Felix argued. "We can't pass for Jews, flea-ridden mantles or no."

"No need," Marcus suggested. He pointed to where Carta festooned the surly-eyed donkey with brass flasks and cook pots. "This is a trade route connecting Damascus with Gilgal and Jerusalem." He passed Felix a flask of walnut oil with which to stain their faces and hands. "We're Syrian merchants...unsuccessful ones, it appears, but unremarkable."

"And if Antipas is right about this man being a rebel and an agitator?"

Felix stopped short of expressing fear, but Marcus understood the implication of the question. The centurion slapped the cloak over his thigh, and his concealed short sword resounded with a metallic ring. "My men will divide into two parties and flank us," he added, "keeping out of sight in the willows. Quintus knows what to do and will come if I signal."

The Jordan, at about the midpoint of its journey from the Lake of Tiberias to the Dead Sea, was a shallow, meandering stream. Between Aenon on one bank and Selim on the other, the river's generally southern course was interrupted by an abrupt turn to the west. For about a quarter mile it pointed at the Great Sea and then pivoted sharply back south again.

It was at this bend in the river that a placid pool formed, screened by poplars. Despite the early hour, crowds of people scurried along dusty lanes, converging on the spot. Keen to extract as much information as possible, Marcus scrutinized the throng.

Most were village stock, sturdy farmers and their families, or craftsmen like potters and carpenters. These could have been on their way to one of the religious festivals the Jews celebrated each year. Some were plainly curiosity seekers, laughing and joking amongst themselves. Others stalked by with intensity of purpose evident in their stride. Single-minded expressions suggested they were earnestly seeking...but for what? Was this religious fervor or political zeal?

Yet this assembly did not look like revolutionaries.

The next circumstance to arouse Marcus' curiosity was the sight of twin groups of obviously well-to-do city dwellers. He signaled Carta to lead the donkey off the path to a grassy verge. Marcus pretended to adjust the pack saddle while making comments to Felix. "That bunch there," he said, pointing to men in brocade robes with large leather pouches called *phylacteries* tied on foreheads and upper arms. The men were proudly displaying their piety with the oversized ornaments containing extracts from the law of Moses. "Pharisees. From Jerusalem by the look of their clothing. They would not come out so far into the countryside if this man, Yochanan, was just another rustic preacher. And their rivals are here as well."

Marcus indicated another knot of fashionably dressed men, more worldly looking... meaning more Roman...in their adopted style. "Sadducees. The temple faction, but don't let that fool you. They aren't pious unless it suits them. The highest ranks of the Jewish priesthood owe their appointments...and their allegiance...to us. These two sects despise each other. If they are both here it only means each side hopes to get this Baptizer to denounce the other."

The disguised Romans moved forward again until reaching a knoll that overlooked the pool in the riverbed. The bank dropped steeply toward the water. Underfoot the dirt of the slope was loose and slippery.

"There must be four or five hundred people here," Felix observed.

"And more coming," Marcus observed.

In the course of Marcus' service he had seen many strange sights and customs. He had encountered Britons who styled their hair with clay and lime into stiff spikes and dyed their skin blue. He recalled dramatically tall Egyptian priests with shaven heads and painted eyelids. But little in his experience prepared him for his first glimpse of Yochanan the Baptizer.

The man emerged from a closely packed group of his followers to stand atop a boulder at the water's edge. He had a mane of coal-black hair that hung below his broad shoulders. His beard, equally untrimmed, gleamed sable. Though his disciples appeared to be dressed in ordinary robes, Yochanan wore a simple tunic of the roughest cloth.

Around his middle was a wide belt, like that worn by a stonemason. The man's face, arms, and legs were sun-browned to nearly the same shade as the leather. Yochanan's eyes swept over the crowd, scrutinizing each onlooker individually and thoroughly. It was an inspection many in the throng found uncomfortable.

"Jewish prophets are said to have called fire down from heaven to consume their enemies," Marcus remarked. "This man fits that description. This is no perfumed soothsayer intent on seducing highborn women. A Nazarite, perhaps. Set apart from birth as a holy man. No razor, no wine, no female companionship. Listen."

Yochanan's voice, as gravelly as the shoreline in front of him, carried up the natural amphitheater of the bank. "The time has come for you to change your hearts! Why bother celebrating the feasts when you have no regard for the One they honor! You say you keep the commandments, when what you mean is you haven't yet broken them *all!* Look inside! You know the truth about yourselves. There is a time coming when everyone will be threshed like wheat and the chaff will be burned up. Do you want to be straw to the fire?"

"The Jews are a strange race if they're eager to hear such talk," Felix observed. "This fellow's more abusive than a nagging wife."

Yochanan continued, "And listen: you can't have a change of heart unless you admit you need it and beg the Almighty to change it for you. No man is so pure that he can do it himself, except in his own eyes! The Almighty is giving you one last chance to transform your hearts," Yochanan said, pivoting and pointing at his audience. "Will you reject this message as you have rejected all the others down through the ages? Do you suppose punishment only happens to those who believe in it?" he roared. "You steal and cheat and betray the people you're supposed to be leading. You sons of snakes. How do you think *you* will escape God's anger?"

One Sadducee drew himself up imperiously. "We are true sons of Abraham," he said.

Yochanan stuck out his chin and in a high, nasal tone that mimicked the religious official he repeated, "We are sons of Abraham."

The onlookers roared with laughter, and the Sadducee colored.

Resuming his own deep-pitched voice, Yochanan stated, "And you comfort yourself every day with those words while you hatch your next plot! Don't you know that the Almighty can make sons of Abraham out of these rocks?" He gestured at the stones poking their tops out of the stream. "Better sons and more acceptable than you," he scolded. "They're already washed clean, and you still wallow in your filth."

"There is no need for Antipas to worry about this fellow," Marcus noted. "The religious types'll tear him apart or poison him soon."

"But his words have a different effect on others," Felix pointed out. "Look."

The first rank of spectators pushed forward until they stood knee deep in the water.

Yochanan's next words still rang up and down the river but had lost some of their severity. "The water in which your bodies are baptized expresses how willing you are for the Most High to clean your hearts. It is the right time for you to do this, because there is someone else coming from the Almighty...in fact, he has already begun his work. You'll never know him if you don't turn away from self-love and humbly admit to the Most High that you need your lives to be healed. He who is coming is much more important than me. All I can offer you is water, but He will clean you with *Ruach HaKodesh*...the spirit of the Ever Living One...and with fire. I was sent to warn you about the harvest, but he will have the sickle in his hand!"

Marcus saw again the gleam of the reaping knife as it flashed toward Quintus. Then by a trick of his memory, it seemed that the blade had been aimed at him. It had been his neck in the way of the sweep of the knife, his life that was in danger. He shook his head to clear it.

"We've seen enough," Marcus said to Felix as Yochanan moved down the row of seekers. Each penitent was pushed under the surface and then lifted with an approving clasp on the shoulders. "It is just what I said. Prophets are ten a penny in this country. He will have his minute of fame and then never be heard of again."

"And this other man he speaks about," Felix questioned. "Is that important?"

Marcus dismissed any significance with a wave of his hand. "This country likes to think a liberator...a messiah...will appear and restore them to greatness. The Baptizer may be a rustic in looks, but he isn't simple in his wits."

"How so?"

"He doesn't claim to *be* the messiah because that would leave him open to a charge of sedition. Clever, eh? And I bet he does every bit of his preaching on this side of the river. Just over there is Perea, part of the territory belonging to Herod Antipas, where our friend the tetrarch could arrest Yochanan without first asking Governor Pilate's permission."

■ ■ ■ ■

Marcus.

Gone.

Alone in her bed, even a few days was too long for Miryam to sleep without dreaming.

And when she closed her eyes, there was Mama sleeping. Smiling in her sleep. Perfectly white, even teeth grinning too wide. Mocking the little girl who stood in the doorway and gaped at her in terror.

"Mama!"

The yellowed shroud stiff with spices. Littered with dried flowers. The fine bones of her hands exposed in the dusky tomb light.

"Mama! I'm sorry! Give me the stones! Don't put them in your pockets!"

No reply. Eyeless eyes, seeing nothing, staring out through the rotted cloth.

Too young Miryam knew all about death.
When she cried out, what angel heard her?
And if Mama's angel came to comfort her? To
hold her against its heart? Would Miryam
not be consumed by fire in its beauty?

"Mama! You were so beautiful! And now..."
What was beautiful had become hideous; the
thing of nightmares.

The child questioned her mother's corpse.

"You must have loved me once in my
small beginnings. Didn't you? Then, why?
Why?"

I remember your arms. Warm and soft.
Your smile. Gentle and patient with my end-
less questions. And surely you knew how
very much I loved you. My eyes followed
you when you moved across the room. I
touched your hair when Father struck you
and you bowed your head, weeping. Do you
remember? You raised your eyes to me.
Grateful even though I was so small. You
reached out and touched my cheek and
then pulled me against your heart... Against
your heart. I heard it beating then. Steady
and certain.

Mama! Wrapped in the yellowed shroud.
Littered with dead flowers. Mama! Do
you hear me now?

Your heart. The pulse of my life.

Your eyes. The mirror reflecting my
worth.

Your love. The rudder steering my
thoughts to heaven and goodness.

The springtimes in my life needed you to be there. The evening star I see still waits for you to come stand beside me and notice and tell me to look up. Music is unheard because the waters rolled over you and you embraced cold waves while I watched on the shore for you to come back!

I was your purpose. Your mission. Yet you turned your back and left me as if I were no more than a pile of stones on the sand.

I was frightened when you died, wrenching yourself from all my tomorrows! But I swallowed my sobbing because El'azar commanded I must.

And then there came a star-filled night when the wind of your accusations gnawed at my face!

Mama! I'm sorry! Give the stones to me! Don't put them in your pockets! Come back!

But you didn't come back. And look at you. Lying beside father. Grinning coldly. Strewn with dead flowers that I once picked.

Whom will I turn to in my need?

Who will hold me now?

Whose face will sleep beside mine on the pillow?

Barak! Oh, Barak! Come back to me, Barak! I can't do this anymore alone!"

Miryam called out, a long cry of anguish. She awakened from her nightmare with the light from Tavita's candle glowing over her.

The old woman said, "Oh, lamb! Wake up! You're at it again! Please, lamb! Wake up! It's long gone! Long gone!"

Miryam, panting, sweating, stared into the light. "The flowers." She sighed. "Always the flowers. The blue ones you helped me pick and lay in her fingers. Remember, Tavita?"

"Yes. I remember, lamb."

"Dead flowers. Still there. Still in her hands. But dead like her. Like me."

"No, lamb. You mustn't."

Miryam inhaled as though breathing were strange to her and she had to think about filling her lungs. "But I am. The stones. Always the stones. My fault."

"Never." The old woman sat on the edge of the bed and, with trembling hand, held a water glass to Miryam's lips.

"I need Barak." Miryam felt emotion constrict her throat as the sense of loneliness overwhelmed her once again.

"Not him, lamb. He never was no good for you."

Miryam sat bolt upright on the bed and flung the cup against the wall. "Yes! I need Barak! I tell you, I need him! I must find a way! I can't go on like this!"

Tavita paled. Her drooping eyes registered a sad fear of what would come if she argued. "It was only a dream. Shall I stay awhile?"

Miryam leapt up. "Get out! Bring me wine! Leave me the light! I must! I will not let my life go along this road! Empty road! I need Barak, I tell you! Just bring me wine!"

HEH

Before arriving at Governor Pilate's capital on the seacoast, Marcus ordered a two-hour halt for spit-and-polish. Carta burnished the centurion's helmet and flicked dust from his master's plume into the cool breeze off the ocean. Marcus and the other members of the squad changed into dress tunics. Swords and pilum heads were polished until they gleamed. The leather of the armor harness was freshly oiled.

It was not only the prospect of being reviewed by Pilate that caused this attention to detail. Arriving in Caesarea always had this effect on Marcus.

Magdala was a sleepy Jewish village and Tiberias the elaborate country retreat of a pretentious man. Caesarea Maritima was a cosmopolitan showpiece. Though small, it rivaled the cultural centers of the Roman world, except for Rome itself.

Herod the Great had spared no expense in his effort to emulate Rome's styles of architecture and tastes in ostentatious display. In a city avoided by his Jewish subjects as ritually polluted, King Herod was free to indulge his own preferences. He also built with an eye toward impressing the Imperial court.

Starting with a site known locally as *Strato's Tower*, Herod raised a masterpiece of Roman architecture. His artisans created stunning contrasts, lavishly setting white marble against the azure of the Mediterranean. He constructed an artificial harbor in sixty feet of water. When finished, it accommodated a fleet of cargo galleys and warships.

A seaside promenade offered the wealthy and powerful a chance to see and be seen. Luxurious baths, theaters, and a circus for athletic and gladiatorial contests catered to self-indulgent entertainment.

So that no one would doubt Herod's gratitude to his patron, set on an artificially raised hill in the center of town was a monument. Transplanted laurels and oaks surrounded a marble temple in which all could pray for the heavenly favor of Caesar Augustus.

Tiberius, though he modestly denied his own divinity, encouraged worship at the colossal bronze feet of his predecessor's statue.

Most of the empire was happy to oblige.

The governor's palace had also been constructed to Herod's specifications and fitted out from an unfettered budget. Jewish subjects complained about the obscene expense of marble statues of naked gymnasts. Mosaic floors of lapis and carnelian depicting bacchanalian romps also offended both moral and fiduciary sensibilities. Herod's supporters merely reminded the whiners of the vast sums expended on the Jerusalem temple. Non-Jews had trouble understanding the purpose of a sanctuary erected to a god who did not even want his name uttered or his image depicted.

Very few pious Jews were invited to visit Caesarea Maritima and still fewer of those accepted. The streets belonged to Greeks and Syrians, Syracusans and Egyptians, Dacians and Idumeans, as well as visiting Romans. All of these admired the sights and had a proper respect for the powerful gods that favored the conquering legions.

On every external wall of each public building bronze medallions gleamed, displaying the benevolent features of Tiberius. Outside the main entrance to the governor's mansion these decorations were of larger-than-standard size. Just in case any passerby missed the point, the authority of the emperor was emphasized by an array of Imperial standards. Each pole also bore his portrait. And below that, a smaller but still prominently displayed roundel depicted the visage of Lucius Aelius Sejanus. *So,* Marcus thought, *the head of the Praetorian Guard and heir-presumptive to Tiberius is already receiving Imperial honors.*

Pilate formally greeted the arriving contingent on the pavement in his courtyard, then dismissed the legionaries to a meal in the barracks. He escorted Marcus and Tribune Felix into his palace.

The three bypassed a library where a phalanx of scribes busily translated Imperial edicts into Hebrew. Other secretaries meticulously copied Pilate's official reports for forwarding to Caesar. Next the trio of men entered the governor's audience chamber, then his private study, where Pilate led the way past his desk. A narrow door revealed a staircase spiraling downward.

At the bottom of this passage a chamber smelled of musty dampness. It was a concealed room without windows where important conversations could be conducted in secrecy. *Or,* thought Marcus, *a place for interrogations to be carried out without interruption.* The floor, tiled in a checkered pattern of light and dark slate, was unfurnished except for four wooden chairs. One of these was already occupied by a hard-eyed man dressed in the black uniform of a Praetorian and wearing the insignia of senior tribune.

But the real surprise was the broadly gloating face of the final occupant of the room. Decimus Vara, lately second centurion of First Cohort, was now also wearing Praetorian black. He stood behind the left shoulder of the superior officer.

"Centurion, this is my new chief military advisor, Tribune Trebonius," Pilate noted. "His aide, of course, you already know."

Vara's smirk was almost unbearable. Now the remark about big changes about to happen was explained.

Marcus was dismayed at the sight but not yet alarmed. Despite Vara's haughty superiority, his new appointment was temporary, subject to confirmation by Sejanus. He still could not act openly against a *Primus Pilus.*

Trebonius' presence in Judea was the most direct evidence yet of the growing might of Sejanus. The Praetorians were specifically designed to be the emperor's bodyguard. In the hands of an ambitious man it was a powerful, intimidating tool, even in parts of the empire far from Rome. Marcus recognized the danger to himself from someone so closely connected to Sejanus.

He also realized that Pilate too had a spy looking over his shoulder.

The governor seated himself but pointedly kept Marcus and Felix standing. "What have you discovered in regard to the man called the Baptizer?"

A formal report then.

Marcus saluted again and supplied a terse summary of what he had seen. "To conclude, Governor," he summarized, "we heard nothing treasonous in the man's words. Primarily he spoke of the obligations of his fellow Jews to reform their worship of their god. Beyond that he urged men to carry out their duties honestly, particularly calling on tax collectors to perform fairly."

Trebonius snorted. "May as well instruct a wolf to leave off eating sheep," he said.

Marcus nodded, then added, "But he did not suggest they should not collect what was owed. He did not challenge the authority of Rome in any way."

"Is that your view as well, Tribune?" Trebonius asked.

The Praetorian did not even ask the governor's permission before making the interrogation his own. Marcus glanced at the Latin inscription set into the floor in letters formed of glistening onyx: *In this room I will be secure in truth.* Was this motto the builder's pledge for the sanctity of the chamber, or was it a warning to those being questioned here?

Felix was either naively unaware of what a dangerous presence they were in or else amazingly serene in his own uprightness. He answered almost blithely, "There is no harm in this preacher. For my own part, I cannot see what causes his popularity! What he offers is sober and without comfort, but the religion of these Jews is strange at best. In all the empire where else is there a slavish insistence that only one god is true? But I agree with the centurion's assessment: we heard nothing that would rouse rebellion."

Trebonius sat back in his chair and Pilate visibly relaxed his shoulders. The two motions, however slight, confirmed Marcus' conjectures. Pilate's administration of the province was being scrutinized.

The Praetorian tribune steepled his fingers together. "You may sit, gentlemen," he said. "It is about the religion of the Jews that we wish to speak. Elsewhere the image of Tiberius is proudly displayed as the living embodiment of Rome...except here in Judea."

Marcus sensed what was coming. The Jewish prohibition against graven images had been respected by Imperial Rome. In purely Jewish cities and settlements the busts of Tiberius did not appear. Jewish practice maintained that coins bearing the emperor's portrait could not be used to pay the required tithe to their temple, but had to be exchanged first. Even the roundels designed to fit on the legionary standards were not displayed except when the cohorts were in camp.

Trebonius continued. "His Excellency Sejanus recognizes that proper respect has not been paid to our beloved emperor. But that is about to change."

So to curry additional favor with the emperor, Sejanus was going to make the stiff necks of the Jews bow at last to this final demonstration of Rome's authority. It was not surprising. Sejanus was known to hate Jews. It was at his urging that Tiberius expelled Jews from Rome some years before on charges of sorcery and proselytizing. Then Sejanus confiscated their wealth for the state and himself.

The Jews were again his target.

Breaking the national will of the Jews would not be easy. A hundred years of Roman influence in Judea had never reduced their resistance to what they saw as blasphemy against their god.

"We will start by correcting a grievous fault left by the preceding governor. My assistant, Vara, suggested that the Imperial fortress of the Antonia display the medallions immediately. You, Centurion Longinus, will take First Cohort and see that it is done. Centurion Vara will accompany you as my representative."

Jerusalem! Marcus understood both the order and its implications. The Antonia stood beside the holy temple of the Jews. Sejanus, through his minions Trebonius and Vara, was not merely challenging their religion, he was going to do it to their very faces.

Trebonius waited for a response.

Marcus had no quarrel with the intent. He had long believed that the Jews were unreasonably catered to in matters that the rest of the empire took for granted.

He also had lived in Judea long enough to know the likely result.

Marcus devoutly hoped that the promise of the floor's inscription was correct: that there was security in telling the truth.

"I will carry out the order," Marcus replied, then directed his next remark to Pilate. "The governor undoubtedly recalls the report of what happened in the reign of King Herod the Great. There was an uprising when he displayed a single golden eagle in Jerusalem."

Trebonius waved away the information before Pilate could reply. "Those vandals were apprehended and dealt with," he said. "And Herod should never have given in to that rabble. The emperor was most displeased that Governor Gratus did not see fit to insist on proper respect for His Majesty, and Governor Pilate is anxious to correct the oversight."

Marcus thought Pilate did indeed betray anxiety, but the emotion he read was not the same as eagerness. Gratus, prefect of Judea before Pilate, had done nothing to offend the Jews. Although the coins minted in his administration carried innocuous images like laurel wreaths and grapevines, still the Jews rebelled. And when they did, Gratus had ordered the crucifixion of two hundred of them at one mass execution.

What Pilate was about to order was a far more serious affront to Jewish sensibilities.

The governor was caught between maintaining the peace and catering to Sejanus' political maneuvering.

And Vara could cloak tale-bearing stratagems with authority as one of the emperor's enforcers of Imperial security.

Where would it end?

Marcus and Felix were dismissed. Bowing, they saluted and left the interrogation chamber. Marcus was grateful to breathe the air above ground again.

■ ■ ■ ■

For Marcus the main attribute of Caesarea was newness. Unlike other majestic cities of the empire, including Rome, Caesarea contained no ruins from previous settlements. It had been constructed all of a piece, from whole cloth. The entire city had the feel of a model on an architect's display table instantly expanded to life size.

This quality of being an idealized monument to Roman superiority carried with it an air of unreality. Caesarea felt something like a stage set. In his present black mood, Marcus was reminded that everyone was playing a role. Few had the luxury of speaking the lines he thought for himself.

Marcus despised dissembling all the while he knew that his career...perhaps his life... depended on it.

The circular temple to Augustus Caesar was no exception to this mood. During the daylight hours it was crowded with travelers intent on seeing the sights. Everyone wanted to report back home that they had worshipped there.

Very few took it seriously.

In the evening hours it was empty and dark, except for the flame constantly burning before the statue of the deified Caesar.

It was also cool and pleasant. Marcus needed the chance to be alone and think.

He reminded himself that he was a soldier. As long as he did not question his orders...as long as he kept his mouth shut and carried them out faithfully...he should be safe.

Should be.

Sejanus had ruthlessly eliminated even powerful opponents by innuendo and lies. Marcus did not count himself among the powerful.

Now Marcus faced three of the man's protégés.

Resting his hand on Caesar's bronze foot, Marcus tried to draw comfort from the god.

Nothing came to him.

Marcus' own personal divinity had always been the spirit of whatever legion he served. Visible in the images on the standards...lions, bulls, eagles...these represented the spirits that protected soldiers.

Marcus did not think it mattered what name was used; Mars or Saturn or something else, the name was immaterial so long as the god being invoked appreciated and blessed courageous, honorable fighting men.

Which was why Marcus was confused. With the addition of Sejanus' face to the poles, even the legion standards seemed sullied.

A voice spoke from the doorway.

"Seeking guidance in your struggle?" It was Vara. "Must have been a shock for you to see me beside the senior tribune today," he said with a sneer. "Can't keep acting better than me now, can you?"

Whether this was to provoke a reaction or just to gloat, Marcus wanted none of it. He attempted to push past Vara, but a meaty hand on his chest stopped him.

"There is no reason for us to be enemies," Vara said. "I might even be able to put in a good word for you. You don't want to spend your life in Judea, do you?"

Marcus plucked Vara's hand away with the same loathing as if he were touching a leper or a deadly snake. "There is nothing I want from you."

"But you have something I want," Vara returned. "Your servant... Carta. Give him to me. Think of it as sealing an improved relationship between us."

Marcus did think of it, and the image he drew nearly gagged him.

With a strangled cry, Marcus leapt forward, his right forearm across Vara's throat. The force of his rush propelled the heavier man backwards, catching his spine across the jutting edge of a marble pedestal. The air went out of Vara with a cry of pain. His heels scrabbled on the pavement, finding no purchase.

Marcus forced his opponent higher. Vara leaned back and back, afraid of having his neck snapped. He struggled to draw breath.

"Keep away from Carta," Marcus snarled, pushing even harder. "You disgust me. And you know what else? If you were so secure with your new patron...so all-powerful...you wouldn't be trying to bargain with me, would you? So I warn you: keep away from Carta and anything else that's mine."

When Marcus stepped back suddenly, Vara dropped to the floor like the entrails of a gutted ox offered to Caesar.

He was still rubbing his throat as Marcus strode away into the night.

■ ■ ■ ■

It was El'azar, Miryam's brother, who knocked on the gate. She heard his voice, urgent and low, as Tavita ushered him into the courtyard and brought him water to wash his feet.

Miryam waited in her bedchamber a long time after she was summoned. She knew he was waiting too.

Studying him through the slats of the door, she watched him drink deeply of his wine and then refill the cup. He stared at his hands in misery, then skyward through the atrium opening above the fountain, as if the sky held the answer to a question.

He pursed his lips and frowned as if he

were inwardly rehearsing a lecture he intended to deliver to his little sister.

Miryam would have none of it.

She brushed her hair and pinched her cheeks for color, then emerged onto the balcony overlooking the courtyard.

At the sound of the door closing behind her, El'azar looked up sharply. He stood.

Leaning against the banister, she extended a hand in inquiry. Why had he come here uninvited?

"*Shalom*, Miryam." He greeted her quietly.

She hovered above him and called down, "Well, big brother. What brings you to my house?"

"You are my sister. I wanted to see you."

"Here I am." She gestured broadly, like an actress receiving applause. "That still doesn't explain why you came."

"I...the whole thing in Cana." He glanced away, sheepishly.

"Well, well. Almost a family disgrace. But you were saved the embarrassment." She did not move from her high perch.

"Come down, Miryam," he asked. "Come down and sit with me awhile, will you?"

"Why should I?" Her tone turned bitter. She glared at him.

"You are my sister."

"So you said. But there's little evidence of it. After all, I am...what I have become. You are a pillar of the temple. Master of great vineyards. Well respected by the..."

"Stop! Please, Miryam! Come down." He moved to the foot of the stairs, imploring her.

She exhaled and shrugged, descending. She did not touch him, nor did he reach out for her. The siblings stood, united only by blood, family obligation, and a common tragedy.

Not love.

Never love.

Miryam led him to the dining room and closed the panel. The walls were decorated with frescos of Roman landscapes. She indicated that El'azar was welcome to sit beside the window, then took her place against the wall opposite him.

"Well then, brother?" she probed. "Where is Marta, my loving sister?"

"Home. Bethany."

"She didn't want to see me?"

He shifted uncomfortably. "She had work to do."

"She would," Miryam scoffed.

"Things to do with the household. Sarah is expecting a child next month and..."

"Ah, yes. Marta wouldn't dare leave her friend to visit her own sister." She sniffed and poured herself a glass of wine. "Well, get on with it, El'azar. I know you're here to scold me."

"That's not why I've come." He scratched his head contemplatively.

"Why, then? You want to make a business deal with your baby sister? Poor widow that

111

she is? Come now, El'azar, there's no love lost between us. Tell me what you're up to. I'll die from the suspense."

He pursed his lips and frowned. "I wanted to tell you... I know... I have not been much of a kinsman."

She snorted in derision. "Well! Confession is good for the soul! Not much of a kinsman! Sell me off to a loveless marriage to make a bond between your estate and that of old Yosef! Shocking! Not much of a kinsman! Father would have been proud of you!"

His face blanched, and he was silent. Then he looked straight at her. "All of what you say is true," he said guiltily. "Yes. I did those things. I thought it was our only hope. You know. Of continuing the family name somehow."

"Of course *I* was the right choice. Marta was too ugly to make a bride for anyone. Who would want her? Especially with the family scandal. So you sold me off, so to speak, to an old man who could not have given me a child unless he picked one off the dung pile of a Roman slum and brought it home to me for a gift. And I lived with your choice for ten years. Now my life is my own. My estates are my own. Not yours, brother dear." She locked him in her disdainful gaze. "If that's why you've come."

"No. Miryam... I came because...everything you say is true."

She laughed at him. "You're telling me it's true? You might have asked me. I knew it long ago."

"Look... I'm trying to say..."

"You're making a poor job of it, El'azar."

"I always have made a poor job of what I wanted to say to you."

"True again, brother dear."

"You were the pretty one."

"And Marta was the hardest worker. And you were Father's one and only son. The center of his world. I was forgotten by everyone but Mama. When she was gone he ignored me. I think you and Marta enjoyed that."

He rubbed his hand nervously across his mouth. "I thought of you the other day. And I wanted to tell you what I remembered. Something about you and Mother."

There was sentiment in his tone. She did not want El'azar, of all people, to lure her to him with sentimental nonsense. He had done too much damage to soften her hatred by bringing up old memories.

She stood abruptly. "Don't, El'azar. Don't."

He went on with it anyway. "You were about six years old, I think..." He paused, as if waiting for her to forbid him to go on. She did not reply and so he continued. "It was after..."

"Don't!" She put up her hand to block his words.

"Let me say this."

"There is no after. Everything stopped. There is only before."

His expression pained, he covered his eyes briefly as though he could read the words on his palm. "I heard you crying for her. No one went to you. Father forbade it. Said you had to get over it. You were so tiny. A little flower. Father's favorite before Mother died. And then every time he looked at you he saw her. He wondered why all over again."

"I won't hear any more of it."

"But it came to me you might wonder why..."

"Why Father was so cold? Why he never embraced me? Never held me or comforted me? Oh, no, El'azar. I never wondered. I was six. Little girls don't wonder. They just wish things were different. Remember?"

"I should have maybe...hugged you."

"You were too busy ordering me around. Father might have...might have spoken to me. I missed Mama."

"That was it. You were...you are...so beautiful. I think Father couldn't bear it."

"Yes. I am like her. A disgrace."

"No."

"Is that why you came all this way? So I could understand why my father hated me? Why you and Marta gloated over me? Why you stood back and rejoiced in my loneliness? Then you...separated me from the only one who ever loved me."

"Barak bar Halfi didn't love you. He used you."

She rounded on him. "Oh? What would you know about love between a man and a woman? Pathetic! I want you to leave, El'azar."

He grimaced. "I didn't come here to talk to you about him. I came to say... I know why...

I mean I understand what you wanted when you went to Barak, and I want to counsel you as your kinsman."

Defiantly she faced him. "I don't need your counsel. I have my own life."

He tried again. "Miryam...you can't have what you are looking for in Barak."

"How do you know what I'm looking for? Who do you think you are?" she snapped.

"He's married."

"So what?"

"Miryam..." He faltered. "Don't make a fool of yourself."

"You mean don't make a fool of you. And Marta?"

"I suppose. Yes. Us too."

"Too late," she said in mock astonishment.

"If you cross this line, Miryam, I will have no choice."

"Well, then. Is that your loving message? Loving brother to errant sister? You've delivered it, El'azar. Now go."

"Miryam... I wish... I wish it were different."

"I wish a lot of things. I wish Mother hadn't left me. I wish I had a brother who had loved me instead of cuffing me on the ear every time I opened my mouth. I wish I had a real family. But I don't. So I take life the way I find it. Unloved. Without much hope. But still breathing. That's me." She squared her shoulders. "Thanks for the grand advice. I'll think about it and let you know what I decide to do, El'azar."

He got up slowly and reached out as if to touch her. She drew back from him. "I'm sorry it's been so...hard on you."

"Save it. I'm standing, aren't I? And I'll have what I want. Good-bye, brother dear. You can find your own way out?"

VAV

It was a little over two weeks before the Passover. All Jews, secular and religious alike, celebrated their ancestors' miraculous deliverance from slavery in Egypt.

During his years of service in Judea, Marcus had heard the stories. How Moshe, the Hebrew lawgiver, was raised as a prince of the Egyptian royal house. How he intervened to stop the beating of one of his countrymen, even though he himself was ignorant of his true identity. How the unnamable god of the Hebrews had, through Moshe, wielded terrifying plagues to loosen Pharaoh's grip on his slaves. How the miracles culminated with the destruction of the Egyptian firstborn when the Angel of Death passed over the houses of the Jews. How the Jews received divine law and national unity during their ordeal in the wilderness and eventually conquered their promised homeland.

Marcus thought the story no more remarkable than that of Rome's founding. Every people had myths proclaiming them to be specially favored by their gods. But why honor a deity who no longer produced results?

This premise was shared by most Romans and accounted for a snickering prejudice against Jews. Why worship a god who so clearly abandoned his people? Passover night commemorated freedom from bondage. What a farce in the face of political reality! The Jews were a subject people. Obviously whatever heavenly forces existed meant them to remain so.

As far as Marcus was concerned, the Jews were welcome to their myths, with one reservation. Every so often the patriotic fervor associated with Passover produced rebellion. Some deluded or power-mad rebel proclaimed himself to be the Jewish Messiah and announced that freedom from Rome was at hand.

It was right and proper that the images of Emperor Tiberius be established in Jerusalem.

Despite this truth, Marcus had to admit that the timing was awkward. Jerusalem, home to 150,000 people, exploded in size during Passover. Almost that number of pilgrims swelled the populace to bursting.

Jewish worship, always centered at Jerusalem, was in Marcus' thinking a routine commercial transaction. It involved the ritual slaughter of animals as a sign of gratitude or to bargain for additional heavenly favors. But during Passover season religious zeal grew in intensity, as did resentment of Rome.

First Cohort marched to Caesarea to await

and receive the Imperial medallions of Sejanus. When Marcus and his troop finally arrived outside the northern wall of Jerusalem a week later, it was surrounded by hurrying crowds of holiday travelers. As Marcus called for a halt the floodtide of pilgrims parted and flowed around the impassive and unconcerned soldiers. The presence of additional Romans outside the city caused no particular comment. The garrison of Jerusalem was always reinforced at holiday times to enforce the peace.

Nor had the faces of the emperor and his favorite caused any problems so far. The standard poles the legionaries carried were still without images, which remained wrapped in linen and leather and were carried with the other baggage.

It was Pilate's plan that the standards be raised on the Antonia fortress during the hours of darkness. That way, he explained to Senior Tribune Trebonius, the first rays of the rising sun would reveal the emperor's benevolent features. The Jews would awake to a grand, already accomplished, and unarguable reality.

It was a nice bit of political maneuvering. Marcus noticed but did not voice the fact that Pilate himself did not accompany the medallions to Jerusalem. Nor did Senior Tribune Trebonius; instead he sent Vara as his representative.

Vara and Marcus had not spoken three words to each other the entire journey.

Marcus used the halt to point out Jerusalem's landmarks to Felix.

The most obvious was the temple built by Herod. The broad expanse of the Temple Mount loomed on Jerusalem's eastern horizon like a gigantic wave poised above the pool of the city. Its polished stone walls glowed bronze in the rays of the setting sun.

"It's huge," Felix murmured at his first glimpse of the dazzling, majestic edifice. "I've never seen anything like it."

Vara, who had ridden in brooding silence most of the way from Caesarea, spat out the comment, "Looks can be deceiving. Anything of beauty is wasted on the Jews. They have no concept of glory anyway. It should be reconsecrated in honor of Augustus."

"Centurion Vara," Marcus said, "would you care to ride ahead of us and alert the post to our arrival? Camp Prefect Salop will accompany you to make bivouac arrangements for the troops."

Marcus knew Vara would want to flaunt his newly acquired status as a member of the emperor's personal guard. He also knew Vara would select the choicest living quarters for himself.

It was a worthwhile sacrifice in order to be rid of the man for a time.

When the Praetorian had departed, Marcus returned to his discussion.

"Vara, as much as I hate to say it, is partly right. Don't think grandeur equals sanctity. You can trust a merchant in any bazaar in the empire more than you can trust the money changers near the temple." Money changers were needed because of the temple tax, required of Jews for the support of their body sanctuary. This levy could only be paid with Jewish shekels, because foreign currency displayed heathen symbols. It was well known that the temple money changers cheated, gouing religious pilgrims on the rate of exchange. They also chared an exorbitant commission. "And if you visit the Court of the Gentiles, hang on to your purse! If the conniving merchants don't separate you from it, the pickpockets will!" Marcus tossed his head. That speech made him sound too much like Vara. Instead he resumed his visual tour of Jerusalem. "That blocky structure...the one with the four towers hanging above the nearest corner of holy mountain...is the Antonia, our headquarters here. It is where the standards will be mounted."

"Where they will be seen by all worshippers going to the temple," Felix noted. He did not elaborate on his thoughts, nor did Marcus intend to be drawn into a discussion about their orders. When Marcus did not respond, Felix asked, "And is the governor's residence there as well?"

It was clear the young tribune had also noted Pilate's absence from this expedition.

"No," Marcus corrected, swinging his arm to point at a low rise to the west of the Temple Mount. Another monumental structure, ringed by high walls and marked by battlements dominated the site. "That is the palace of Herod the Great. It is home to the governor whenever he visits Jerusalem." Once again there was no editorializing, no attempt to elaborate. "We have work ahead of us tonight. Let's get on with it."

■ ■ ■ ■

Centurion Avi Shomron was an old man who had worn himself out in the service of Rome. His eyes were contracted into a permanent squint from fifty years in the desert sun. He was almost bald, with a fringing circlet of white tufts that matched his patchy whiskers.

Nominally in command of Fourth Cohort, in reality he oversaw only the Antonia. The troops of Fourth Cohort patrolled the trade routes to the south and east of Jerusalem, protecting caravans of frankincense traders and slave merchants. Its far-flung responsibility stretched over Jordan into Nabatea and Arabia and southwestward to the borders of Egypt.

Such constant travel was left to younger and fitter men. Shomron stayed in Jerusalem with a reduced garrison of a hundred soldiers. While Jerusalem was the most holy city to the Jews and their capital, it was not the headquarters of the Roman prefect. Therefore enforcing the law was primarily the duty of the temple police: Jewish guards working under the direction of the Jewish high priest, Caiaphas.

Shomron limped across the barracks chamber and thrust a cup of wine into Marcus' hand. "They won't stand for it," he said. "And nearly Passover? Pilate must be crazy. Unless he's *trying* to provoke them and in that case

121

I say good for him. Here's to the governor."
He hoisted a brimming goblet and drained it.

Marcus raised a cautionary hand. Vara was not present, but Tribune Felix was. While Marcus had found no duplicity in the young man, he thought Shomron's words dangerous.

The three officers had been up until late supervising the placement of the standards on the outside walls of the Antonia. Nor did completing that task end their concern. Much of the rest of the night watch had been spent poring over a plan of Jerusalem. Marcus identified locations where squads of soldiers would be stationed. These groups represented additional security forces, in case an outbreak of rioting should develop.

As dawn neared, Shomron and Marcus dispatched the guard details to their assignments. Marcus, unsatisfied, reviewed the flashpoints one more time.

Undeterred by the thought that his words might be reported back to a critical superior, Shomron surmised, "I bet High Priest Caiaphas was not even consulted. Fat old gasbag...probably bust something when he hears."

"From anger?" Felix guessed.

Shomron chortled and slapped his thigh. "From fear! Gratus...him that was governor before Pilate...used to sell the priesthood to the highest bidder...four claimants in ten years, including Caiaphas' father-in-law. Everybody knows the present man's in our pocket. There is no way they'll believe he did not consent to this. Be lucky if his own supporters don't stone him to save their scrawny necks from the mob."

Shomron explained that although he was born in the region, the religious turmoil made no difference to him. As a Samaritan he hated Jews even more than they hated Romans.

After all, the Samaritans were regarded by the Jews as despised, half-breed apostates. And since Shomron also was a mercenary in the pay of Rome, the hostility applied many times over.

"But why provoke them deliberately?"

"To crush them!" Shomron said savagely. "Crush them utterly! Arrogant, overbearing Jews! Ship them off as slaves. Mark my words, it'll have to be done eventually."

"What do you say, Marcus?" Felix asked.

Marcus gestured at the outline of the city spread out on the table. It was covered with charcoal-drawn circles and slashes to show where trouble was expected when daylight unveiled the medallions. "I don't read minds," he said, "so I won't guess what the governor intends. But Shomron is right that there will be disturbances. Some of the more hot-headed Jews are close to exploding already. The robes of their chief priests are stored here, in this building, under our 'protection.' To the pious...Pharisees like I pointed out to you...our presence in the same building already defiles the very cloth. What do you think will happen when..."

Shomron pointed out the window. "When

123

the sun comes up?" he queried, indicating the silver band that outlined the mountains of Moab.

■ ■ ■ ■

Spread out three stories below Marcus' view from the Antonia was the north pavilion of the Temple Mount. Beyond this spacious square reared the towers and bastions of the sanctuary itself. The first rays of dawn picked out white-robed priests going about their duties. As yet there was no crowd of worshippers, nor any indication that those present had noticed anything amiss.

As the sun illuminated Zion, handfuls of pilgrims arrived. The Court of the Gentiles, the plaza surrounding the sanctuary, was dotted with the devout and those who served them. Low, melodious psalms greeted the day like a cool and pleasant breeze. The south facade of the Antonia, facing the temple grounds, remained buried in its own shadow. So far the medallions were unremarked.

Soon the bellowing of bulls and the mutter of sheep being led to the slaughter disturbed the morning's tranquility. The actual altar was hidden from Marcus' sight by a courtyard wall. Behind this enclosure the black smoke of the sacrifices billowed upward into the sky.

A man in a red-and-brown-striped robe stood at the top of the fourteen steps just outside the Court of the Women. It was he who first appeared to notice the additions to the Antonia's walls. Marcus was looking right at him when he shaded his eyes, stared, then grabbed the arm of a fellow worshipper.

The violent gestures and exaggerated movements of excited speech attracted the attention of others. Soon the north terrace thronged with a rank of Jews facing the Roman fortress. More worshippers poured out of the courtyard of the slaughterers than entered. Others streamed from the gates leading to the temple storerooms of oil and firewood.

People flowed around the temple buildings instead of entering them. Onlookers crowded the plaza, their original purposes forgotten. As Marcus watched, the number of the outraged swelled from twenty-five to fifty and appeared about to double again.

Pointing fingers changed to shaking fists. The hymns of thanksgiving soon became shouts of "Sacrilege! Sacrilege!" A brace of lambs driven into the eastern gate caught the sense of danger. They bolted from their handlers.

At the first alarm the money changers on Solomon's Porch looked up from their counting tables. They swept orderly piles of denarii into iron-bound strongboxes and bellowed for the guards. Apprehensive merchants dealing in ceremonial animals gathered protectively in front of the pens ringing the courtyard. Fistfights broke out, and the angry chant swelled in volume.

Somehow news of the disturbance was communicated to the cramped streets of the city sprawling below the mount. Earlier the ramps leading upward toward Zion had been occupied by orderly queues of pilgrims. Soon they were packed with others coming to see the desecration for themselves.

Temple police in dark tunics and conical helmets appeared on the scene. At first they tried to silence the chanters. But as Marcus watched, it became clear they were confused and uncertain what to do. Obviously outnumbered, they formed a thin line between the sanctuary and the Antonia, then melted away when rocks were thrown.

"Felix," Marcus said to the tribune, "make the rounds of every post. No more people allowed on the mount. Prevent any more from going up the ramp from the city. When the entries are secured, the area is to be cleared. No exceptions."

"Where will you be?"

It was the instant that separated a career military man like Marcus from a young man whose future was really in politics. "I'm going down there," he said in answer to the question. "To see if this can be stopped before it goes any further."

■ ■ ■ ■

Surrounded by his squad of handpicked First Cohort legionaries Marcus marched out of the Antonia. His route lay along the northern face of the Temple Mount. Though he sensed the urgency of regaining control of the rapidly deteriorating situation, Roman discipline asserted itself. Legion military doctrine taught that the steady tramp of hobnailed boots cowed unruly civilians more than a hurried approach. A detachment of confident, determined soldiers reconfirmed Rome's dominance in a way out of proportion to their actual numbers.

Before dawn the troops had dressed in full battle array. Each man carried his ocher-colored shield emblazoned with the silver-winged lightning bolt insignia. Every legionary also carried a pair of javelins. At each soldier's right side was his short sword.

The colonnade that enclosed the temple precincts had portals in the four walls surrounding it. The Tadi Gate broaching the north wall was virtually never used because of its proximity to the Roman stronghold. Jews on their way to worship did not want to be defiled by contact with even the shadow of the Roman Antonia.

A pair of frightened temple guards were stationed on the inside of the gate. Through the grillwork Marcus saw that the north courtyard was more packed with irate protestors than before. "Open the gate!" he demanded.

"But sir," one of the Jewish sentries asserted, "we have no orders to admit you."

"Open it, or my men will break it down," Marcus said tersely.

The gates, hinges creaking from long disuse, flew apart with remarkable speed. "Two men here, Quintus," Marcus ordered. "See that no one comes in behind us. Forward."

A sea of fists gesticulated above every prayer-shawl-draped head.

Quintus was not intimidated. "Make way there," he bellowed. "Way for the centurion! Make way!"

Four legionaries advanced, pressed a hole into the mob with the bosses of their shields, then stamped their feet and pivoted so as to widen the gap. Another pair of soldiers pushed to the apex of the flying wedge, stamped, and also pivoted.

Marcus proceeded at a measured pace into the space that continuously appeared in front of him.

"Blasphemy! Sacrilege!" A wild-eyed man, his red beard flecked with spittle and his voice hoarse from shouting jumped into Marcus' path. "Graven images are an abom—"

The remaining syllables were not completed. Reversing his pilum, Quintus jabbed the butt of the spear into the protestor's midsection. As the protestor's breath escaped with an agonized gasp, he sank down, clutching his stomach.

With surprise, Marcus recognized the man. It was the same fellow Quintus had flogged for swinging the sickle. Marcus wondered fleetingly if he should have ordered his execution after all.

But there was no time to think further on it now.

Spearpoints glittered in the morning sun. The progress of the Romans was inexorable.

The mob was angry. Nevertheless, no Jew

was prepared to throw himself onto a sword—at least, not yet. But Marcus knew how easily anger became violence when left unchecked.

Affixed to a marble pillar at the base of the fourteen steps leading up to the sanctuary was a sign written in Hebrew, Greek, Latin, and Aramaic: *Gentiles are not permitted to pass this point, on pain of death.*

Marcus was fully aware how outnumbered his men were. A wrong move in the midst of this multitude and the hostility would boil over into bloody conflict. His senses acutely tuned to the importance of the next few seconds, Marcus stopped three paces short of the warning column and turned to face the mob.

"People of Jerusalem," he said. "Listen to me!"

The crowd was not inclined to give their attention to a hated Roman, certainly not at this moment. Marcus stared back at them without speaking further. The nearest rank of protestors averted their eyes from his unflinching gaze and grew still.

The hush spread outward from the center. Eventually the raging voices farther back in the throng were quieted.

"Jews," Marcus said. "You see where I have halted. I respect your beliefs. I am not here to disturb your worship, but this rioting must cease."

"Those images disturb our worship!" boomed a protestor. It was the same Jew in the red-and-brown-striped robe Marcus had spotted from the Antonia. "It is against our law! And next

129

week is the Passover!" A furious roar of approval greeted these words.

"I am here to discuss the matter with your priests," Marcus said. "I am here to preserve order...and to prevent bloodshed." There was no mistaking the threat implicit in the words. Romans who spoke of blood to be spilled never referred to Roman blood.

"What if we storm the walls and take those cursed portraits down?" argued the outspoken agitator.

"Mark that one," Marcus said in an aside to Quintus, then loudly, "Think carefully before you do anything hasty."

From three sides of the square came the crash of sword hilts on shields as the rest of First Cohort appeared at the gates. A thunderous drumming echoed around the courtyard as three columns of legionaries advanced. Felix led the advance from one direction and Shomron from another. Vara, his sword slashing the air, appeared from the third. The Praetorian was shouting, "Kill anyone who makes a false move!"

Caiaphas, the high priest, ran toward the scene. The *cohen hagadol*'s gold-embroidered sash hung crookedly from being hastily knotted. The hem of his robe was torn from where he had caught his heel in it as he bustled out of the sanctuary and down the steps.

Marcus greeted the man respectfully. "I have come to discuss the images of our emperor," he said. "Will you precede me to the Antonia and wait for me there?" Caiaphas, his pale cheeks and forehead dripping with perspiration, nodded.

"But first, tell your people to go peacefully," Marcus said, jerking his chin toward the armed ring of legionaries encircling the worshippers.

Caiaphas did as he was told. Sullenly the crowd began to disperse.

"Round up ringleaders for punishment," Vara insisted.

Marcus thought of two Jews he could denounce: the violent older brother and the man in the striped robe.

But turning them over to Vara meant crucifixions. Marcus was certain that such a bloody outcome was not what Pilate had in mind.

Instead he gestured at the throng of hundreds of angry-eyed Jews. "Would Praetorian Vara care to indicate which ones he means?" Marcus inquired.

■ ■ ■ ■

The standoff remained tense, but the show of force coupled with the restraint demonstrated by Marcus prevented a slaughter. As soon as he could, Marcus withdrew his troops to the gates of the Temple Mount. They restricted the entry of worshippers to twenty-five at a time. Thereafter just a number equal to those who had completed their sacrifices and left the premises were allowed to enter.

The temple guards, reinforced in number,

cordoned off the plaza north of the sanctuary. Worshippers were permitted to go about their business but were prevented from getting a closer look at the offending medallions. No Jews were allowed to congregate in groups larger than a minyan of ten.

For the time being the crisis was past.

When Marcus arrived back at the Antonia, he found Caiaphas and a circle of agitated, bustling aides. The Jews were inside the room housing the Jewish ceremonial robes.

By tradition and out of respect for Jewish customs, Gentiles did not enter the chamber where the high priest's vestments were stored. Thus the space, fragrant with cedar-lined closets and incense, formed an island of Jewish sanctity within the Gentile fortress.

But the fact that Caiaphas chose to wait inside the vault was not lost on Marcus either. On more than one occasion in Jewish history officials of the priesthood had taken refuge in the Roman citadel. For over two hundred years Jewish high priests had often been the tools of their foreign overlords.

Caiaphas was certainly no exception. Holding his office at the sufferance of the empire, he knew it was in his best interest to see that no hint of revolt reared its head. If he succeeded in keeping the peace, the rewards of office were substantial. As long as things stayed peaceful, he was permitted wide latitude in dealing with civilian, domestic affairs.

But let him fail in his responsibility, and his tenure could end immediately.

The high priest had used the time since he parted from Marcus to regain his composure. He was a vain man, whose naturally gray hair was dyed jet-black. His face resumed its normal expression of superiority. When he stared down his long nose, his customary pose, a censorious crease formed between his eyebrows.

"Why was I not informed before this…this…" Stopping short of using a perilous word like *outrage,* Caiaphas substituted a haughty wave of his hand. He gestured toward the south wall of the Antonia where the medallions hung.

"Is it necessary for His Excellency, Governor Pilate, to ask your permission before honoring the emperor?" Marcus asked.

Raising an imperious forefinger like a pedagogue correcting a child, Caiaphas turned stiffly toward his flock of obsequious attendants. "Surely His Excellency recognizes how difficult it is to govern these unruly subjects."

An appropriate murmur of agreement rose.

"In fact," Caiaphas continued, "the emperor himself knows how ignorant and superstitious most of these people are. Isn't that so?"

Another concurring buzz.

The high priest turned back toward Marcus. Neck, shoulders, and back moved as one inflexible unit, as if he had a spear shaft connecting hips and head. The upraised hand remained posed in a declaration of his veracity. "As the Almighty is my witness," he said, "we long to do all proper reverence to the emperor…and to the renowned Lucius Sejanus. We of the better classes know that there is no real offense in images of our emperor, who is adored here as indeed he is throughout the world. However, we must bring such uncultured, unschooled folk as these along gradually. They think that these very modest, harmless, entirely fitting adornments are somehow improper."

"Are you proposing that the medallions be removed?" Marcus asked. "Such an action would dishonor the emperor and cause shame to the governor."

"I never...wouldn't think...must be another..." Caiaphas sputtered. "Is Governor Pilate in Jerusalem?"

Marcus shook his head. "Caesarea."

"I will write to him, explaining the difficulty. Perhaps it is merely the placement of the standards that is a problem. Superstitious people don't like to have the heir to the divine Augustus staring over their shoulders as they pray. And the governor must remember that next week the celebration of Passover is coming. Already pilgrims are gathering, making the maintenance of order that much more difficult for me."

"No doubt," Marcus commented wryly. "Write your letter. In the meantime the temple restrictions I have imposed will remain in place...and so will the medallions."

■ ■ ■ ■

Tavita's jowls sagged more than usual as she handed the message from Barak to Miryam.

It was clear the servant did not like what was coming.

Miryam shot her a look of warning. Best to say nothing. Best to keep it to herself. No matter what happened between Barak and herself, Miryam did not want to see even a glimmer of disapproval from the old woman. "Leave me alone," she ordered. Tavita, who had busied herself making the bed, grumbled an unintelligible response and left the room.

Miryam went to the window but did not break the seal or unroll the papyrus. She watched two wild ducks with a tribe of new hatchlings swimming among the reeds at the edge of the lake. If such insignificant creatures could have an hour of happiness, why shouldn't she?

Of course Barak's letter would be cloaked in a pretense of respectability. He would speak of business and his interest in discussing the possibilities she mentioned: Saffron. Crocus bulbs. Spices.

All the while he would know and she would know: if he came to Magdala it would be for a far different reason than either could admit openly.

They would divide themselves between the truth of their passion and the coarse deceit of infidelity. He would come to her bed with the unspeakable fear of being caught. After reveling in their desire, he would flee the scene. Glancing furtively over his shoulder, he would pretend he had been somewhere else.

Miryam toyed with the scroll, which no

doubt contained the impeccably proper reply. Yet she was sure it meant something else entirely. Did she really want to open it, knowing Barak as she did? She loved him. She had always loved him. But she had learned that a man beloved, who yielded to her temptations, was still far from a man who loved her in return.

She thought of Marcus for the first time in days. There was no pretense in him. He simply was hungry for her, and she spread herself to be his banquet. She enjoyed every minute of his pleasure because he had never spoken of love. There was no illusion of caring for the other.

But Barak in her bed was all about pretending. She knew that misery and longing would come hand in hand; he would taste her flesh, then slink away into the shadows. Most of the time she chose to believe the illusion of undying love. At night, alone, her body reached for him; ached for his touch.

But today, in the broad light of day, she held the unopened message up and wondered whether to break the seal.

Was this not the answer to all her wishes? To have him back again?

Or was it simply a foolish dream?

Maybe it didn't matter. There had been no one else in her life when she needed someone so desperately. Barak had been everything to her. She needed the illusion. Needed to believe in spite of what she knew. The lie was better than her emptiness.

She slid her thumb beneath the red wax seal and broke it open.

The words on the page were stiff and formal but clear. He was coming to her.

"To: Miryam, widow of Magdala
From your humble and obedient servant,
Barak bar Halfi..."

■ ■ ■ ■

Marcus had been up for two nights and two tense days. After visiting and revisiting the posts ringing the Temple Mount, he was at last soundly asleep. He finally relinquished the watch to Shomron and Felix. His strict orders called for him to be awakened at once, should any disturbance erupt.

The more Marcus observed Felix the more the young tribune impressed him as cool and capable. Once again he regretted being saddled with Vara. Vara's first inclination upon entering the sacred ground of the Jews had been to order drawn weapons. The Praetorian had to be forcibly restrained from commanding a charge into the heart of the crowd. Since that time he had not stopped prating about making examples to teach the obstinate Jews a lesson.

In order to rid himself of such annoying thoughts, Marcus directed his imagination to Miryam. Once the Passover season was done and Jerusalem emptied out again, Marcus believed, he and First Cohort would go back to Galilee. The thought of returning to

Miryam's bed excited him. He went to sleep pleased with his success in quelling the near-riot. Miryam would be a well-earned reward.

■ ■ ■ ■

Just after midnight a storm rolled across Jerusalem from out of the desert. Thunder paced around the Judean hills like the tramp of an encircling army. Hail pelted the ramparts, making the guards hunker down behind whatever shelter they could find. Pebble-sized chunks of ice rattled off their helmets like shot from a celestial sling.

Despite what Marcus had coached his mind to display, his dreams swirled with images of conflict. He saw again the hatred in the eyes of the throng outside the temple. Anger reached toward him like flames.

And then in his sleep he was back in the forest east of the Weser River. The thunder translated into his nightmare as the drums of the Cherusci tribesmen. Hail clattering against the slender opening of his casement window recalled the impacts of the arrows. Men were cut down to the left and right of him. The howl of the wind carried the war cries of attacking Teutons and the screams of butchered Romans....

The battle line of legionaries faltered, nearly broken. Centurion, optio, and guard sergeant all lay dead in a welter of gore and mud. Incessant rain sluiced their blood into the river to mingle with dead bodies. Drowned Romans, dragged under by the weight of their armor, littered the Weser.

Marcus and a weary handful of others were the extreme left of the Roman force. If they were overwhelmed, then the entire army of General Germanicus would be pushed into the river and destroyed.

"Stand! Stand!" Marcus' voice croaked. The remaining Swiss mercenary allies fled. The volley of arrows slowed. Another attack erupted from the woods. Black shadows moved against the gray curtain of rain.

A pair of Cherusci burst into view. One, a giant of a man swinging a two-handed axe, split the skull of a wounded Roman.

The other attacker selected Marcus, drew back his arm, and darted a spear. It clanged off the boss of Marcus' shield, then both tribesmen were on him.

Marcus caught a blow from the axe with his short sword. The clash of metal nearly dashed his weapon from his hand. He sensed the second assailant circling, looking for an opening to thrust at him from behind.

Bracing himself for another shock from the axe, Marcus' foot slipped in the mud and he pitched sideways. The clumsy sprawl saved his life as the battle axe swept over his head.

Scrambling inside the next swing, Marcus buried his sword up to the hilt in the Teuton's stomach. The man fell forward, wrenching the blade from Marcus' grasp. No weapon! Where was the other attacker? His left foot touched the shaft of the spear. The fingers of his right hand *groped in the mud, coming up with the battle axe.*

A noise from behind. Roll!

The point of the spear came up as the Cherusci lunged. Then out of nowhere a hand grasped his shoulder!

"Master, wake up."

Marcus flailed wildly, knocking someone away.

"Master, it's me, Carta."

Sitting up on his pallet, Marcus cleared his head of the haunting vision. Thunder boomed, recalling him to time and place.

"Carta," he said. "What is it? Is there trouble? Are the Jews rioting?"

"No, master," the boy replied. "A message. A rider from Caesarea. He says it is from the governor. Urgent."

Calling for a taper from the torch blazing in the hall to light his oil lamp, Marcus unfolded the wooden binding enclosing the wax tablet. A message not even committed to parchment meant urgency indeed.

Jewish protestors in Caesarea, he read, *have surrounded the governor's mansion. Return at once with First Cohort.*

ZAYEEN

The rainy season was supposed to be over. Yet Marcus endured hours of riding through shrieking wind and punishing hail. He ordered two changes of mounts, one in Shechem and again in Megiddo.

Marcus, Tribune Felix, and a squadron of cavalry troopers co-opted in Bethel arrived in Caesarea Maritima at mid-morning. The rest of First Cohort were behind on the road somewhere, stoically trudging and quietly cursing their soaked-through state.

The scene in the courtyard of Pilate's palace in Caesarea was extraordinary. It was packed from portico to gateway, from garden to colonnade with Jews. All were male, all were silent, and all had walked a day and a night from Jerusalem to reach the seacoast.

There had been no vandalism. The statues of naked muscular athletes and voluptuous maidens in Pilate's courtyard were covered with Jewish cloaks, but no damage had been done. The Jews were not rioting. There was no stone throwing or shaking of fists...they just stood.

There was another entry into the mansion.

Pilate, when he met Marcus in his office, was clearly nervous. Senior Tribune Trebonius and the other Praetorian soldiers were away in Damascus to meet with the Syrian prefect. The resident cohort assigned to Caesarea was also absent, dealing with pirates operating out of Sidon. The number of soldiers remaining in Pilate's household guard were merely a handful.

"And there must be five hundred of them...those Jews...out there," Pilate said. "What happened in Jerusalem?"

Marcus explained what transpired the morning the medallions were discovered. He also said that the day following relations had been taut but without violence.

"It's because they're here," Pilate asserted. "Here, threatening me. When I woke up, there they were. Waiting. Waiting."

"Have they threatened you, Excellency?" Felix inquired.

Marcus pictured the mass executions carried out by Governor Gratus: a forest of crosses hung with bodies like a whole orchard of rotting fruit. "Have they?" Marcus repeated the question.

"Their presence is a menace," Pilate replied, an edge of panic to his tone. "They say they want to speak to me. They aren't even supposed to come to Caesarea...they have defiled themselves. Who knows what might happen next! Go out there. Talk to them. Find out what they want."

Marcus knew he was being sent out as the sacrificial lamb. As the officer most identified with the placement of the medallions he was being offered to the mob. If he was not torn limb from limb, then Pilate would consider what to do next.

A Roman's commitment to duty allowed Marcus no alternative.

A rhythmic murmuring entered the courtyard-facing window. Governor Pilate spoke Latin and Greek but very little Hebrew. "What's that?" he demanded. "What're they saying now?"

Marcus cocked an ear. "They're praying, Excellency. As soon as they've finished, I'll speak to them."

Felix volunteered to accompany him. Since they might be walking toward their death, it was a striking gesture. The two officers left Pilate surrounded by the cavalry troopers to supplement his security detail.

Before stepping out the portal onto the terrace, Marcus paused as an odd thought struck him. "Ironic," he said.

"What do you mean?" Felix asked.

In that moment Marcus decided the young man was completely trustworthy. "It's ironic that the governor didn't go to Jerusalem when he knew there'd be protests over the standards...so the protest has come to him. A commander can't hide from the consequence of his actions, even if he tries."

The bobbing heads stopped; the singsong prayers ceased.

"Here we go," Marcus said.

Though the protest had so far been entirely peaceful, instant hostility crowded the square at Marcus' appearance. A knot formed in his stomach. There! He spotted the man in the striped robe who had harangued the worshippers on the Temple Mount. And there again! The red-haired man felled by the blow to the stomach and his younger brother.

The back of Marcus' neck prickled. Squaring his shoulders, he took a breath. "Jews," he said in a booming voice. "Why're you here, disturbing the peace? You should leave at once. Return to your homes."

"I, bar Abba, will speak for all," the striped-robed man suggested. "We've come to seek an audience with Governor Pilate, but he's refused to see us."

Bar Abba. "Son of the father." Surely a false name chosen to hide the man's real identity as well as for its symbolic overtones. "The governor is a busy man," Marcus responded gruffly. "Give your message to me, and I'll see that he gets it."

Bar Abba snorted. "Centurion, you, of all people, must already know why we are here! We have a law..."

"You have many laws," Marcus said. "More than any other people on earth, I think." He hoped the quip would reduce the strain.

No one smiled.

"We have a law," bar Abba continued, "a law handed down by the Almighty, which says we aren't permitted images of man or beast."

"But I am a Roman, and such a law doesn't apply to me. Or would you make the whole world obey your laws? Or should the Antonia, which is Roman, have to follow your rules?"

"The presence of the images is a sacrilege to our worship. They offend the Almighty."

"There is precedent in your history for your god to defend his own honor," Marcus said. "Why not wait to see if he'll strike them off the building himself?" Even as he spoke he remembered the violence of the storm the night before. He shook away the thought, hastily reasserting his authority. "We also have laws. We're bound to honor the emperor. You are likewise obliged to honor him. Or are you encouraging rebellion?"

"No other governor has offended us in this way," bar Abba said, ignoring Marcus' question. "Does Governor Pilate wish to *cause* a rebellion?"

"Is that a threat?" Marcus said fiercely. "If it is, you'll regret it."

There was no reply, forcing Marcus to speak again.

"What do you want?"

"We want the standards removed."

"And what'll you do if they aren't?"

"We'll stay here 'til they are."

"Know this," Marcus said. "The governor will consider your petition, but not if you continue this affront to his dignity. So far you've not been harmed in any way, but you must leave now, or you may not be able to leave later."

The challenge was plain: depart at once, peacefully, or risk being carried out on the points of Roman lances.

Bar Abba shook his head. "We aren't afraid to die," he said. "Remove the standards..."

"Or else what?"

Bar Abba shrugged. "Or else our blood is on the governor's hands."

■ ■ ■ ■

When Marcus reported the conversation with the man who called himself *bar Abba,* Pilate flew into a rage. "Extortion! They can't threaten me! Who do they think they are?" Part of his hostility was then directed at Marcus. "What did you do up there in Jerusalem to cause so much trouble? How could you take a simple assignment and botch it so badly?"

This was not the time to remind Pilate that Marcus had merely been executing orders. "They say they won't leave unless the standards are removed," Marcus repeated. Pilate could not duck the present problem by placing the blame on Marcus.

"Won't leave unless!" Pilate blustered. "Do they think they can haggle with me like a spice seller in the bazaar? Drive them out. Use whips...swords if necessary...but I want my courtyard cleansed of their foul presence at once." As an afterthought Pilate added, "Keep the bloodshed to a minimum."

There it was: exactly the situation Marcus successfully avoided at the Temple Mount. Since it came as a direct order, this time there was no escape. The command to keep the bloodshed to a minimum was a foolish post-script. It was a provision designed to let Pilate shift the responsibility if things went bloodily wrong.

When Marcus cleared his throat, Pilate whirled round on him. "Do you object to the command, Centurion? Are you going to argue with me also? Or don't you think you and the cavalry troopers are enough to face a band of unarmed Jews?"

"No argument, Excellency," Marcus soothed. He was thinking how *band* was an inept choice of words to describe a cohort-sized group of nearly five hundred men. And who said they were unarmed? "Your word is law. But I do have a suggestion."

"What?" Pilate said suspiciously.

"Wait 'til tonight. They'll be hungry and thirsty. When they're sleepy as well, it'll be much easier to create panic and confusion. We will stampede them."

"Approved," Pilate said grudgingly. "But do it."

■ ■ ■ ■

Hours of preparation passed. Marcus gathered the troopers and explained his intent. Pilate would not allow his household guards to join the battle. He claimed they needed to be kept in reserve in case the mansion was attacked. Counting himself and Felix. Marcus had twenty-five Romans to confront the mob of Jews.

"On my signal," Marcus said, "we sweep in from three sides: portico, colonnade, and garden. Not from the street gate. If we leave them an avenue of retreat, they'll take it. If they have none, they'll fight."

"Why not kill them?" one of the troopers growled.

"Whips before swords, by order of the governor," Marcus stressed. No sense trying to discuss the bigger picture of national repercussions. Sometimes having an order to fall back on made things easier. "Make all the noise you can. Shouts, trumpets, you understand. Then lay about you with the lash. Herd them like sheep. Don't draw blades unless they show weapons of their own."

"I don't like it," the same trooper muttered. "Dirty Jews will knife us in the backs."

"You are relieved," Marcus said firmly. "Report to the stables and remain there. Anyone else? Any man I see not following my instructions completely will forfeit one year's service credit and feel the lash himself. Any takers?"

There were no more complaints.

The blare of trumpets and the clash of spear butts on shields shattered the vessel of night into shards of terror. Men, jostled out of sleep, crashed into each other. Jews knocked down other Jews before the first Roman raven ever fell on a protestor's shoulders.

To add to the panic, some of the troopers who spoke Hebrew shouted, "Run for your lives! They're killing everyone!" even though the most blood spilled so far came from a score of broken noses.

For the first few moments of the night-watch encounter it seemed that Marcus' plan would be an unqualified success. Ten or so Jews, those nearest the gate, bolted into the street outside. They pelted east away from Caesarea.

Hardier souls, or those too hemmed in to escape easily, were encouraged by the whistle of the raven whips. To the sounds of panic were added cries of pain as the troopers laid about them. The Romans indiscriminately slashed faces as well as backs.

The protestors scrambled over each other in their haste to get away. Then the voice of bar Abba rang out, "Sit down! Sit down!"

Directly in front of Marcus, a man whom he had been successfully driving dropped to the ground. The dark form turned lumpish as the figure crouched, covered his head with his cloak, and buried his face in his arm. When Marcus belabored the man's shoulders with the whip he produced grunts of pain, but no further attempt to flee.

Around the courtyard the result was the same. The Jews did not lift a hand in their own defense, but neither did they run away. It was like lashing unresisting sacks of grain.

Defeated in his initial strategy, Marcus called for lights. Flickering torches illuminated a hellish scene of armored demons whipping unmoving victims. "Stop!" Marcus called.

Picking out bar Abba's striped robe from the rest, Marcus drew his sword and crossed to the leader. He kicked others out of the way as he went. Grasping bar Abba by his hair, Marcus jerked the man's head up. "Get out," he snarled into bar Abba's face. "This is your last chance!"

To Marcus' surprise, the man straightened his back and tossed back his cloak. With deliberate care bar Abba parted the folds of his robe and bared his throat to the light. "Kill me," he said. "Kill us all. We are willing to die rather than let our temple be defiled."

Marcus' arm drew back, the point of his short sword aligned right below bar Abba's chin.

Around the plaza the other troopers did the same. Each prepared to execute a Jew with a deft blow.

Each Jew calmly awaited the stroke.

To Marcus' utter consternation, protestors not yet facing drawn swords threw back their cloaks, presented their necks, and demanded, "No, kill me first! No, me!"

The Roman soldiers would have to slay twenty or so Jews each to complete the night's gory work.

Marcus let the tip of the blade droop. "Withdraw," he bellowed to the legionaries. "Do you hear me? Withdraw."

He was baffled. Was the placement of a handful of inoffensive medallions worth dying for? Were the faces of the emperor and his favorite a greater sacrilege than the cheating and stealing that regularly accompanied temple services? If men could die with such composure in the midst of such hypocrisy, what might they do for honor that rang more true?

If a leader appeared who could unify and rally the Jews behind a real cause...like reestablishing their independent kingdom...the whole empire would have trouble containing the force of their uprising.

It was a serious threat to consider.

For the time the protestors had won, but there were no shouts or cheers. The noise that pursued the chagrined Romans back into Pilate's mansion was the sound of prayers.

■ ■ ■ ■

Three days passed.

The protestors remained in the courtyard. They were allowed no food or water except what they had carried with them from Jerusalem.

There had still been no defacing of the governor's property and no carnage. The crowd made little noise apart from times of prayer.

At dawn on the day after the aborted attempt to use force the rest of First Cohort had arrived. Ringing the palace grounds, some legionaries plainly itched for the chance to end the confrontation by force.

Vara, the chief voice calling for a swift and vicious end, was not alone in that sentiment. Pilate was virtually a prisoner in his own mansion. Afraid he would be attacked if he tried to move, the governor was even more frightened of making a mistake.

Pacing from office to library to audience chamber and back again, Pilate dithered about what to do next. Felix offered no advice; Marcus was again at odds with Vara.

"Drive them out with whips," Vara urged.

"And if they will not go, use swords and spears."

"They *won't* go," Marcus asserted. "When we tried scourging them into leaving, they simply sat down and exposed their necks for the blade. If we kill one we must expect to have to kill them all. Wait. Sooner or later hunger and thirst will drive them out."

"But they can't stay," Pilate said, stalking his shadow across the marble pavement and then being trailed by it in turn.

Marcus knew the predicament Pilate was in. It was a dilemma of his own making. In attempting to curry favor with Sejanus he had broken precedent by insisting the medallions be installed. Now he was caught. No matter what he did next he risked the emperor's displeasure. If he capitulated, he might be branded weak and easily intimidated. If he used force, almost certainly armed insurrection would follow. Maintaining order in all parts of the empire had always been Tiberius' highest priority.

Finally, driving Pilate's sense of urgency was the imminent return from Syria of Senior Tribune Trebonius. Making no decision would be seen as the worst possible character flaw. What if the Praetorian stepped in and resolved the conflict in Pilate's place? Surely that would mean a quick exit for the governor and an ignominious return to Rome.

What way out would also save face?

"Excellency," Marcus suggested, "the Jewish Passover is almost here."

Pilate threw up his hands in frustration. "What of it? Would you like me to become a Jew so I can side with them?"

"Perhaps the centurion has become a Jew himself," Vara inserted with a sneer. "Or perhaps his Jewish mistress has tainted his judgment."

Marcus bit his lip, but Pilate made a angry gesture that said he did not want to be bothered with squabbling over trifles.

"This is the worst possible time to spill Jewish blood," Marcus pointed out. "These are not criminals or ferocious rebels. We are speaking of a religious controversy. But let them die over this matter and a clever preacher..." Marcus paused long enough for Pilate's thoughts to also turn to Yochanan the Baptizer, then continued, "a clever preacher will call them martyrs, sacrificed in the name of freedom like the lambs on their Passover."

"Give me answers," Pilate demanded. "I don't need to be reminded of the rest."

Marcus knew that whatever advice he offered would hang around his neck forever. If it turned out badly, he would be the one sent to oversee tar caravans for the rest of his career. But, hoping to prevent bloodshed, he plunged ahead anyway. "Be magnanimous. Ignore these people for a few more days. Send a message to High Priest Caiaphas about a special favor from the emperor. To honor their holy day you will withdraw the standards to the inside of the Antonia where they will not offend. That way you will not be seen as negotiating with rebels. Caiaphas will be even more in your debt than before, since he will appear to share in the amended order. The emperor will continue to be honored on Roman premises while the peace of the province is restored without any military action."

"A gesture for their Passover," Pilate mused. "Yes. It will work. Caiaphas will also emphasize that their lives are being spared as part of this Imperial grant. And if they are as religious as they claim, they will hurry off to return to Jerusalem in time for the celebration. I knew I would come up with a solution." Pilate bellowed for his secretary to join him.

Marcus slipped Felix a wink, but Vara glowered. "One more suggestion," Vara said, interrupting Pilate's dictation.

"Yes, what?" Pilate said, annoyed at the intrusion.

"So there is no repetition of this kind of affair, why don't we arrest this bar Abba fellow and the other ringleaders? Make examples of them."

Marcus knew the sort of example Vara had in mind.

"A good suggestion, Praetorian Vara," Pilate complimented.

"Excellency," Marcus cautioned, "bar Abba has been a voice urging restraint. If this affair ends peacefully, we should keep an eye on him but take no further action."

His head tilted in contemplation, the governor eyed Marcus with suspicion. "A Jewish mistress, eh?" he muttered. "Go away, all of you. I'll have additional orders later."

KHET

Word of the events in Jerusalem and Caesarea reached the town of Magdala. Miryam listened to the recounting with detached interest. Life was much more than Roman politics and the fanatical religion of her own people. The temple had long ago become ruled by priests who served with the tacit approval of the Roman governor. Religion was, she believed, a tool to keep the ignorant populace under control. This was in direct opposition to her brother El'azar, who prayed daily for the coming of a messiah to liberate Israel and cleanse the temple. Her lack of concern was another source of conflict between Miryam and her siblings.

She had guessed that Marcus was somehow involved in the events of the past weeks. Otherwise he would have been back in Magdala and once again trying to get into her bed. He would be surprised at how she had changed in the intervening time since their last meeting.

She decided she would tell him in person that it was over between them. She was in love with another.

Marcus would take it pragmatically. He enjoyed her, but he was the type of man who would have no trouble finding another woman to take her place.

It was late afternoon, three days before the eve of Passover. Miryam had been watching for the approach of Barak bar Halfi and his family since mid-morning.

They were hours later than their scheduled time of arrival, but Miryam did not mind. Perhaps they would be persuaded to stay the night at her villa in Magdala and resume their journey to Jerusalem the next day.

A dozen imagined scenarios ran through Miryam's mind. All of them concluded with Barak taking her in his arms and promising that somehow they would find a way to be together.

At last Miryam spotted Barak and his family among the hundreds of pilgrims making *Aliyah* to the temple.

Through the haze she could see Barak's band was small. As Miryam's tenant, he was a poor man. His wife and youngest daughter perched on a donkey, which he led. Two other daughters, as plain in face and form as their plump little mother, walked along behind. The day was hot, the road choked with dust. No doubt Barak's wife would be caked with grime and sweating. A contrast which would work to Miryam's advantage.

Miryam hurried to her room. She washed and anointed herself with her most expensive perfume, then put on a fresh linen shift. Could Barak fail to notice the difference between his ordinary wife and Miryam's extraordinary beauty?

She would offer him her renewed love with one additional enticement.

Thousands of Persian crocus bulbs were stacked and locked away in a storage room in her barn. Freeman, short sword at his side, stood guard over the treasure she would give Barak.

Could any man refuse the combination of wealth and passion? No man Miryam had ever known. And Barak bar Halfi had always been governed first by passion.

She brushed her hair and braided it. Barak had always enjoyed taking the ribbon from her thick plait. How his eyes had glowed with desire as she shook her hair free and let it cascade over her shoulders.

Would he have the same image when he saw her again? Ten years had passed, but she had so much more to offer now. She had learned how to drive a man to the edge of madness and then satisfy every longing. She would make Barak remember, make him hungry for her again. Then she would teach him more about passion than he dreamed existed.

And his wife would never suspect.

Everything was ready in the courtyard. Clean basins of water for washing feet. Food. Drink. Cushions beside the fountain in the foyer. She had also made a bed in the barn behind the sacks of bulbs. Just like old times.

She smiled when she heard Barak's voice at the gate of the villa. True to the plan, old Tavita greeted the family, ushering them into the open vestibule and calling house servants to wash their feet and make them welcome.

Miryam waited upstairs, cherishing the sound of Barak's voice. Flushed with excitement, she drew a deep breath to steady herself. It would not be good to appear too eager.

Tavita called to her from the foot of the stairs. "Mistress! Mistress Miryam! Barak bar Halfi and his family have arrived."

This was Miryam's cue to enter. One last glance in the looking glass. A swift brush of a stray lock of hair. Then she emerged. She had rehearsed it a thousand times. Pleasant grace. Move with elegance down the steps. Interested but not too eager. Extend the hand. Greet Barak's squat mud-hen wife and daughters first. Ask if they had been properly cared for. Was there anything they needed? How was the journey? Hot for so early in the season, was it not? Address Barak coolly, as though this was pure business.

Barak, in response, exhibited uneasiness, and hovered at his wife's shoulder. As he introduced his daughters and his wife, he did not look Miryam in the face. "My wife, Eve. And from youngest to oldest here are my girls." He named them, but Miryam forgot the names as soon as she heard them.

Barak's eyes darted around the opulent dwelling. His thoughts were obvious to Miryam in spite of pleasant small talk: *She's come up in the world. Wealthy. Friend of Romans. Mistress of an estate and a villa. Mistress of other things as well. I'm still a lowly tenant farmer.*

"Jerusalem will be more crowded than usual." Miryam took a seat on a cushion and invited the others to follow suit.

Eve babbled, "Oh yes! Everyone is talking about it! Our men facing off with the Roman governor in Caesarea over the shields they hung on Antonia tower! Imagine! They backed down all right. Barak would have gone, but I told him he shouldn't. Not being a married man with daughters. What if the Romans had killed everyone? Then I would have been a widow. My daughters orphans at the mercy of charity."

Miryam continued to smile and nod through this vapid recitation. She noticed that Barak stirred uncomfortably as Eve went on and on.

Miryam patted Eve's hand sympathetically. "You are a wise woman to keep him close." Then she added, "Where will you stay in Jerusalem?"

Eve exclaimed, "I thought you knew! With your brother, El'azar, and your sister, Marta! We were wondering if you were going along."

Miryam did not say El'azar had not invited her. "I have so much business here, I'm afraid."

"Even during Passover?" queried Eve. "Poor dear."

Barak interjected, "Great estates mean great responsibilities, my dove. Isn't that right, Miryam?"

Miryam answered sadly, "It's almost more than one woman can manage." It was time to get to the point. "That is why, Barak, I have asked you to stop by. I have a business proposal to make."

Barak stared down at his feet. "Yes. The bulbs. Saffron." Why would he not let himself meet Miryam's steady gaze? He took his wife's hand in his own. Was he trying to resist the temptation Miryam knew he must feel?

"My late husband had plans for planting and growing saffron in Galilee," Miryam lied. Old Yosef had nothing to do with this. "He thought it could be a success with the right man in charge."

Eve's round face brightened with enthusiasm. "Barak is such a hard worker. I know Master Yosef always looked on my husband kindly. It is so good of you to follow through with your husband's wishes."

Barak interrupted quietly. "I'm not sure this is right for me. I don't know enough about it. Such a delicate crop."

Eve argued, "My husband is too modest. He is an incredible farmer. As your revenues must tell you."

Barak continued, "The saffron must be harvested exactly on the right day. One freeze and the entire crop could be lost...."

Miryam knew why he was resisting. He was afraid of getting involved with her. And he knew it was inevitable. Miryam let Eve chatter on. No matter what Barak felt, Eve would have her way. They would take over the twelve fallow acres in Cana. The crocus bulbs would be planted. Saffron would be harvested. They would be rich.

"Then it's settled," Miryam said, bringing the discussion to a conclusion.

Eve beamed. "You won't be sorry. Barak is an honorable man. A hard worker and..."

"Yes. Good!" Miryam brushed his rigid

hand with her fingers. "My late husband would be so pleased."

Barak was pale as he nodded his agreement.

"The day is late," Miryam sympathized. "I'll have the servants make rooms ready for you. No use pressing on. We have so much to talk about."

At this, Barak rose suddenly to his feet. "No! No...thank you. I...we have made arrangements down the road... I mean...we must push ahead."

Miryam smiled, pretending not to care. It would have been so much easier if he had agreed to stay the night. Her chance to present him with the other half of her bargain was slipping away.

She patted Eve's arm. "If you must go, well then... But you're welcome. And do try to stop in on your way home." She winked at the daughters. "Now, we have prepared a table for you. Through there." She indicated a doorway into a dining area where a feast was spread. "Go ahead. Wash up. And I'll just steal your husband for a few minutes. I'd like to show him what has arrived from Persia. And the contract of course. I have it ready for his signature."

Eve and her daughters, oblivious to Miryam's real motive, were too grateful for words. Miryam knew that Barak's wife had called her a whore right along with everyone else. But here she was, for a few Persian crocus bulbs, sending her beloved down the garden path!

Away they went to the table. That would add a few pounds to their ample backsides.

Miryam and Barak were alone.

She took Barak's arm. He pulled it back. She gave him the knowing smile of an old friend as if to say, "I won't hurt you."

Chagrined, he nodded and meekly trailed her out to the barn.

Freeman, his face stern, stood to attention and unlocked the door. Miryam dismissed him. His weathered face puckered into a scowl as he obeyed. The old man had guessed, of course, what lay in store for Barak bar Halfi.

Miryam led. Barak hesitated. The barn was dark. Warmth surged through her as it had ten years ago when they were alone.

"Over here." She moved toward the heaps of crocus bulbs.

He remained rooted. "What do you want with me?" he asked in a resigned voice.

Turning to face him, she tossed her head as though he had insulted her. "I want you to harvest spice. Then you'll be rich and I'll be richer."

"You were at the wedding."

She shrugged and sauntered back to face him. "So?"

"You know what they would have done to you?"

"El'azar gave me some idea." She reached around him, brushing the small of his back with her fingertips. "Strip me and stone me for a harlot? Is that it?"

He pushed her away. "I love my wife."

"You love me. You know you love me." She moved to embrace him, sliding her arms around him. "You can't forget what we had any more than I can forget." She drew him into the shadowed space.

"You've made a mistake. I made a mistake. Coming here..." He did not respond to her touch, but she felt the hammering of his heart.

She raised her face to his. "We can have it again. Barak! Everything I have is yours...everything!"

His eyes hardened with desire. Lips parted as he stooped to kiss her.

Miryam melted with the fire of longing. She had won! Everything she had dreamed of would now come true.

And then...

A shriek sounded from the entrance. Barak jerked his head up in horror. He shoved Miryam hard, sending her sprawling to the floor.

Framed in the doorway were Eve and her daughters, a plump hen surrounded by her chicks!

"You are a slut. Always have been." Barak acted the part of an outraged man of honor as he towered over Miryam. "We have been offered another orchard and a house. We'll be off your land by the new moon."

"Barak!" Miryam pleaded. "No! Barak, don't..."

Snatching up a handful of dust, he flung it at her, stinging her eyes. "And that is my answer to your spice!" He strode from the barn. Grasping Eve by the elbow, he propelled her away from Miryam, from the house, and from Magdala.

■ ■ ■ ■

Marcus stood again in the Court of the Gentiles on the Temple Mount. It was one day before the beginning of Passover, but the tension that had gripped Jerusalem a week earlier had dissipated.

Everywhere he saw cheerful looks, and occasionally triumphant smirks, quickly concealed.

He turned around to study the walls of the Antonia where the last of the medallions was being removed. As Marcus watched, the shield bearing the face of the emperor slid upward, then over the parapet of the Antonia. It was like watching a bronze lizard crawling to safety.

Over his shoulder Marcus noticed sunlight winking on the gilded cornice of the Jewish sanctuary. He was glad he was not superstitious. To someone more gullible it might appear that the god of the Jews and the divinity of the Romans had been face-to-face and the Hebrew deity had triumphed.

Marcus did not believe in omens...much.

He believed in force and tolerated politics. Both of those elements he understood. For that reason he offered sacrifices to whatever local gods he encountered, even if he thought it an idle gesture, without real significance.

It never hurt to play it safe.

The Jews certainly saw the events of the preceding week as a vindication of their righteousness. A heightened air of celebration surpassed the usual holiday merrymaking.

The Jews had no idea what dangerous ground they were on. Coercing Pilate had succeeded, but the governor had been made to look bad in the eyes of Sejanus and the emperor. Marcus suspected Pilate had several second thoughts. Maybe slaughtering the protestors in his courtyard would have been preferable.

In any case, future Jewish protests could expect less tolerance, even if the issues raised were of more significance. They had used up their measure of mercy and should not expect more.

"And what a stupid cause to be willing to die for," Marcus muttered aloud.

"Master?" Carta asked. "Did you speak?" The youth was obviously enjoying the sights of the city.

Marcus grimaced. "It was nothing," he replied. Pointing at the animal pens, he handed over a silver denarius. "Go buy a pair of doves for us." Gentiles, while not allowed to enter the sanctuary premises, were permitted to send offerings in to the god of the Jews. "Remember," he added as Carta set off, "count the change. You should get fourteen pennies back."

Short measures, damaged goods, imperfect animals, clipped coins: all these corrupt practices characterized the holy mountain of the Jews. Once again Marcus shook his head at the irony. The emperor's face polluted their worship, but cheating and deceiving their fellows apparently did not.

At least Marcus also had reason to celebrate. Even under Pilate's suspicious eye he had acquitted himself properly. Soon he could return to Galilee and Miryam. He would try to forget about Jerusalem, politics, and every Jew except one…and she would make him forget anything else troubling.

A loud crash interrupted his reverie. This was followed by shouting and punctuated by cries of pain. Through the crowd of holiday pilgrims it was impossible to tell for certain, but the disturbance appeared to come from the direction of the money changers' tables.

Another riot was breaking out, and Carta was somewhere in the middle. What if the Jews were merely pretending to be pacified? What if this was the real rebellion? Marcus slapped the sword hilt hanging at his left side but did not draw it yet. He sprinted toward the noise of the tumult.

Another crash! A flock of doves, suddenly released from an overturned cage, exploded upwards in a riot of panicked flapping. Marcus dodged a pair of lambs bolting toward him.

Jumping up on the bottom rung of a corral fence, Marcus peered over the milling throng. He saw the knotted cords of a whip flick up and slash downward. A voice with an arresting tone of authority shouted, "This house is supposed to be for prayer...to worship my father! But by lying and cheating you have made it a home for thieves!"

The lash whistled again, and another cry of pain rent the afternoon air.

Like thousands of tiny cymbals, coins spattering on stone rang a discordant music. Whooping and yelling, people bent and scooped up bouncing pennies. A groan of anguish connected more to the disappearing money than to the scourging wafted upward.

Someone seemed to have been reading Marcus' mind. More corruption was produced by deceitful people falsely claiming to honor their religion than ever came from bits of inanimate brass.

The pounding of drums summoned the temple police.

Marcus racked his brain. Who would do such a thing? Not the Sadducees; they were too entrenched in the present system. Not the Pharisees; lavish displays of religion were their style, not angry demonstrations. Zealots? But this matter did not concern politics; it was internal religious dissension.

The plaza between Marcus and the tumult was packed with onlookers. Some appeared shocked, some curious, some openly applauding.

Others were hostile, angry. One handsome, dark-haired man shook his fist and shouted what could only be violent threats.

Since Marcus could not move closer, he ascended another rung of the fence. Could it be that Yochanan the Baptizer had turned militant after all? Had Marcus guessed wrong?

Marcus got the barest glimpse of a tall man with a whip raised in his hand. The fellow's face showed the flush of indignant fury. A thinner face, not so weathered. Not the Baptizer then.

Marcus was relieved.

Then a group of men, apparently the troublemaker's friends, closed around him and hustled him away. Out the eastern gate they went, just before the temple guards belatedly appeared on the scene.

Things were not quieting down. The instigator may have departed, but the uproar continued. Money changers grabbed bystanders by their lapels as if to shake loose the pocketed coins. The animal merchants called for help in rounding up their roaming charges. The temple police stood around uncertainly, harangued on all sides and baffled as to what action to take.

As Marcus hopped down, something clicked against his heel. It was a bronze coin that had rolled or been kicked halfway across the courtyard. He bent and retrieved it. The edge clearly showed the marks of a file where part of the metal had been scraped off. On its face was the visage of Tiberius.

This had not been a good day for the image of the emperor.

Carta tugged at his sleeve. "I saw it all," he said urgently. "I was second in line at the dove sellers when this man appeared like a fury.

He shouted and whipped them. You should have seen them scramble to get away!"

"Did you hear his name?"

"Yes," Carta replied. "His friends who took him away before the guards came called him teacher. *Rebbe Yeshua*, they called him."

"Anything else?"

"One of the money changers was talking to a priest. He said they'd get even with that Yeshua of Nazareth if it was the last thing they did."

Nazareth was in Galilee. Marcus hoped this incident was merely the ravings of an unfettered madman. He hoped whatever rebellion might follow would stay here in Jerusalem and not follow him back home.

"Do you have to report this to the governor?" Carta asked.

Marcus thought about that. Go back to Caesarea? Tell Pilate that even though the shields were down, things were still not under control in Jerusalem?

"No," he replied with finality. "This is just another example of a Jewish religious fanatic. No concern of the governor. Let's go."

■ ■ ■ ■

While three quarters of Jewish families in Galilee swarmed to Jerusalem, Miryam brooded alone in Magdala. She knew Barak would see her brother and sister over the holiday.

Distance had partially shielded Miryam's siblings from the gossip surrounding her. Several days' travel between their home in Bethany and Miryam's estate in the north diluted scandal to a degree.

But Barak would arrive clothed in indignation and self-righteousness from his encounter with Miryam.

Would Barak tell El'azar what had happened?

Would Barak's wife whisper to Marta the details?

Miryam felt sick with the thought of Barak and her brother discussing her as if she were a sort of renegade. She knew Barak well enough to understand that he would protect his own reputation first. He had always been weak in that way. It mattered to him what people thought.

She forgave him anyway. She loved him in spite of the fact that years before he had let her go under to save his image of respectability.

Now Miryam had no respectability left to save. So why did she care what her brother thought of her? Why should she wish that she was going to be home with her family for Passover when they disapproved of her?

But she did care. She did wish. The holiday approached, and Miryam was left out.

As was the custom, Jewish servants were excused to spend time with their own families. The Passover *seder* was the ceremony in which supper was eaten while reclining. Since servants usually ate standing up, this was a sign that every Jew was free in the eyes of the Most High, regardless of social status. *Pesach* was meant to be a celebration of freedom from bondage. Every Jewish servant was ceremonially free from servitude and allowed to dine with members of his own kin, reclining like a king at his own table.

In the scowl of the Freeman Miryam saw his loyalty to her had disintegrated. He took his leave to head home to his daughter's house in Cana. His curt farewell left Miryam with the distinct impression that he did not know if he would be back. And if he came back, he did not know if he could remain in the service of a woman who had forsaken Torah so completely.

Miryam had planned on giving him a gift of a few denarii to buy his holiday meal. After reading the resentment in his eyes she withheld her generosity. What right did her servant have to judge her behavior? He could find his own lamb to sacrifice and purchase wine and matzo with his own funds. Let him go then and recline at his daughter's table like a rich man. For the seven days of Passover he could pretend he was the master of his life and did not need to be employed!

Who was left at the villa? Besides old Tavita there were three Syrian housemaids and their half-wit husbands who tended the livestock.

The house was a gloomy place. Tavita displayed her ire by slamming in and out of rooms, growling at the Syrians, complaining about her bones and her feet and her age—and the fact that she was left to do the work of twenty.

As a child Miryam had loved the Passover. She had been the most eager among her siblings to search the house for leaven. She had understood that cleaning each bread crumb from every corner had been like clearing away the sin in her heart.

Here beneath the cupboard, a small lie.
There in the corner, a bit of anger.
On the shelf, a bad thought.

Life had been simple when the broken pieces of her soul had been crumbs, easy to sweep into a pile and burn in the yard.

Now?

Shattered pieces everywhere. Too many to gather. Too many to count. Throw the broken parts away and there would be nothing left of her at all.

There was no starting over.

This year there was no pretense. Miryam did not bother to clean the leaven from the house. What was the point? She did not order the lamb to be selected and killed or the blood of the lamb sprinkled on her doorposts. The angel of death would pass by, see it, and laugh at the joke. There was no passing over her sin.

Too much. Too often. Too big. In spite of vows made to be better. Promises to herself broken time and again.

She had given up.

Wasn't that a kind of freedom? she reasoned. Accepting her chains? Wasn't that better than pretending she was something she could never be?

But still, in quiet moments, she wished she

could start over somehow. Sweep her soul clean. Be someone else. Someone...good.

The joyous celebration of freedom in the Passover mocked Miryam of Magdala.

She was in bondage to loneliness, a slave to obsession, desire, and passion. And there was no one who could set her free.

TET

A day before Passover a messenger sent from El'azar arrived outside Miryam's gate in Magdala.

The youth had been given strict instructions. He was to deliver the letter into the hand of Miryam personally. No servant of the household could take it from him.

Tavita offered to pay him and take the parchment to her mistress. The mistress of the house was in ill health, confined to her room, the old woman explained.

None of this mattered to him.

Next Tavita invited him to wait in the open courtyard.

He would not enter.

She attempted to coax him, offering a tall glass of lemon water to quench his thirst.

He refused to drink.

Remaining steadfastly rooted in the middle of the street, he was visible to everyone who passed by.

Shielding his eyes from the harsh glare of the sun, he would not let the shadow of Miryam's wall touch him.

Tavita knew without explanation that the lad was obeying the old proverb, "Better to burn with thirst in the blast of the sun than to find shade in the house of a harlot."

With a sigh the old woman closed the gate and tramped up to rouse Miryam from her long sleep.

She was thanked by having a shoe and an oil lamp heaved at her head by her mistress. Miryam, who had not left her gloomy bedchamber in two days, was in no mood to get up or to see anyone. A string of curses followed the old woman back down the stair, across the courtyard, and out to the messenger once again.

"My mistress is ill as women sometimes are. She won't see you. Give her brother's message to me, and I'll see she gets it."

He shook his head resolutely. "I'll wait."

Curious stares from two fishermen. Heads together, they muttered something about the whore of Magdala. Tavita scowled at them.

The messenger shrugged. "You see why I can't come in."

The old woman slammed the gate once again. With renewed determination she hobbled across the vestibule and up the stair. This time she remained on the balcony outside Miryam's shuttered room and addressed her through the door.

"He's still outside in the street. People are

174

starting to talk. He won't leave until you take El'azar's letter from him. He will be there until you take it in your own hand. He won't enter. You know what that means."

Then she stepped back as Miryam, eyes blazing with fury, hair wild, charged out in her shift.

This was not the first time Miryam had sunk in the mire of depression, only to be aroused by rage. Loneliness and self-pity had festered into roaring hatred. Smashing a vase, she cursed the messenger and the people of Magdala who passed her villa. She damned El'azar and Marta for betraying her. Calling on the ground of Cana to turn to salt, she blasted everyone but her beloved Barak.

Every insult planted in her heart had blossomed into a tangle of thorny hatred.

She stormed to the gate and yanked it open with a crash.

There she stood, a madwoman, uncombed and unwashed, snarling at El'azar's messenger like a cornered stray.

The youth took three steps backward. He gawked at her. His mouth worked, but he could not speak.

Then, timidly he asked, "Madame... Miryam Magdalan? Sister of El'azar of Bethany?"

"Who else should I be?" she shouted. "Idiot! My maid told you I am sick! Sick with a blinding headache! What do you want?"

Clearly frightened by her appearance and demeanor, he fumbled to retrieve the roll of parchment. "From Master El'azar of Bethany," he blurted. "He says... I'm not supposed to wait for your answer." Thrusting the scroll into her hand he bolted up the road without looking back.

Miryam retreated to the walled refuge of her house. As the heavy gate smashed shut, she stood trembling behind the high walls. She stared at the message from her brother as though it contained a sentence of death.

And then she looked up. The eyes of the house servants were fixed on her, waiting.

"What are you staring at?" she shouted. Then she ran up to her room. The clang of the bolt resounded through the building as she locked herself in.

Three long minutes passed in utter silence as she read the note.

Then she began the wrenching wail of a woman in mourning.

■ ■ ■ ■

The religious holiday in Jerusalem had not been about worship of the Hebrew God. It was indeed about pure politics, Marcus concluded.

The Passover week was now finished, and peace had been preserved. It was as good an ending as could be managed.

That was Marcus' assessment. Imperial dignity was bruised, but Imperial might had not been seriously challenged. Everyone knew Pilate could have ordered a bloodbath in Caesarea, just as Marcus could have launched one on the Temple Mount. Neither event had occurred, and the Jewish political leadership was relieved.

Sometimes simply showing the fist was superior to using it.

The high priest, Caiaphas, was totally unconcerned about the lives of his countrymen. He saw men like bar Abba, Yochanan the Baptizer, and Yeshua of Nazareth as troublemakers. He would have welcomed their execution.

Marcus knew this for a fact.

There were several conferences between the civil authorities and the religious leadership about maintaining the peace. Each was attended by the pompous high priest. At every meeting about rebels and unrest, Caiaphas trotted out his favorite saying: "Better that one man die than that the whole nation suffer." With this stale proverb he assuaged his conscience each time a rebellious Jew was handed over to Roman justice for punishment.

If Rome had massacred the protestors, there would have been open rebellion. That would have meant the end of Caiaphas' lofty position.

Caiaphas preferred judicial murder to be used selectively. He was right in his view of sacrificing a few to preserve the whole. A small number of Jews crucified as an occasional example kept the populace controlled. Mentally Marcus shrugged it off.

Only one thing continued to trouble him. He knew that he had lied to Pilate, and by now Pilate knew it too.

Marcus had convinced the governor to make a concession over the standards. He had asserted they would still honor the emperor by hanging images on Roman territory inside the Antonia instead of outside it.

That was not true and would never have worked.

Pilate had forgotten that the religious vestments of the Jewish high priest were stored in the Antonia.

As far as fanatic Jews were concerned, the presence of the emperor's portraits were even more defiling *inside* the walls of the Roman fort. Caiaphas had insisted that the images be completely removed, otherwise more Jews would undoubtedly offer their throats for cutting.

Having witnessed the scene in his own courtyard, Pilate believed the high priest and complied. Once more under the cover of darkness, the standards were bundled up and carted away. By now they rested back in Caesarea.

So Marcus had invented a necessary fiction in order to get Pilate to agree to the "compromise." Unfortunately, the governor had certainly discovered the ruse and knew that Marcus was the perpetrator.

Marcus did not feel he had any choice. If he had not prevented a mass execution, he would have been blamed for the revolution that followed. This way he could only be held responsible for a bit of damaged pride.

How serious was that?

Returning to Galilee as soon as possible looked better and better.

On his last day in Jerusalem, he was again summoned to a meeting with Caiaphas. The topic was state security.

It probably meant another request for more troops. Caiaphas would argue that to ensure calm he needed more temple police. This would mean an arrangement whereby the Jewish leader administered additional money collected in taxes.

Marcus had no doubt that much of the increased budget would find its way into Caiaphas' own pockets, or those of his sons.

Standing beside a half-empty water reservoir outside the wall of the Antonia, Marcus doubted that Pilate would approve the claim. The province was in dire need of public works projects, especially roads and improved water supplies. Pilate would argue, truthfully for once, that he could not part with a single denarius.

Despite the fact that the rainy season had recently ended, Jerusalem's cisterns were half empty. It would be a long, dry summer. And future droughts would be worse unless alternate sources of water were created. Marcus had heard talk that Pilate was planning an aqueduct, but it was all speculation so far.

Not far from Marcus a handful of kneeling legionaries laughed as they played dice. Someone had scratched a game board on the paving stones. Each throw of the cubes advanced a player's marker toward the winning square, the one depicting a crown.

The prize for the victor was a blue cloak, probably extorted from some Jew, and now disputed over by the parties involved.

The legionaries, laughing at a crude joke, acted carefree and unconcerned.

Seeing how lighthearted they were, Marcus wondered if he would have been happier to remain a soldier and never become an officer at all.

As he stared moodily into the murky pool the high priest's entourage swept up behind him.

Caiaphas had recovered his arrogance. With stiff posture and waving forefinger, he carried himself with his accustomed haughty gravity.

Caiaphas was accompanied by Vara. Marcus knew the bear-like, hulking Praetorian was in Jerusalem but had so far managed to avoid him.

In his glistening black breastplate with its engraving of silver curlicues, Vara was a living monument to vanity.

Arrogance was one of the traits common to the Praetorian guards. It was part of what Marcus despised about them.

Vara took the lead in speaking. "Centurion Marcus Longinus! I have instructions for you."

Technically Vara had no authority to give orders to Marcus, but from the deference given him by the high priest's lackeys, clearly he had convinced them of his importance. This was not the time or place for Romans to show dissension toward each other.

Marcus' temper rose. "In regard to...?"

Beside Caiaphas was a Jew in farmer's dress. He was dark, thickly bearded, and handsome as Jews went, Marcus observed. The man looked vaguely familiar.

Caiaphas introduced him. "Centurion, this is Barak bar Halfi. He's going to work for us."

An informer, then. The sole reason the high priest employed commoners was to obtain information.

That explained Vara's interest as well.

But why should it be of concern to Marcus, who was returning to his duties in the Galilee?

"Bar Halfi was on the Temple Mount during the recent disturbance caused by a certain Yeshua of Nazareth," Caiaphas explained.

Yes! That was where Marcus had seen the man. Barak bar Halfi was among the angry, fist-waving, self-righteous mob shouting down Yeshua's interference with temple commerce.

Bar Halfi puffed up with self-importance. "And I have been a witness to other performances by this charlatan. I was present in Cana when he managed some sleight of hand with water and wine to convince the ignorant rabble of his miraculous powers. He needs watching, this one. He's up to no good."

It was typical for informers to enhance their status and their pay by making the object of the surveillance as sinister as possible.

"Yes," Caiaphas resumed. "We've decided to keep track of this Nazarene until we know what he's up to. Crowds have gathered to hear him speak, and that may lead to unrest.

Some of the followers of Yochanan the Baptizer have even joined this new troublemaker. Bar Halfi is taking up a lease on a farm in Nazareth near the close kin of Yeshua. He will furnish regular reports on them."

Such reports could lead to arrest and execution. Roman political technique included assassination. Kill the leader and the crowds disperse.

"And you, Centurion," Vara addressed Marcus, "are directed to lend any assistance bar Halfi needs and to receive this information for transmission to me." Stepping closer to Marcus, Vara added, "I suggest you handle this correctly, Marcus. Governor Pilate is already unhappy about the deal he struck over the standards. It made him look like he backed down to a mob...and he blames you."

Marcus had no reason to think well of a Jewish teacher, especially one who caused a near riot in the temple marketplace, but he could not help feeling sorry for the man. If the high priest and Vara were both suspicious of Yeshua of Nazareth, it was merely a matter of time before they found a way to eliminate him.

■ ■ ■ ■

It was after dark when Miryam heard Marcus and Tavita talking. She could not make out all their words but understood the meaning by the tone of voice. El'azar's letter was mentioned and then, Tavita told everything. "...his name is Barak bar Halfi."

Marcus was first incredulous and then angry. Was he angry at Miryam? The voices told her he was. They said other things too. He would hate her when he saw her. He would see the ashes of grief in her uncombed hair, see the tear she had made in the fabric of her garment above her heart, and he would mock her.

He, being a Roman, had no concept of a Jewess sitting *shiva* during the prescribed mourning period. When El'azar's letter arrived, Miryam had covered the looking glass, drawn the curtain, discarded her shoes, and refused all nourishment except dry bread and water. She did not light a lamp or sleep on a bed.

She had done everything correctly except the reciting of *kaddish* for the dead.

No. She could not bend her mind around the words of *kaddish*.

Impossible. When she opened her lips to pray, seven voices shouted her down. She covered her ears to shut them out, but finally she realized their accusations came from within her.

Even Marcus would hate her after this, they said. Mourning and praying could not bring Miryam back from her sentence of death. Her own brother, El'azar, and her sister, Marta, had declared that Miryam was dead to them. El'azar had written that she must never contact them again or call herself their relative. She was a disgrace, a shame to their family, for trying to tempt Barak bar Halfi into adultery. From this day on, Barak, his family, El'azar, Marta, and all the righteous of Israel would count Miryam's name among the dead each year at Yom Kippur.

There was no coming back to life from such a sentence. So Miryam was left alone to mourn for her lost self.

Marcus knocked, softly at first. He called her name. She did not reply.

He rapped more insistently. "Miryam!" he called.

Angry. Yes. Angry at her.

The voices told her he would strike her for the unfaithful thoughts she had toward Barak. He would slap her and tell her that not even a Roman could stand such a slut. She should stop pretending and start charging for her services. At least that would be more honest.

Now he was pounding, slamming his fist against the wood and shouting her name.

Perhaps he would kill her. It would be a mercy if he did. Save her the trouble.

When his shoulder heaved against the door, the jamb splintered. The bolt flew across the room, narrowly missing her head.

He stood framed in the opening, panting as he clenched and unclenched his fists.

She raised her eyes to him.

"By all the gods!" he breathed. "Miryam! What have they done to you?"

Tavita, carrying a lamp, hovered in the corridor. Marcus took the lamp from the old woman and came near to where Miryam sat in the ashes.

His face was twisted with fury, his eyes bright and wild as he stared at her.

Yes, the voices told her, he would kill her for a harlot. One stroke of his sword, and it would be over.

She bowed her head and tugged at the collar of her gown to reveal her neck.

He carefully placed the lamp on the table where El'azar's parchment lay open. Picking up the scrap of paper he read the words and cursed. Then he dipped the corner of the scroll into the flame and let the thing burn his fingers before he dropped it to the ground.

"How long has she been like this?" he asked Tavita.

The old woman's voice quaked. "All through Passover, sir. Now two days past it."

Marcus grunted. He moved near to her, towering over her. He reached down to touch her matted hair.

Surely he would strike, the voices crooned.

"Miryam." His turn was imploring. He knelt beside her. Lifted her chin with his finger.

It was plain her faithlessness had broken his heart. Soon he would let rage overpower him.

He brushed gray ash from her forehead and cheek. He ordered Tavita to go away and close the door. Then he asked, "Why have you let them do this to you?"

Miryam could not answer. Who did he mean? The voices? El'azar? The rest of them?

"I've seen enough righteousness these past weeks to make me sick," he said disgustedly. "Lunatics! All of them! They lie down before the governor and beg to be killed over a few

Roman images looking down on their temple. Hypocrites! In the very same temple the priests and the partisans rob and steal from poor people who have come to worship their God. The merchants, there by permit, pay a percentage of their take to the priests!" He stroked her arm. "These are the sort who have cast you out."

Miryam managed to croak, "I am dead to them."

He wrapped his arms around her and cradled her against him. "And better off for it."

"Cast out...guilty."

"And they aren't? The day before Passover started I saw one Jew who seemed to understand the hypocrisy of it all. A Galilean from Nazareth. A madman, I think. Or maybe one of your prophets. He made a whip and drove the money changers from the temple court. Dumped their tables. I'd like to have such a man in my cohort...but he won't go down well with the priests. His name is Yeshua."

The rest of what he said was drowned out by a long wail as the voices in her mind shrieked in torment. She covered her ears with her hands until at last they quieted. Like spectators in the stands, she knew they were watching her, waiting.

For the moment, however, Miryam could hear clearly. She found her voice. "No respectable person will receive me. Where will I go?"

"Little hypocrite. So it's about what people think, is it?" He scooped her up in his arms and threw back the curtain. Striding onto the balcony he carried her down to the shore and waded into the water. "Look at you! Covered in soot! Wallowing in this show of grief. Fooling even yourself! All the while you never intend to change! You're no Jew. You're built to give a man pleasure, and I will be the man you give it to! No, Miryam, you're not alone. You're on the other side of the line. Everybody's guilty. Everybody's rotten when you strip away the pretense. You're just sorry you got caught!"

With that he dropped her into the water. She came up sputtering, sobbing with anger. He had ruined everything! She had intended to pine away with self-pity.

"Why did you do that?" she demanded.

"Because you need a bath. There's a dinner being held at the house of another Jewish outcast. We're going. Levi the tax collector. You know him."

"I wouldn't be caught dead in his house."

He pushed her back when she tried to stand. "Get over it. Stop lying to yourself. You are everything they say you are. A slut? Yes. And I am glad for it."

Covering her face with her hands she wept. "I wish I was...a good woman...something else...something better. Don't you understand, Marcus?"

"Well, you're not. I'm not. Nobody is. Nobody can be. So give up. You don't love me. You don't love anything but yourself. That's why we suit one another. We're two of a kind, you and me. Now wash yourself. Dress in something to tantalize every man who sees you. You're mine now. Property of Rome. I claim you with a kiss." He drew her out of the water and kissed her hard on the mouth. "So, Miryam of Magdala. You're the woman of Marcus Longinus, Centurion of Rome. I'll kill any man who trespasses on my property. If you're unfaithful to me again...remember what I'll do to him."

■■■■

Miryam and Marcus arrived late to the banquet.

She was dressed, Roman fashion, in a long white linen tunic with a border of gold. The drape of the fabric off one shoulder accented her slender neck and voluptuous figure. Thick, dark hair was woven with gold thread that gleamed in the light.

Marcus, tunic cleaned and armor polished by Carta, exuded an air of authority and strength.

The house of Levi Mattityahu was a large, white, two-story villa built on a hill overlooking the lake and the city. The fishermen of Galilee derisively called the place *Sodom*.

It was a social gathering place for the wealthy outcasts of Israel. Levi's frequent guests were men and women of considerable means and low reputations.

They despised the common folk of Galilee.

Likewise, the population feared their power

and prayed for the day when they would be turned to pillars of salt in a sea of brimstone.

For the moment, however, Levi Mattityahu and his guests were alive and well.

The food and entertainment rivaled that of the finest houses in Rome. Torches blazed from marble pillars that supported the portico around the open courtyard. On the balcony musicians played while reclining guests were served from silver platters.

Miryam and Marcus entered unannounced and unnoticed.

Miryam recognized only a few at the gathering. She had met Kuza, the steward of Herod Antipas, through her husband's business dealings. She had never seen Kuza smile in his service to Herod, but tonight his wide mouth was open like a braying donkey's as he laughed at some joke Levi told.

Kuza's young, auburn-haired wife, Joanna, was between her husband and their host. Her pale skin was flushed with drink. She patted Kuza's cheek affectionately.

As for the other fifty-some guests, they were a strange combination of overdressed Jewish tax and customs officials replete with new money. The rest were Roman civil servants and soldiers junior in rank to Marcus. Their women rounded off the group. These females were not common whores from the wharfs of Magdala. They were, rather, mistresses of the conquerors, displaying their wealth in gold jewelry and expensive clothes.

Tonight, Miryam knew, by coming to the

home of Levi Mattityahu she had become one of them. One by one-faces turned toward her, mouths turned up in cynical smiles.

So, they seemed to say, the lady in the great house with the great family name has finally quit pretending to be better than everyone else.

Miryam Magdalen, the whore of Marcus Longinus, had finally shown her true colors.

And what choice did she have? Her banishment from her family had demolished even the pretense of respectability.

Marcus leaned close to her and brushed his lips against her bare shoulder. "You put them all to shame, you know," he whispered. "Beautiful. Beautiful."

He was pleased with her appearance. The way a soldier is satisfied that his horse is best in the rank, or the hilt of his sword has a jewel unlike any other. Miryam knew what she had become. An object. A belonging. She did not doubt that Marcus would carry out his promise to kill any man who tried to take her from him.

Levi hailed them, standing and rushing to clasp Marcus' hand.

"I thought you weren't coming!" he cried. Then his eyes swept over Miryam appreciatively.

Marcus slipped his arm around Miryam's waist. "I've been away awhile. We had some catching up to do."

Levi guffawed and winked. "Like I said, I'm surprised you came at all with such a feast spread out before you."

Miryam flushed at their joke. But what right had she to feel shame? It was true. And she was what Levi imagined her to be—what everyone had called her all along.

Marcus asked, "You know Levi, don't you Miryam?"

"Everyone in Galilee knows Levi," she remarked coolly. "Taxes on my orchards paid for seven pillars in his courtyard and that fountain."

Levi laughed again, unashamed of the way he made his fortune. "And tonight I'll give a little of your fortune back to you! Come sit! Eat! Kuza is filling us with tales about the latest messiah to take Jerusalem by storm!" He indicated two spaces near Kuza and Joanna at the head table.

"Lunatic, you mean." Joanna bit into a stuffed date and examined the remaining half. "*Shalom*, Miryam. I've lost a wager over you. Kuza bet me two drachmas you'd be coming along with Marcus tonight. I thought it would take a few more weeks."

So everyone knew about Barak. About El'azar's letter, and her banishment.

Miryam held her head erect. "Marcus has been telling me for some time that Levi served the best food and wine in Galilee."

"And in Judea," Levi volunteered, draining his cup.

Miryam inclined her head slightly in agreement. "Not even the steward of Herod Antipas can compete with the banquets of Rome's most successful tax collector, eh?"

Kuza and Joanna caught her insult. Kuza tossed it back lightly. "Where does he get this, Joanna?"

Joanna studied the jeweled fingers of Levi. "Levi steals boldly from the estates of many. Including...Miryam Magdalen!"

Levi passed Miryam a platter of pheasant. "So you see, dear lady, we've been eating the best of your table for years. Without conscience or remorse I'm afraid. It's about time you joined in the fun!"

Joanna leaned near to Miryam and whispered, "One condition to joining our exclusive band."

Miryam caught a glint of compassion in Joanna's eyes. Could she understand how desperate Miryam was? How alone? "What is that?"

"Conscience and remorse are not allowed." Joanna patted Miryam's hand and lowered her voice more as the men talked over them. "My husband, Kuza, is Idumean, like Herod Antipas. My father is a priest from the line of Aaron. He disowned me years ago. It hurt for a while. But Kuza is good to me. And I have my little boy, Boaz. You could do worse than Marcus. You'll find you could do worse than us. At least we are what we are."

Miryam's gaze lingered for a moment on Joanna's clear blue eyes. Had she found an ally in her loneliness? Another woman who understood what it meant to live outside the rules? Miryam did not reply.

Joanna's mouth curved slightly in a smile of genuine acceptance. The two would be friends.

Levi, who had already had too much to drink, bellowed the question, "Herod Antipas is like his father, isn't he, Kuza? I mean at heart he simply won't tolerate the raging rabble for long, will he?"

"I would say," Kuza pondered, "Yochanan the Baptizer might well be served up like one of these pheasants one of these days. Especially if Herodias has anything to say about it."

"Why so?" Marcus asked. What was Herod's mistress's connection to the Baptizer?

"Haven't you heard?" Kuza returned. "No, this happened while you were away. Seems the prophet is not content telling common people to change their wicked ways. Sometimes he even tells highborn folk exactly what wickedness he means."

Joanna leaned over to Miryam. "Delicious scandal! Herodias left her husband...who just happens to be half-brother to Antipas! The Baptizer denounced her and says openly that Herod Antipas should throw her out. She'll have the prophet's head for that."

"What do you say, Marcus?" Kuza asked. "You were on prophet patrol these last two weeks. Managed to get through Passover in Jerusalem with your skin intact. Tell us, then. Galilee and Judea are crawling with Jewish fanatics. Are they a threat to the Roman empire, or simply to the pride of Herod and his women?"

"The Baptizer was not in Jerusalem as far as I know," Marcus said at last. "But there was one interesting encounter. A man...some sort of rabbi...took a whip and beat up the money changers and animal sellers. Called them thieves and the sponsors of thieves. Tipped over their counting tables."

Levi threw up his hands in exaggerated horror. "How could he treat money with such disrespect?"

There was a round of chuckling, but Joanna said to Miryam, "Driving out the money changers. I remember my father quoting the *Tanakh*...the holy Scriptures...which say that when Messiah comes, he will cleanse the temple. Could this man think he is a messiah?"

"Any idea who he is?" Kuza asked Marcus.

Marcus shrugged. "Only something Carta, my servant, overheard. Seems some of the aggrieved merchants called him *Yeshua of Nazareth*, so maybe you have a messiah from right here in Galilee."

"Yeshua of Nazareth!" Levi mocked. "A carpenter's son."

Miryam's mind clicked back to the wedding at Cana. Could the man they were speaking of be the same Yeshua she overheard speaking? "There was a Yeshua who performed some magic..." she began.

"That's the one!" Joanna confirmed. "Turned water into wine!"

"Ho!" Kuza shouted. "That's the kind of messiah we need!"

The party-goers howled at this.

"Now," Kuza continued, "if he can magically produce bread to go with the wine, we can all retire."

"Exactly!" Joanna agreed. "Levi, you must invite him to your next party! Maybe he would perform for us."

"Not a chance!" Levi said, a mocking, sour look printed on his face. "No one who knocks over counting tables will ever sit at my dinner table!"

YOD

Wildflowers spread out in a riot of color on the distant hills across the sea of Galilee. Blooms called *Farewell-to-spring* splashed bright pink along the ridges and swales.

Miryam was sorry to mark the passing of spring. Marcus was packed, ready to return to duty. She still had not told him her secret. For two months she had suspected it, hoping, yet also fearing, it was true. Now she was certain. After the winter solstice, she would have his child.

Carta waited at the gate with Marcus' horse.

Miryam and Marcus sipped wine on the patio of her villa and watched as fishing boats with russet sails scudded across the water. She did not care any longer if the fishermen saw her sitting openly with her Roman lover.

"How long will you be away?" She stroked his wrist seductively as she imagined his hands touching her through the thin linen tunic she wore. She did not want him to leave.

"Not long. Pilate's dispatch says it's routine. Some Jewish matter. Immediate attention, he says. I don't know."

The sight of Marcus Longinus and his servant Carta coming and going from Miryam's door at all hours was no longer a top item of gossip in the city of Magdala. A baby in Miryam's household would kindle the fires again.

In anticipation of her confinement she had hired a Roman from the household of Herod Antipas as her steward. He had come highly recommended by Kuza. Now all business offers and counteroffers came through him. She no longer had contact with the common people. This insulated her from Jewish insult and animosity.

Farmers sold their produce to her at rock-bottom prices. Miryam then passed the merchandise along at double her cost to feed the enormous household of Herod Antipas and the Roman garrison at Tiberias. She dealt personally with Kuza, Herod's steward. By now Kuza and Joanna were frequent guests at Miryam's villa.

"What will you do while I'm gone?" Marcus kissed Miryam's wrist, but his eyes smoldered with suspicion.

"I've sold the new crop of figs to Kuza. That's settled. I can relax a bit. Joanna is bringing little Boaz to stay for a few days."

Through mutual loneliness Miryam and Joanna had been drawn to each other from their first meeting at the house of Levi Mattityahu. Their status as outcasts from respectable society created a strong bond. Miryam was closer to Joanna than she had ever been to her own sister, Marta. And Joanna's four-year-old son, Boaz, adored Miryam.

New friends and Marcus' companionship had calmed Miryam's fears in the weeks since the dinner at Levi's house. The disembodied voices that had taunted Miryam with shouts and commands were only whispers now. On the long nights when Marcus was away she still had uneasy stirrings in her thoughts and occasional nightmares. Because of this, she was grateful Joanna and little Boaz were coming to stay at the villa.

But why was Marcus so sullen this morning?

"The nights...we'll drink and talk. She'll catch me up on court gossip." Miryam mopped her brow. "It's almost too hot to sleep. Summer's here."

"And all this time I thought you were the reason I was burning up."

Suddenly she feared he would not come back to her, that this was their last moment together. She leaned toward him and searched his face. "We should go to the seashore when you come back. It'll be cool there. What do you say? Playing in the waves by moonlight."

"You'll miss me?"

"You'll come back, won't you?" Why did she feel so desperate?

"If you think I could resist such an invitation..." He stood. Towering over where she sat, he touched her cheek and recited the words of Propertius:

> *"I waged noble war in your thighs.*
> *Either with you, or for you with*
> *my rivals,*
> *I shall always be at arms: no*
> *peace with you can please.*
> *Rejoice for none is as fair as you:*
> *you would grieve*
> *If there was one, but you may*
> *with cause be proud...."*

She wrapped her arms around his waist and whispered, "Stay, Marcus. We have time... Stay... Carta can wait."

"But Herod Antipas can't. Pilate won't."

"Stay," she teased, knowing she had aroused him. "Tell them you had to practice your swordsmanship."

He knelt in front of her, his face level with hers. She wrapped her legs around him. His face was tense. Was he angry at himself for wanting her when there was not time enough to take her? Or was there something else? He kissed her hard and she experienced coils of fire unwinding.

And immediately Marcus was the one in control.

Her eyes brimmed and her breath quickened. She had to tell him about their child. "Marcus... Marcus? I am sure I am pregnant."

Suddenly he drew back from her. When she clung to him, he pushed her away.

"And who is the father?"

She gasped. "You! You are! Marcus, there has been no one but you! I swear it!"

He studied her with a cool disdain. Hooking his fingers in the neck of her gown, he tore the fabric away.

"Marcus! No!" she cried, and attempted to cover herself.

"This is what your precious Barak bar Halfi turned down? The man would have to be made of ice." Rising to his feet, he saluted her. "You said his name in your sleep last night, Miryam. My sword will be sheathed until I return. And then I will run you through. Believe it. I will make you forget him."

With that, Marcus turned on his heel and left.

■■■■

There were no tears left to cry.

Miryam hugged her knees as she sat on the sand at the water's edge. Hours passed. The glare of the sun burned her skin. Old Tavita came out, imploring her to listen to reason, to come inside.

"Grieving again? And this time for love? But many a woman has had to bid her lover farewell for a while! Your good master...your dove... Marcus Longinus will be back! Please, Miryam!"

The old woman's voice seemed far away, as though she were calling to Miryam from across the lake. "Come in!...bid your lover farewell!... Marcus farewell! Grieving again! Come in! You will burn!"

There was the Sea of Galilee, flat like a sheet of molten lead. Why not fill her pockets with stones? Wade in? Let the water flood her lungs and draw her down?

Marcus would come back...and she would be gone. Tavita would tell him Miryam had vanished into the Sea of Galilee one night.

Why had she told him about the pregnancy? She should have known he would never believe the child she carried was his.

If she was dead, would he be sorry he left her so cruelly? She had begun to believe Marcus was her savior. But had he stayed with her merely to satisfy his appetite?

One thought kept her moored to life. Perhaps she would miscarry. And if she did not? Marcus had promised to come back and run her through. If she could not convince him of her faithfulness, she would die by his hand and welcome death.

Joanna arrived. Miryam heard her and Tavita on the balcony.

"And he left her? Just like that? The swine!"

Waves lapped Miryam's ankles. She rested her head against her knees. Joanna's indignation was a balm to her injured soul.

The piping voice of little Boaz called to her, "Aunt Miryam! We're here! Can I go swimming?"

Miryam raised her head and drew a deep breath, returning from her inner thoughts to reality. She was thirsty. How many hours had she been baking in the sun?

Boaz ran to Miryam and threw his arms around her neck. "*Shalom!* Aunt Miryam! I am excited to see you! I was excited since Mama told me we could come visit! Mama says we will stay here for five sleeps!"

"*Shalom,* Boaz." Miryam's parched throat croaked out the words. She embraced the child and fingered his pale blond curls.

Joanna's shadow fell over them. "Look at you," she scolded. "Miryam! Tavita says you've been sitting here like a stone since he left." She flipped the torn edge of Miryam's tunic and cursed. "He did this?"

Miryam nodded, not trusting herself to speak.

Joanna fumed, "The swine! They're all swine. Men are. Marcus is. And a Roman swine is the worst sort. Get up. Get dressed." She helped Miryam to her feet and enfolded her in her arms. "You're too good to fall to pieces like this."

Miryam buried her face in Joanna's shoulder and wept. *Oh, friend! My friend!*

Boaz tugged on Miryam's arm, then patted her leg. "Mama? What's wrong with Aunt Miryam?"

"Nothing a little wine and common sense won't fix." Joanna stroked Miryam's back. "Hush now. Hush. It's never as bad as it seems, is it?"

Oh yes. This time, Miryam thought, *it is.*

■■■■

Was Miryam really pregnant? Whose child did she carry? Marcus might have believed it was his except that, on the last night they were together, she had been dreaming of the Jew, Barak bar Halfi.

His anger, already steaming, boiled over. The more he thought about her infidelity and the consequences, the more irate he became. He had warned her, hadn't he?

Had it not been for the urgent order from Pilate, Marcus might have gone back and killed her!

Who did she think she was? Hadn't he treated her well? Hadn't he raised her above common whoredom and the life she deserved?

And now she betrayed him for some insignificant Jew? A hireling! A spy!

If he could have reached Barak bar Halfi's throat just then, he would happily have strangled the man and blamed it on Jewish rebels.

Perversely, he was also angry with himself. When had he ever let a woman disturb him so? None of them were faithful, none worth losing sleep over.

A duty to perform was exactly what he needed to help his mind return to proper ways of thinking. He was sorry that the assignment was not more clear-cut and straightforward.

The text of Pilate's order raised a number of questions in Marcus' mind. He was to proceed immediately to Selim on the Jordan.

There he would overtake a company of troops belonging to Herod Antipas, then go south with them into the region of Perea.

Apparently Herod Antipas had received word that Yochanan the Baptizer was east of the river, preaching in the tetrarch's domain. The Jewish prophet was baptizing where he could be arrested by Herod Antipas without the permission of Rome.

Pilate was afraid that Yochanan might be "accidentally killed while resisting arrest." Pilate did not care about the life of a wild-eyed Jewish preacher. He was, however, sticking to his determination to make no martyrs. The governor did not want Herod Antipas creating any either. Marcus was not to participate in the capture. His duty was to accompany Herod's men as an observer only. He had no authority and no official standing, but realized he was about to become the Baptizer's shield.

It was one more task that could easily land him in trouble. If he interfered with Herod's men, then the tetrarch could complain to Pilate. If he failed in his mission and let Yochanan get killed, he would also have to answer for it.

Vara was waiting for such a slip.

Marcus stared at the ceiling. It was impossible to win. Maybe the gladiator motto was right after all: *In life, grasp anything you desire whenever you can, and die a glorious death. Nothing else matters.*

"Come on," he said brusquely to Carta. "Roll up my things. We are heading out tonight."

■■■■

It was late. The rush of waves against the sand kept an even cadence as nightbirds called from the garden.

The bedroom was bathed in the soft light of three candles.

Miryam and Joanna lounged on the cushions and talked in whispers.

Little Boaz slept soundly on the window seat. Strands of blond hair fanned across the pillow.

Sweet, sweet, Miryam thought as she fixed her eyes on the sleeping child. How blessed Joanna was to have such a son.

Miryam rested with her head in Joanna's lap. Joanna brushed her hair as they talked. The women had consumed two carafes of wine and were mellow but not willing to give up the night.

"I used to dream of having a little girl." Miryam took Joanna's hand and pressed it to her cheek. "Someone to hold the way I wanted to be held after my mother...after she was gone."

"The only time I can hold Boaz is when he's asleep. He's on the move every waking minute," Joanna countered.

"Even that much. To be able to rock my baby to sleep and say, you know, this is my child. Part of me."

The two tenderly observed Boaz.

"He has kept me sane," Joanna confided. "I love Kuza. Gave up everything to be with him. My family... But he has other women. I know it. Everyone in the court of Herod Antipas keeps mistresses. Like a stable of horses. Yochanan the Baptizer is preaching a lost cause if he thinks they'll ever change."

"How do you stand it?"

"Once I tried to leave. Kuza and I had an argument about some little whore. Herod had grown tired of her and passed her along to Kuza. So I packed up Boaz and went to my father's house. Hoping, you know. But Father wouldn't see me. I heard my mother crying inside. Begging. But he sent a servant out to tell me that me and my half-breed, bastard child were dead to the family, thank you very much. And would we please never darken the door of their righteous house again." Silence. "So here I am. No place to go. No one to ask forgiveness for my mistakes. My father wouldn't listen anyway... I've spent my life looking for someone to really love me. Know me. For such a long time I believed it was Kuza. I think he loves me as much as he is able. But Boaz is my comfort. He is...everything. I don't think I understood about love until I first held him."

Miryam blinked at the guttering flame of a candle. She rested her hand on her stomach and thought about the child she carried. She wanted children one day. But not now. Not like this. Not if it meant giving up Marcus. "Marcus will never believe it isn't Barak's child."

Joanna snorted. "Why should you care?"

"Because...I...I do care for him."

205

"You love him?"

"He gives me pleasure. I miss him when he's not here. I would be sorry if I lost him. I think... I wouldn't want to go on living. Who do I have to go to? If you hadn't come when you did, Joanna... You and Boaz..."

"You would have had a terrible sunburn." Joanna tried to ignore the implication.

"If I lose Marcus..."

"Look," Joanna offered. "Let's not sit around here and wait for him to come back. We can go to Judea for a while. The miracle worker is there, you know? The Rebbe Yeshua. The carpenter's son from Nazareth. He is a wonder. Healing cripples and giving sight to the blind. A prophet some say. The Sadducees and their talmidim hate him. My father must be foaming at the mouth. But it might be fun to go to Judea and see for ourselves."

"I'm not blind or crippled. I need a miscarriage. I need Marcus back." Miryam sat up glumly. "If Yeshua the miracle worker can't do that for me, I'm not interested."

Joanna pressed her fingers to her temples. "You give me a headache."

"I don't want this baby unless I can have Marcus too."

"It's not that hard to get rid of a baby." Joanna sighed with resignation. "Women at court do it all the time."

Miryam sipped her wine. "How? Tell me. You know about these things. I have heard of it, but...tell me then."

Joanna shrugged. "There is a priest."

"A priest? But Torah says abortion is…"

"Yes. Murder," Joanna finished, then hesitated to see if the word had any effect on Miryam.

"Tell me!" Miryam insisted.

"He's not a *cohen*. Syrian. He keeps an altar to Molech. He lives across the lake. Herod Antipas goes to him for divination. But there are other matters. He has medicine…it causes miscarriages."

"How long does it take?"

"The women I know have left Tiberias by boat and are gone a few days. They drink a potion. Made from rye grass, they say. A simple formula. It causes labor to start. But it's expensive."

"I don't care. I want to be able to tell Marcus the whole thing was a mistake!" She grasped Joanna's wrists hard. "You've got to help me with this!"

■ ■ ■ ■

Joanna knew more about the priest of Molech than she was willing to tell at first. As the night wore on, however, more details emerged with each glass of wine.

The priest of Molech practiced his craft in a ruined temple in the wilderness of Golan near a village called *Gadara*. The site was a few hours' walk from the Greek city of Hippus on the eastern shore of the Sea of Galilee.

The priest was a necromancer, a medium who

spoke to spirits of the dead. It was said he could read fortunes in the entrails of animals.

Free from the Jewish authority in Jerusalem, he chose his domain in the territory ruled by Philip, the half-brother of Herod Antipas.

The ancient altar of Molech stood high on a rocky ridge. The idol's hideous stone face scowled toward Israel. A fire was stoked in its bronze belly to consume the sacrifices placed in its red-hot arms.

Worshippers from Syria, Samaria, and Lebanon made frequent pilgrimage to consult the priest and make prayers and offerings to Molech.

Wealthy Jews as well as poor tenant farmers from Judea and Galilee often visited this place in secret. They brought pregnant mistresses with them and unmarried daughters who had heaped disgrace upon their families. The medicine of Molech's apothecary frequently saved Jewish relatives from the scandal of unwanted children.

The diviner would not accept silver or gold in payment. A donkey laden with grain, olive oil, and fine wine was his fee. As for Molech's appetite, it was satisfied in a way convenient for everyone. The aborted infant, often still living, would be placed in Molech's outstretched arms and burned.

In this way the disgrace of immorality within the House of Israel vanished in curls of smoke rising over the mountains. The law against fornication could at least *appear* to be kept. Life could go on without disruption or embarrassment.

Joanna elaborated these facts about Molech's high place to Miryam. It was a grim and unpleasant spot.

Joanna implored her, "I'm sorry I told you about it at all."

"You've saved my life." In Miryam's mind was the hope that the necromancer could speak to the spirit of her mother. Perhaps she would receive some message, some guidance and comfort. The voices in Miryam's head began to hum their approval, urging her to go!

"Wouldn't it be better to come to Judea with me? To hear the rabbi from Nazareth? Maybe even tell him about the baby? Ask him what to do? He's a merciful man, they say. And wise. Maybe you could have the child secretly and make some arrangement for its upbringing? A school in Alexandria? Half the bastard children in Rome are being brought up incognito."

That was not the issue, Miryam argued. The one thing that mattered to her was keeping Marcus. Yeshua of Nazareth was a holy man. Surely he would denounce her as a harlot. Miryam was in no condition to be humiliated further. What would it change? Instead, she would make a pilgrimage to the altar of Molech. And when she returned, her problem would be solved.

Joanna decided, rightly, that this was no place to take little Boaz. Friendship notwithstanding, Miryam would have to make the journey on her own.

No servants could be trusted with such a secret. Not even old Tavita. This was Miryam's crisis. She would see to it herself.

■ ■ ■ ■

And so it was arranged. Miryam packed clothing to imitate the style of a wealthy Greek woman. She bronzed her skin with walnut oil and put on layers of heavy veils. Finally she practiced speaking Aramaic with a thick Greek accent. Her disguise would be convincing enough to fool the ignorant bumpkins on the fishing quays of Magdala, she thought.

The lake was calm. She slipped from the side gate of the villa and strolled past Tavita, who was returning from the market. The old woman did not look twice.

Her confidence soaring, Miryam walked quickly to the fishing district. There she found two brothers from Capernaum cleaning their nets. She recognized these two. John and Ya'acov bar Zavdai had gained notorious reputations as brawlers along the lakefront. They were known as *Sons of Thunder*. She and Tavita had once seen them take on five traders from a caravan who insulted their sister in the marketplace. Like all fishermen on the lake, the two worked stripped to the waist and were deeply bronzed by the sun.

John was bear-like and coarse-featured. His nose had been broken in some past fracas. His thick black beard was braided, brown hair tied back. Ya'acov was fair-haired, short, and stocky. Quieter than his younger brother, he was, nevertheless, a force to be reckoned with in a squabble. The two would be safe to travel with, Miryam reasoned.

Confident in her disguise, she explained that she was called away to the bedside of her dying mother in Hippus on the eastern shore. Three days' wages for the journey. Were they interested?

They conferred a moment, agreed upon the price, and within the hour, set sail.

■■■■

A brisk wind came up, swelling the sails. Perched in the bow of the fishing boat, Miryam let the spray cool her. Afternoon light danced on the blue waters. She kept her gaze steady on the eastward shore where the white buildings of Hippus gleamed.

Hippus had existed from the time of Alexander the Great and the Greek empire of the Seleucids. When the city was captured by the Jews in the Maccabee rebellion, its pagan temples had been razed to the ground.

One hundred years later it was rebuilt by the Roman general Pompey. Its population was a mix of races and languages from all over the Roman empire.

Among the Jews, both Hippus and Gadara retained reputations for evil and sorcery.

The Galileans, coarse and vulgar, ignored their passenger. Thinking she spoke mostly

Greek, they talked with open disdain about Rome's appointed rulers. They gossiped about those Galileans who had given up their boats and nets to follow after religious fanatics like Yochanan the Baptizer on the Jordan.

What was the point? they scoffed. And now Andrew, brother of Shim'on, had taken off after Yeshua of Nazareth! Shim'on was left to fish and support the family on his own.

Everyone had been saying the Messiah would come in their lifetime, yet the world went on as usual.

Some in Galilee put their faith in bar Abba, the Zealot. He had led the protests in Jerusalem and Caesarea against the idols of Rome. And then there were the bandits in the hills. The mere mention of them struck terror in the hearts of tax collectors and non-Jews who traveled along the road from Magdala to Damascus. Yet bar Abba and the robbers were merely a thorn in the flesh of Rome.

It was the religious fanatics, like Yochanan the Baptizer and more recently Yeshua of Nazareth, who made the Romans and their appointed Jewish priests and political rulers squirm. From the Temple Mount and from royal palaces they watched and listened as reports poured in of miracles and vast crowds of followers.

Popular sentiment had grown for Yochanan, who preached repentance, a turning away from following after the Roman lifestyle. The chief sinners in the land, cried Yochanan, were Herod Antipas and his mistress, Herodias!

The market stalls of every village buzzed about Yeshua, the rabbi of Nazareth, who drove the money changers from the temple. On that same day the Rebbe went on to heal one hundred cripples, it was said.

How Caiaphas, the high priest, and the Sanhedrin hated him! Overturning the tables was bad enough. But how could they fight a man who restored the sight of a blind girl? Since the days of the prophets, no one had experienced such a thing! Surely the people would follow after this Yeshua and usurp their authority!

Ah well. And what did any of it have to do with two poor brothers fishing on the Galilee?

Had the fish multiplied since the Rebbe from Nazareth had spent time at the lake? No.

Had his presence brought some blessing to the waters? No. Yeshua was off in Judea, and everything in Galilee was as it had always been.

"Except some days we get lucky, eh?" whispered Ya'acov. "An easy way to pick up three days' wages."

"You think she's going to her mother, do you?" asked John, stroking his beard.

Miryam did not turn but listened to their speculation.

"She smells like a garden."

"Everything else about this journey smells like fish."

"Greek? Or Syrian? She is very dark."

"I fancy dark meat."

"Rich. Her hands are soft. I helped her

into the boat. Never done a day's work from the feel of her hands."

"A courtesan. Kept by a rich man. Not the marrying kind if you ask me."

"Why does she travel alone? No servant."

Silence. The brothers contemplated their passenger. A few murmured words passed between them, and then they laughed.

Miryam felt the color rise to her cheeks. Had they guessed the identity of their passenger? Had they deduced the purpose of her journey to Hippus?

She pretended not to notice as their whispering grew ever fainter.

Inwardly her own voices mocked her.

You are a fool to think you could keep this a secret. Everyone will know soon enough that you went to the priest of Molech. They'll cover smiles with their hands when you walk by. There is no escape from your reputation. No redemption for a whore. No coming back from the road you took.

Fill your pockets with stones. Hire a boat. Sail to the center of the sea and slip overboard. That is the only way to end the pain!

The city loomed ahead. Soon she would be out of their boat. She would find an inn and stay the night before traveling on to Gadara and Molech's shrine.

This bronze god would be merciful. It would accept her sacrifice without question.

KAF

The city of Hippus was part of the Decapolis, the league of ten Greek cities which were centers of trade and culture mostly to the east of the Jordan River. Sixty years before, it had been given as a gift to Herod the Great by Augustus Caesar.

The structures lacked the grandeur of Caesarea's majestic buildings, but it was, nonetheless, a modern and thriving city. The streets were paved. Public baths, temples, and buildings for commerce were faced in polished marble. Shopping arcades with covered porticos surrounded the city center. Inns were plentiful for travelers.

Miryam secured a room at an inn that Joanna said was used by the courtesans of Herod's court. She paid enough for five nights' lodging plus food to be brought up to her. It was a clean, elegant, restful place, and its elderly Greek proprietor was discreet. The bedchamber overlooked a fountain in the inner courtyard.

Giving instructions to the innkeeper, she arranged for the hire of a servant and a pack animal to carry oil and wine as far as Gadara.

The servant, an uneducated Syrian peasant, had had his tongue cut out years before by a Nabatean bandit. His silence was thus guaranteed. He was to wait for Miryam overnight. She would travel on alone to the shrine and take the potion. Within hours she would pass the child. The ordeal would be over and forgotten.

She would ride back to Hippus, where she would rest a few days before returning home to Magdala.

"I have relatives in Gadara," she explained, attempting to maintain some pretense of respectability.

It was clear from his expression that the proprietor of the inn knew the truth.

There was a brothel across the road. The whores and fine ladies often traveled to Gadara to "visit relatives." He smiled slyly and shrugged as if to indicate it was none of his business.

Miryam slept fitfully the first night. Music and laughter from the brothel kept her awake. She thought about the baby and wondered if it was a girl or a boy. Doubts crept in, only to be whispered away by voices urging her to get it over with!

Turning her face to the pillow, she imagined what it would be like to hold her baby. Then she pictured Marcus. How angry he had been! She wept bitterly, finally sleeping from the exhaustion of grief.

Before daybreak the innkeeper knocked on her door. He brought warm bread, dried fish, and pomegranate wine for breakfast. The servant and his donkey waited downstairs. Gifts of wine and olive oil were loaded and ready.

The innkeeper made it easy. "You have

paid me well. It is only six miles up the highway to the village of Gadara." Then he added sympathetically, "If you should want to go farther? Perhaps you want to make prayers and offerings at a certain shrine? Inquire into your future? Or buy some potion for your health? You will see the shrine among the boulders above the village. My servant will take you where you tell him. And he will bring you back here to rest when you are ready."

So this was a highly organized business. That fact somehow comforted Miryam. She was not the only woman in trouble who came here for a solution. And there were plenty of participants ready to dispense compassion and assistance for a fee.

■ ■ ■ ■

Despite having a mission to perform, Marcus' mind did not grow easier. Instead he brooded and fumed. He beat Carta when a saddle roll slipped, even though he had tied up the bundle himself.

With Marcus mounted on horseback and Carta on a donkey, the two traveled fast for the next two days. They did not overtake Herod's soldiers at Selim, nor at Amathus, still further south. In fact, they did not catch up with the company until the morning of the third day, at the Jordan River crossing between Jericho and the Perean city of Julias.

Except for their helmets and spears, it was

difficult to distinguish between the tetrarch's four soldiers and the worst cutthroats from the bazaars of Damascus. This was not surprising since Herod Antipas did most of his recruiting from among the toughs of the Syrian souks. The Herodian mercenaries were as likely to knife their commander in his bed as to obey a distasteful order. That simple fact explained why they soldiered for Herod Antipas and were not invited to the better pay and benefits of a Roman auxiliary legion.

"Who's in charge?" Marcus demanded.

"I am," growled a squat, one-eyed man. "And since we're on Perean soil, what's it to you?"

"Be very careful, my friend," Marcus warned, his anger soaring like the temperature of the air rolling in from the desert. "I am here as the personal representative of Governor Pilate and by his order." Marcus flicked his grapevine swagger stick against the greave that protected his shin, then stepped to within two paces of the man.

"Am I supposed to be impressed?" replied the Herodian trooper with a sneer. "I..."

Marcus' anger boiled over. He was no longer concerned with any consequences, political or otherwise.

The soldier's contemptuous reply stopped midsentence. His face was a stiff scornful mask, but there was terror in his eyes.

The point of Marcus' dagger was under his chin. Marcus had distracted the man's attention from the draw of the blade by the slap of the swagger stick.

"Yes," Marcus rejoined, prodding the man up onto his toes with short jabs of the knife's sharp tip, "yes, you are. Let's begin again. What are you doing here?"

To the stench of the man's unwashed tunic was added the acrid reek of fear.

"We are here to seize the troublemaker known as Yochanan the Baptizer," the detachment's leader admitted. "It is the tetrarch's right."

"Just so," Marcus agreed. "Provided the Baptizer is on this side of the river. Otherwise you will not disturb him in any way. And if you do manage to arrest him, I will accompany you for a time...just to see that he doesn't break free and injure you, or call down fire on your heads."

Antipas' soldiers did not like this development. The other three exchanged furtive looks. Marcus paid particular attention to this trio. All wore leather strings about their necks from which concealed daggers were suspended. Pilate had been right about Yochanan's probable fate; these were hired killers.

"I'll have those weapons," he insisted. He poked their commander again. "Tell them quickly, while you have a tongue to use. Carta, pick up those knives. And the spears as well."

Now he had done it.

Though Marcus would never betray any weakness to these cutthroats, he realized his anger had gotten the better of him. Irritation at the foul, back-stabbing assassins had provoked him into open confrontation with them.

Marcus had no regrets.

Contract murderers who would slaughter unarmed prisoners were no allies to Marcus, even if their ruler was an ally of Rome. Repercussions were of no present concern either, but he recognized his own life was in danger, as well as the Baptizer's.

"I will go with you," he repeated. "Move out."

Low clouds scudded past overhead, as if hurrying somewhere with nothing to stop them. It came to Marcus that events in his life were unfolding in much the same way. He shook away the thought as he would a bad dream. He put no stock in omens or feelings.

A half mile upstream from the river crossing they found Yochanan, in the middle of an audience numbering several hundred. The Baptizer stood on the trunk of a gnarled willow that projected over the water at a low angle.

He was, to Marcus' regret, still on the Perean side of the border.

Though he had heard the Baptizer speak only on the one earlier occasion, Marcus recognized the gravelly voice at once.

"You are right to be sorry for your past wrongdoing," he heard the preacher saying. "And even more right to be afraid for the consequences. Suppose you have an orchard and in it a fig tree that you water and care for year after year. And each season it produces only small, sour figs. What do you do?"

Someone in the crowd yelled, "Cut it down and replace it with another?"

Yochanan's massive head nodded vigorously, tossing his lion's mane of black hair. "And you would chop it up and toss it in the furnace. Listen: there is someone nearby who has an axe already in his hand. I am merely giving you a warning, but he is the owner of the orchard. Look at your own life and answer: how much longer will he wait to strike? Listen to what the prophet Isaiah says: 'Clear a road through the desert for Adonai!' Do you think he means building roads as the Romans build them? No! The prophet is saying, level the road into your hearts! The Almighty is trying to enter your life. Will he be able to get there? Or is the way to your heart blocked with things you hold on to, like pride and arrogance and a guilty conscience?"

The sharp tang of sage blew in off the desert. In the moist places on the riverbank the milling crowd crushed wild mint underfoot. The scents mingled like incense offered in a temple.

"Then what should we do?" the same onlooker asked.

"If you are going home to supper and pass a beggar who has nothing to eat, you must share with him," Yochanan asserted. "If he is dressed in rags while your closet is full of things you no longer wear, don't wait. Give him what he needs! And don't say, 'Someone else will come by soon... I'll let them do it.' No! You could have gone home a different way, but you didn't. The Almighty has made that beggar your duty and nobody else's."

The leader of the Herodian soldiers snarled at Marcus, "He's east of the river. We can take him!"

"Wait!" Marcus ordered. "What's the hurry?"

A man dressed in the tunic of a temple guard was among the listeners. As Marcus watched, the soldier pushed his helmet up on his forehead and stepped into the water below Yochanan's perch. "What about me?" he asked. "What do I need to do?"

Marcus was surprised to find that he was leaning forward expectantly, awaiting the reply.

"Don't bully people," the Baptizer answered. "Don't use your authority to force money from them. Don't arrest men on trumped-up charges and tell lies about them in order to get a reward."

The troopers of Herod Antipas grimaced at this exchange. "What is this?" their one-eyed leader spat. "How much of this do we have to hear?"

Every accusation Yochanan delivered rang true. Marcus wished the denunciation applied solely to men like the hired killers, but he recognized his own past misdeeds in the words of the prophet.

Raising his swagger stick like a warning finger, Marcus bent his head toward Yochanan to indicate he was not through listening yet.

The Baptizer added, "Don't follow the

example of leaders who live corrupt, immoral lives. Don't think that because someone has a high position his wrong actions can be excused. Take that sack of corruption, Herod Antipas. He has shamefully wronged both his wife and his brother by living with that whore, Herodias. Do you think the Almighty is not paying attention?"

"Come on," the chief of Herod's men muttered, looking Marcus squarely in the eye. "We are going to carry out our orders *now!*"

Marcus could not legally interfere. He might not be able to stop them anyway.

The bazaar toughs retrieved their spears from Carta's donkey.

Shoving through the rear ranks of the spectators, the mercenaries caused a stir. Voices raised to protest the violent handling turned to shouts of warning for Yochanan to flee.

The temple guard, in water up to his waist, called for someone to pass him his weapon. After receiving it he stood at the water's edge, ready to defend the Baptizer.

Others, seeing this action, bent and picked up stones and chunks of driftwood.

A woman screamed and grabbed the hand of a child.

Herod's soldiers lowered the points of their javelins. They were prepared to skewer any—even women and children—who got in their path.

The one-eyed man roughly shoved an elderly priest aside.

Bloodshed was seconds away.

Carta said, "Master, do something!"

It was at that moment that the Baptizer intervened. Calling to the temple guard, Yochanan merely asked the man to steady him as he stepped into the water and waded ashore. He started to walk toward Herod's men. His followers closed around him, barring his way.

In a gesture unusually gentle for such a powerfully built, angry-sounding man, Yochanan touched each on the shoulder while looking into their eyes. "I knew this time would come," he said. "Go where I told you. Find the one I told you to find. Do what he says to do. Don't worry about me. Nothing can happen to me that was not written long before. And remember what Isaiah wrote: 'Don't be afraid to say to the cities of Judah, Here is your God! Here comes Adonai Elohim with power.'"

Relieved that they had gotten off so easily, Herod's men hustled Yochanan up the slope and out of sight of the crowd. Two of them walked backwards the whole way, concerned that the throng would change its mind and attack them.

"Where are you supposed to take him?" Marcus asked. "Back to Tiberias?"

"No," was the reply. "To Machaerus."

■ ■ ■ ■

The sun was just rising.

The prosperity of the Roman empire was evident everywhere.

Miryam followed her mute escort through

the motley crowd of foreigners who crammed the quays of Hippus. Bawling camels and babbling human dialects added to the hubbub.

Heaps of merchandise from the caravan routes of the east waited unsheltered in the open air to be loaded onto small ships and carried across the lake to Tiberias, Caesarea, and even on to Rome.

Crates of fruits and vegetables grown on the fertile farms of Galilee were unloaded from boats to be taken to the markets of Hippus. Piles of Judean grain and corn lay exposed to rainless skies.

In all this Miryam could see only the flocks of children darting in and out of the crates. Babies balanced on the hips of women bargaining with the fruit sellers. A toddler, wrist tied to the apron strings of his mother, buried his face in the woman's cloak when Miryam smiled at him.

For a minute the longing and doubts returned. Her heart urged her to turn back from her mission, to buy passage home, to have Marcus' child.

The servant turned and scowled at her as though he heard her thoughts. With a jerk of his thumb he pointed to a cramped alleyway off the main street. Miryam hesitated, listening to a boat owner calling out for any who wished passage to Galilee.

And then the image of hope was broken. A Roman soldier, prostitute at his side, strode through the throng. The eyes of respectable women filled with contempt as they passed.

In a flash Miryam remembered that this was how the world saw her. She was the whore of a Roman. A child born out of wedlock would be an object of scorn. Better...more merciful...to be done with it.

Eyes downward, she followed the servant and the donkey up the cobbled street toward the hills of Golan.

■■■■

It was nearly noon when Miryam and the servant reached the outskirts of Gadara. The village was a squat, shabby collection of dwellings in stark contrast to the prosperity of Hippus.

Far below them the harp-shaped lake shimmered in the haze of evaporating water as the sun beat down unmercifully.

On the high plateau of Gadara, a herd of swine grazed among the last of the wildflowers. The stench was overpowering. The air buzzed with the monotone of flies swarming around heaps of animal excrement.

The escort spread his hands as if to ask if she wanted to stop. He held a fist to his lips and tilted his head back in pantomime. Did she want to drink? Or rest?

She did not.

He raised his face to the barren, rock-strewn mountain in the east. Shielding her face against the glare, she spotted the enormous obelisk of the ancient pagan temple. A thin wisp of white smoke trailed upward.

Miryam nodded. Molech was waiting.

"We'll go on then," she said.

Her porter shook his head from side to side and tied up the lead rope of the pack animal. He grabbed the donkey's tail and placed it firmly into Miryam's hand. She was to hang on tightly, and the animal would draw her up the steep slope.

So. She would go alone from here.

His scrawny face full of pity, the porter surveyed her from head to foot. Then he pointed toward an enormous gnarled oak in the center of the swine pasture.

He would wait for her there.

■ ■ ■ ■

Much to Marcus' relief, he encountered a company of Fourth Cohort troopers returning from Arabia. By redirecting them to accompany him, both he and the Baptizer arrived in Herod's citadel alive.

Palace and fortress, Machaerus was located seven miles east of the Dead Sea. Enlarged and improved by Herod the Great, Machaerus had been a stronghold by a caravan route into the spice regions since much earlier times.

It was also one of the grimmest structures in one of the grimmest locales Marcus had ever been. Positioned on a rocky hill rising sharply from barren surroundings, it was enclosed on all sides by ravines.

Around the base of the hill Herod the Great

had built a ring of defensive walls and towers. He then topped the natural summit with an inner bastion, including towers ninety feet high.

The royal palace was in the center of the out-cropping. Beneath it were cisterns hundreds of feet deep. These swelled with rainwater in the wet season, enough to last the summer. The arrangement made the place practically siege-proof.

It was said the elder Herod built it in case his unpopularity resulted in riots and he had to flee from Jerusalem.

Machaerus was an almost invincible retreat.

It was also an inescapable prison.

Marcus saw Yochanan escorted into a cell in the lowest tier of the fort's rooms. Set into the walls were shackles, but the Baptizer was not confined in them.

The jailer was a Jew.

That fact made it easier for Marcus to discharge his duty with some expectation that the prophet might survive incarceration. Putting on his most stern voice Marcus intoned, "Rome has taken official notice of this prisoner. Therefore, see that no harm comes to him, and that he is fed properly."

The official readily agreed.

It was all he could do. Marcus believed his presence had thwarted an assassination that would have occurred between the Jordan and Machaerus. But as to the future? Who could say?

Before taking his leave of the fort, Marcus bade farewell to the prisoner. "You did a brave thing at the river," he said, "surrendering as you did. If your followers fought, you might have escaped in the confusion, but many others would have died."

The Baptizer shrugged. "It may be that my work is done. That is for the Almighty to decide. I know that it is now *his* time; it is no longer mine."

"Who is this you are talking about? I heard you order your followers to find this mysterious other. Will you tell me?"

The Baptizer's gaze penetrated Marcus. "He is Yeshua of Nazareth."

LAMED

On the return trip from Machaerus to Galilee, Marcus first met Yeshua of Nazareth face-to-face.

It was at the forks of the Jordan, just north of the Jericho crossing. Marcus and Carta rested for the night near where the dusty wadi stretching up to Beth-nimra reached the river.

In the morning they awoke to find large crowds of people flowing up the valley. "As if the river were running backwards," Carta remarked.

That comment reminded Marcus of some Jewish folklore. A story told how when the ark of the Jewish god reached the Jordan's bank opposite Jericho, the waters reversed their direction for some miles upstream. About to this very spot, he reflected.

Then Carta asked, "Is the Baptizer free, and did he get back here ahead of us? What else can draw this many people together?"

Remembering the subterranean cell in which Yochanan had been secured, Marcus doubted it.

Besides, the makeup of the throng was different.

Where the Baptizer's audience had been mostly healthy adult men and women, this group was more diverse and less fit.

There were scores of cripples hobbling on crutches or aided by friends. Blind beggars advanced in file, each with a hand on the shoulder of the one ahead.

Children were also present, scores of them.

Marcus thought he had guessed the explanation. "This may be the man the Baptizer spoke of," he explained. "We'll go listen." He did not say that if Yeshua of Nazareth was another prophet like the Baptizer, Pilate would want an account of his preaching.

The Baptizer had offended Herod Antipas but had not actually broken any Roman law.

This time sedition might be easier to prove. Yochanan had been a popular figure. If Yeshua spoke against the arrest, he might rouse his hearers to revolt.

Perhaps a second arrest would closely follow the first.

Marcus still could not see Yeshua. There was

a natural pulpit of rock perched beside the river, but it was unoccupied. Yochanan would have been in that very spot.

Baptisms were taking place along the creek, but none of those performing the ceremony of repentance were the right man either. Maybe Yeshua had already heard of Yochanan's capture and fled, leaving others to do his work for him.

"Where is the teacher?" he asked an old woman who hobbled past on a crooked stick.

Since he was a Roman officer, she was afraid to answer. Then, bracing her knobby hands on the cane, she raised her head and looked around. "No soldiers?" she asked in a quavering voice.

Marcus shook his head.

That distinction seemed to convince her that Marcus had no hostile intent. "He has already finished speaking for the morning," she said. "But just find the biggest group of children. That's where you'll find *him.*"

On a gently sloping space of sand Marcus spotted the same tall, dark-brown-haired man he had glimpsed on the Temple Mount. The fellow was seated on the shore. Two young children sat on his lap, and three stood close behind his shoulders.

Was this the same man who had lashed the money changers?

A precocious boy of about five stepped forward until he was right in front of Yeshua. With a challenging grin, he extended a double handful of round, flat rocks.

Yeshua accepted the dare. Gravely selecting a stone, he called out a good-natured warning to those in the water. Then, drawing back his arm, Yeshua made his toss with a flick of his wrist.

The rock skipped twice, took a giant bound, and splashed down in midstream.

The five-year-old, beaming, made his choice of weapons. His throw skipped three times, then dribbled across the surface for three more.

Yeshua clapped his hands. "Well done!" he said to the child.

"Again!" the boy called happily.

From behind Marcus came a family: mother, father, and twin girls about age seven.

And in the arms of the father, a third child.

They passed close enough for Marcus to see clearly that the youngest, a boy of two, was not whole. His neck was kinked, his head tucked tightly against one shoulder. His eyes were crossed, incapable of focusing, blurring his view of the world, which only offered him pain. Spittle from the corner of his mouth stained his father's tunic. Arms and legs were interlaced as if he were a newborn. At the instant the group passed by, a convulsion seized the child. A spasm passed through his whole frame, twisting his torso into a crumpled ball. His mouth opened as if to scream with the agony, but what emerged was a pitiful whimper.

Marcus made a sign against the evil eye.

In Rome such a monstrosity would never have been allowed to live this long. Deformed or spastic children were summarily deposited on the banks of the Tiber. There they died of exposure or were eaten by animals. Though it was not spoken of, sometimes they were used as sacrifices in rituals supposedly forbidden but still practiced.

Marcus understood why cripples and blind beggars came to see itinerant preachers. Sometimes they were gullible enough to hope for a miracle; mostly they played on the sympathy of the crowd to get more alms.

But this! What could that father have been thinking of to reveal his shame to the world? If this Rebbe Yeshua had any care at all for suffering, he would direct the man to a spot where the child could be drowned and forgotten.

The twins appeared footsore and weary. Flanking their obviously exhausted mother, they glanced around and down, around and down. Marcus knew they felt every eye on them, probing their grief. Probably the last two years of their young memories were scarred from being the objects of pitying stares and unguarded commentary.

How far had that family walked to reach this remote spot? What cruel hand had extended this false hope? Surely this tragedy had lost any possible optimism about its conclusion long before. Why resurrect any expectations?

The father trudged down the slope with a singleness of purpose. Marcus knew the expression. He had seen it on the faces of mortally wounded soldiers. Men who knew they were finished had that look as they dragged

their shattered limbs over the ground, determined to gain one more yard, draw one more
breath.

News of the family's arrival moved faster than
they. The throng parted for them, not helping,
but moving aside as if they were lepers.

Marcus wanted to see how Yeshua would
react to this farce.

He was startled. The teacher was already up,
moving quickly toward the man and his
pathetic burden.

Yeshua caught the father mid-stride. His arms
passed under the body of the child, embracing
the man as well. Together they sank to their
knees. Their heads nodded together, foreheads touching over the small form of the
boy.

At last the father relinquished his grip,
dropping back on his heels. He was spent. He
had delivered his charge; at last he gave in to
fatigue.

The crowd had grown so watchful that
Marcus could hear the ripples passing in the
stream. He heard Carta's breath catch in his
throat.

The cords on the sides of Yeshua's neck
bulged, as though the child's pain was his
own.

What was happening? How would this end?

Time felt utterly stationary. No movement,
no words disturbed the concentration.

Then came the tiniest relief in the tension:
Yeshua's head lifted ever so slightly. The
strain on his shoulders visibly eased.

It was on the mother's face that Marcus first recognized that something extraordinary had occurred. From being almost opaque, her features changed from an expression of bewilderment to one of indescribable joy!

Yeshua stood.

The child's legs hung over the crook of his arm...and they were straight, not contorted.

For an instant Marcus thought the child was dead. Then, over the sound of ripples and hushed breathing, came a piping call. "Thirsty, Mama. Thirsty."

The riverbank erupted in shouts of wonder.

The mother rushed forward, grabbing the child from Yeshua's embrace.

The twin girls, faces streaming tears, clung to their mother. Over and over they called "Mama, Mama," and the name of their brother, Samuel.

The father, his face buried in the sand, grasped Yeshua by the ankles.

Yeshua knelt again, raised the man up, bracing him by clasping his shoulders. For an instant his hand lay on the man's forehead: a blessing. An accolade for...for what? Belief? For love that refused to give up?

What had happened here? Marcus had seen the child. This was no beggar's trick, no feigned illness.

Now that once-crippled child was sitting upright in his mother's arms. Clear-eyed and straight in every limb, he patted her face with concern for her tears.

Then Yeshua turned the father about. After

first restoring the man to his mended family, Yeshua led them away from the crowd. Marcus heard him tell his followers to allow no one to disturb them.

What was this he had witnessed? There was no one he could speak to about it, no one with whom he was free to voice his bewilderment.

Glancing at Carta, he saw the boy quickly wipe his face with his hand, then turn away.

"Come along," Marcus said gruffly. "We've wasted enough time." Then he thought of something. The centurion called to one of Yeshua's men, a curly-haired Galilean kneeling beside the river. "You there," he said. "Tell your master that Yochanan the Baptizer has been arrested...taken to Machaerus. He may be in danger himself because..." Marcus stopped himself from babbling. "Just tell him."

■ ■ ■ ■

The steep path to Molech's shrine was well worn from the feet of many travelers. But today Miryam was alone on her journey.

She was scared, the way she had been as a girl when her father told her about the idols of the Canaanites that ringed the mountains above Israel.

She had no faith in superstition and had long ago denied the existence of the One God of her Jewish ancestors. Still she experienced a sense of foreboding. The air grew thick as she neared the image of the deity which, in her father's stories, had always been the embodiment of evil.

Go on! Get it over with! You have nowhere else to go! No one to turn to! No one who cares! the voices said, urging her on.

Sweat streaked her face as the donkey aided her up the switchbacks. At last the trail opened onto a plateau that overlooked the Jordan Valley and Galilee to the west.

A ring of giant stone pillars surrounded the twenty-foot-high image of Molech. A broad face grimaced in a terrifying mask. The blank eyes were wide. The stone mouth gaped.

It was easy to see how the ignorant might believe and be frightened. But she would not let herself run in panic. Her visit was a practical matter, and Molech was nothing, a thing of stone. Her father had told her idols are made by human hands: the face carved by a man, the fires of sacrifice lit by a man.

It was the spirit and heart of man, he had said, that turned lifeless things into gods to be worshipped.

The flame in the belly of the idol had almost died. Smoke had dissipated, but the smell of burning flesh was strong and unpleasant.

Where was the priest?

She halted and grasped the lead rope of the donkey. Wind from the west stirred, cooling her. Dry grass made a hissing sound in the breeze. The mule lowered its head to nibble heads of wild grain.

From the boulders above the shrine came the thin piping of a flute.

"*Shalom?*" she questioned, forgetting the pretense of her Greek identity.

The music, plaintive and mystical, played on.

She called again. At last the song ceased. Minutes passed. Stirred by the breeze, the leaves of an oak tree rustled. The donkey snorted, blowing away dust with its nostrils.

A man, his face and head clean-shaven, appeared among the rocks. His chest was bare. Camel hide was wrapped around his waist and secured with a belt of snakeskin. A leather pouch hung like an apron.

Flute in hand, he leapt from rock to rock, observing her curiously. He licked his lips as though she were a meal he was about to devour. She looked away, uneasy at the frankly lascivious stare of his black eyes. She resisted the urge to flee back to Hippus.

"A Jew-ess." He drew his words out, caressing each syllable on his tongue. "Come to offer sacrifice to Molech, son of Beelzebub? Great enemy of the God of Israel?" he mocked.

"I heard of you from someone in the court of Herod Antipas." She could not look at him as he danced nearer to her.

He shouted a laugh. "That one! A good customer! Well then!" He touched her face and she drew back. He laughed again at her response. "You have a weighty problem." He strode around her, sizing her up.

"Yes," she replied in a barely audible voice.

Tears stung her eyes. Horrible man. Leering. Undressing her with his eyes. She had made a mistake!

You can't run away now. He is the only one who can help you!

"I am the only one who can help you." He repeated the words of her inner voices. "You cannot run away."

She ventured, "What...is your name?"

He leaned close and whispered, "Legion." His lips brushed her ear. "And your name... is...*mourning*. And the name of the thing you carry...is...*nonenity*."

She pushed him away as a surge of fright and dark pleasure coursed through her. "I should not have come here."

Don't say that! Where else will you go?

Her legs grew weak. She sank to the ground.

Legion parroted the inner voice. "Do not say that! Where else will you go? I am the only one who has the cure for this sickness! Nonentity would destroy your life, so you must end his existence! It is you or him. To accomplish that it is me, or nothing."

How did he knew she was pregnant? She tried to ask him, but words failed her. She could not move or speak.

Helpless, she watched as his bare feet strode around her three times. He began an incantation in a language she did not understand.

Then he removed a vial from a pouch that hung from his belt.

Kneeling beside her, he slid his hand along

her body from head to foot. He raised her head and pressed the vial to her lips, urging her to drink the bitter liquid down.

"Your body...sweet...," he murmured. "No room for children. No... You are meant to be a home for others of a different world. Seven, waiting for this hour of your final surrender."

He waited as the potion took hold. She felt consciousness ebb.

She sobbed once, aware he was caressing her. Then he picked her up and carried her...somewhere...somewhere...

■ ■ ■ ■

Was she awake? How long had she been in the cavern? Was she dead? Tangible darkness pressed in on her senses. She lay alone on the hard floor. A reed pallet was her bed. It was cold. Where were her clothes? She wanted a blanket. Why was it so cold?

Somewhere far away a baby cried and cried.

A dream? A hallucination conjured by the potion?

Miryam strained to see, but the inky black curtain surrounded her.

Nearer she heard the whisper of a child. *"Mama? Don't let them take me! Mama? Where are you?"*

Yet another, older child explained impatiently, *"What's the difference? We're all going up the funnel."*

Miryam gasped as a labor pain seized her.

She panted through the agony, then stuttered, "Bring a light. Who is there? Where are you going?"

The antiphonal chant of two young children replied to her question:

"There is no light here."

"The fire."

"Smoke up the flue."

"Babies in the arms of Molech."

"Up the slope we walk, crying for our mothers."

"The fire."

"We are ashes now."

"He will burn us and still want more."

"Beelzebub."

"Lord of the flies."

"To destroy the Promise."

"He slaughtered the babies in Egypt."

"But Moses escaped. In Bethlehem too he butchered us all."

"The Son of the Most High escaped!"

"Beelzebub envies the innocent."

"So the innocent die first!"

"Mama? Will you burn me on his altar?"

"He kills me in your womb."

"To defy Adonai, the Eternal One, you offer me up. Mama?"

"What was."

"What is."

"What will be."

"We children..."

"Tiny hands and velvet skin."

"Hold me, Mama! Mama?"

"Kiss my cheek and sing me to sleep."

"We babies..."

"...are the true martyrs beneath the throne of Adonai."

Contractions grasped her lower back, then clamped around her middle like a vise. Unrelenting, the pain held her until she could not breathe. The warmth of blood and water trickled from her as the drug worked to expel the baby.

"Marcus!" she sobbed. Her voice echoed back from the depths of the cavern where Legion had carried her. She held her arms up to the vacant air. There was no one to comfort her. No one to guide her from this place.

Distant voices of demons crackled and hissed like snakes. They claimed her soul forever. There was no going back. No turning away. Hope was dead in her.

MEM

Pre-dawn light filtered through the opening of the cave where Miryam lay on the pallet. The scent of smoke drifted in.

Her head throbbed as though she had drunk too much new wine. Her stomach cramped, but the discomfort was no worse than in her usual monthly courses.

She was relieved that she had ended the pregnancy early. It was over and done. She could forget it and get on with her life.

Images of a dream flashed in the back of her

mind. She tried to remember what the voices had said. But the details escaped her. She was left with a vague sense of uneasiness.

Were there children here?

Remembering parts of her nightmare, she opened her eyes cautiously. A large basin of clean water and a towel was near her head. Her clothes lay neatly folded nearby. Within reach was a basket of fruit and a jug of water, but she was not hungry.

She was seized with panic. Was someone watching her? She wanted to go home, to be home!

When she sat up abruptly, the space around her spun. She waited, then, rising slowly to her feet, braced herself on a ledge as she washed and dressed hurriedly, preparing for travel.

Groping toward daylight she emerged from the den. A thin ribbon of smoke rose from the hideously grinning idol.

The morning sacrifice had been made. The priest who had taken the offering from Miryam's body was nowhere to be seen.

She was utterly alone.

A cold wave of nausea washed over her. She retched bile and moaned as she remembered the first part of her dream. Children, yes. They had spoken to her, accused her.

But there was more. What was it? She could not remember.

"I want to go home," she slurred.

The donkey, relieved of its pack, was tethered to a tree outside the circle of plinths.

Miryam staggered to the beast and untied it. Leaning heavily against it, with the help of the mute guide she made her way weakly down the path to Gadara and then to Hippus.

■ ■ ■ ■

Marcus and Carta rode without speaking for a considerable part of their journey back.

It was the boy who finally broke the silence.

"Master," he said softly, urging his donkey up alongside the black horse. "What did we see back there at the river? I mean, what exactly happened?"

What indeed?

Marcus had been pondering that question ever since witnessing the actions of Yeshua of Nazareth.

By disposition and training, Marcus was a skeptic and a cynic. Centurions were just like other men: some were superstitious and others not, but all were hardheaded and none were easily impressed.

The most disturbing thing about the event was that the child's healing made Marcus question his own senses. Marcus had survived battles and achieved distinction by exercising cool, clear judgment.

Before answering Carta, Marcus reviewed his memory again.

Once in Macedonia Marcus had witnessed a Thracian healer cast evil spirits out of a man who convulsed and frothed at the mouth. There were gasps of astonishment and applause when the man stood upright, spoke normally, and pronounced himself delivered.

Later that night Marcus had also seen the fully recovered victim and the healer drinking together in a tavern and dividing the take from the crowd.

The recollection did not apply here.

That the child had been ill, seriously ill, was not open to question. Marcus had seen men in all stages of life and death, and he knew he could not have been fooled about the child's condition.

Then, too, there was the evidence of the family's behavior.

Their grief and despair was unfeigned. They were at their last hope and it showed.

What then?

Could a switch have been made? Marcus had seen Egyptian magicians supposedly turn sticks into live snakes and back again. Was it possible that Yeshua substituted a healthy child for the other in some sort of grotesque conjuring trick?

In front of the parents, hundreds of onlookers, and Marcus' own eyes?

Not possible.

What options did that leave?

No matter how he turned the matter over in his mind, Marcus was forced to conclude that he had witnessed something supernatural. Something outside his experience.

"I can't explain it," he finally admitted to Carta. "And it's not merely what we saw happen to the child. There was something unusual about the teacher himself. He did not care about the praise of the crowd. I've never seen someone demonstrate such power and yet want nothing for himself afterward."

Marcus lapsed into thought. He did not see Carta nod slowly and allow the donkey to drift back a handful of paces.

But it was not solely the miracle Marcus pondered.

It was also the pain in the faces of the child's father and mother.

Before the intervention of Yeshua of Nazareth, those parents had no reason to expect anything for their child other than suffering and eventual death. Yet, instead of resenting the distress the damaged child had caused, they lavished their concern on him.

What was in the parents' hearts to make them care so for their children?

Marcus had seen still more in the father's face. He knew the man would gladly have given his own life in exchange for his son's healing had that sacrifice been required.

Marcus wondered if the baby in Miryam's belly could be his after all.

He would have to think on it. Perhaps he had spoken too hastily to her. Perhaps he had been too harsh and quick to anger.

It was an unusual thought.

■ ■ ■ ■

Marcus' internal debate over Yeshua of Nazareth and the child's healing stayed with him for much of the journey. Besides Carta, with whom could he discuss the unnerving occurrence? Most of his colleagues in First Cohort would believe he had been too long in the Judean sun.

Perhaps Felix would be interested. The young tribune was not violently prejudiced against Jews. He had also been impressed with the demeanor of Yochanan the Baptizer, even if the Roman was not receptive to the austere message. Felix would listen to his tale of another Jewish preacher, particularly since this one was perhaps more intriguing than the first. Over a skin of wine they could discuss what Marcus had seen and what it meant.

Marcus considered sharing the story with Miryam. But they had parted on such bad terms that he could not come to any conclusion about it.

The events of the past week had almost driven the memory of their conflict from his mind. Some of his thinking had certainly changed. Marcus was no longer adamant that she had betrayed him.

Had he wronged her? Was she truly carrying another man's child or was it his own?

If the baby was his, what would it look like?

A boy, of course.

Broad-shouldered and hearty, naturally, but perhaps with his mother's tawny skin and captivating eyes.

The notion grew on Marcus. His thinking progressed from the all-consuming love he had seen lavished on the stricken child to the relationship between the steward Kuza and his wife, and their son, Boaz.

Maybe it was time for him to be a father.

Carta recalled him to the present. "Master, we are nearly at the crossroads. Do we turn aside for the night or keep on?"

The most direct route from the Jericho region back to Caesarea Maritima struck across Judea toward the northwest. Skirting the border between Judea and Samaria, the caravan trail passed near the fortified city of Neapolis.

Outside the town was a rock quarry. Once it had supplied limestone slabs for building blocks, but it had fallen into disuse. Now the area was a garbage dump and home to wretched outcasts like lepers.

It was also the place of public execution.

On the edge of the reeking pit two crosses were silhouetted against the sky. Two bodies hung from them.

It was not unusual for thieves or murderers to be dispatched by crucifixion. Summary justice was swift when the wrongdoers could be captured. In many parts of the empire the law-abiding populace applauded the order and security that Rome provided.

Such was not the case in Judea.

The Jews had a saying in their religion that anyone who was hanged from a tree was especially cursed. This made crucifixion a particularly strong deterrent when used judiciously.

Misused it had the completely opposite effect.

The Jews were so horrified by the punishment that they would refuse to give evidence even against a notorious brigand if he was under sentence of death.

Marcus was also disturbed by the sight, but not because it offended him. It bothered him merely because he had been enjoying his daydream. His position as *Primus Pilus* obligated him to inquire about the circumstances.

Between the two uprights stood a lone soldier on guard duty. He appeared bored. Crucified felons sometimes took a long time dying. Days passed before their lungs clogged with fluid and they finally drowned, unable to hoist themselves up on their pierced feet for one more rattling breath. Anyone attempting to aid a crucified man incurred the same penalty, so there was really nothing to be guarded. Roman attention to legal detail merely required the sentry's presence.

It also meant the two wretches were still living.

"Hail, Centurion," the legionary saluted at Marcus' approach.

Marcus acknowledged the greeting. "And what are these guilty of?" he asked, expecting to hear a catalog of crimes.

"*Maiestas*," was the reply.

Marcus started. *Maiestas* was a charge of defaming the state or the emperor. It was used against political opponents because only being accused of it was tantamount to a conviction. Suspected rebel leaders could be executed for *maiestas* when their other activities could not be proven. All it took was the testimony of "witnesses" to illicit conversations slandering the emperor or his government.

In Rome even listening to such conversations made one liable to prosecution.

It was said that Tiberius raised a charge of *maiestas* against a man for carrying a coin bearing the emperor's face into a privy.

Disrespect was punishable by death.

It was not anything Marcus expected to hear in a backwater province like Judea, especially when the region was at peace.

For the first time he thought to peer up at the faces of the condemned.

What he saw gave him another shock. Though bruised, bloody, and cracked from dehydration and exposure, the features of the first man were recognizable.

It was the older brother from near Pella, the one who had been flogged for swinging the sickle. Marcus had seen him twice since: on the Temple Mount and in Pilate's courtyard.

And now here again, nailed by hands and feet to wooden beams. There was a choking gasp and a shudder as the man lurched against the nails. He bit at the air for a morsel of breath.

"What?" Marcus stammered. "Who ordered this?"

"Praetorian Vara," was the response. "That one you're looking at and the other offended the dignity of Rome. They are made examples."

Who was the other?

Turning to see gave Marcus the third and greatest jolt. It was the younger brother, not much older than Carta. The one whose attempted flight from enforced service had precipitated the crisis in the first place.

"This one was no rebel," Marcus said through gritted teeth. "Take him down."

The guard glanced nervously around. "Pardon me, Centurion," the sentry apologized, "but you know it is not permitted. The order for their executions was properly signed, and Praetorian Vara himself witnessed the carrying-out of the sentence."

Of course he did, Marcus thought. *He probably enjoyed every hammer stroke and anguished cry.*

Marcus looked at Carta. His servant's face was a frozen mask, expressing nothing.

He turned again toward the boy on the cross. The head hung forward on the chest, mouth drooping open. "He is already dead," Marcus noted. "Take him down."

"But the other is not," the guard protested. "The order says both must die before either is removed."

The older brother was beyond being able to speak, but there was mute appeal in his eyes. "Break his legs," Marcus ordered tersely.

It was an act of mercy. Breaking the legs hastened death because the condemned could no longer struggle upward. Untying a leather pouch from his belt he threw his coin purse at the soldier's feet. "See that they are properly buried," he said.

"Sir?" the legionary queried, eyeing the money. "Rebels?"

"Buried!" Marcus snapped. "Not thrown into the quarry. When I return here I will ask. And I better hear that my order has been obeyed!"

■ ■ ■ ■

Marcus caught up with Vara in Caesarea.

A group of dignitaries, including Governor Pilate and Senior Tribune Trebonius, gathered outside a newly constructed granite building. One of Pilate's public works projects, the structure was to be the mint for Judean coinage.

The ceremony of unveiling the inscribed cornerstone was in progress. In chiseled letters four inches high the memorial inscription announced that Pontius Pilate, Governor of Judea, was responsible for the construction. The mint was dedicated to the glory of Emperor Tiberius for the benefit of the citizens of Caesarea.

Vara, his bald head gleaming in the sun, stood at the rear of the assembly.

Marcus grabbed him from behind and yanked him out of sight behind a scaffolding. "Where did you get the authority to order crucifixions?" he asked harshly, turning Vara to face him. "Are you mad? Every effort for the last year has been aimed at keeping the peace and you jeopardize it? Why?"

Vara stared coldly into Marcus' eyes. "Take your hands off me," he demanded.

Recollecting that this was no time to be brawling, Marcus released his grip.

"So, Centurion Longinus," Vara said matter-of-factly. "You have finally gotten back. You must have come across the rebels I executed at Neapolis."

"What rebels? I saw two Galilean farmers, one of them barely a man."

"Really?" Vara retorted, raising his bushy eyebrows. "They were seen in the governor's courtyard with the ringleader bar Abba. It is known that they were also involved in the disturbance in Jerusalem."

"What of it? The whole matter ended peacefully."

Scornfully Vara replied, "I suggest that you keep out of affairs of state and stick to policing camel traders. It was decided that bar Abba and the prominent agitators should be arrested."

So Vara's view had prevailed. After Marcus thought the issue was settled, Pilate had reversed himself. He had decided to show the fist of Roman control.

"Unfortunately bar Abba himself escaped," Vara continued. "He is hiding in the hills with a gang of cutthroats, but we'll get him soon. We caught the two brothers just beyond Neapolis."

"But they live near Pella," Marcus asserted. "They weren't fleeing! They were simply going home! Did they offer any defense?"

"Against *maiestas*?" Vara said with a laugh. "Slandering the emperor? As the centurion should remember..." A significant pause followed these words, then, "*Maiestas* has no defense. It only requires two witnesses to be proven. Thereafter sentence is automatic and execution immediate."

"And you were one of the two?" Marcus said, clinching his jaw. "What a mockery! Who was the other?"

"Tribune Felix," was the reply.

So Felix had been turned! The young officer Marcus believed honorable had been bribed or threatened into supporting the Praetorian. The whole thing made Marcus taste bile in his mouth. All he wanted now was to offer his report of Yochanan's arrest and get back to Galilee.

Making a gesture of disgust, Marcus pushed himself away from the scaffolding and from Vara.

The Praetorian called after him. "And Centurion, I am the chief officer enforcing the laws regarding *maiestas*. Once you warned me about withholding information. Now I warn you. Governor Pilate seems to think you are useful. But if I hear you knew more about the rebels than you let on..."

Pilate did not see Marcus. The governor was with important guests at the celebration following the dedication. An inattentive secretary listened to Marcus' report as he dictated it and recorded desultory notes on a wax tablet. The space on the tablet ran out before the account. "That's more than enough," the secretary said, his head cocked toward the sounds of merrymaking coming from the banqueting hall. "His Excellency will contact you if he requires more details. If you'll excuse me, I am invited to the feast."

Marcus was not summoned to the dinner. Though night was already falling, he and Carta left Caesarea that same hour.

NUN

It was twilight of the fifth day following the abortion when Miryam finally left the inn at Hippus in the company of the mute guide. Night passage back across the lake had been arranged with Jewish fishermen who had been forced to remain on the east shore during the day of rest.

It was ideal. She would arrive home under cover of darkness. There would be no chance for curious neighbors to question where Miryam had been.

Old Tavita would continue to believe that Miryam had simply gone to Capernaum to visit Joanna for a few days.

Only Miryam and Joanna would know the truth.

Fully veiled, Miryam stepped onto the quay to board the fishing boat. She was surprised to see that John, Ya'acov, and a third fellow manned the craft.

"You!" cried John, reaching out to help

her board. "Did your mother recover?" It was a logical question since she was not dressed in mourning clothes.

"Yes." Miryam noticed the enigmatic smile on the lips of the deaf-mute. She shot her guide a sharp look and paid him. He remained grinning on the quay to listen to Miryam's lies.

"I'm glad of it," remarked Ya'acov. "There's a summer fever going 'round. Half of Capernaum is down with it."

"I'm returning to Magdala. The home of a friend. The villa of Miryam of Magdala."

The trio exchanged surprised looks.

The third fellow, brawny and stripped to the waist, eyed her skeptically, examined the deaf-mute, and then stared back at her. "What are you doing in the company of that one?" He raised his arms and grimaced, then shouted at the servant as though he were a dog to be chased off.

The deaf-mute started and ran from the quay. The third fisherman laughed and returned to his work.

"This is our partner, Shim'on," John explained with amusement. "He's a madman, enjoys scaring helpless creatures. But never mind."

Shim'on defended himself. "That one's a demon and a cutpurse. Hires himself out as a guide to take...ladies to...." His eyes widened and he did not finish stating his case against the deaf-mute. There was no need.

John and Ya'acov blinked stupidly at Miryam. This was indeed the fellow who guided the whores to the shrine at Gadara.

Perhaps the mother of their passenger had not been ill. Maybe she had no mother.

Miryam's anger rose at the flagrant curiosity of these ignorant peasants. Why did they stare at her? What business was it of theirs where she had been or why? She picked her way over nets and rigging to the bow of the craft.

The trio of fisherman stayed as far away from her as possible. In their murmur Miryam heard Shim'on speculate that his wife would kill him if she ever found out what sort of cargo he had carried across Galilee.

What sort of woman called Miryam of Magdala friend? Was she a concubine of Herod? they speculated. It was clear she was something more than a common prostitute. Richer. Dressed like a lady.

They clasped hands and made a pact to tell no one they had brought her on their boat. Good enough.

They lapsed into low, urgent conversation about the events of the past week in Judea. Arrests and the crucifixion of two Zealot brothers who had associated with bar Abba. The imprisonment of Yochanan. Were Yeshua and his group of talmidim also at risk? This question was turned over and examined from every angle. Andrew, the foolish younger brother of Shim'on, was following the new teacher. What did this all mean?

Rome and Herod Antipas were clamping down on any possible rebellion. Bad news for everyone. Fishing had been abysmal, but what point was there in running off to follow a rabbi and offend Imperial Rome? Shim'on determined he would find his brother, throw a net over him, and drag him back to the real world.

Everywhere across the lake the lamps of night-fishing boats winked on like fireflies.

The three fishermen knew each boat and crew even in the dark.

"What if they see we've got her onboard?" Shim'on hissed. "I'm not lighting the lanterns."

Miryam covered herself with her cloak and went to sleep.

Later she heard the big fisherman mention Miryam of Magdala and the Roman centurion. His comments were followed by laughter.

Miryam had fooled no one.

■ ■ ■ ■

The wall at the rear of Miryam's estate was too high to scale in his armor.

Marcus had given much thought to his reunion with her. As late as it was, he craved the comfort of having her close. He did not want to return first to Tiberias. There he would be overwhelmed with demands for details of his mission.

He had to see her now, tonight.

Marcus also rejected the notion of going to the main entrance. If he did, he would have to go through a charade. He would have to address her through servants, pretending to call on the mistress of the house on a matter of Roman business.

It would mean delays and artifice and deception.

Marcus was in no mood for games. He was ready to tell Miryam that they should forget what was past. And that he wanted her in his life, no matter what.

It never occurred to him to ask her. He would tell her, and that would be that.

Things were no longer steady in Judea. After years of being mired in the least-interesting territory in the empire, suddenly everything was upside down. The influence of Sejanus was overwhelming the province. Vara was promoted to a dangerous position. Marcus had encountered something beyond his rational senses.

All that had been reliable had stopped being so.

Before any more time passed, before any more misunderstanding could intervene, Marcus needed to add Miryam to the short list of dependable things in his life.

"Unless you want me to land on my head," he instructed Carta, "hold him still."

It had been a while since Marcus had last done this maneuver. While Carta held Pavor's bridle, Marcus stood upright on the horse's back. The animal snorted and shied sideways. "Easy!" Marcus scolded gruffly. "Steady!"

With the additional height Marcus climbed easily onto the top of the stone fence. "Let Pavor graze," he called to Carta, "but don't let him wander off. I'll be back."

Clasping sword and dagger so they would

not ring against the chain mail, Marcus leapt down from the wall. Landing on the turned earth of a flower bed, he made no more noise than might follow the dropping of a slender tree limb onto a mossy bank.

Brushing himself off, Marcus got his bearings and located the stairs to Miryam's bedchamber.

■ ■ ■ ■

The light from Miryam's window drew Marcus like a moth. Even before he set foot on the stair he pictured her in her chamber. In his thoughts she was wearing the yellow shift. Her hair was unbound and brushed into a lustrous cascade that hung over one shoulder. She was seated on her divan. The glow falling on her skin gave her an unworldly beauty.

The meeting Marcus pictured was intense, passionate, all-consuming. The noise he made on entering would alert her to his presence. She would turn, at first in alarm. An instant later she would run to him. She would make little cries of excitement that he would stifle with kisses. He would sweep her up in his arms and carry her to the bed. Previous quarrels would be forgotten.

The night air was intoxicatingly sweet. He could not tell if the scent was of flowers in her garden or Miryam's perfume swirling out to greet him like the touch of her nails on the back of his neck.

Exquisite torture! He wanted to rush into

the room and take her as if storming an enemy stronghold. Yet at the same time he held back, unwilling for the vision to end.

The stair tread creaked under his foot. He was one step from the top. Surely she must have heard the noise. What if she was frightened and called for the servants? That would spoil the planned reunion!

"Miryam," he called softly. "Don't be afraid. It's me."

There was no response.

He moved to the portal and stood in the entry.

She was not seated on the divan. On her dresser the flame of a single oil lamp flickered.

Was she sleeping?

He peered into the gloom where the bed lay blanketed in shadow. "Miryam," he repeated. "It's Marcus. I'm back."

A different image replaced the first. He would touch her shoulder where she lay sleeping, and she would turn to him. She would draw him down and...

The bed was unoccupied, the covers unmussed and unoccupied.

Marcus flopped into the chair that stood between bed and desk. Where could she be at this hour? Irritation came over him, even as he recognized its foolishness. He had sent no message, given her no warning of his arrival. She could hardly have anticipated his unexpected appearance.

But where was she?

Marcus' imaginings collapsed in frustration. Then another notion took over. The actual situation was almost as good. Now he would be in her room waiting for *her*. Think how astonished she would be! Think of that beautiful face, all confusion and surprise. She would want explanations, but soon enough the details would be unimportant, swept aside in the physical reality of his presence.

Marcus unhooked dagger and sword and set them aside. The cingulum apron jingled as he dropped it to the floor. He squirmed, pulling his chain-mail armor over his head, leaving him clothed in his dark-red tunic.

A jug of wine stood at hand. Marcus considered the dainty blown-glass Damascene chalice that was near it and rejected its use. Popping the flagon's stopper with his teeth, he took a long draught. That would help pass the time.

He hoped it would not be long.

Idly he hooked the toe of his sandal in the latch of a chest and flipped it open. Her clothing.

Leaning forward, he lifted an armful of silk. The aromas of saffron and frankincense swirled around him. Stirring uneasily in the chair, he gulped another mouthful of wine.

Where was she?

What if she was staying away overnight with Joanna?

Tossing the clothes back into the chest, Marcus slammed it shut.

Another swig of wine.

He toyed with a tortoiseshell comb on her dresser, put it back, and picked up a pot of kohl eye shadow.

A splash of wine fell from the flagon, scattering drops over the dresser's surface. Marcus cupped his hand and swept the puddle toward the edge.

His fingers landed on something protruding from the shelf beneath the desktop.

Marcus tugged absentmindedly at it. It was stuck and resisted his efforts. Yanking more vigorously, Marcus popped it loose.

A scroll of parchment, too large for the narrow space, had been jammed into the shelf. A strip of papyrus caught in a crack and peeled off as he removed the scroll.

Squinting, Marcus recognized Miryam's handwriting. He moved the clay lamp closer to him as he unrolled the message.

Dearest Barak, he read.

Flaming arrows exploded in Marcus' brain. Like the inescapable scorching mixture of tar and sulfur shot from Parthian bows, the horror of her betrayal pierced him keenly. Whichever way he turned his feelings, the infamy of her actions scalded him, tormented him.

She was a viper, a jackal, a demon.

She did not deserve to live!

Marcus raged inwardly, throwing the scroll from him. It rolled beneath the bed. Stooping, he grasped the handle of his dagger. He would kill Barak bar Halfi. He would slit his throat and gut him like a fish. He stabbed the point into the top of Miryam's dresser, upsetting the pot of kohl.

But what if bar Halfi had been taken in by her wiles just as Marcus had?

She was to blame. Who knew how many men had been caught in her deceit? How many others had she enticed, snared, tortured, and discarded?

Retrieving the scroll, Marcus sat down on her bed. He gulped another mouthful of wine. Brooding, he pondered the different ways she could be killed, hunting for the method that would give the most satisfaction.

■ ■ ■ ■

The moon set early, leaving starlight to guide the sailors.

On nights when there was no moon, by law each city along Galilee was required to keep navigation lamps burning along the shoreline. Jar lamps were placed in windows of stone structures at regular intervals. By the heavens and these lights merchant sailors and fishermen could identify dangerous shoals and safe harbors.

On the grounds of Miryam's villa a navigation lamp was kept in the window of the stone gardening shed. The servant tended wick and oil faithfully.

That tiny beam of light guided Miryam's boat directly to the sandy beach in front of her house.

The white crescent of beach was plainly visible in starlight. A convenient place to land.

Miryam paid John and Ya'acov the agreed-upon fare.

Shim'on jumped out to guide the vessel into the shallows.

John helped her from the boat and passed on the bundle of belongings. The water was cool and only knee deep as she waded onto the beach.

She turned to thank the three sailors, but they had already pushed off and vanished into the obscurity of the night. The less said the better. Their reputations and marital happiness depended on secrecy.

So they said nothing to her. She was comforted by the fact that if these three brave fellows so much as saw her in the marketplace they would turn and run the other way.

Home. The air was scented with flowers.

So much had happened since she left the week before. Her problem was solved. Marcus would come back the way he always came back to her. Everything could go on the way it had been. No complications. No commitments. She knew her relationship with Marcus was not about love. It was about pleasure and company. When they made love she was thinking of someone else....

She studied the constellation the Greeks called *The Archer* as it dipped into the west. It was known in Judea as *The Lamp,* and its spout seemed poised to spill oil over the hill country where Barak bar Halfi now lived. They had taken a rundown farm near Nazareth, she had heard. Was he happy there? Did he ever consider his shabby life and think about what might have been if his wife had not interrupted them that day?

"Barak," she breathed, studying the stars. "I haven't forgotten."

SAMEKH

The door to Miryam's bedchamber was open onto the balcony. The lamp was lit as if her arrival was anticipated.

She climbed the exterior steps but remained in the shadows until she could see who was inside.

It was Marcus. He sat on her bed with his arms crossed. His face frozen in a scowl.

So he was still angry at her.

Clearing her throat, she signaled that she was there. His lips tightened as he looked up.

"What are you doing here?" She entered.

"Where were you?"

She held up the damp hem of her robe. "Swimming."

"I've been here three hours."

"You should have let someone know." She tossed her bundle onto the bed beside him.

His eyes flashed. "Where were you?"

"You mean where have I been the last few days?" She smiled coyly. "With Joanna."

"Liar." He leapt to his feet like a savage guard dog running to the end of a rope.

She turned away as if his rage did not intimidate her. "You're drunk," she replied dismissively.

He charged, grasping her upper arms in a viselike grip. "And what if I am? Drunk. Drunk enough I could kill you! I say you're a liar!" he said menacing. "And a whore!"

Suddenly she was afraid. He was out of control. Beyond reasoning with. She kicked against him, scratching his face and trying to free herself. "You're hurting me! Marcus! Let go of me!" She bit his arm, drawing blood. He shook her loose with a roar.

He held her for a moment, then grasped her hair, yanking her head back until she cried out with pain. "I should break your neck. Rid the world of you. Liberate every man you keep dangling by your will!"

"Marcus!" she cried, knowing he had the strength to do it. "Don't!"

He entwined his fingers in her hair. "Or I could crush this pretty head between my hands. The Jews would thank me. Rome wouldn't care."

His grip tightened. Her head ached. "Marcus!" He was capable of carrying out his threat. "All right! I wasn't at Joanna's!"

"Who were you with?" His breath was foul with wine.

"I went to..."

"Where were you, slut?"

"Gadara! I went to Gadara! To get rid of..."

"Was he there?" Marcus took the parchment from his belt and slapped her across the face with it. "Tell me!"

She sobbed. "No! I went to...get rid of..."

The parchment scroll slammed across her

cheek again and again. "Where did you stay with him? Where? I told you I would kill any man you were unfaithful with! And I'll lay the two of you in your grave together!"

"No! Marcus." She struggled against him, but he was too strong. "Marcus! Please... Gadara... I went to...get rid of...the baby!"

Her confession was like a body blow. Marcus shoved her hard, sending her sprawling. He towered over her, clenching and unclenching his fist as he gripped the papyrus sheet containing her profession of love for Barak.

Furious, she rubbed her cheek. How she hated him! She cursed him and spat. "I've been to the shrine of Gadara!"

Hands fell limply to his sides as the meaning became clear to him. Staring at the guttering flame of the lamp, he shook his head from side to side and winced almost imperceptibly.

He murmured, "It's not...what I wanted."

Her hatred for him boiled over. She threw herself at him, beating her fists against him, then clawing his face. He stopped her attack with the slightest effort, grabbing her wrist and holding her.

She fought like an animal, shrieking and cursing him until at last she lay exhausted at his feet.

He eyed her with a cool disdain. "I almost pity you," he said. "Beautiful, unnatural creature that you are. Almost...pity." And then he spread his hands and looked up, as if addressing the heavens. "Is this all there is to it?"

She panted. "What are you talking about?"

"My life," he replied hollowly. Wiping his hand across his face like a man waking from a dream, he turned away from her and left the bedchamber. By the time she got up he had vanished.

■■■■

Marcus strode across the garden, belting on sword and dagger as he went. Heedless of the noise their confrontation had made, Marcus was unconcerned that he and Miryam had roused the household.

Just let one of her servants try to stop him from leaving!

Kicking aside a bucket that stood in his path, Marcus threw up the bar of the gate latch and slammed the door open.

His rage burned like the fire of a forge, tempering the metal of his resolve. It was better that he did not kill her. Better she be left to think on what she had done, what she had lost.

Better too that she not be regarded with compassion, even in death. Let her bear all the consequences of her treachery.

Nor would it have to be Marcus who spread the news. Slaves were notorious gossips. In two days the whole of the Galilee would know how Marcus had rejected the whore of Magdala and why.

Carta emerged from under the shadows of trees, leading their horses by the reins.

"Master?" the boy queried. "I heard shouting."

"Don't!" Marcus warned. "Not a word."

"But..."

Lashing out, Marcus cuffed Carta a back-handed blow. The clout landed on the servant's ear, staggering him sideways. "Not a word."

Undeterred, Carta choked out, "Your face."

Marcus put his fingertips to where his cheek felt seared with a hot iron. His hand came away moist, bloody from where her talons had scarred him.

"It's nothing," he muttered, mounting Pavor. The horse, scenting blood and sensing fury, danced around in a circle. "To Tiberias," Marcus ordered. "Keep up as best you can. I want to be there before the watch changes."

It was Marcus' own reputation that was uppermost in his mind. How would he be regarded when the news came out that Miryam had betrayed him with a Jewish farmer? Barak bar Halfi was a grubber in the earth, with dirt under his fingernails and the odor of sheep on his skin.

Halfway back to Tiberias Marcus had it figured out. He would make light of it. Miryam was a common whore, nothing more. Marcus had never thought of her in any other way.

And the scratches on his face?

He would quote Propertius—

> Our lamplit brawl last night delighted me...
> Be rash, come on, attack my hair,

And mark my face with your
shapely claws...
Indubitable signs of sincere affec-
tion.

That should answer any questions.
And then?
He was tired of her, nothing more. There
were other whores.
But only he would know how much more
deeply than the scratches ran the wounds.

■ ■ ■ ■

Marcus had rejected her, accused her, ridiculed
her to the world. Miryam heard her servants
discuss the brawl among themselves. It wasn't
long before the tale of their violent parting
spread into the surrounding town.

The Roman centurion had wearied of her
unpredictable behavior, her rages and fits of
weeping. He despised her fearful clinging
and loathed her unfaithfulness. Like everyone
else who associated with Miryam for any
length of time, he had seen the truth of what
she was.

Turn the physical beauty of Miryam inside
out to look at her soul and she was a hideous
hag.

Half-mad. Self-centered. A liar. A cheat.
Adulterous. Covetous.

The final evidence of her condemnation
came from three fishermen hired to bring her
back from the east shore. In spite of their

effort to keep it quiet they had been seen by others on the lake that night. The truth of their journey came out. Miryam had arrived at the quay in Hippus in the company of an outcast. Everyone knew this fellow and what he did for a living. There could be no doubt that she had presented the fruit of her womb to the demons of Gadara.

The Freeman, who had been a faithful servant for years, left her service within the week. Others of the household likewise resigned. Only the steward and Tavita remained. A replacement staff of four Syrians were hired. Lazy, slovenly people without respect, Tavita complained.

Even Tavita barely spoke to Miryam. The old woman went about her duties sullenly. She stayed because she had nowhere else to go. She barked orders at the Syrians, who resented her and commented behind their hands whenever Miryam left the room.

With each day that passed, Miryam sank further into depression. She no longer ventured out to the marketplace. She remained in seclusion, blaming Marcus for her loneliness and isolation.

Since the hour Marcus left, she alternated between fury and despair. She slept restlessly during the day. Each night she awoke to the hiss of seven voices urging her to end her life.

She kept an expensive alabaster bottle of pure nard for the anointing of her dead body. Through the steward she purchased a hewn tomb overlooking the lake. A peaceful place to rest. She wrote out instructions regarding her burial; what Tavita was to dress her body in; what songs would be sung...

What stopped her from ending it? The thought that she had one friend remaining in the world. One person would come to mourn her. That friend was Joanna.

Today Joanna sat beside her on the shore as Boaz darted in and out with the waves.

"The common people. They hate us. They wish evil on anyone who has more than they have. You've got to pull yourself together," Joanna admonished her.

Miryam hugged her knees and stared out onto the glare of the lake. "Am I worse than anyone else?"

"Of course not. Half the women at court have had affairs. More. I'm approached frequently. That's why I stay in Capernaum. Affairs always end badly. One person always hates the other. That's part of the entertainment. A play by Homer is nothing compared to the passion and pain of real life. They'll tire of gossip about you and move on to someone else."

"When?"

"When you take another lover. Or when Marcus does." She shrugged.

"I don't want *any* lover. I want Barak bar Halfi. That's what started this."

"If you don't mind my saying it, why would you want him? He's poor. Mired in his religion."

"A good man."

"No such thing exists."

"He is."

"Not if he comes to your bed, he's not." Joanna grinned.

"I know he loves me."

"Love? You still believe in that? Even after the man has spurned you twice? Well then, you're hopeless."

"I want to be loved." Miryam winced. Yes. That is everything she had ever wanted. The desire for love consumed her. It had always been beyond her reach. "You're a cynic."

"Maybe. But at least I'm not the one thinking about hanging myself. Life for me is as good as it is possible to be. Kuza may entertain himself with other women. It saves me the trouble. But I have my son. He is my life. What more do I need? Bo is everything."

"Barak would be faithful to me."

"You believe that?" Joanna snorted. "Peel away the Jewish righteous exterior and he's probably as lascivious as Herod. Rotten. Stinking like the dead. The difference is, Miryam, your Barak really cares what people think. Now what happens if you win him back to your bed? Take away his respectable public persona? I'll tell you. He would be leaping from female to female like a ram servicing a flock of ewes."

Miryam defended him. "I won't hear it! He's not like every other man! I saw it in his eyes! Barak still cares for me! If it weren't for these religious Zealots preaching from every corner of the territory..."

"It's a game. You know that." Joanna pressed her lips together and stared at a fishing boat making for land. "It's the job of fanatics to keep everyone stirred up. You're right about that, Miryam. Whose business is it who Herod Antipas wants in his bed? And who cares what he does? Yochanan the Baptizer is a doomed man. Herod's mistress won't be satisfied until he's silenced. And it's his own fault. Why didn't he keep his mouth shut? All this stirring up is going to get a lot of people hurt."

Miryam rested her cheek on her knees and closed her eyes. "Everything has gone wrong for me."

"It just feels like it," Joanna consoled.

"No. I mean it. When will I be able to show my face again?"

"When you quit caring what people say. You're quite the hypocrite. I say that out of friendship."

"I dread seeing Marcus again."

"Be comforted. He's out of favor."

"Oh?" Miryam said, pleased by the news.

Joanna supplied the gossip about Vara, Felix, and the machinations of the Praetorian guard. "In short, he's been too sympathetic to the Jewish population."

"Not with me, he hasn't."

"You're a Jew by birth only. Oh, well. Kuza thinks Marcus will be transferred unless Vara finds a way to have him crucified for treason." She laughed, but Miryam was uncertain if she was joking.

"Either way is all right with me," Miryam remarked. "Give me a hammer, and I'll drive the first spike."

Joanna glanced at her sideways. "He must have truly hurt you."

"No," she denied, "only my pride."

'AYEEN

In the heat of the afternoon, thunder clouds reared up like stallions fighting in the eastern sky.

Old Tavita carried lunch to the arbor where Miryam and her steward labored over quarterly accounts. Revenues from the groves in Cana were down by half in the three months since Barak bar Halfi had left his orchard. The new tenant had not been diligent. The midsummer harvest of figs was a bitter disappointment.

"He says the trees have stopped bearing fruit," the steward said, reading the farmer's explanation. "He says the grove is cursed."

Miryam sipped her wine and studied the distant horizon. The hills of Gadara were blue in the afternoon haze. "Cursed." Her lips curved in a bitter smile. "Implying what?"

"Implying? I don't think he's implying anything. The trees look healthy enough. The orchards around are bearing fruit. But this grove is barren."

She threw the cup across the garden. "Is he saying that my orchard won't bear fruit because it is mine?"

Flustered, the steward closed the wax tablet and sat back abruptly. "Not at all…it's just…he is reporting the fact…"

"That the fig groves of Miryam of Magdala are barren! And my wheat fields. And my vineyard in Capernaum. All barren. As I am barren. Is that what they are saying?"

"The wheat was sown in the rocky field. Poor soil. A difficult situation at best."

"My enemies planted weeds in the field to ruin me."

"The Khamseen often carries bad seed from the wilderness to our fields.…"

"Superstition!"

"A fact every farmer knows."

"Winds from Gadara!"

"You're not the first to lose a crop of wheat to weeds."

"And maybe you think I am cursed? And my lands and orchards too?"

"No…I meant…"

"If you can't wring a profit from these ignorant tenants, maybe I've misplaced my trust in you."

"Please, Lady Miryam…" He stared at his feet, then shot an imploring glance at Tavita, who waited patiently beside Miryam. It had been a very unlucky year for the estate. The bad fortune had begun when two hundred ewes of Miryam's flocks had miscarried.

The religious in Galilee declared that such

events were proof of a verdict from God upon the unrighteous. This Yeshua, with his pious teaching, had power to turn the earth against those he did not approve of, it was said.

Even though there was no evidence, Miryam believed her flocks had been poisoned by her enemies. Other wealthy friends of Rome had also suffered financial reversals in the last months.

"You'll show me some improvement or find yourself out of a job," she snapped. "Get out of my sight."

He lapsed into frustrated silence.

Tavita stepped between them. "You're tired, lamb."

The steward slunk from the garden.

Miryam covered her face with her hands. She had a headache. "Who can I trust?" she muttered. "Where can I go?"

Tavita gave her a message tablet. "A courier brought it from Joanna in Capernaum. I thought she might have cheerful news for you."

Miryam opened it and studied the message hastily pressed into the wax. It was not good news.

...Come to me in Capernaum, dear friend. Our sweet son, our only son, is dying. The court physicians of Herod Antipas have kindly come to examine him. Yet they say it is hopeless. Our Boaz sleeps near the sleep of death. Kuza is frantic with grief and sinks hourly into deeper despair. He will not be consoled. I cannot say how much time our

precious baby has. But I will need your company. Come quickly!

Joanna

■ ■ ■ ■

The Capernaum home of Joanna and Kuza was large and lavish, designed in the Roman style. Like Miryam's villa, it was built around an open courtyard and a central fountain. The portico's walls and pillars were polished marble, the floor around the fountain encircled by a mosaic vine, hung with clusters of blue lapis grapes. Common rooms faced the shoreline.

With the sound of the waves in the background, the villa exuded the impression of serenity, perfection, and pleasure. How could such tragedy come within these walls?

After receiving Joanna's entreaty, Miryam arrived in Capernaum in the early evening. The house was surprisingly calm in the face of the imminent death of the master's heir. Miryam had witnessed death many times, and usually the street outside the unfortunate home was crammed with mourners. Their keening was often deafening.

Not in Kuza and Joanna's home, however. This was proof of their separation from the rest of the citizens of Galilee. They had no real friends, merely political acquaintances, allies, and enemies in the court. A lonely existence, Miryam thought. Little wonder Joanna had pleaded for Miryam to come.

Herod's doctors had gone.

Marcus' tall black horse was at the gate.

Carta, reins in hand, stood by, waiting while the centurion made a call of condolence.

The sight of the youthful servant renewed Miryam's sense of fury against her former lover. She would have to see Marcus inside, but she would simply pretend he was not there.

She swept past Carta, who smiled shyly and bowed as she passed. Miryam did not acknowledge him.

Her knock was answered by a thin, solemn doorman who ushered her into the courtyard. The plaza was empty except for a handful of servants gathered in a tight knot.

"I was sent for by your mistress."

The house steward nodded and led her to the dark bedchamber where little Boaz lay.

Marcus and Kuza stood framed against a window in the purple twilight.

Kuza wept openly as Marcus glared almost angrily at the dying child. Boaz, his belly bloated, his complexion like ashes and lips colorless, struggled to breathe. Blond curls were straight and damp with the sweat of agony. His frail body seemed dwarfed among the bedclothes.

Joanna sat on the floor beside him. Eyes red from hours of weeping, she mourned the imminent loss of her baby in abject exhaustion.

She held his limp hand to her lips, looking up only when Miryam whispered, "Boaz."

There was no doubt the once-lively little boy was past hope.

"Miryam?" Joanna spoke her name and in it was the question: *How can this be? Why has this happened? Can God be so cruel as to take away my reason for living?*

Miryam rushed to her side, brushing by Marcus as if he were a stranger. She felt his sad eyes follow her as she knelt beside Joanna and embraced her.

Joanna spoke slowly as she fought for control. "Oh, Miryam! The physicians say some organ in his belly has ruptured. The bile and poison have spread...everywhere. My poor baby. My baby. He screamed and screamed for me to help him, but there was nothing I could do! The doctors gave him juice from poppies to kill the pain. Oh Miryam! Boaz! What can I do? What can I do? My light is going from my life... I'm going to lose him!"

Joanna collapsed in Miryam's arms with sobs so deep that Miryam wondered if her heart would not break from it.

Kuza fell to his knees, clasping his hands together in agony of soul and mind. "We are being punished by the Eternal!"

Marcus scowled. "What kind of fiend is this Hebrew god, who murders children as judgment on the mother and father?"

"A god without pity," Miryam replied bitterly.

"It is his will," Kuza said in a barely audible whisper.

Marcus cursed as he crossed his arms. "You're all crazy. All Jews. You're crazy."

Miryam thought perhaps he was talking to her. She stared at him, daring him to say more.

He would not look at her as he strode to take Boaz's hand. He caressed it for a moment, then said in a strangely tender voice, "But never mind! Maybe there's something to be done. Someone who can help."

"Nothing to be done." Joanna shook her head from side to side. "My life ends when he breathes his last."

Marcus overrode her. "In Judea I saw the rabbi from Nazareth work some sort of spell. He healed a child...a cripple...with my own eyes I saw it. And now this Yeshua of Nazareth has come back to Galilee."

Kuza raised his head and grasped Marcus' arm. "Where is he? How can we find him? I will crawl on my knees...if only..."

Marcus seemed determined. "He's staying in Cana by last report. Come on, Kuza. We'll ride all night. We'll fetch him back here and make him work his magic on Boaz."

■ ■ ■ ■

Joanna, who had once been strong and confident in the way she faced life, crumbled before Miryam's eyes.

The boy's breathing became more labored as the hours passed. Joanna, hands clasped, pleaded with a deity who was too far away to hear or help.

Her beloved Bo would be a supper for worms by this time tomorrow. The weight of that reality was crushing. Again and again Miryam asked herself how and why such a thing could happen. She struggled to control her own emotions.

She had come to love the bright little boy. She looked forward to his visits. He cheered her with his affection for her. Now even that comfort was about to vanish from her life.

Miryam found herself anxious for the ordeal to end. Wouldn't Joanna be better off when his suffering was over?

At midnight Boaz began to stir from his drug-induced stupor. He cried out in pain and moaned pitifully, "Mama! Hold me! Mama! I hurt!"

Trembling, Joanna dripped the prescribed drops of poppy juice onto his tongue and then held him, rocked him as she sang his favorite lullaby.

He lapsed again into unconsciousness as Joanna stroked his hair and kissed his brow. "O Adonai," she breathed. "Take me instead. I am the one who should die. Not this innocent soul. Blessed are you, O Adonai! Hear my prayer! Spare my son! Punish me instead!"

Impossible request, Miryam knew. Pathetic. Agonizing. In the history of the world that petition had been prayed millions of times. Who ever heard of God answering? One person could not take another's infirmities upon himself and die in that person's place!

And how could a mother bless Adonai in the face of losing her child?

Joanna was losing touch with reality.

Pity and grief began to take hold of Miryam against her will. She remembered Boaz brushing her hair on the seashore while Joanna told him stories. He had wrapped his arms around Miryam's neck and kissed her cheek. She had laughed and told him he was the light of her world, and there was no sun shining but him.

Love like this was the surest path to pain!

And now? His hurts had become Joanna's. Miryam's friendship with Joanna had brought an added burden of sorrow and loss. Miryam wanted to run and hide. Forget it all. Pretend Bo was not dying as she watched helplessly! When all the grief in the world reflected in Joanna's imploring eyes, Miryam turned and left the room.

A thought came to Miryam: *why not give him a few more drops of the juice to aid him on his way?*

She contemplated that option for a long time. Such an act would be a mercy. End the suffering.

Then she heard Joanna say, "O Most High! Adonai! That you would help Kuza and Marcus! That they would find the rabbi and bring him here to help!"

This was the ultimate absurdity for Miryam.

No magician from Nazareth could call Bo back. Why had Marcus taken Kuza on such a hopeless journey? Was it to get him out of the house, away from the convulsions and the flood of sorrow?

Perhaps.

Kuza would come home. His son would

rest in the peacefulness of death. It would be finished, and the poor man would not have witnessed the worst of it. Joanna was more resilient than her husband. Women were always better able to cope in such matters.

The muttered vows of Joanna became an irritation.

"O Adonai, that you would hear my prayer and have mercy…"

Mercy? From the God of Israel who opened the earth to swallow those who opposed him? The raging voices inside Miryam's head railed against the cruelty of a God who would allow such suffering!

Joanna caressed Boaz and choked out, "God of Israel, I will give my life to you if you will hear and answer! I will make sacrifice at the temple in Jerusalem each new moon! I will…"

Miryam snapped, grasping Joanna's shoulder. "Stop it, Joanna! Stop! It's hopeless! You are talking to the air! There's no God to answer you! There's no mercy in this except…soon his suffering will end."

Joanna's head bowed as she wept again. "Then widen the mouth of my baby's tomb and make room for me! I'll be with him in heaven soon enough."

Heaven? Was this Joanna's last illusion?

Yes. Well, then. Let her cling to that at least. If it comforts her, let her hold on to heaven.

Throughout the long night Miryam watched distant lights on the lake as fisherman lit the bow and stern lamps on their boats to lure fish into the nets.

All the while the voices hissed this lesson in Miryam's thoughts: *There now. That's what hope and love will get you. A little light and you think it's the sun. Instead you end up trapped in a net with a thousand other fools. You're drawn in, gasping for air, and gutted. So. That's where love leads. Love will leave Joanna gasping and gutted! To believe is to invite destruction!*

Better to be a realist. Was she bitter? Yes. But hadn't life taught Miryam that it was safer not to expect goodness? Or mercy? And especially not love?

Look what love had done to Joanna!

Miryam told herself she was grateful she had no child, no one she cared about. Life was too uncertain. Hope was the light to draw her in. Love was the net. Trust was the knife in the fisherman's hand.

■ ■ ■ ■

Pavor, Marcus' black horse, struggled up the slope. He was lathered and panting. Kuza's mount, though it came from the royal stables of Herod Antipas, was no less winded.

From Capernaum to Magdala the route lay along the lakeshore, level and fairly smooth. They had made good time despite the darkness.

After passing Magdala, the road to Cana wound upward into the Galilean hills. The boulder-strewn trace twisted and turned in and out of canyons. Nowhere was the path wider than a cart track, so without a moon, the pace slowed.

Marcus suggested they set their course by a star. Orange-eyed Arcturus lay ahead of them in the west, on what he estimated was a direct line to Cana. They could save time by forsaking the road and striking cross-country. He thought they would pick up the highway again where it joined a better-marked caravan route.

It was a mistake.

In less than an hour they were lost. Marcus could still see Arcturus glowing overhead, but the wadi they followed swung abruptly northward. When they tried to climb out of the canyon again, the opposite wall proved impossible to scale.

They wasted another hour hunting a different way out, before giving up and retracing their steps.

Getting back took another hour, but it felt as if ten had come and gone.

All the while the tortured image of little Boaz hovered in front of Marcus' eyes.

Why had he suggested such a futile mission? The boy was clearly dying, was probably already dead.

He had brought Kuza out here in the middle of the night. The steward was no soldier, no hard-edged campaigner, but a courtier with soft hands and no reserve of strength. From the sound of the older man's labored breathing, Marcus might be killing his friend too.

Kuza had not complained, had not asked for a rest. His desperation to do something for Boaz drove him on.

In any case it was hopeless.

What had possessed Marcus to encourage Joanna and Kuza to expect anything other than the boy's death?

If the two men did not plunge over a cliff and break their necks...

If they were not set upon by bandits and their brains bashed out with stones...

Even if they completed their fool's errand, it could make no difference. This night would simply prolong the time before Kuza recognized and accepted the inevitable loss of his only child.

Yet what would Marcus do if it were his child?

He dug his heels into Pavor's flanks. "Come on," he urged Kuza. "It's more level here. Kick him up and follow me."

■ ■ ■ ■

When Miryam awoke on the balcony it was almost dawn. The sky in the east was streaked with pastel shades of amber and russet. There would be a storm over Galilee by evening, she thought.

The sails were unfurled. Small craft scudded home from the long night of labor.

Miryam rose and went into the room where Boaz still lay in his mother's arms.

Joanna raised her face toward Miryam. She shook her head as if to say it would be over soon.

"Have you slept?" Miryam asked.

"No."

"Would you like me to take over for a while? You can get a bit of rest."

Joanna's eyebrows rose slightly as she gazed down at Bo. He was so little in her arms. His head rested on her breast. "No. No, thank you. I know...this will be the last I'll hold him. I can't sleep. Can't put him down. This will have to last me a lifetime. And...Marcus and Kuza won't make it back in time, will they?"

"No," Miryam answered truthfully.

Miryam touched the child's brow. He was burning with fever. How had he made it through the night? Had it not been for the potion, the pain would have killed him. But here he was. Taking one shallow breath every five seconds. His belly was swollen to bursting. Surely it would break open and his insides would spill out if this did not end soon!

Joanna gazed at the little boy tenderly.

Was she finally accepting the inevitable?

"I was angry at him four days ago. He broke a vase, and I sent him to his room without supper. I shouted at him, and he cried. Oh. What I would give to take it back." Her smile was sad as she remembered. "I've wasted my time with him. Wasted. Thought I would always have time to spend. I forgot to notice him. Forgot to really listen. And now there's no time to make amends."

"Could I get you anything to eat?"

"No."

"Is there anything?"

Joanna brushed his matted hair with her fingers. "I have nothing in the house to anoint his body."

"I'll send Carta to my house to fetch some.

I've got an alabaster bottle of perfume. Pure nard from Alexandria. I've kept it. Saving it for something. I don't know why. Fit to anoint a king. So, if you will let me, it will be my offering."

■ ■ ■ ■

It was noon when Carta returned to Capernaum from Miryam's house. The youth, carrying Miryam's alabaster bottle of perfume, was ushered into the bedchamber where Bo lay.

Carta's sensitive face reflected sorrow as he stood wordlessly observing mother and son. Bowing slightly, he asked, "May I speak, Lady Joanna?"

She inclined her head in permission.

"All night I have asked the unknown god, the great god, to speed my master on to find the teacher. If only he could come here. We saw such wondrous things!"

Joanna, who had given up, managed a sad smile. Boaz would be gone with the hour. Even if they found Yeshua, they could never get him back to Capernaum in time.

Miryam stood abruptly, interrupting this futile prattle. "Thank you, Carta. You have brought what we need." Miryam picked up the bottle as if to say that soon they would be anointing Bo's body. It was time to bury hope.

"Yes, Lady Miryam." Carta bowed again and backed out of the room.

Boaz opened his mouth in a strangled cry.

His eyes widened and rolled back in his head. He arched his spine and began to convulse in his death throes.

Joanna cried for help.

Miryam rushed to take him from her arms and carry him to the bed.

Joanna cried, "Don't, don't don't, don't!"

Bo grew still again after a few moments, and Joanna sank to her knees.

"Go on," Miryam urged. "Get in bed."

Racked with sobs, covered with his vomit, Joanna lay down beside him.

Miryam hovered near the two. What use was she? Kuza should have been there. Once again she inwardly railed against Marcus for taking Kuza off on such a hopeless quest.

"How can I help?" Miryam implored. Tears streamed down her cheeks.

"There's no more to be done. I know it. Leave me alone with him." Joanna wrapped her arms around his tiny body and tucked him close to her. "He'll go to sleep in my arms one last time. And I can say...*Shalom.*"

Miryam nodded. "I'll be outside when you need me." She tried to find some word of consolation but could no longer speak. Emotion choked off her words. She patted Joanna's arm and retreated to the arbor.

PEH

It was just past noon when Marcus and Kuza dragged themselves into Cana. Both horses were lame. Pavor had only a stone-bruised hoof and would recover. But Kuza's mount had bowed a tendon and might always favor that leg. Marcus could not even imagine how the steward would explain that fact to the irascible Herod Antipas.

For the past two miles they had been walking, leading the horses. Their pace was slower than Marcus could have crawled.

On top of his sense of futility, Marcus also had the guilty sense of having made matters worse.

Even if they found the teacher, this Yeshua of Nazareth, what would they say to him?

Sir, please heal an obviously dying child?

And where is the boy?

Just an all-night ride away from here, but won't you come anyway? You'll be just in time to say some comforting words over a very small corpse.

It got more preposterous with each grinding, dirty pace.

Marcus rubbed his hand over the stubble on his face. He blinked hard and wiped his bleary eyes.

Kuza continued to trudge forward persistently, one step after the other, limping like the horse.

Marcus could not bring himself to say anything negative, not after they had come so far.

There was a commotion up ahead. Marcus recognized the place. It was a rocky field that belonged to Miryam.

On a knoll in the middle of the field a crowd had gathered. Perched on a rock atop that low hill was the slim, dark-eyed man Marcus recognized as Yeshua of Nazareth. All around him, sitting on the ground, were concentric rings of listeners—five hundred or more of them.

Marcus pointed out the rabbi to Kuza. "There he is," he said.

Kuza stared and nodded but did not move.

Marcus knew what he was thinking. This fellow did not look like a renowned healer or a powerful wizard.

Kuza frowned and bit his lip. Marcus saw his brow furrow with concentration as he made up his mind. The steward swayed with exhaustion and put his hand on Marcus' shoulder to steady himself.

The steward of Herod Antipas was used to giving orders. He did not ask favors of Jewish peasants, nor did he expect kindness from them in return.

What if this teacher spurned the request?

Could you demand a miracle and get one?

Kuza stumbled forward.

They reached the edge of the crowd.

Marcus saw hostility on many faces.

He halted at the back of the gathering. Perhaps Yeshua hated Romans. The teacher might refuse to speak to Kuza if he knew the two men had come together.

Marcus let Kuza go on alone.

The steward's voice croaked from the dust of travel. "Sir!" he interrupted, his voice almost inaudible at first. Then he called out across the heads of the crowd more firmly, "Sir! Will you help me? My son...my only son...he's dying!"

A murmur of resentment passed through the crowd. They caught sight of the royal seal of Herod Antipas glistening on the chain around Kuza's neck. What right did this man, this servant of Herod, have to ask anything of Yeshua? Sinner. Cheater. And why would Yeshua answer the request of such a swine?

A man in the crowd shouted at Kuza, "Your master arrested Yochanan the Baptizer! You have no right to ask the rebbe for anything!"

Kuza cried out to Yeshua, "Sir! I have no one else who can help me!"

Love for a child was the great leveler. All the power in the world could not save the son of Herod's steward.

And so he too was a poor man and a beggar.

Yeshua stood and dusted himself off.

With a gesture and a glance he quieted the hostile crowd.

Kuza's words tumbled out one on top of the other. He did not care that everyone was watching, that his words would doubtless be carried back to Herod Antipas.

"He's terribly sick. The doctors have given up. They say he's going to die. I traveled all night to find you. Please...I'm begging you! If you can help him, please..."

Yeshua stooped, taking a boy from the arms of his mother. The child was almost the size and age of Boaz, Marcus thought. Yeshua spoke quietly to the child, then hefted him high onto his shoulder. The boy clasped his hands on the broad brow of Yeshua and laughed.

The life of a child was what Kuza was asking for, the action seemed to say. And then Yeshua grasped the feet of the boy and the two began to wade toward Kuza through the crowd.

Face-to-face with Yeshua, Kuza fell to his knees and bowed his head.

Yeshua turned and scanned the crowd, as if daring anyone present to deny this father the life of his son.

No one spoke. All objection ceased.

And then Yeshua spotted Marcus. Marcus felt Yeshua's eyes boring into his as if to ask why he had come.

With a start, the centurion recognized that Yeshua was speaking directly to *him*—not to Kuza, not to the others, but directly to him.

"You people," Yeshua said sadly. "Unless you see signs and miracles, you won't believe."

The recollection of what had transpired at the river with the miraculous healing of the two-year-old came flooding back. That was why Marcus had suggested this journey. That was the reason for seeking out Yeshua of Nazareth.

But had they found him too late?

Kuza's outstretched hands trembled as if he were an old man. There was no time left for debate. "Please," he implored. "Sir, come down to Capernaum before my child dies!"

Marcus had seen this before, back at the river. The crowd waited in anticipation.

Kuza remained on his knees.

The teacher took the boy from his shoulders and passed him to one of the talmidim.

Grasping Kuza by the arms, Yeshua raised him to his feet and studied the steward's anxious face. Kuza's eyes locked on the steady gaze of the rebbe. Tears flowed down Kuza's cheeks.

"Go on home," Yeshua said earnestly as he clasped Kuza's arm. "Your son...is alive."

That was it? There was no thunderclap, no brilliant light in the sky. Yeshua had not even said the boy was cured. Just that he was alive. Was it a guess? Or worse, was he merely saying something to get Kuza to leave?

Marcus was dismayed.

Obviously Kuza did not take the meaning that way. He wiped away his tears. "Thank you," he repeated again and again. "Thank you. When you come to Capernaum you must stay with me."

Marcus saw Yeshua's face break into a smile.

Hesitantly at first and then with increasing confidence, Kuza smiled back.

"Go home," Yeshua instructed once more. "I will be pleased to stay with you and your family when I come."

■■■■

Peacocks strutted through the garden in search of Boaz, who had delighted in feeding them every morning. Kuza had raised them with Herod's dinner table in mind. But Boaz had made them pets and placed himself in front of the birds when the butcher had come to fetch them.

Bo had won that contest. Now who would protect the birds, Miryam wondered?

The frame of the arbor dripped with grapes. Sunbeams filtered through the broad leaves, splattering light on the stone bench where Miryam lay.

Marcus had once held her and kissed her here after a banquet. They had talked about Joanna and Kuza and their precious boy with envy.

Wealth, position, prosperity, power: none of that amounted to anything compared to Bo's traipsing around the lawns with a flock of peacocks in pursuit.

The grounds of the villa already seemed deserted. Without the bright spot of Boaz, what did any of it mean?

Near the water's edge a peacock stretched its neck and gave a shrill, eerie wail. From around the garden peahens and peacocks joined in an almost human sound. Something like laughter, or the babble of conversation in a crowd, Miryam thought. Peahens chuckled as peacocks spread elaborate tails, flapping and crying as they hurried toward the house. The din was deafening.

Did they know that their young master had died?

Then a shriek emanated from inside the villa.

Joanna shouted, "Boaz! Oh, Boaz! Little Bo! My son! Oh, my son!"

Miryam sat up, certain this marked the end. A weight pressed on her as she stood and turned to where peacocks and a score of peahens clustered around the base of the steps.

Then she saw why the birds had hurried to the villa!

She gasped and reeled back at the sight of little Bo standing barefoot in his white linen robe at the top of the steps!

Behind him, Joanna clung to the door frame for support. She sobbed as she gaped at him.

Could this be?

He was whole and well. Fully healed.

Miryam wondered if she was seeing his spirit.

Then Bo grinned down at his hungry audience.

"*Shalom*, birds. I'm sorry I missed your breakfast. I was sick, you see. Sleeping a lot. Dreaming. Be patient, birds. I'll have bread for you in a bit."

■ ■ ■ ■

Kuza was impatient, eager to get home. He chafed at being delayed by the lame horses. Locating a wealthy olive grower who was a tenant on land owned by Herod Antipas, he ordered the man to care for both his mount and Marcus'.

Next he found two horses for hire. Lavishly laying out denarii, he took them for the ride back to Capernaum.

Through all these transactions Marcus had the gravest misgivings. What were they hurrying home to find?

If Marcus had been worried about Kuza's shattered hopes on the outbound journey, he was even more concerned now. Kuza had taken the promise of the itinerant country preacher at face value. How crushed would the man be when he returned and found his son dead?

Had Kuza been turned in his wits? Had the night ride been too much for the man? Was he in need of healing himself?

Marcus had seen men go crazy with the pain of wounds. He had been near soldiers gripped by fever who had to be restrained from stripping off their clothing and running into snowstorms.

Had something like a fever assaulted Kuza?

The journey back was much easier in daylight. There were no wrong turns, no missteps. Despite Kuza's urging, Marcus found himself wishing he could postpone their arrival.

The centurion analyzed his sense of dread. He had experienced something unusual at the Jordan. That much was true.

But this instance was something else again. This time Yeshua had not even seen the child, had not touched him or been within twenty miles of him. No healer Marcus had ever met…genuine or bogus, holy man or charlatan…would ever agree to such a trial of his powers.

Yet Yeshua seemed to regard the miracle as an uncomplicated request. As if at the very instant of Kuza's asking, the supernatural deed was already accomplished.

There was another difference between the two events.

Marcus had not known the family of the sick child by the river. He had never seen the boy before and probably would never meet them again. He would never know if the child relapsed into drooling spasms five minutes after leaving the scene.

But Boaz was another matter.

He had seen the five-year-old climb into Joanna's lap and watched her respond with unparalleled love. Even Kuza, who could cow merchants with a glance and devastate debtors with a word, swelled with pride when he ruffled the boy's golden curls.

And then there was the child's effect on Miryam. Miryam, so self-assured and self-centered, always softened when Boaz called her "aunt." When the boy hugged her around the neck, she looked vulnerable…something she would never admit in a thousand years.

In short, the difference was that Marcus *knew* Boaz. Marcus understood what a hole would be left in the lives of people he cared about by the boy's death.

They were about halfway between the Horns

and the outskirts of Magdala when a fast-moving speck appeared in the distance.

Kuza took no particular notice, but Marcus' heart sank.

It was Carta, riding as Marcus taught him. The youth's elbows were held close to his body, and the pressure of his knees kept him moving as one with the galloping mount.

There could be only one reason for such speed: Boaz had died. Kuza was being urgently summoned home to deal with a Joanna prostrate with grief.

"Kuza," Marcus said, wanting to warn him, to cushion the blow somehow. But by then Kuza had recognized Carta and spurred forward.

Carta saw them. He shouted something, but the *Khamseen* blowing across the lake crashed in Marcus' ears, scattering the words.

Joanna must be desperately ill, Marcus thought wildly. Perhaps she had attempted suicide? "Kuza, wait!" Marcus yelled.

"Master!" he heard Carta at last. "Lord Kuza! Master! Boaz is alive! He's alive!"

■ ■ ■ ■

Had there ever been such a reunion?

Such joy!

In the courtyard beside the fountain, Kuza and Joanna embraced their son. They wept and praised the Most High together. The light of the torches appeared to burn more intensely as Kuza held Bo and kissed his face.

Miryam, Marcus, and Carta stood apart

and watched awkwardly. They were outsiders, observers of the miracle, but somehow unable to comprehend what it meant.

Miryam felt Marcus' penetrating gaze of sorrow and longing and...something else. Regret? Pity?

He touched her arm, but she ignored him, turning away.

What right did Marcus Longinus have to pity her?

She left the house and went outside. The wind blew her hair, whipping her face. A storm was brewing, stirring the lake into a froth.

No lights from fishing boats were visible tonight; likewise she had no light of hope to draw her back to Marcus. It was over between them.

She made her way through the darkness to the arbor. Rain began to patter on the leaves of the grapevine. Marcus followed her to the shelter but remained outside, taking the full force of the growing gale.

She was hidden in shadow. He called to her, "Miryam! I want you to come with me!"

"Why should I go anywhere with you?"

"Something has happened...This...today. Boaz."

She countered defensively. "What has that to do with me going with you?"

"The powers of this man... I want you to see him. Hear him..."

"Then what?"

"I want you to see for yourself." His words were tinged with amazement. "Then maybe..."

"Maybe what?" she challenged.

"Maybe he can help," Marcus finished lamely.

Fury consumed her.

Who was Marcus to tell her she needed help? "Go see this healer yourself!" she shouted. "I'm not sick! You're the one, not me!"

He did not reply for a while. Vines thrashed in the power of the storm. "Yes. You're right." He remained rooted as the rain became a torrential downpour. "I didn't mean... I wasn't saying it's only you...maybe it's everyone. The world, maybe. I don't know. The truth is, Miryam, I'm a Roman...not even worthy to ask him."

And what was she?

Shunned by her own people, she was worse than a Roman. She was a Jewish traitor, a collaborator with the enemy. She had invited a centurion to share her bed; she had murdered their baby and offered it to Molech!

Marcus could not help what he was. But Miryam!

A righteous prophet like this Yeshua, a holy man, would pick her out of the crowd from afar. He would gather stones himself and pass them out to the people. He would point at Miryam and shout that the whore of Magdala must be stoned to drive evil out of Israel!

How could Miryam explain to Marcus that her guilt separated her from the God of her fathers, from her family and her people forever?

How many of the laws of Moses had she broken? Long ago Miryam had lost count of the lies she told herself and others.

Miryam remained mute, considering Marcus' confession. At least he had finally admitted he was a swine. She found satisfaction in that, but she would not forgive him for it.

He pleaded, "If you could only hear him. He healed Boaz."

"Bo is an innocent child. Why would he refuse if he had the power? And I am saying if...we don't know what he did. I'm content with my life the way it is," she finished, knowing her sins had created a gulf so wide she could not cross over.

"I have been a fool." He turned on his heel and left her.

She had no more tears to shed for him. As he strode up the steps into the torchlight of the house, she whispered, "Farewell." She was not sorry to see him go.

TSADEE

The trickle of the fountain cooled the autumn heat beating on Miryam's roof She sat on the stone rim by the water and studied her young guest in a way that told him she was paying rapt attention.

Boaz acted unaware that something extraordinary had happened to him.

He had been sick and now he was well.

In a dream, a beautiful voice had sung to him, telling him he was loved, telling him to be well, to get up and feed his hungry peacocks.

He had obeyed.

That was what he knew.

Scrubbed and dressed in his finest, he stood squirming in front of Miryam. He held a bouquet of peacock feathers in one hand and her alabaster bottle of perfume in the other. He placed the ointment beside her. "You forgot this, Mama said." And then he proudly thrust the feathers forward. "These are for you."

Miryam took the items from him gravely. "Lovely. Did you find them yourself?"

"They're everywhere on the garden path. Long ones and short ones."

How grateful she was that the ointment had not been needed for Bo's burial! "Thank you, Boaz. And I'm very happy you're well." She embraced the boy. "And how are your peacocks?"

"Not at all happy," Bo replied gravely.

"They're molting. Cranky fellows. Losing their pride all over the grounds," Joanna added. "Bo gathered these especially for you." Then she pleaded, "Miryam, come with us to Nazareth. The teacher's mother lives there. Kuza knows about it. He hears at court where he is and what he's saying. Herod Antipas has spies who keep the court informed. I want to see this teacher with my own eyes. See if what they say is true... And I want to thank him... Secretly of course." She attached a veil across her face. "You see, I'm a peasant today. Kuza could be reprimanded if Herod's lackeys identified me."

Enough time had passed that Miryam had begun to doubt whether the night ride of Kuza and Marcus to Yeshua had anything to do with Bo's recovery.

She had pondered it and decided that the boy had simply reached some sort of crisis. He had survived, and everyone was pleasantly surprised. No magic. No miracle. Just a happy twist of fate.

"Nazareth?" Miryam screwed up her face. "There's not even a decent place to stay in Nazareth. We'll be sleeping under the stars."

Bo clapped his hands and jumped in anticipation at the prospect of sleeping outdoors under the stars.

Joanna dropped the veil. Her features radiated with joy and light. *Like a woman in love,* Miryam thought.

"I have to thank him properly." Joanna had a donkey loaded with gifts. "Show him Boaz. Tell him what it means to have my son back." That's when Miryam knew. Joanna was going to Nazareth with or without Miryam.

"And what if the good rebbe had nothing to do with Bo's recovery," Miryam asked, at last expressing her recent doubts.

Joanna gave her a quizzical glance. "You can't mean it."

"But I do. What if?"

"Bo was dying."

"What do Herod's fellows say about him?"

"That he's got...power."

The voices in Miryam's mind shouted a hundred accusations. Too many to discuss. "Maybe his power is not a good thing."

"Not good?" She placed an arm protectively around Bo's shoulders. "How could saving my son's life not be good?"

"Maybe he uses sorcery, I mean. A spell to make Boaz sick and another to make him well."

"Why would he do such a thing?"

"Kuza is Herod's steward. Herod Antipas arrested that wild man...the Baptizer. Maybe this teacher had a point to prove."

"He gave me my son's life."

"Maybe."

Joanna dismissed Miryam's comment. "No matter what you say... I saw with my own eyes..."

"Doesn't matter." Miryam brushed her fingertips over the surface of the water. "I can't come. I've got business to tend to."

Joanna searched her face. "Miryam? Why not hear him for yourself?"

"I'm as curious as the next person. But I can't."

"You mean you won't."

"All right then, I won't."

"What are you afraid of?"

Miryam's resentment built. Why was Joanna pushing for this? "Afraid?" She denied it, but her voice shook.

"Yes. To go to Nazareth."

Boaz piped, "Go with us, Aunt Mir. We'll sleep under the stars. It'll be fun."

Barak's face leapt, unbidden, to her mind.

"My new tenant in Cana is about to ruin my fig grove and... I can't."

The child was disappointed.

Miryam did not tell Joanna that she could not make this pilgrimage to hear the teacher. What if she met Barak in the crowd by accident? Worse yet, his wife.

Joanna knew. "It's that man you told me about, isn't it? The lover who betrayed you. Or his wife who caught you...that's it. He lives near there, doesn't he? Isn't that what you said?"

Miryam closed her eyes and put a hand to her mouth. She nodded once. "If his wife were to see me... You know, she already turned my brother and sister against me. Barak wouldn't betray me... I know he wouldn't." This was at least halfway true. She believed Barak still cared for her, but he was too weak to act on it. When his wife found them together, of course he had to turn his back on Miryam. She did not hold him entirely responsible. One day soon she planned to talk with Barak, but on her own terms. "Joanna, if I was recognized..."

Joanna exhaled with relief. "Why didn't you just say that? You can wear a veil. Dress plainly, like me. And if you see this Barak or his shrew of a wife, you can go off somewhere. No one will know."

Miryam could not admit that she was more frightened of Yeshua and his power, regardless of whether that power sprung from good or evil sources.

What could he reveal about her? No doubt, if he was a righteous man, he would strip away her last shred of pride and show the world who she really was. She would be his example. The day's lesson on what qualities made a wicked woman.

But Joanna and Bo would not be denied her company.

"We'll stay at the back. So you can get away if you have to," Joanna argued.

"All right. I'll come with you," Miryam conceded. "Now have some lunch, you two. I'll pack a few things."

■■■■

Kuza led Marcus for a stroll around the garden of his Capernaum home. The trees shimmered with the colors of autumn. The flock of peafowl pecked among the fallen leaves, plucking each aside and inspecting what lay beneath.

The house and its grounds were deserted. Joanna and Boaz were off to Nazareth to see the healer, Yeshua. The household servants except Kuza's personal manservant had gone with them. Marcus did not mention his certainty that Miryam had gone to Nazareth to see Barak bar Halfi and not Rebbe Yeshua.

Kuza and Marcus were alone.

"It's good that we have this time to talk uninterrupted and without being overheard," Kuza explained. "This may be our last opportunity for a while. That is, you may not want to be seen with me."

Marcus waited for the steward to clarify his meaning.

"Herod Antipas is furious that I went openly to Yeshua to beg a favor," Kuza explained. "It doesn't matter to the tetrarch that my son's life was at stake. I am accused of using bad judgment. Since the tetrarch ordered the arrest of Yochanan the Baptizer, Herod Antipas is especially sensitive to public opinion. And I have crossed him."

"Are you in danger?" Marcus asked.

"Danger?" Kuza repeated. He denied the assertion, but his worried look contradicted his words. "No, but I need to stay out of sight for a time. I have not been discharged from my post. Perhaps the tetrarch will forget about my indiscretion if nothing new reminds him of it. But I will understand if you want to keep away from me."

Waving aside the suggestion, Marcus explained, "Rome has no particular interest in Yeshua of Nazareth. I don't see how being your friend can harm me."

Kuza laid his hand on Marcus' arm. "Don't decide too quickly. Herod Antipas is looking for any excuse to execute Yochanan. Mark my words: he will find one. That said, anyone connected to the Baptizer is also suspect."

"And how does this touch the rabbi?"

"Don't you know?" Kuza said with alarm. "The two men are cousins. Kin. Yeshua and his followers are already being watched by Herod's spies."

Marcus' thoughts jumbled. Vara was using

the charge of *maiestas*...defaming the emperor... as a way of eliminating people. What if Herod Antipas took the hint and applied the same accusation to Yochanan? It was not a difficult leap then to associate Yeshua with an identical indictment.

And Marcus, a Roman officer, had been the one to take Kuza, Herod's royal steward, to meet with Yeshua. It was common knowledge that they had traveled by night. Innuendo and suspicion could supply the rest.

Kuza studied his friend's face. "You see," he said kindly, "it's not as easily disregarded as you might think."

Shaking off his brooding study, Marcus replied gruffly, "I'm in no jeopardy. As long as I stay in Galilee and do my job, there will be no cause for complaint against me. But I understand your situation. Now, you mentioned there's a favor you would like from me."

"Yes," Kuza agreed, nodding. "I owe a debt larger than I can ever repay. I've thought of something. You have training as an engineer, true?"

Marcus admitted that as a Roman centurion he had practical experience overseeing building projects like barracks, aqueducts, and bridges.

"The synagogue here in Capernaum needs a new roof. The community is prosperous, but the Jewish population isn't large. The expense of it...you know. I'm part Jewish myself, but Joanna suggested we should honor Israel's God. If I donate the funds to do the repairs, will you conduct a survey to see what is needed?"

Marcus readily agreed. "And besides that," he added, "put me down as a subscriber to the gift. I also want to express gratitude to the gods for Bo's healing."

■ ■ ■ ■

Miryam's feet hurt. The two-day journey that separated Magdala and Nazareth was painful enough in a jolting oxcart, but walking the seventeen-mile distance was worse. Joanna insisted that in order to appear to be commoners they had to travel that way. No servants either; just the two women and Boaz.

Bo skipped ahead of them at times, running off to investigate rabbits among the rocky slopes or blackbirds perched on thornbushes. It was impossible to tell that the five-year-old had ever been ill in his life, much less near death.

They spent the first night at an inn in Gath-hepher. In Miryam's opinion she had seen cleaner stables, but here the choice was not a matter of pretense: there was no other inn to be found. Miryam did not spend much time fussing with the dusty mat or the hard floor. The bedbugs kept her awake instead.

Morning found them up early and walking south in the shadow of Mount Tabor. They reached Nazareth well before sundown marked the start of the Sabbath. There was an inn, cleaner than the first. It was crowded, but they succeeded in obtaining a room, just as the hazzan's blasts on the shofar announced the coming of the day of rest.

The next morning the unpretentious hamlet was crowded with people, all hurrying in the same direction. "What is it?" Joanna asked a passerby. "What's happening?"

"Rebbe Yeshua will speak in synagogue at service," was the reply. "Everyone wants to listen to him."

"Come on, Miryam," Joanna urged. "We can hear him, and then I can take Bo to meet him after!" Joanna's voice contained barely suppressed excitement.

Studying the village, Miryam made a quick assessment.

True, it was a beautiful spot, an area of lush pastures and fertile fields. Nazareth perched on a hillside. It was protected by Mount Carmel from the wintry storms blowing off the Mediterranean. Nazareth had expansive views stretching across the Valley of Jezreel to the south.

So much for the positive side of Miryam's impression of the place.

But at barely five acres in extent, the whole of Nazareth proper was tinier than her most modest-sized orchard. Its lone dusty street was sparsely lined with one-story homes and one-room shops. A squat synagogue was the lone structure large enough to stand out from the rest. Even the religious building was dwarfed to insignificance by the limestone backbone of the ridgeline.

Nor would the town grow much larger, bordered as it was on one side by a sheer cliff.

So this was the rebbe's hometown, Miryam thought. She had never seen a less likely place for an exalted man to be from. Her lack of enthusiasm was evident.

Joanna was undeterred. "I want to meet Yeshua," she asserted.

Miryam also had someone she wanted to see, but it was not Yeshua. She scanned the throng for Barak bar Halfi.

Bo tugged at her elbow. "Come on, Aunt Mir!" he chided impatiently. "There won't be any room left!"

He meant room left in the women's gallery of the synagogue.

How long had it been since Miryam dared to go to a worship service? What would her welcome be if her identity became known? And if the teacher was truly a righteous man, would he not know what sort of woman she was? Would he not pick her out from the crowd and shout his condemnation?

Despite her objections she allowed Boaz and Joanna to pull her along. She was curious about the teacher, and the lattice that separated the women's section from the men's would hide her from his view.

On the way up the street they overheard conversations in the crowd.

"There's his shop," someone noted.

There was no air of mystery about Yeshua's shop, no grandeur such as one might expect for the edifice of a healer or a worker of miracles. What she saw was a single room with an awning stretched over poles. A sign in Hebrew announced that it was a woodworker's place of business.

She gave it a closer inspection as she passed. A pair of chairs, with sycamore frames and woven-reed backs and seats, showed evident pride of craftsmanship. On a shelf was a display of ornate amber-hued olive-wood boxes, each with perfectly fitted joints. Many of them sported inlaid patterns of dark oak or walnut. On a few the carpenter had worked designs in reddish almond wood.

Miryam admitted to herself that if the items she saw were the product of his hands, Yeshua was a fine artisan. There was nothing sloppy about his workmanship.

The entry to the women's gallery was at the side of the synagogue. The doorway was already packed with people who could not be squeezed inside. "Are you sure you want to do this?" Miryam repeated. "Wouldn't it be easier to see him after? Instead of fighting through that crowd?"

Joanna was adamant. "We've come all this way."

Miryam shrugged. There was no arguing with Joanna when she was in her role of mother hen. "Then let me handle this," Miryam suggested. "Excuse me," she said at the rear of the swarm. "Watch out for my nephew, please. Look out for the boy. Watch out."

Each time a woman turned sideways to see what the problem was, Miryam pressed through the opening created. Dragging Bo and Joanna behind her, Miryam succeeded in entering the gallery. It was a cramped passage that stood along one wall of the synagogue, separated from the rest of the sanctuary by a lattice-work screen.

That was close enough. Miryam thought. She pushed Joanna and Boaz ahead of her so that their noses were pressed against the partition. After all, Miryam was not the one interested in seeing Yeshua.

She carried on an inner dialogue with herself. What was she doing there? Such a waste of time. It was farcical and distasteful to be packed in with these smelly common folk for the doubtful thrill of hearing a country preacher. *You are better than this,* she told herself. Then she winced. Did she really believe that?

Miryam studied the attentive faces: mothers holding babies or lifting up small children to see.

Her inner voices scolded, *You have no business being here at all.*

Peeking around Joanna's head, Miryam caught a glimpse of the synagogue's main space through a triangular gap in the screen. A forest of bobbing heads covered in prayer shawls swayed in devotion.

And yes, there was Yeshua, the same man she had glimpsed in Cana at the wedding. He was seated at the end of a row on the opposite side of the room, facing her. Miryam could see him clearly.

A wisp of brown hair fell across his high forehead from beneath his prayer shawl. He had a strong jaw, kind, dark eyes, thick brows, a straight nose, and large, callused-looking hands. He seemed at home, relaxed, as he greeted the elders who filed in around him.

Beside Yeshua a boy of about thirteen fidgeted nervously. Miryam guessed that today the boy was to be called to the *bema* to read for the first time. The boy wiped sweat from his brow and exhaled. Yeshua nudged him slightly, smiled, and nodded. It was a gesture in which Yeshua told him that every man in Israel had done this and that he would do well. The boy smiled back in appreciation.

A hush fell over the congregation and the service began.

Much to Miryam's annoyance, the prayer leader for the day was an elderly man whose quaking voice could scarcely be heard above the crowd's murmuring.

Impatient, she looked away from the lectern and scanned the rows of men seated on wooden benches and crammed in the aisles on the stone floor. It was when she craned her neck to peer around Joanna's other shoulder that she spotted Barak bar Halfi. He sat on the platform in a place of honor called "the seat of Moses."

Miryam's heart jumped. He was almost close enough to touch.

Then another thought struck her. If Barak was present, then his slug-of-a-wife Eve must be in the same gallery with Miryam! Miryam plucked at her head scarf and adjusted her veil, fearing discovery.

Instantly the discordant whine of seven voices began to hammer in her brain. *We told you you shouldn't be here! Run! You'll be discovered and humiliated! You have no place here! Leave! Go back to Magdala!*

Then the *Shema* began: "Hear, O Israel, the Lord our God is one Lord," burst from close to a thousand throats. Those at the back of the room and those packed around outside the building did not start with the others. The declaration not only rolled over the listeners, it continued to stream back and back until it sounded as if the hills themselves were shouting.

Miryam buried her face in her hands as the voices dissolved into one hideous, discordant shriek inside her head. No longer were her thoughts coherent. She felt as though she would pitch forward. She would have fallen had it not been for the press of others holding her up.

Then everything around her subsided. The voices that tormented her were driven back. She clung to the lattice and breathed in as she attempted to regain control.

Joanna whispered, "Are you unwell?"

"Too hot," Miryam replied. But it was more than that. Much more. She wanted to escape from the gallery, to run back to the safety of her own house. But there was no getting out.

The shammash, the synagogue's attendant, a burly, thick-bearded, red-faced man, approached the dais. In his brawny arms he carried the carved oak chest of the Ark. Reverently he opened it and removed a cylindrical object wrapped in fine linen. The big, rough-hewn fellow cradled the Torah scroll.

For an instant it resembled a baby swathed in blankets.

Miryam's head swam and she tottered. She shook her head and made the picture go away.

Miryam's eyes shifted to the uncovered roll of the law. The shammash held it aloft and with deliberation pivoted so all could see. She remembered when, as a child, the display of the Word of the Lord had sent a thrill of excitement up her spine. How long had it been since she believed?

What nonsense, she told herself. Or was that another's voice speaking?

Now she looked quickly away, substituting instead the delight of drinking in Barak's face!

She would have him again!

More prayers, more blessings, more proceedings.

Then Barak bar Halfi, new member of the congregation, was called to the lectern to read a Scripture portion. Miryam was thrilled, not because she was following the service, but because she wanted to stare at Barak.

The Torah scroll was unrolled to the book of the beginning—B'resheet.

Reading from the story of Avraham, Barak recited:

"They came to the place God had told him about; and Avraham built the altar there, set the wood in order, bound Yitz'chak his son and laid him on the

altar, on the wood. Then Avraham put out his hand and took the knife to kill his son."

This was the most dramatic part of the passage. Miryam glanced at Yeshua. At the sound of those words he pulled his prayer shawl close around his face. His features lost in shadow, he sat with his head bowed, as if in serious thought.

Barak continued:

"But the angel of Adonai called to him out of heaven: 'Avraham? Avraham!' He answered, 'Here I am.' He said, 'Don't lay your hand on the boy! Don't do anything to him! For now I know that you are a man who fears God, because you have not withheld your son, your only son, from me.' Avraham raised his eyes and looked, and there behind him was a ram caught in the bushes by its horns. Avraham went and took the ram and offered it up as a burn offering in place of his son. Avraham called the place Adonai Yir'eh, 'Adonai provides,' as it is said to this day, 'On the mountain Adonai is seen.' "

"The Word of the Lord." Barak kissed the scroll, then sat down. He had done well.

He is more than a farmer, Miryam thought. *And soon again, he will be mine.*

The Torah reading was followed by commentary and explanation and a translation from Hebrew to Aramaic. Miryam was absorbed in her own thoughts.

Yeshua's head remained bowed, his face obscured from view. Was he praying? Sleeping?

Visibly trembling, the thirteen-year-old boy was called up to read from the Tehillim. In a quaking voice that broke in and out of manhood, he read from the eightieth psalm:

"Shepherd of Israel, listen!
You who lead Yosef like a flock,
you whose throne is on the cherubim,
shine out!
Before Ephraim, Benjamin, and
Manasseh, rouse your power;
and come to save us.
God, restore us!
Make your face shine, and we will be
saved!"

The words roused Yeshua. He lifted his chin and smiled at the boy. The rebbe's face shone with pleasure. So Yeshua approved of the second reading. The boy was reassured.

After yet another blessing, the prayer leader's palsied voice invited Yeshua to come up and read the Haftarah, a section from one of the prophetic books.

Yeshua stood. Gravely he accepted the wooden-handled pointer with the silver tip, which looked to Miryam to be the only expensive bit of ornamentation in that backwater place.

The scroll was opened to the book of the prophet Isaiah.

When the same clear voice she had heard in Cana began reading, there was a low humming in her head. It was as if the voices could not articulate any words but were still trying to divert her attention.

Yeshua began to read, and yet he was not reading at all. With a gaze that embraced everyone in the room, he spoke the Word as though he had memorized it.

> "The Sprit of Adonai is upon me;
> therefore he has anointed me to
> announce Good News to the
> poor;
> he has sent me to proclaim
> freedom for the imprisoned
> and renewed sight for the blind,
> to release those who have been
> crushed,
> to proclaim a year of the favor of
> Adonai."

Everyone waited for him to continue, but he did not. Utter silence descended on the people as they considered the reading. Yeshua rolled up the scroll and handed it to the shammash.

Then Yeshua spoke, gently, as though he were trying to explain the meaning to a child. "Today, in your hearing, this passage of the *Tanakh* is fulfilled."

Every eye in the synagogue, even Miryam's, was drawn to the calm, serious features of the carpenter from Nazareth as he stepped away from the platform and took his seat.

"What does he mean, today it's fulfilled?" queried the large woman behind Miryam.

Her companion shrugged and whispered

back, "*Meshugge*. Him and his mother. Always have been."

"Yes, but what can he mean?" continued the first. "After all, who is he, the son of Yosef the carpenter, to be talking of fulfilling things?"

"Hush!" Joanna hissed urgently. "He's speaking again."

Yeshua said, "No doubt you will quote to me this proverb: 'Physician, heal yourself!' Do here in your hometown what we heard you've done in Capernaum." Yeshua glanced toward the lattice, toward Boaz, toward Joanna, toward Miryam, as if he could see through it and view their faces clearly.

Miryam shivered. In Capernaum?

Bo had been healed in Capernaum, even though Yeshua had not been there! Was he speaking of that? Who was he staring at? Who was he speaking to? She saw Joanna grasp Bo, tears running down her face.

Yeshua continued, "Next you'll say, 'Now do the same miracles here.' I tell you the truth, a prophet is not without honor except in his own country. When Elijah was in Israel, and the sky was sealed off for three and a half years, so that the land suffered a severe famine, there were many widows; but Elijah was sent to none of them, only to a widow in Zarephath in the land of Sidon."

The woman behind Miryam muttered, "What's he saying? That we're not good enough to see miracles here in Nazareth? That we don't measure up to Capernaum? That we aren't as good as them?"

Miryam studied Barak. He did not receive Yeshua's message well. His face was irate, hate-filled.

Another woman chimed in, "And it's not as if he's anybody! Isn't he the carpenter? Haven't we known his family forever? Scraping by, like the rest of us! And the other sons of Yosef, Yosef the Younger and Ya'acov and their sisters and brothers? Eh?"

The voices in Miryam's head trilled triumphantly. Joanna had been wrong about Yeshua. He was nothing. He was arrogant. What right did he have...?

Fists raised in fury. The murmur became a challenge. Barak bar Halfi stood up before the congregation and deliberately tore the fabric of his robe's lapel. He cried out, "Blasphemy!" Other men leapt up and did the same.

Over the rising tumult Miryam heard Yeshua say, "There were many people with leprosy in Israel during the time of the prophet Elisha; but not one of them was healed. Only Na'aman the Syrian, was healed."

A clamorous rank of men, led by Barak bar Halfi, surged forward. He and several others seized Yeshua by the arms and the husky shammash grabbed him from behind.

Were they were going to stone him? Kill him for blaspheming?

Inside her head a chorus of exaltation buzzed and cheered.

Joanna rattled the lattice screen and shouted, "No, stop! Stop! Here is proof! He saved my son in Capernaum! Please! Don't do this! Stop!" Her pleas were lost in the shouting.

Bo sobbed. "What are they doing, Mama?"

The women in the gallery struggled to escape. By the time Miryam emerged, the men of Nazareth had dragged Yeshua away from the center of the village toward the edge of the cliff.

Miryam recognized Yeshua's mother from the wedding at Cana. She was no longer smiling. "Stop!" she cried, attempting to break through the crowd. "Don't do this! Please, dear friends! Oh, please!" Over and over she pleaded with her neighbors for her son's life.

Miryam knew they weren't going to take the time to stone him. But she joined the chorus of accusers and shouted, "Stone him!" Miryam laughed, enjoying the show. The mob went wild! She was certain they were going to throw him off the precipice. And then it would be over. This great healer, this miraculous godly man, would not be able to save himself. Being righteous was no better than being wicked, Miryam thought. Either way people would find a way to despise you. And what they despised they would seek to destroy.

It was impossible for Miryam to separate the howling of the crowd from the shrieking in her head.

At the brink of the sheer drop the crowd halted. On one side of Yeshua was the shammash, on the other, Barak bar Halfi.

The shouting of the throng stopped, but not the screech of Miryam's inner voices.

Kill him! Push him over! He's no one! Arrogant! Full of pride! Who does he think he is? The Messiah?

Yeshua gazed into the eyes of the synagogue attendant.

Yeshua knew the man. He knew them all. These people who were determined to kill him...they had watched Yeshua grow up! And Yeshua knew them each well!

Even from a distance Miryam could see the shammash withdraw his hands from the teacher. In evident confusion he covered his eyes and stumbled backwards.

Then Barak. Barak had encountered Yeshua that night in Cana, at the wedding. So why did Barak hate him?

Yet with Yeshua's steady examination of Barak's face, Barak released his hold as if he had been burned. His arms hung limply at his sides.

Yeshua stepped from between the two men. No one else moved forward to take him.

Suddenly all the attackers stepped back. No, fell back, cleaving a path through the mob.

For an instant more he searched every familiar face. His mother called his name in grief, but he did not acknowledge her voice.

The teacher strode from the brow of the hill into a stillness as complete as a tomb's.

Turning his back on Nazareth, he walked away from his hometown toward the north.

■■■■

The event in Yeshua's hometown marked the end of Miryam's relationship with Joanna. Miryam found her companion brooding on a boulder overlooking Nazareth.

Joanna's red-rimmed eyes simmered with anger. She refused to look up when Miryam called to her.

Bo dabbled in a shallow stream, sending sticks floating away in the current.

"So much for your holy man," Miryam said cheerfully as she sat down beside Joanna. "Worthy of a circus in Rome. Except he got away with his life."

Joanna did not reply. She moved the hem of her robe so it would not touch Miryam...as if Miryam were unclean. Joanna fixed her gaze on Bo.

Surprised by the rebuff, Miryam said, "All right. What did you expect?"

Joanna turned her quiet fury on Miryam. "You're mad."

Miryam tried to shrug it off. "We've known that for some time."

"You were screaming. Laughing."

"I don't remember that."

"Yelling that he should be stoned."

"Everyone was."

"I took Bo away so he wouldn't see you. Wouldn't witness it if they killed the man who saved his life."

"You don't know that he healed Bo. It could be coincidence. I've always thought so."

"Shut up. I know what he did. Kuza knows. Yeshua is…"

Incredulous, Miryam plucked a handful of grass and flung it in indignation. "He's an arrogant charlatan. These people know him better than anyone. They know what he is. Not a prophet. He makes chairs and cupboards and inlaid boxes for bar mitzvot and birthdays." She snorted. "The wife of the innkeeper says his mother was pregnant before she married. And there's a lot of speculation about the father." She laughed, feeling vindicated somehow by another's tainted past.

Joanna's eye's narrowed. "An accusation against him…coming from you! Even the devil is laughing at that."

"Well, at most he's a clever magician."

"And at worst?" Joanna challenged coldly.

"A self-deluded…"

"No. No more. I won't hear it." Joanna stood precipitately and put her hand out to silence Miryam. "Look, I don't want you around Bo anymore. You're crazy. I thought Yeshua could maybe help you."

"Me?" Miryam mocked.

"And maybe help me. Maybe he still can."

"Ah. Now I understand. Sure. You came up here to seduce the famous rabbi. Fill up your miserable life?" Miryam was angry now, stung by Joanna's disapproval.

Joanna simply stared at her in stony silence. "You are beyond hope, Miryam," she finally said dully.

Flustered by the attack, Miryam tried to turn

it around. "I've been saying that for years."

"I reject you. And what you stand for. I turn my back on you." Joanna repeated the words spoken in the rite of exorcism.

"Joanna…friend," Miryam protested.

Joanna's tone was menacing. "Don't call me friend. You're not welcome in my home, Miryam. If you see me in the street I will turn away. Save yourself the bother. Don't approach me. Don't speak to my child. Pity is wasted on you. Your brother and sister were right to reject you. You are…yes…I see it…a bottomless pit… You say you only want to be loved? You don't know the meaning of the word. And when love gets close enough for you to touch it, you imagine…somehow… you think…it must be something else. Something as filthy and trivial as you are. You are dead to me."

"Don't!" Miryam covered her ears with her hands.

Joanna pressed her palm to her brow in exasperation. "I don't need this."

Joanna called Bo sharply and stormed out of the field.

She was gone from the inn by the time Miryam returned.

Miryam went back to Magdala alone.

KOOF

The rainy season of late fall had just begun as Marcus and Kuza reviewed a set of drawings of the Capernaum synagogue. The charcoal sketches rendered on papyrus were spread out on a table in Kuza's dining room. "These pillars appear to need bracing," Marcus said, indicating the row of seven columns supporting the eastern wall of the structure. "I'm concerned about the weight of the gallery."

Joanna entered the room, trailing Boaz, who was eating a dried fig.

Noticing Marcus, she frowned, bit her lip, and appeared to come to a decision. "Bo," she said to the boy, "go and play in your room for a bit."

Marcus and her husband glanced up. Sending Bo to play was usually the prelude to a lecture.

"Marcus," Joanna said. "You heard what happened in Nazareth?"

Marcus acknowledged that he had received information about how Yeshua of Nazareth had again provoked a riot. He understood that the teacher had nearly gotten thrown off a cliff because of it.

He did not add that he got the news in a letter written by Barak bar Halfi. Bar Halfi noted that he had nearly eliminated any problem with Yeshua once and for all. The letter concluded that Barak was sorry to have failed, but he would still be doing his duty as an "observer."

"Some religious disagreement," Marcus commented lightly. He had no intention of revealing that Barak was a spy in the employ of the priests and paid by Rome.

The subject was a personal dilemma for him. Knowing how highly Kuza and Joanna thought of the rebbe from Nazareth, he did not want to admit that Yeshua was being watched. Neither could he betray his oath to Rome. At best he could keep a lid on matters. He hoped Yeshua would do a better job of staying out of trouble in the future.

He admitted to himself it was probably a futile hope. He concluded dismissively, "The business in Nazareth is no concern of mine...or Rome's."

This was the connotation he had attached to his own version of the incident when he forwarded it to Pilate.

"But Miryam *is* your concern," Joanna responded hotly.

"Not any longer." Marcus turned his attention to the plans.

"Something happened to her."

"What's that to me?" Marcus said.

"She's not herself."

"Miryam of Magdala is no concern of mine, insane or not," Marcus said brusquely.

Kuza tried to hush his wife. Circling behind Marcus, he laid his fingers across his lips and glared at her.

Joanna could not be silenced. "She was

cheering when Barak bar Halfi took the lead in wanting to kill Yeshua. And this after seeing Bo healed. I lost my temper with her. But...something terrible has taken hold of her. I'm worried about her."

Coldly, Marcus said, "She and this bar Halfi were lovers. You aren't really surprised she sided with him, are you? Didn't you know that's why she went to Nazareth? You couldn't really think she wanted to meet Yeshua? You know it was bar Halfi's baby she got rid of."

Glaring at Marcus, Joanna replied in disbelief, "It was *your* child. She hadn't been with anyone else but you since you two met."

Kuza said, ineffectually, "Joanna, don't be rude to our guest...our friend...the *Roman* officer..."

Staring Marcus in the face she asserted, "The only reason she went to Gadara was to keep you. She thought getting rid of the baby was what you wanted!"

"It never was," Marcus said doubtfully.

"I was with her the night you left her so cruelly. It was *your* child, Marcus. And you're the reason she went to Gadara. She was desperate to keep you. It's driven her quite mad, you know." Shaking her head sadly, Joanna left the room.

■ ■ ■ ■

Miryam blamed Yeshua for her breach with Joanna. But perhaps what had broken one relationship could mend another.

One last hope.

One last chance. The solution came to Miryam as she wandered through her house late at night. She would make herself an ally in the war against Yeshua.

She sat down to write Barak.

Dear Barak,
I have heard the report how in Nazareth you bravely led the people to drive out the false prophet Yeshua from the synagogue. I have seen how wherever he goes he divides people and families. He has come to reside in Capernaum and fools flock to him like lost sheep needing a shepherd. Like yourself, wise teachers question him and declare him a servant of Beelzebub. I myself have lost a good friend who believes he performs miracles and proclaims his raving as truth. She will not speak to me because I do not agree. Now word has come that your friendship with my brother, El'azar, is also severed because of your opposition to Yeshua. I am sorry to hear this, for I know how El'azar valued your wisdom. I wish you to know that not everyone in my brother's family believes as El'azar does. Barak, you may rely on my undying friendship as well as my agreement with your position on these matters. Yeshua is a danger to us. I congratulate you on your defense of what is right. If ever you are in Magdala, please call on me. I wish to make amends for my stupidity.

Miryam

■ ■ ■ ■

It was late when Tavita awakened Miryam with a soft rapping on her door. "Get up. Get dressed."

"What is it?" Miryam was groggy from too much wine. "Has something happened?"

"You have a visitor," said the old woman, dipping the flame from her lamp onto the wick of Miryam's candle. "Barak bar Halfi is here."

"Barak? Here?" Miryam sat bolt upright. "Alone?" Less than a week had elapsed since her letter!

In a tone thick with disgust and sarcasm the old woman answered, "Alone. He says he just arrived in Magdala, and that you have some unfinished business. Something about crocus bulbs and saffron."

The bulbs had been stored in sacks in the cool cellar. Still good. Dormant. Waiting for sunlight and attention to make them blossom. Like her love for Barak, Miryam mused. "Tell him I have to get dressed. Tell him I'll be down in a bit. Show him to my private garden. Let him sit beside the fountain."

Tavita scowled and closed the door. She knew there was no point in arguing.

Miryam glanced in the bronze mirror. Her bare skin glowed golden through the sheer fabric of her shift. Running a comb through her thick tresses, she arranged her hair to cascade loosely. She let the strap of her garment fall off one shoulder. Pinching her cheeks for color, she smiled at her reflection. A hint of fragrance was daubed on her throat, wrists, and temples. She was certain he could not resist her.

Wrapping a shawl around her in the pretense of modesty, she descended the stairs quietly. For a minute she hung back in the shadows to observe him.

A single lamp flickered on the table beside a carafe of wine and two goblets. Barak bar Halfi, his head slightly bowed, stared intensely at the flame. Miryam had seen that look before. He was thinking about her. Wanting her. But he would play a game with her, pretending to have come out of courtesy.

The breeze ruffled her garment, carrying the scent of her perfume to him.

He inhaled, raised his head, and searched the shadows for her.

Clutching the shawl close around her, she emerged into the light and let him drink in her image. He swallowed hard at the sight of her, then glanced away. Then, blinking rapidly as though he had been blinded by a lightning flash, he gazed back at her. This time he did not turn away.

"I don't know why I came." He stood slowly and spread his hands in helplessness.

It was a lie. He knew why. She knew. The game had to be played out. They would pretend, as if they were simply innocent victims caught in an irresistible current carrying them away.

She smiled and took a hesitant step toward

him. She lost her grip on the shawl. The fabric fell around her bare feet.

Barak's eyes swept over her with desire. His lips parted in astonishment. He knelt to retrieve her covering and remained there to worship her. She placed her hand on his head in a kind of acceptance of what was to come. His fingers closed around her calf. He moaned and rested his head against her.

Each move was a superbly choreographed dance of resistance and yielding, protest and urging. The illusion of helplessness was somehow maintained.

Did he take her against her will?

Did she tempt him more than he could endure?

Was it really anyone's fault?

Was it not right that the first man who had ever known her would love her in spite of his wife and children? Miryam had not chosen to be separated from Barak. That choice had been made for her.

Did it matter to him that others had found comfort in her bed? No. Every kiss said that this was right, that it was as it always should have been.

Of course they would keep it secret. He had an aura of respectability to maintain even if Miryam did not. But he would come to her again and again in secret.

That night, as she lay in his arms, she knew Barak was everything she had been looking for.

■ ■ ■ ■

All winter long Miryam found pleasure in Barak's company. It was pleasure tempered by fear, however.

And then he changed in his attitude toward her.

Barak's visits became sporadic. His conversation was terse, lovemaking almost perfunctory. Had he tired of her so soon?

For the third time in a month he put off coming to Magdala. He sent word that his wife was suspicious and he had to be careful.

Could Miryam not understand that his reputation and life were at stake? Adultery was an offense punishable by stoning. He could not divorce his wife yet. The time would come, certainly, but Miryam would have to trust him and be patient.

She was not patient. Her waking hours revolved around thoughts of Barak's next meeting with her. When she slept, she dreamed of him. Often she awoke on fire for him, reaching into the darkness for him.

When he was with her, she could not bear for him to leave her for a second. When the inevitable time came for him to return to Nazareth, she wept and begged him to stay even an hour longer. He called her childish and dangerous. She accused him of not caring for her. She told him she could not go on living if he left her again.

Her veiled threat of suicide was met by his stony indifference.

Maybe he wanted her to go through with it. Maybe his life would be easier if she was not around.

She sat down to write about her fears. She questioned him bluntly. Did he still love her? Did he want to see her? Her patience was at an end, the note read. If he did not come soon she would close her door to him forever.

■ ■ ■ ■

It was a simple reply to Miryam's question, scrawled in the same cramped hand Miryam had so cherished in her youth.

She rolled Barak's scrap of papyrus into a scarf and tied it beneath her heart. She was happy for the first time in months. She spoke kindly to the servants and hummed as she gathered late springtime flowers from the gardens. No one knew the reason for the change in her. Old Tavita might have suspected, but if she did, she kept it to herself.

His words were meant for Miryam alone.

Coming to Magdala. Will be there alone in the midnight watch. Third day after the new moon. Be at orchard gate.

■ ■ ■ ■

A swath of countless stars glittered against the dark sky. The slim smile of the moon was barely visible.

Long ago the household staff had shuffled

off to sleep. Only the fishermen of Galilee were awake tonight. The lights of their boats beamed and bobbed in the distance as they worked to lure their catch into the nets.

Miryam bathed in the lake and smoothed perfumed oil on her skin. She dressed in a thin silk shift that clung to her body.

She re-created every sensory pleasure the way Barak liked it. Windows were open wide to the balcony. A soft breeze in the trees mingled with the sound of waves and chirping crickets. Her bed was made up with fresh, crisp linens that smelled like the pleasant time of summer before the days of scorching heat. There was barely enough light from a lamp for Barak to see as they made love. He would not forget this night. She wanted the image of her to burn in his mcmory.

Before midnight she left the house and walked out through the olive orchard to wait beside the gate. The air was fragrant with the scents of flowers and sage from the hills.

Constellations drifted across the dome of the sky.

A half hour passed, and Barak did not arrive. An hour and he still was not there.

At first she was angry. How dare he keep her waiting when she wanted him more than the next breath?

And then she began to fret.

What if something had happened to him? The bandits of bar Abba were active between Magdala and Nazareth. What if he had been beaten and robbed?

She imagined him calling her name as he lay on the roadside with no one to help him!

And then she heard a voice call playfully, "Miryam?"

She suppressed a cry of joy as she drew back the bolt and threw open the gate. She fell into the arms of a shadowed figure, wrapped in robes. She could not see his face.

"Where were you?"

He stopped her question with an urgent, probing kiss.

Desire for him overwhelmed her.

He embraced her, caressed her roughly, even as she tugged him into the seclusion of the orchard. He kicked the gate shut, stood panting for an instant, and then pushed her onto the ground.

"Not here," she protested. "Barak? Please..."

He did not reply. He clamped his hand over her mouth and tore at her clothes. She struggled weakly against him as he forced himself on her, pinning her beneath him. Stones and gravel tore into her flesh.

She fought harder. "Barak! Don't!" Her cries were muffled from the clamp of his hand on her mouth.

He laughed, enjoying the fight, aroused by her pain and horror.

In that instant she knew the terrible truth!

"Who are you? I want Barak! Let me go!"

She tried to scream, but her attacker slammed his fist into her, knocking the wind out of her. Two hard slaps across her head left her dazed, unable to resist. Minutes of agony passed, broken by her sobs.

And then it was over.

The attacker stood and rolled her over with his sandaled foot.

"Good," he said. "Not exceptional, as bar Halfi seemed to think you would be, but good enough to satisfy Rome."

It was clear from his dialect he was a Roman. Had he killed Barak? Exacted a last confession from him that he was coming here to be with her?

"Where is Barak?" she pleaded. "What have you done with him?"

He grasped her wrist and jerked her to her feet. "He said you'd have a bed made up. A lamp lit so I could see you in the light."

"You've killed Barak! I know it! Let me go! Please!"

She bit his wrist, attempting to escape. He roared and grabbed her hair, restraining her easily. "He said you were full of fire. I always wondered what it was about you that drew Marcus Longinus like a moth to flame. Yes. You seared his wings."

"Marcus!"

Another laugh. "I serve with him. We're old friends. My name is Vara."

She knew of the Praetorian centurion Vara. His reputation for cruelty was unsurpassed. "Please let me go!" she begged.

He shook her and clamped his hand hard over her mouth again. He hissed in her ear, "Barak told me the way to your bed. His wife came with him to Magdala, you see, so he couldn't make it. Frightens easily, that one. I offered to tell you in person. Barak won't be along. You like the message so far? There's more, Miryam. Much more to come. I will show you the Roman way as you have never seen it."

As Vara dragged her toward the dim light of her own bedchamber, she knew there was no escape.

RESH

True to his words to Kuza, Marcus buried himself in the work of running the military district of Galilee. He increased the number of patrols and followed up every report of banditry. First Cohort was never allowed to idle. If they were not on assignment, Marcus ordered vigorous training exercises.

He himself was up at dawn practicing with javelin and sword. His days lasted until late each night, reviewing and writing reports.

The combination left him little time to worry about either politics or Miryam. He was exhausted every night, but the arrangement suited him.

In the spare time he permitted himself, he supervised the repair of the synagogue in Capernaum. The restoration was more extensive than originally anticipated. The structure's walls required bracing before they would support the refurbished roof. He added that repair to the project as well, then secretly contributed from his own funds to make it possible.

The legionaries who accompanied him looked askance at the whole proceeding. The idea of a Roman officer assisting Jews at one of their houses of worship was preposterous. The Syrians in Marcus' command thought Jews were atheists since they denied the existence of all gods but one. Why a Roman would show so much interest in the religion of the Jews was incomprehensible.

The Samaritans in the cohort were even more scornful. They were especially incensed when Marcus made them haul and stack building material for the project. He did not try to get them involved in the actual labor of repair, since their presence would have defiled the building.

Besides, they were difficult enough to manage as it was. Wagonloads of bricks for the synagogue mysteriously fell and cracked. Tar somehow got mixed with the lime for the mortar, rendering it unusable.

And whenever they thought they could get away with it, the Samaritan troopers were openly hostile to the Capernaum Jews.

Marcus himself never entered the synagogue, but he reviewed plans and drawings on a table in a tavern across the street. That was where he was sitting one afternoon when there was a commotion outside.

A loud shot was followed by a crash, a cry of pain, and gales of laughter.

Evidently three of the Samaritan legionaries were amusing themselves by throwing rocks at the Jewish laborers. Then one of them got a bright idea. Waiting till a hod carrier with a armful of bricks ascended a ladder, the Roman soldier kicked the scaffolding.

The Jew fell fifteen feet. By sheer good fortune the building blocks dropped away from him. The man was not killed, but his arm broke when he landed on it.

Marcus burst out of the inn in time to catch sight of the three soldiers guffawing and pointing. He grabbed the first one he came to and threw him headfirst into a wall. The second turned just in time to get Marcus' fist in his teeth. Down he went.

The remaining soldier saw the fate of the other two. Spreading his hands, he pleaded, "Centurion, we meant no harm. A bit of fun, is all."

"Fun, is it?" Marcus demanded. "I'll have your hide off! I'll..."

A sharp call interrupted the catalogue of punishment. "Centurion Longinus!"

It was Praetorian Vara, arriving in town at the head of a column of cavalry. At his side rode Tribune Felix.

"What's this?" Vara said scornfully. "Brawling with your own men?"

In no mood for verbal antics, Marcus snapped, "I'm disciplining them. No concern of yours."

"But it is," Vara corrected. "You men clean yourselves up," he said to the legionaries. "Marcus, a word with you."

The burly Vara dismounted and entered the tavern while Felix remained outside. Marcus had no choice but to follow.

Once inside, Vara wasted no time launching into his message, which it plainly pleased him to deliver. "You haven't caught bar Abba yet, have you?"

Bar Abba had gathered a group of rebels and was fighting a guerrilla war against unarmed caravans and isolated farmhouses. He had murdered a few of his countrymen known for being Roman collaborators.

Despite frequent forays into the hill country by Roman patrols, the local farmers always managed to warn the radical leader before they ever got close.

"No," Marcus admitted. "But the last report said he was down in the desert beyond Perea. Not in our territory at all."

"But you wasted time working on a Jewish synagogue?" Vara clucked his tongue. "And you took one of Herod Antipas' royal stewards to consult a sort of Jewish preacher? Very questionable activities."

So the news about the visit to Yeshua of Nazareth had gotten back to Caesarea.

Marcus said nothing.

"Finally," Vara said slowly, relishing the trouble Marcus was in, "about the two rebels I executed at Neapolis...a lawful sentence with which you tried to interfere... I've learned that you previously had a violent encounter with them. Not only did you let them go unpunished, you didn't report the matter to headquarters."

Felix had truly stabbed him in the back and twisted the blade.

When Marcus still made no comment, Vara concluded, "If it were up to me, I would have you broken completely...or worse. But the governor has decided to merely reduce your rank. You remain a centurion of First Cohort, but you are no longer *Primus Pilus*. As a matter of fact, you have a new assignment altogether: you will oversee the collection of taxes for Capernaum, while still keeping an eye out for rebels, of course."

A menial job. A guard sergeant and a half-dozen troopers would be enough; it was no position for a centurion.

Arguing would be the same as disobeying an order, so Marcus stood mute.

"No comment?" Vara goaded. "By the way, I enjoyed having your Jewish whore. She was not the best, but she fought back enough to be diverting."

Marcus clenched and unclenched his fists. If he so much as threatened Vara, the bully would call out. Marcus knew the troopers had been told to expect such a summons.

By tomorrow Marcus would be nailed to a cross on the Tiberias parade ground.

Vara stuck out his lower lip. He was plainly disappointed that Marcus did not rise to the bait. "One more thing," he added. "I'm sure you can't afford a servant in your newly reduced circumstances. Plus, you'll be short of cash. I fancy the boy. Why not sell him to me for, say, thirty denarii?"

Marcus trembled when he spoke. "Get out," he said.

Vara's booming laugh mocked Marcus long after the Praetorian remounted and rode away.

■ ■ ■ ■

Because of Marcus' efforts to refurbish the synagogue, the Jews of Capernaum were used to seeing him around their city. Some actually smiled at him now when they passed him on the street. Others, like Shim'on the fisherman, scowled and turned away.

Yeshua remained in the area. At first he spoke publicly only in the synagogue. There were no outbreaks of hostility like the one in Nazareth. Capernaum welcomed Yeshua with open arms.

Marcus had avoided hearing the rabbi's teaching. He had been told by Kuza and others that Yeshua sat on a sawhorse amid the scaffolding and piles of building material as he preached. The teacher did not demand a choice seat in a freshly painted hall; he remained cheerful and unpretentious.

According to Kuza, Yeshua expressed satisfaction that the synagogue was being repaired.

For an unknown reason, Yeshua's approval pleased Marcus. He could not explain it but admitted to himself that he felt it.

Then because of the stories of miraculous healings, people from as far away as the Decapolis started coming to hear Yeshua.

347

Normally placid Capernaum, with its six thousand residents, counted another thousand people in its environs on any given day.

The increased notoriety caused a change in the teacher's habits. The synagogue no longer held the audience, so increasingly Yeshua spoke out-of-doors.

Merchants and innkeepers had no complaints. They kept track of Yeshua's whereabouts in order to direct newcomers to the local celebrity. Nazareth's loss was Capernaum's gain.

Two days before Sabbath, Marcus rode up from Tiberias with Carta jogging alongside. They came to a cove of the Sea of Galilee even as Yeshua arrived from the other direction.

It was a pleasant spot, the hillside dotted with wild olive trees and sycamore figs. Marcus and Carta took up a spot in the shade.

Tall reeds growing in clumps at the water's edge framed the blue of the lake and the mountains on the far shore. On either hand two of the broad-waisted, high-prowed fishing boats were drawn up on the gravel. In one of them, repairing some rigging on the single sail, were the bar Zavdai brothers, John and Ya'acov.

Beside the other vessel Shim'on and his brother, Andrew, were scrubbing a net. His tunic kilted up high on his thighs, Shim'on was fussing with a tangled part of the mesh. His face showed frustration that only deepened when Yeshua and his audience flowed over the hill and down toward him.

"Can we stop and hear him, master?" Carta asked. "For a short time?"

Marcus indicated that he was in no special hurry. As long as they stayed at the rear of the throng there should be no problem.

The number of people gathered around was too large and the shoreline too flat for Yeshua to be seen by anyone farther back than three rows.

Marcus saw Yeshua approach Shim'on. The teacher gestured toward Shim'on's boat. He seemed to be asking a question.

At first the big fisherman denied the request. He shook his shaggy head and gestured down at the net.

Yeshua appeared to repeat the appeal.

Behind him, standing on the side of the beached craft, Shim'on's brother called out. "What will it hurt? I can help you with the net now and fix the rigging later. Let the master use the boat."

Shim'on frowned angrily. Marcus knew the fisherman's reputation. He was a headstrong man who liked being the one who made decisions.

Marcus also knew there was friction between the two brothers. Andrew was already openly interested in the teachings of Yeshua and had traveled with him. Shim'on complained that Andrew was taking too much time away from their business and leaving too much work for one man.

In any case, being seen as discourteous in the presence of a thousand witnesses was too much even for blunt Shim'on. Slamming down the snarled net, he snapped at Yeshua to get in and yelled at Andrew to get out and help.

Together the brothers pushed the vessel out from shore. In the boat's rhythmic rocking Jesus stood upright, steadying himself by holding on to the mast. "Listen!" he said. "The time has come! God's kingdom is near!"

Marcus' ears perked up at that. What did the teacher mean about God's kingdom? Was Yeshua referring to a place beyond this world where the gods lived? Many religions taught that there was a life after this one. Many sects promised devout followers a time of bliss to make up for what they had suffered on earth.

But a *kingdom?*

Too many previous Jewish rebels had associated their freedom movements with restoring a kingdom ruled by the Jewish God.

Marcus hoped he had not misjudged Yeshua. The man acted genuinely good and, even more important to Rome, genuinely harmless. But this line of talk could prove dangerous.

Yeshua continued, "Turn to God from your sins and believe the Good News!"

Relaxing, Marcus unconsciously patted Carta on the shoulder. No threat of sedition in this kind of speech.

Shim'on pointedly ignored Yeshua's preaching. The fisherman continued to repair his net, even though his brother had stopped to listen.

As Yeshua continued to speak, Marcus

reflected that the teacher echoed the statements of Yochanan the Baptizer. Yet there were differences. Marcus could not exactly define them, but one idea circled in his head. Yochanan had spoken of the need to change your ways in order to be ready for something that was coming. Coming soon, certainly, but still in the future.

Yeshua made it sound as if the something...whatever it was...was already present, nearby, within reach.

When Yeshua finished talking, he prayed aloud.

Then he said to Shim'on, "Thank you for the use of your boat."

Shim'on made a dismissive gesture, as if no thanks were needed.

Yeshua was not through. "Row out and let down your nets."

Looking up from his work, Shim'on stared at Andrew and waggled his hand next to his ear. *Meshugge*, the gesture said. Slowly, the way one would explain something to a slow-witted child, Shim'on replied, "You know, rebbe, we already fished all night. We worked hard, too."

Yeshua grinned good-naturedly, even though Shim'on was playing to the crowd.

Marcus, though not a fisherman himself, understood the futility of the plan. By day schools of fish fled to deeper water, far out in the lake. They did not rise near the surface to feed...and to be caught...until after nightfall. That's when they were attracted to the bright lights on the fishing vessel shining in the darkness.

Shim'on was telling the audience that Yeshua might know Torah, but he didn't know anything about fishing. He continued, "We caught nothing...not a single stinking...not even one tiny fish, see? All we caught were knots and tangles."

It was at that point that Shim'on grinned doubtfully up at Yeshua's face.

The crowd sensed Yeshua would not preach anymore that day. Since no miracles appeared to be coming, they started to drift away, back over the hill toward Capernaum.

But then something happened. As Shim'on and Yeshua looked at each other, Shim'on's blustering tone changed. Marcus moved closer to hear his words. With evident confusion Shim'on said, "But if you say so, I'll let down the nets."

His brother stared at him. "Well?" Shim'on bellowed. "What are you waiting for? Help me. Don't stand there!"

"Master," Carta said, "shall we go?"

"Wait a bit," Marcus suggested. "Just a while longer."

In the part of the lake where they were, the lake bottom dropped precipitously not far offshore. Marcus watched as Shim'on and Andrew heaved at the oars, their shoulder muscles bulging as they pulled.

After a time Marcus saw Yeshua raise his hand. *Here,* his gesture said.

Shim'on and Andrew lowered the net over

the side. The weighted edge tugged the mesh into the deep while a set of floats kept the other side from sinking.

Yeshua leaned over the side of the craft and peered into the depths. His face, reflecting the brilliant light from above and the glare off the water's surface, seemed to glow.

Oars moved in rhythm, like a miniature galley ship on the high seas, as the brothers rowed in a circle, closing the loop of net back on itself. Then Shim'on hauled at the line closing the bottom of the pouch.

Marcus saw Shim'on standing upright, in a posture anticipating no more effort than he might use to coil a length of rope. As the centurion watched, the fisherman's face reddened with effort and strain. Bending over, Shim'on grabbed a bundle of net with both hands and struggled to raise it barely waist high.

"Hey!" Marcus heard Shim'on's bellow cross the water. "Ya'acov! Get John! Bring the other boat! We need help out here!"

When the other vessel drew alongside the first, all four men heaved and struggled to draw in the net. The space of water between the two craft appeared to be boiling! By squinting his eyes Marcus saw hundreds of fish leaping into the air and falling back.

The bellow of boisterous laughter floated across the waves. Using baskets of woven reeds, the four men scooped load after load of fish into Shim'on's boat. Soon it began to settle noticeably lower in the water.

There were yet more fish in the net. John

and Ya'acov started dumping the catch into their own craft...until the gunnels were barely a handspan above the surface.

Marcus saw Shim'on's face jerk up in astonishment. Flinging the basket away from him, the fisherman approached the teacher and sank to his knees.

Yeshua nodded once and placed a hand on Shim'on's sun-bronzed shoulder.

What passed between them? Marcus wondered. He wished he could somehow share it.

Marcus strained to hear the words each man uttered, but the sense of it was lost in the lapping of the waves.

Carta stood pale and trembling at the water's edge. "Something...important...is happening, I think."

Marcus cleared his throat as if to disagree. It was his duty to deal with fact, not emotion. Just a lucky catch. Or was it? In broad daylight? With no lamp to draw the school up from the murky depths to the surface?

Marcus felt it too: something important. But what did it mean?

A slight breeze rose from the east, carrying on it the scent of lavender.

The centurion and the youth watched for a minute longer, then turned away without an answer.

SHEEN

As Miryam moved through the crowd at the Magdala marketplace, she was aware that Jewish men turned away, shielding their eyes, at her approach. Jewish mothers yanked their children back, lest they brush against her. Roman soldiers nudged one another, grinned, and leered at her. They whispered and raised their eyebrows, studying her as though she were naked.

On more than one occasion she stopped to talk with handsome soldiers or pale foreigners from the north.

Often a man ended up sharing her bed for the night.

Word of her passion and beauty spread even as her spirit collapsed in the months since the brutal rape. She no longer had to search for company. Companionship came to her with gifts and stories of faraway lands. She dined with strong, rich, and worthy men. Sometimes she offered herself as dessert. Those who were unworthy she merely teased and tantalized and turned out without satisfaction. Of course, rejected suitors did not admit that they had been sent away unfulfilled.

Miryam of Magdala became a legend whom men discussed over wine in the taverns of Alexandria and Rome and the villages of Gaul.

The fantasy far overreached the reality of her performance as a courtesan.

She was as mad as she was beautiful. Her unfortunate suitors learned that about her before the evening's entertainment ended. Sexual encounters invariably ended in rage or hysterics. More than one hurried from the house with bloody claw marks on his face.

This was a secret about her which somehow was never revealed when one fellow compared notes with another. Perhaps each man thought he had been the only one to disappoint her.

In Magdala she stopped trying to bargain with Hebrew merchants. They ignored her and threw any merchandise she touched into the charity basket reserved for lepers.

No one cried "unclean" as she passed, but even the touch of her shadow was countered with the sign against the evil eye.

And so she was surprised when the piping voice of a child cried out to her, "Aunt Miryam!"

She turned to look. Was the voice calling her?

"Aunt Miryam!"

It was Boaz, darting through the crowd! Running straight to her with his face full of delight and his arms wide, he flung himself against her in a joyful embrace! Cognizant of the shock around them, she did not respond at first. She stood rigid, rooted in the belief that she was indeed unclean and unworthy to be touched by a child.

"Aunt Miryam!" Boaz grinned at her. "Where have you been? Mama and I went to your house. You weren't there. The old woman said you went out looking for something. We've been searching for you for an hour!"

Miryam raised her chin defiantly as she caught Simon the Pharisee scowling at the encounter. She sank to her knees and wrapped her arms around Boaz. "I am glad to see you, Bo. You're bigger."

"Yes." He clenched his fist and made a muscle to show her. "Feel this. Uncle Marcus says I'm strong enough to fight a lion with my bare hands!"

"Fine. Well done. Very strong indeed."

"And Uncle Marcus says..."

His words were lost to her as she thought about Marcus. It had been so long since she thought of him at all. Apparently he remained close to Joanna and Kuza. He had not been excluded.

Emotion constricted her throat. It had been so long... But she could not let the jackals around her see that she cared.

That she was lonely.

Through the crowded aisle, beyond a heap of limes in a stall, came Joanna. Her fine red hair gleamed in the sunlight. Her face was the same and yet...something had changed about her. She was happy, radiant.

Joanna raised her hand in greeting as though nothing had ever happened. "Miryam! *Shalom!* Oh, Miryam! We've been looking all over for you!"

Miryam, suddenly self-conscious, withdrew her arms from Bo and stood, expecting confrontation. She said nothing.

357

Why was Joanna so excited?

Miryam could not speak to her in public.

Joanna grasped her by the elbow and propelled her from the market. "I hope you're done with your shopping."

Miryam did not tell her that she had not come to buy today.

Loneliness had driven her into the throng in search of someone she could sell herself to.

Joanna headed for a copse of trees beyond the synagogue. Bo urged the two woman on. Like a puppy, he ran ahead, darted back, circled them, and ran ahead again. He leapt onto the trunk of a fallen tree and declared that they would now sit down together in the shade and talk.

"Sit." Joanna's excitement was tinged with gentleness. Or was it sorrow?

Bitterness simmered in Miryam. "Why are you here, Joanna? Don't you know that just speaking to me is anathema?"

"Forget that."

Miryam countered, "I'd like to. But no one will let me forget it. So? Why are you here?"

"I've been thinking..."

"A dangerous thing."

Joanna laughed at the barb. "You're right."

Bo piped, "The rebbe is coming to our house tomorrow to teach! To our own house. I told Mama I want you to come hear him too."

Miryam fixed her gaze on her hands. She did not dare look up, lest the child see her disdain at such a suggestion. How dare they come here to drag her to hear the very one who had caused the rift in their relationship? "The rebbe."

"Yeshua," Bo sat down beside her. "The one who made me well."

Joanna said, "Bo thought of you first. I mean when we talked about who we should invite he said that Aunt Miryam should come. After all, you were there when Bo was healed."

"Yes. I was. And when Yeshua's neighbors in Nazareth decided he was a charlatan..."

"Miryam, come," Joanna said quietly. When she instructed Bo to go play by the water's edge until they were done talking about things women talk about, the boy obeyed reluctantly.

Resentment choked Miryam. She had been without a friend since that day in Nazareth nine months earlier. "And after that my best friend told me she never wanted to see me... And that she never wanted her child to come near me. With good reason, as it turns out. You know what I have become. Oh well, I suppose I have become more of what I was. Not worse. Only...more of it. You had good reason."

Joanna let her run down. "No. I did not. I was wrong."

Miryam shook her head from side to side. A parade of men drifted through her mind. "No. You were not wrong. And your rebbe would be the first to throw the stone at me."

"He's not like that."

"I've never seen a rabbi who isn't."

Joanna took Miryam's hand and tried to lift her chin. "If you came to hear him, you would know. Miryam...he's not like anyone else. Not anyone. He somehow sees people's hearts."

"Well, then! That lets me out! What a view he'd have if he looked into *my* heart. So much... Is it my mother's madness, do you think? I am not as brave as she was. At least she put an end to her unhappiness. I'm alive. So much gloom... Not even room for me anymore. I don't know where I went. Maybe I was never...never anything but lies and...and..."

"Come home with me, Miryam. Yeshua can help you sort it out. Find yourself again under all that."

"Nothing left," Miryam said flatly.

"Come home with me and Bo, Miryam. And if you don't like it, you can leave. But you won't find what you're searching for in the marketplace. Or in a man."

"What *am* I searching for?"

"What we're all searching for. Love. Mercy. A way to start over. To be born again, with a soul bright and clean. Perfect, like a newborn baby."

"No earthly power can give me that."

"Only come. Just as you are. Hear what he has to say," Joanna urged. "Come. See for yourself. Or you will never know if you missed your chance."

■ ■ ■ ■

Marcus stood halfway down the length of Kuza's columned courtyard, and stared at the decorative pool that doubled as a cistern in the center of the terrace. The pillars and sliding panels that formed the roof glowed from the torchlight, giving the central space pleasant illumination while allowing corners of thick shadows.

Kuza, fearful of how Herod Antipas would react if his steward openly embraced the rabbi from Nazareth, was not present. Even so, the interior of the plaza was packed to capacity with people eager to hear Yeshua. Joanna had delivered a hundred invitations.

By Marcus' estimate, fully seven times that many were present, spilling out onto the front steps and into the gardens. Joanna made it clear that all were welcome. She had no inhibitions about accepting Yeshua into her home; in fact, she was widely known to be one of his supporters, donating money and provisions to the itinerant teacher.

Yeshua spoke on an extraordinary theme: The Almighty has unusual expectation of human conduct.

"Love your enemies!" Marcus heard Yeshua say. "Do good, and lend, expecting nothing back! Your reward will be great, and you will be children of *Ha'Elyon*...the Most High: for He is kind to the ungrateful and the wicked."

This was unlike any message Marcus had ever heard. Every other religion seemed to be about gaining power over your enemies—not giving it away.

At a shrine in Rome dedicated to Jove Optimus Maximus... Jupiter the highest and the greatest of the gods...there was a sacred spring which stopped flowing. When the priests of the cult investigated they found it clogged with votive tablets tossed into the pool by the worshippers seeking the aid of the deity.

Fully half of the prayers inscribed on bits of tins were curses:

Jove, I know Drusus bribed the judge to rule against me. May his servants strangle him in his sleep.

"Show compassion," Yeshua commanded. "just as your Father shows compassion."

The differing groups gathered in Kuza's house demonstrated how futile this message was. Some were bitter rivals who no doubt prayed for their opponents to be crushed.

In one corner, smug and self-righteous, were the hyper-pious. Marcus recognized Simon the Pharisee and his cronies. Some had even come from Jerusalem to join the inquiry.

Directly across the pond from Simon was a cluster of men belonging to the temple faction. Lawyers and scholars of Jewish tradition, they bitterly hated the Pharisees.

Also present were others like himself, those completely outside Jewish religious society. Levi Mattityahu stood nearby.

Both the Pharisees and the temple faction looked askance at the Roman and the tax collector.

And, in a corner, Marcus spotted Miryam. She appeared unwell, thin and withdrawn.

Knowing what had happened to her with Vara and since, he was not surprised.

The flickers of the torches made her outline waver, as if Miryam were a candle about to gutter out. She gave the impression that the next blow, whatever it was, would extinguish the flame of her life, leaving a wisp of smoke to mark its place.

Marcus admitted to himself that, as much as he tried to deny it, he felt a sense of responsibility for her. He was aware her own treachery had led her to the pit in which she was trapped. Even so, he could not help sensing that he had been part of pushing her in.

Yeshua said, "There was a man who had two sons. The younger one said to his father, 'Father, give me my share of the estate.' So he divided his property between them. Not long after that, the younger son got together all he had, set off for a distant country and there squandered his wealth in wild living. After he had spent everything, there was a severe famine in that whole country, and he began to be in need. So he went and hired himself out to a citizen of that country, who sent him to his fields to feed pigs."

Marcus saw the cosmopolitan politicians and the puritanical Pharisees raise their eyebrows and twitch their robes. He knew one group was offended by the notion of a freeborn man taking on any menial labor and the other by the thought of having daily contact with unclean animals.

Marcus doubted that this story carried weight with the religious types, but Levi Mattityahu paid close attention.

Continuing his story, Yeshua said, "He longed to fill his stomach with the pods that the pigs were eating, but no one gave him anything. When he came to his senses he said, 'How many of my father's hired men have food to spare, and here I am starving to death! I will set out and go back to my father and say to him: Father, I have sinned against heaven and against you. I am no longer worthy to be called your son; make me like one of your hired men.' So he got up and went to his father."

Miryam had retreated even further into the shade. Her own family had rejected her utterly and, from what Marcus gathered, felt entirely relieved and justified to have done so. Whom did she have to go home to? What would her welcome be?

Yeshua resumed, "But while he was still a long way off, his father saw him and was filled with compassion for him; he ran to his son, threw his arms around him and kissed him."

And that was how the Almighty regarded lost, wicked, rebellious humans?

Marcus noted that most of the pious frowned at this story, but others nodded with approval.

Yeshua was set to take up his tale again when there was a disturbance in the center of the courtyard. Part of the sliding cover that gave a choice of sunshine or shade to the terrace was removed. A rectangular object was being lowered by ropes tied to its corners.

Extraordinary!

Marcus reached for his sword before recalling that he was not wearing it. Was this a robbery? An attack by rebels?

From above came a voice shouting, "Take the stretcher! Guide it down!"

Four men stepped forward to oblige.

What they received was a pallet on which lay a young man. As the stretcher came to rest on the flagstones, Marcus saw that he was about twenty years of age. His upper body, chest, and shoulders were sturdy and muscled.

His legs were withered and twisted. It was obvious he was paralyzed below the waist. "Rebbe!" the spokesman on the roof yelled. "We couldn't get in the door! We had to come this way!"

Was a miracle about to happen? Many of those attending the gathering were hoping for such a possibility.

A way cleared for Yeshua to pass through the throng and reach the side of the pallet. Bending over the paralytic, Yeshua extended his hand. The young man grasped it eagerly.

"Friend," Yeshua said.

An expectant hush fell over the assembly. What word would he pronounce? Would he be successful at healing someone so obviously genuinely crippled in front of so many witnesses?

"Friend," Yeshua repeated, "your sins are forgiven you."

There was a heartbeat during which the silence remained intact.

Marcus saw Miryam's head jerk backward as if she had been slapped in the face.

Then the room came alive with muttering. Though no one spoke loudly, hostile murmurs crisscrossed the floor like scurrying rats.

The countenance of Simon the Pharisee turned red. Marcus knew the man thought Yeshua had uttered blasphemy.

Though they would never admit to agreeing with the Pharisees about anything, members of the temple party wore matching scowls. It was clear they shared the opinion that since only God can forgive sin, no one, least of all a country preacher from Nazareth, should speak of it.

Yeshua betrayed no concern over the crowd's antagonism. In a voice full of authority he queried, "Why are you turning over such thoughts in your hearts? Which is easier to say? Your sins are forgiven you? Or get up and walk?"

Marcus thought about that. Forgiveness of sin was interior to a man. No one but the sinner could know how paralyzed and twisted was his soul. No one but the sinner could ever recognize that he was pardoned. But to grant release from physical captivity to someone whose entire world was a confined rectangle of helplessness...

"But look!" Yeshua commanded. "I will prove to you that the Son of Man has authority on earth to forgive sins." Gazing down into the hopeful eyes of the young man, he said, "I say to you: get up, pick up your stretcher, and go home!"

Pandemonium!

The cripple did not haul himself upright on Yeshua's arm as if dragging on a rope.

No! He leapt to his feet!

The same feet that had been contorted and turned in stood flat on the pavement. The calf muscles were smooth and healthy, the knees straight.

No trace of his deformity remained!

If the enclosure had been full of grumbling before, it now echoed with shouts of amazement.

Simon the Pharisee stood stock-still, with his mouth open.

Another Pharisee fell to his knees. With arms upraised, he recited the acclaim, "Blessed art thou, O God, King of the Universe, who has permitted us to live to see this day!"

At Marcus' side, Levi grabbed his hand and wrung it. Tears streamed down the tax collector's cheeks. "Forgiven! Forgiven!" he said in an awed whisper.

Marcus turned to see Miryam's reaction.

But the space beside the pillar was vacant. She was nowhere to be seen. Did she believe herself too depraved ever to be forgiven? Was she too afraid even to hope?

■ ■ ■ ■

Forgiven?

Like a lash the word drove Miryam from the gathering. She pushed her way through the packed congregation as they pressed forward to see and hear what the rabbi would do next.

Behind her, cheers of wonder erupted. She did not look back but fled sobbing into the darkness.

Forgiven?

Easier to put the legs of a cripple right than to make her twisted soul straight!

To forgive her sins would require a miracle of making whole what was irrevocably broken. Her soul was in a million pieces. She had shattered it herself. She had told so many lies she could no longer remember the truth. The shards of her existence shimmered like fragments of glass smashed against a stone.

All flash and color in the sun.

But without purpose, practical use, or meaning.

A danger to any who might touch her.

There was no going back. No changing who she was or what she had become.

The voices in her heart mocked her with the word: *Forgiven!*

Unlike the prodigal in Yeshua's story, her family had not left the door of welcome open to her. No one waited on a hill or searched the horizon for a sign of her return. On the contrary, they prayed she would not come back!

Like the young sinner in Yeshua's story, she was starving to death, eating the swill of the swineherd. But there was no happy ending. It was too late for her!

Too late!

She ran wildly into the blackness of the night.

The voices of the crowd echoed hollowly behind her: *Joy! Wonder! A miracle!*

But it was not Miryam's miracle! Oh, how simple it would be if her legs were paralyzed! If someone would carry her into the presence of the rabbi of Nazareth and lay her at his feet! Then he could see what was broken in her life and repair it, make her whole, tell her to get up and walk!

She felt pursued, hunted!

The presence of evil nipped at her heels, urging her to escape Yeshua and those who followed him. His light would simply illuminate the blackness of her heart. The stark glare of truth was more than she could bear!

The sounds of celebration diminished as she jogged on without looking back. When the lights of Capernaum had faded in the distance behind her, she slowed and, gasping for breath, staggered toward home along the moonlit track.

Minutes passed. She heard the hollow clip of a horse's hooves approaching. Glancing furtively over her shoulder, she made out the distinct outline of a Roman helmet. Moving quickly to the side of the road in search for a place to hide, she crouched behind a boulder and held her breath.

The horse halted.

Someone called her name.

"Miryam."

It was Marcus!

She did not reply. Her heart pounded in terror; blood rushed in her ears.

"I know you're there," Marcus probed. "I saw you at Joanna's. Why did you run away? Come back with me."

Crickets chirped in the grass behind the road. Miryam covered her face with her cloak and pressed her cheek against the rough surface of the boulder.

Marcus tried again, coaxing her to show herself as one might speak gently to a frightened animal.

"I won't hurt you," he said.

She did not believe him. After all, she had figured out what must have happened the night of her betrayal. Barak couldn't betray her, so it must have been Marcus who shared intimate details about her with Vara. What pleasure Marcus must have taken at Vara's tale of her rape! He had his revenge. And how she hated him!

"Why didn't you just kill me? Why turn your Roman hound loose on me?"

"What are you saying? Miryam? Come back with me. Come speak to the rabbi. He can help."

"Help what?" she threw back in his face.

The horse pranced nervously at the sound of her words. "Help you," Marcus replied softly.

"I don't need help," she said, resentment in her voice. "I'm not crippled."

There was thoughtful silence. Then Marcus dismounted and moved slowly toward her. "Miryam... I think...this is someone...you can tell him...anything. Everything."

"What difference would it make?" she shouted. "Go away, Marcus!"

"What have you got to lose?"

"I am...it's too late for me to try."

"Try? I'm not asking you to try. Talk to him. Listen to what he has to say." He took another step closer.

Should she run? "Stay back, Marcus! Stay...away..." She stood up. Her fists clenched, she was ready to fight. "All right then, draw your sword! Better you killed me before, as you threatened, instead of sending Vara to do your bidding! It would have been more merciful if you had killed me!"

"Miryam." He was ten or so paces from her when he stopped. "You can't think I had anything to do with Vara!"

She yelled, "Don't pretend you didn't!"

"It wasn't my doing."

"You were jealous of Barak! It was you who sent Vara to my orchard! You knew I would open the gate. Knew I would think it was Barak. You knew what Vara would do to me! You thought I would blame Barak for this! But I figured it out! It took some time, but that's the only thing that makes sense."

The centurion squared his shoulders and lifted his chin slightly in comprehension. When he did not deny her accusation again, she took it as an admission of his guilt.

He clasped the reins of his horse and sprung into the saddle. The animal snorted and danced, sensing its master's tension.

"Go on then, Miryam, believe what you

want," he said scornfully. "You're blind, you know. You created the illusion of your own truth. You've been sinking in a quicksand of lies and half-truths about yourself for so long you won't even notice when the mire closes over your head entirely."

"What is truth?"

He held his anger in check. "Good question… I don't know yet… No. Not yet." He laughed. "But here's a better question. If I *did* know, would you care? Or are you too happy wallowing in self-pity and misery to want to climb out and start over?"

She scooped up a handful of dust and flung it at him. "Go away! I hate you! Do you hear me? I hate you!"

Whirling his horse around, he galloped toward Capernaum, leaving her to find her own way to Magdala.

TAV

In some ways Marcus did not mind his demotion. Now that he was no longer *Primus Pilus* of First Cohort and his sole responsibility was supervising taxes and toll collections for Capernaum, his duties were practically nonexistent. Instead of accountability for the five hundred troopers of First Cohort, now he supervised a squadron of twenty. There were fewer reports to write, and that meant fewer headaches.

That was how Marcus rationalized the change.

Truthfully, the downgrading hurt.

No one had yet been assigned to replace him, but Marcus assumed the post would eventually go to a political crony of Vara's.

Marcus had also lost the accommodations that went with the title. His new home in Capernaum consisted of four tiny rooms. In one Carta did the cooking. In another cramped cubicle was a wooden foot locker, a bed made of rope mesh, and a stand for Marcus' armor. There was a corral out back for Pavor.

The *corona obsidionalis*, the bronzed wreath of heroism, hung atop the rack suspending his sword and dagger.

At least no one could take away that emblem.

It was all that remained of Marcus' pride in his years of service to Rome.

Reaction among the troopers was mixed. Everyone hated Vara and believed that Marcus had been handed a raw deal. On the other hand, many of the legionaries hinted that by being too friendly with the Jews...too easy on them... Marcus brought the reduction in rank on himself.

Marcus was too good a soldier and too proud to take any of them into his confidence. With no one to whom he could unfold his thinking, he drove himself to more exercise. Beyond that, he brooded a lot and drank more than he was accustomed to.

He sat on his bed doing both when Carta tapped at the door frame.

"Master," the youth said, "there are two Jews here to see you."

"What do they want?" Marcus inquired gruffly. Probably it was nothing. Marcus realized that Jews like to wrangle. There had already been three impassioned discussions about the proper shade of paint for the refurbished synagogue. Most likely this was a deputation seeking Marcus' endorsement for their side in the conflict.

"They would not say."

"Well, ask them to come in."

"I already did. They respectfully declined because it would defile them."

Marcus snorted. That was as good a perspective on this wayward province as you could find in one sentence. People came to him for assistance but refused to enter his dwelling because it would pollute them.

Setting aside his first response, which was to tell them to go to Sheol, Marcus reflected that he had nothing else to occupy his time. Why not see what they wanted?

Of the two men waiting patiently in the sun, one was nondescript, squat, and furtive-looking. He was clearly frightened at speaking with a Roman.

But the other was someone Marcus recognized. It was the sparse-bearded, Greek-featured disciple of Yochanan the Baptizer.

"What is it?" Marcus asked.

"Centurion," said the fine-boned man in a melodious voice, "I am Philip of Bethsaida. My companion's name is Avram of that same place."

Acknowledging the greeting, Marcus added, "And I have seen you before. You were at the river with Yochanan the Baptizer."

Philip admitted that the assertion was correct, while his companion looked even more nervous. The response was not surprising, since every Jew believed that Rome had spies everywhere. Marcus had just demonstrated the truth of that conviction.

Philip was undeterred. "We have heard that you are a fair man who deals justly with our people."

Marcus grimaced. Helping Kuza fulfill a vow was one thing...being tapped for other Jewish charities was something else. Best to put a stop to this nonsense right away. "You must be mistaken," he said, waving the wineskin dismissively. "Besides, I have no time...."

"Please," Philip interrupted. "Hear me out. We were talmidim of Yochanan. Now we follow Yeshua of Nazareth."

They had Marcus' attention. "Go on," he said.

"We are concerned because we have not heard from Yochanan in all the months he has been imprisoned. None of our letters have been answered, and we are concerned that he may be ill."

Remembering the dismal depth inside Machaerus in which the Baptizer was confined, Marcus agreed the surmise might be correct. Cautiously he commented, "So? Yochanan is the prisoner of Tetrarch Herod Antipas. You will have to go to him for information."

Avram appeared ready to bolt. Philip laid a hand on his arm. "We don't want to make things worse for Yochanan," he noted. "But you were there when he was arrested and thrown in jail. You could get in to see him, couldn't you?"

Without speaking for a time, Marcus admitted to himself that he probably could visit Yochanan. Since he could claim he was still under orders to track the associations formed by Yeshua of Nazareth, he even had an officially acceptable justification for the trip.

But why should he?

Maybe it was because Marcus wanted to pose a question that perhaps only the Baptizer could answer.

"Tomorrow at dawn," he said crisply. "Be ready to travel fast. We will make the round-trip journey in a week." To Carta he said, "You stay here this time. I know you want to go hear Yeshua speak. You have my permission. If a messenger comes for me, tell him I am following an investigation but will return soon."

■ ■ ■ ■

Gaining entrance to the catacombs beneath Machaerus was not difficult. Marcus merely reminded Herod Antipas' guards of his earlier warning that Rome had taken official notice of Yochanan the Baptizer. He implied that this was an official visit.

No one even bothered to ask who Philip and Avram were. The three men were admitted to the fortress and conducted by torchlight into the dungeon.

During his years of service stretching from Gaul to Persia, Marcus had witnessed much cruelty, many loathsome diseases, and hundreds of prisoners. He had executed men without flinching and slept soundly afterward.

But the changes he noted in the Jewish prophet disturbed him.

Yochanan did not move when the cell door opened. Sitting with his back to the passageway, he scratched a mark on the wall with a fingernail. "Set it down and go," he croaked in a voice hardly recognizable as human.

"Rebbe," Philip said with alarm. "It's Philip. Philip and Avram."

The eyes that turned, blinking and watering, toward the flame, had sunken so completely that little spark of life remained.

Yochanan's skin was pasty white. His hair and beard were twisted and snarled into fist-sized knots. His arms, once muscled like those of a metalworker or stonecutter, were as thin as a sapling's branches in midwinter.

Marcus rounded on the jailer. "I thought you were to see that no harm came to him!" he hissed angrily. "Why has he been starved?"

"Sir," the guard explained, "Herod Antipas ordered that he be fed...but no one can make him eat. I leave his bowl full, and when I return, it's not been touched!"

Once, in Rome, Marcus had viewed a bear

captured in the forests of Gaul. Though at first the animal was ferocious, as the duration of its captivity lengthened into months, it pined away. Given the finest cuts of meat, eventually it refused food. Even live prey thrust into its cage had no effect. It crouched in its own filth, its hair fell out in clumps, and its flesh developed running sores.

In the end it was killed for its hide. When the furrier tried to flay the beast, holes tore in its paper-thin skin. The whole stinking mess had to be discarded.

Yochanan was like that bear. He had lived outdoors, slept under the stars, roamed freely. The Baptizer not only performed ceremonies with purifying water, he lived with cleanliness as part of his daily regimen.

Now this.

Resting on his knees, rocking back and forth as if praying, the Baptizer reached out imploring arms. "Philip," he begged. "They will not give me any news. Is he the one? Was I wrong? Should we be looking for someone else?"

"We wrote you," Philip said. "We reported faithfully. Crowds are coming from all over the Galilee and even farther away."

"They don't give me letters," Yochanan returned. "No letters. No messages. No word."

Marcus stared at the guard.

"Orders," the jailer replied. He spread his hands.

Political prisoners were routinely kept isolated from communication with those outside. It was not unusual.

"Yes, but is he the one?" Yochanan repeated.

This was exactly the question Marcus had traveled a hundred miles to ask. "You are talking about Yeshua?" he inquired.

Yochanan nodded.

"But what do you mean, is he the one? The one what?"

The Baptizer stopped bobbing. Squaring his shoulders, he raised his chin. "You," he said, studying Marcus' features. "You were here before...the Roman."

"Yes...but who do you think Yeshua of Nazareth is? What does it mean?"

"Do you know the word *HaMashiach?*" Yochanan asked.

"The Jewish Messiah...a fabled future king?"

Yochanan lifted a bony finger. "Not just a king," he corrected. "The Son of the Most High. The one our prophet Isaiah spoke of: '*A highway will be there, a way, called the Way of Holiness. The unclean will not pass over it, but it will be for those whom He guides... Those ransomed by Adonai will return and come with singing to Zion.*' He will be one sent by the Almighty to reconcile mankind to Himself."

Philip broke in, excitedly, "Yeshua is doing amazing things!"

Yochanan searched the face of his follower. "But is he the one? Others have done wonders and spoken the right words, but they were not the Deliverer. I must know. Go to him! Ask him. You," he said abruptly to Marcus. "Will you send me word of what you see and hear? You will tell me the truth and not what you think I want to hear."

What would happen if the jailer reported that Marcus illegally gave the prisoner information? That he was asked by a captive...a political undesirable...to break the laws of Herod Antipas and his oath to Rome?

"I will," he said, disregarding his worries. "You are not the only one who wants the truth." Inexplicably a flash of concern came to Marcus—not for himself, but some unexplained apprehension. He sensed an urgent need to return to Galilee. To Philip he said, "You and Avram return together. I must ride on ahead."

■ ■ ■ ■

As the seasons turned toward fall again, Miryam failed like the withered grass of the hillsides. It was days since she had eaten well.

Old Tavita, her arms heaped with plates of food, scurried in to Miryam's room in the morning and out again in the evening. She clucked her tongue and fumed that the food was hardly touched. Miryam would melt away, she fretted. She would grow sick and die if she refused to eat. And then what would the old servant do? Where would she go? Who would take care of her since she was old and childless and without family?

Tavita's pleas went unheeded.

Miryam had hardly spoken since the night

she fled from Joanna's house in Capernaum. She was too hopelessly locked in her sins to find a way to escape. She accepted that she was unworthy to beg the rabbi of Nazareth to forgive her. And if she did, what would he say?

Stop sinning?

She could not change.

There were no longer tears or bouts of weeping. Her grief was too profound even for that.

A sort of calm determination settled in. Miryam gave strict orders not to be disturbed. When Joanna came to call, she was turned away at the gate.

Miryam no longer contemplated a life without love. She no longer contemplated life at all. She spent her time thinking of her mother. Finally she understood why Mama had done what she did.

Miryam remembered Mama clearly. The silence. The furrowed brow. Sometimes sad looks thrown at Miryam, El'azar, and Marta. As a young girl, Miryam had carried her mother's unexplained pain even though the other children did not seem to notice.

Miryam recollected the morning at the shore when she gathered the prettiest stones and carried them to Mama as if they were jewels. Round ones. Oblong. Flat. Smooth. Mama had held each one up and thanked Miryam. *Her voice is sad. Why?* Miryam could remember thinking. Then Mama had filled her pockets with them and waded out into the water. Nothing dramatic. She simply had not looked back when Miryam called to her. She had walked straight into the depths and let the weight of the stones carry her down.

The water was not even deep. But the stones…the stones held her down even though she might have wanted to breathe.

Minutes passed with Miryam screaming on the beach. Screaming for help.

Long, flowing tresses floated upward. Dark locks uncoiled, marking the spot where Mama drowned.

Miryam stood crying for her to come back! *Come back!* By the time the men waded out to drag her in, Mama was dead. Skin blue. Eyes open. A strange smile. She looked beyond the little girl who clung to her hand and begged her not to go away. Stones spilled out from her pockets onto the sand.

So this was death. Cold. Hard. Unresponsive. And where had Mama gone?

El'azar told Miryam at their mother's tomb that the scribes believed there was no heaven or hell. Therefore Miryam should not worry about Mama burning forever in a distant lake of sulfur and brimstone. Neither should she imagine that Mama was waiting for her beneath a tree in Abraham's bosom. There was simply the long sleep of oblivion. Nothing to fear.

Still Miryam wished. Wished it were different. That Mama would come back and hold her.

And now? Miryam was grateful she had no children to leave behind. She would not do to a child what her mother had done to her.

To be abandoned was to be betrayed. Was there any act so cruel as that betrayal?

Everyone whom Miryam had ever loved had abandoned her.

Was it Miryam's fault? Would it have been true if Mama had loved Miryam enough to go on living? If Miryam had childhood memories of sandcastles on the beach instead of stones in her mother's pockets? Miryam could not say.

Barak had reminded her that adultery was a sin punishable by stoning to death. So be it. Miryam would choose the stones that would end her life.

She strolled the thin ribbon of beach in front of her house day after day and considered which she might gather to exact her punishment. Round. Oblong. Fist-sized. Smooth.

It would be over quickly. And yet she could not find the courage to put them in her pockets and wade into the water.

What if Barak came to her door the hour after she drowned? What if she had a chance for happiness and the stones held her down? It would be a just sentence, certainly, and also the one way she could be free of yearning for something she could never have.

■■■■

By leaving Philip and Avram to return from Machaerus on their own, Marcus accomplished the journey to Galilee in two days. Dusty and sweaty, he unbridled Pavor, slapped the horse into the pen, then plunged up to his shoulders in the watering trough.

He rose, sputtering and calling, "Carta! I'm back. A towel, boy! Quickly!"

There was no answering shout.

Shaking the drops from his hair he yelled again, "Carta!"

The figure that emerged from the house was not the youth, but Kuza. "Marcus," said the steward in a halting voice. "There's been...the boy is..."

Marcus crossed the distance separating them in three strides. Grabbing Kuza by the shoulders, he demanded, "What is it? What's happened?"

Kuza shook his head. "We just found him. He's been hurt," he said. "Joanna is with him."

"Hurt? How?"

Kuza gestured toward the doorway. "Look inside."

The front room of the cottage was a shambles. The cooking pots were overturned. Wineskins had burst, spattering their contents. Crushed into one empty skin was the clear imprint of a legionary's hobnailed boot.

The door to his bedroom hung crookedly from one torn leather hinge.

Inside the chamber his chest was splintered, clothing strewn about the room. The armor rack was upended in one corner.

Hanging from a broken leg of the overturned stand was the *corona obsidionalis*. The wreath greeted him in mocking derision.

And on the floor and the walls more dark red splashes.

This time they were blood.

Joanna barred the entry to the cubicle where Carta slept.

"Marcus," she said, "his face is...you may not recognize him."

Swallowing hard, Marcus pushed past her.

On a cot, his face the same color as the lime-washed walls, lay Carta. At least Marcus identified the curly auburn hair.

The features were one large wound: eyes blackened and swollen shut, nose shattered, lips and cheeks gouged raw as if scraped across the paving stones. The boy's breathing came in ragged gasps.

One eye opened the barest slit.

"Master," Carta croaked. "I fought him. He was too strong for me. He...he hurt me, bad." There was a sob, charged with shame. "I couldn't get away, and then..."

"Did anyone see?" Marcus challenged, whirling on Kuza.

Putting up his hands as if to defend himself from the centurion's rage, the steward denied it.

Marcus stepped nearer, doubting that Kuza was telling everything he knew.

"What?" he insisted.

"It was dark...neighbors heard screams...a large man riding away..." Kuza stopped and took a shuddering breath. "Some say...a Roman...wearing black."

Vara!

Joanna, not as apprehensive of reprisal as her husband, confirmed it, then drew Marcus from the room. "The boy did not want you to know who did this. He is afraid for you."

"Will he live?"

"It was a beast who did this and not a man," she said flatly. "An animal. He did unspeakable things to the boy...."

Marcus understood.

"Will Carta live?" he repeated.

Joanna sighed heavily. "His neck is broken. He cannot move arms or legs."

Marcus took one last look, then turned and shoved Kuza out of the way, heading for the corral. The steward trailed Marcus outside, pleading, "Marcus, don't mention that I..."

The centurion was already gone, Pavor's hooves thundering away into the night.

■■■■

Galloping out of Capernaum, Marcus had one thought in mind: revenge. He would find Vara and strangle the man with his own hands.

He should have done so much, much sooner.

Carta was battered beyond recognition, horribly violated, and crippled for life, if not killed.

The image haunted him. A fury he had not experienced since the battle of Idistaviso possessed him.

Kuza said the attack happened before sunrise, perhaps not long before Marcus arrived. If only he had gotten back sooner! If only he had taken Carta with him to Machaerus!

It was the seventh hour of the morning. Vara could not be far ahead. He was probably headed to Tiberias. Marcus would seek him there first, but he was prepared to trail Vara as long and as far as necessary to exact vengeance.

Passing through the hamlet of Genneseret, Pavor scattered a plodding camel caravan. Shrieks and curses pursued him as several of the camels bolted, spilling cargo and flinging handlers.

There was no plan to Marcus' action, no reasoned outline of what would happen. Blind rage consumed him. Unconsciously he wrung a handful of the horse's mane as a substitute for Vara's throat; the Galilean countryside disappeared from his sight as the miles flew by.

At the barracks in Tiberias he burst past the sentry at the gate. The man had to dive aside to escape being trampled. Tossing the reins into the air, Marcus vaulted from Pavor's back before the horse skidded to a halt directly in front of the officers' barracks.

Guard Sergeant Quintus appeared in the doorway. Seeing the murderous look on the centurion's face, he attempted to block Marcus' entry. "Where is he?" Marcus insisted. "Vara! Where is he?"

Quintus tried reasoning. "Centurion... Marcus... I know what happened. But you can't go in...."

That was the information Marcus needed. Ducking his head, he rammed his shoulder into Quintus, driving the older man backwards into the wall. "Stay out of my way," he warned tersely.

Down the corridor.

A pair of voices echoed from behind a closed door.

Vara!

"The trap will work," Vara insisted. "As long as you, bar Halfi, don't foul it up."

"Don't worry. In Jerusalem she'll come to me where I say and when I say. Just have *him* there."

Marcus burst in.

Barak bar Halfi was between Marcus and Vara. Alarmed at the centurion's appearance, bar Halfi tried to scramble out of the path of the rampaging centurion. The two men collided, giving Vara a chance to bellow for help!

Striking bar Halfi in the face with his elbow, Marcus knocked Barak to his knees. Leaping across the intervening desk, Marcus lunged for Vara.

The Praetorian slashed at the air with his dagger and roared again for assistance, all the while backing up.

Bar Halfi bolted out a side door.

Marcus was so determined to strangle Vara that he had not drawn a weapon.

As Marcus closed with his opponent, Vara plunged the point of his knife into Marcus' forearm.

Ignoring the wound, Marcus drove his fists into Vara's jaw, beneath the man's chin. Vara's head snapped back, and Marcus' fingers closed around his windpipe.

The shaft of a pilum struck Marcus in the back of the head, stunning him. Quintus tackled him from behind. Two legionaries pinned his arms, dragged him away from Vara, and forced him to the ground.

The Praetorian straightened up, rubbing his throat. "I'll see you crucified for this," he said. "After I have every inch of skin flogged off your carcass. Take him away."

"Not so fast," demanded Tribune Felix from the hallway. "What is this?"

Rapidly recovering his composure Vara asserted, "Centurion Longinus blames me for his demotion. His resentment got the better of him, and he attacked me without provocation."

"Is this true?"

Marcus expected no assistance from Felix, whom he had once thought could be a friend, but who then had betrayed him. Bitterly he said, "Ask him what he did to my servant...if you don't already know."

"To Curta?" Felix queried. "No, I don't know. What about it, Vara?"

"The centurion was not at his post in Capernaum. His slave refused to answer my questions or take orders from me. I punished him as was proper."

"He raped the boy and broke his neck. And I will kill him for it, or die trying," Marcus retorted.

Felix regarded Vara with a fixed stare.

Shrugging, Vara said. "What of it? It's a slave. I intended to discipline him, but perhaps he was weaker than he appeared. What is the proper payment for a slave? Thirty silver denarii? Here, take it." He flung a leather pouch on the floor. "But the centurion must be flogged for assaulting me."

"Give me five minutes alone with him," Marcus snarled. "Then you can do whatever you want to me."

"Take the centurion to my office," Felix ordered.

His head spinning from the blow, Marcus tried to make sense of this. What office did Felix have in Tiberias?

The young tribune continued, "And Praetorian Vara, I think it is time for you to return to Caesarea. I will give you a two-hour head start, which should be enough for you to get behind enough guards to protect you."

"A report...," Vara began.

"For your sake, I hope not," Felix concluded. "Get out!"

Tied to a chair in what had once been his office as *Primus Pilus,* Marcus had no choice but to listen to Felix's explanation. The tribune removed his own scarf and bound Marcus' arm. "I am the new commander of First Cohort," he said. "No matter what you think, I did not betray you, nor have I sided with the Praetorians. My family has some influence in Rome. Governor Pilate decided to hedge his bets in case Sejanus ever falls out of favor with the emperor."

"What happens to me?"

"Nothing, if you go back to Capernaum

and leave this feud alone. Vara cannot hurt you in Galilee...but I cannot protect you outside it."

Marcus grimaced. "I think you have the order exactly backwards," he said. "But I will obey your command."

ALEF-BET

The mountains on the east shore of Galilee loomed large in the early-morning light. A mist hung low over the water.

Miryam raised her head and searched the horizon toward Gadara. She thought of the baby she might have had. What would he look like? Would he have the same crooked smile as Marcus? Would his hands be square and strong? Would he turn his head at the sound of her voice?

She had destroyed the one human being who might have loved her.

Whose child had been sacrificed to Molech today? she wondered.

Was there even one glimmer of hope for the likes of her?

The face of Yeshua came to mind. She squeezed her eyes shut, trying to force the image from her. But she remembered the compassion in his eyes as the paralyzed man lay before him at Joanna's house.

What had he said?

"Your sins are forgiven...."

Who gave him the right to say such a thing? No one could forgive sins but the Lord of Mercy, *Adonai!* And yet...

If only! If only!

If only Yeshua would look at her and speak such words and somehow make them true!

Miryam stared at the heap of stones beside the water's edge. She knew what she had to do.

One hope. One last chance to meet him. Her choice was simple: to speak to him and perhaps find some reason to live, or stay here alone and die!

■■■■

About fifty men and women were gathered around the door of Marcus' house as he arrived in Capernaum. Had they come to await news that Marcus Longinus had killed Praetorian Vara?

Had Carta died? Marcus wondered. Had they come to mourn the boy in silence? Or was this the deathwatch?

All eyes probed him as he dismounted. A stranger led Pavor to his stall.

What was this? Tears of compassion streamed down their faces. Without speaking, they had spoken. *"Hayedid!"* they seemed to say to him! *"Friend."*

Ranks parted for him in respect, forming a straight path to the open door of the house.

He could not make eye contact with anyone, lest they see how near to breaking he was.

He paused in the doorway, leaned a minute on the frame as he gathered his courage. He caught the nearness of death. The inevitability of losing Carta closed around his heart like a vise as he entered. It was as though he had come to the boy's tomb. The floor was swept, debris cleared away, furniture righted.

Joanna appeared at the portal to the compartment where Carta lay. She beckoned for Marcus to come quickly.

He stumbled forward, as though caught in a terrible dream. Joanna and another older, plump woman were there with Carta. Joanna sat at his feet, the other at his head. Joanna's companion had eyes that brimmed with sorrow as she viewed the child—as though Carta were her own son.

Carta would have liked the way she gently stroked his hair. Yes. Had he been aware of her tenderness he would have been pleased.

The boy still lived. His fragile body lay covered by a sheet. Arms were exposed at his sides. His breath came in grating wheezes, like tearing strips off frayed cloth.

Carta was so nearly somewhere else, so barely still present. All that remained, it seemed, was to wind him in grave clothes and cover his face forever.

Marcus dropped to his knees and carefully took Carta's hand. He kissed the limp fingertips and placed the open palm against his cheek. Emotion choked Marcus. His chest seared from holding back the flood that threatened to overwhelm him.

Marcus could not bear to look at Carta's battered face. He kept his gaze riveted on Carta's hands. Familiar. Unchanged by the ordeal. There was the scar on his palm from the day Carta cut himself while peeling an apple. Marcus had stitched the wound himself and called Carta a brave lad because he had not flinched. It had been so easy. Carta had believed Marcus could fix anything, make everything right. He was so young, on the verge of manhood. He had recently adopted Marcus' manner of walking, of talking. Often when he cleaned Marcus' armor, he tested the sword when he thought Marcus could not see him.

All the while Marcus had been secretly pleased with Carta's adoration and trust that Marcus could accomplish anything.

But there was no mending this. No changing it. No calling it back. Even the authority of a centurion could not hold back a child from the grave. Neither the might of his sword nor the power of the bronze gods of Rome could intervene to save him.

There was just one who could intervene, but Marcus could not ask him.

Marcus was not a Jew. Yeshua had come to heal his own people, not the Roman overlords who defiled every precept of the Hebrew religion by their very presence.

"Kuza has gone," Joanna broke the silence. "This is Mary of Nazareth. She came to watch and pray with me."

Marcus knew the risk for a Jewish woman to enter the home of a Gentile and a Roman. Here was courage. He croaked. "I thank you for it."

Mary replied quietly as she brushed Carta's hair with her fingers, "I also have a son."

"Yes." Marcus bobbed his head in acknowledgment. "Carta is...yes. He is my only son."

Joanna explained. "Mary is the mother of Yeshua, Marcus. Staying at the fisherman's house. She came when she heard what was done to the boy."

Marcus covered his face with his hands as the flood finally washed over him. "Oh, dear lady...," he began haltingly. "Your son, Yeshua, is the one hope I have. So I have no hope at all. I'm not a Jew. I'm...the enemy of your God and your people. How could Yeshua help the likes of me?"

Mary stood and placed a hand on Marcus' heaving shoulder. "Courage," she urged. "You must at least ask, or you'll never know."

"Marcus, you must send for him," Joanna encouraged.

Marcus wiped his tears away. He raised his head and groaned in agony as he studied Carta's broken features. "My son! My boy! Carta, oh, Carta! If only I were worthy to ask!"

"You can't change what you have been. Just what you will be. Now get up," Mary commanded. "The child will die if you don't go boldly."

Marcus rose stiffly and took off his sword.

Mary went with him to the door. She stood at his right hand in silent support of his petition.

The crowd of onlookers had grown. On either side of the path stood Philip and Avram, whom Marcus had taken to visit Yochanan in Machaerus. Near them were three elders of Capernaum's synagogue.

"We just arrived. We heard about your boy," said Avram.

An elder added, "How can we help?"

Marcus cleared his throat. "Please, friend... I have one hope...that you will present my case to the Lord Yeshua. Tell him Carta lays paralyzed. He is fourteen. Still a child. Tell him my boy will die if he doesn't heal him. Tell him please...for me that I..." Words failed him. He tucked his chin and swallowed hard.

Philip and Avram exchanged looks. With a nod, they were followed by the elders of Capernaum as they made their way from the town to seek Yeshua.

■ ■ ■ ■

The marketplace of Magdala was nearly deserted. The fishermen's stalls were empty, the shoreline littered with nets.

Miryam asked a grizzled Nabatean wool merchant, "Where's everyone gone?"

"They've run off. This miracle worker is bad for the wool business, I can tell you. Now if I was a baker or a seller of produce? Then I would take my trays of food and have a captive market."

"But where are they?"

"Some are carrying their sick kinfolk to him. Others have gone to see wonders and hear the Nazarene rebbe teach. They'll be straggling back soon, and I'll be here when they arrive."

"Where does he teach today?"

The Nabatean shrugged as if he did not care, then pointed north. "Along the highway. Toward Capernaum. A mile or so. But he'll be nearly finished by now."

■■■■

Miryam walked north for two hours along the highway. At last she came to the fringe of a crowd spread across a broad, open farm field like a blanket. The stubble of a grain crop had been plowed under. The ground was soft and cool. Children played happily on the opposite side of the road. Miryam guessed there were at least ten thousand people there. Differing manners of dress identified them as coming from Jerusalem, Judea, the coastlands, as well as from Galilee.

A contingent of twenty Roman soldiers stood near the back of the gathering as Miryam approached. They were there to intimidate, in case the rebbe urged the people to rebel against Rome. And yet they too were listening.

Yeshua spoke from a boulder on the edge of the field. Miryam, far from the rebbe, sank to the moist earth to watch and listen.

How could she get near enough to speak to him?

Shim'on, Ya'acov, and John, the three fishermen who had sailed her home from Gadara, stood near Yeshua.

This was troublesome for Miryam. How could she approach Yeshua when they were there? They certainly knew who she was and what she had been up to.

"Go back home," an inner voice urged her. *"This is hopeless...."*

"A fool's errand! You'll never reach him!"

"And why should he forgive you anyway?"

"Who does he think he is? To forgive? Impossible!"

"What are you looking for? Miryam? Whore of Magdala? What do you think you can find here?"

She opened her mouth and managed to stammer aloud, "Something...some...hope...something to...believe again..."

Heads swiveled to peer curiously at her. She fell silent under their disapproval. The accusations in her head shrieked louder, and she fought to hear Yeshua above them. His words pierced her heart like a shaft of light penetrating the darkness.

Then she spotted Levi Mattityahu, the most notorious tax collector in Galilee. A good friend of Marcus! She had been to supper at his house! Levi sat in rapt attention at the rebbe's feet! Lucky day! If only she could manage to get to Levi, he would introduce her, help her.

Yeshua's voice was clear, resounding like

a trumpet against the backdrop of hills. It echoed in sharp argument with the inner voice that commanded Miryam to run from this place.

She dug her fingers into the ground, rooting herself in the furrow.

Yeshua seemed to be speaking to her.

"How can I live again?" she whispered through gritted teeth.

"...*But I tell you who hear me, Love your enemies. Do good to those who hate you. Bless those who curse you. Pray for those who mistreat you. If someone strikes you on one cheek, offer him the other as well. If someone takes your cloak, don't stop him from taking your tunic. Give to everyone who asks you and if anyone takes what belongs to you, don't demand it back. Do to others as you would have them do to you.*"

The inner argument began afresh. How could these words apply to her? Didn't she deserve the scorn of her family and neighbors?

Do something kind to someone who hates me? Give? Bless? Pray? Miryam knew that anything she offered would be spit upon.

The words of Yeshua were lost to her then. She strained to hear them, but they spun around and whirled away like dry leaves caught in the wind.

She was seized by a scorching headache. Covering her ears, she attempted to drown out the clamor in her brain.

It was no use. Scraps of phrases rang like a spoon against a brass pot.

Don't judge and you will not...
Don't condemn and you will not...
Forgive and you will be...

How much more? How long could she hold on? The sun was fierce. Too bright. She was nearly blinded as it dipped behind Yeshua. She could no longer see him in the glare.

The good person brings good things out of what is stored in his heart. The evil person brings evil things out of what is stored in his heart. For out of the overflow of the heart he speaks...

There was nothing good that Miryam could find in her heart. How could she practice what he taught? It was hopeless! She managed to whisper, "Help me, Lord!"

Then she heard his melancholy voice reply clearly, *"Why do you call me Lord, but you don't do what I say? The person who comes to me and hears my words and puts them into practice? He's like a man building a house who dug down deep and laid the foundation on rock. Then a terrible flood came. The torrent struck and the waters rose but the house wasn't even shaken because it was soundly built. But the person who hears my words and doesn't put them into practice is like the man who built on sand. The minute the torrent struck the house it collapsed and was completely destroyed."*

Destroyed. Yes. That was her life. The floods had come, and she was without foundation or strength to resist. She was drowning.

Drowning on dry land. Gasping for breath even before she put stones in her pockets and waded into the water.

So. It was over. Yeshua had finished teaching, and Miryam had barely heard any of what he said. She buried her face in her hands and remained on the ground while people stood up around her. Groups began to drift away home to their routine lives and mundane problems.

Long minutes passed before she looked up.

About a thousand lingered. A handful of supplicants gathered closely around Yeshua.

Perhaps if she waited? Went forward to stand quietly near him until everyone else was finished? She could talk to him. Tell him...everything! Ask him what she could do; how she could live again!

Her heart raced as she picked her way through the milling crowd and across the furrows toward the rebbe. She could hear him talking to his close followers. The three fishermen stood with their backs to Miryam. They were like a wall separating her from Yeshua.

If only! One word from him! One!

Forgiven!

She could see the top of his head. Dark hair in wisps against his forehead. Yeshua was nodding, listening attentively to two men as they queried him: "Yochanan the Baptizer sent us to ask: Are you the one who was to come? Or should we expect someone else?"

Miryam moved closer. There he was! She

could almost touch him! Yeshua smiled and fixed his gaze on them. "Go back to him and report what you've seen and heard. As the prophet Isaiah has written, *'The blind receive sight. The lame walk. Those who have leprosy are cured. The deaf hear. The dead are raised. And the good news is preached to the poor.'*"

"Sir," began Yochanan's talmidim, "The man who took us into Machaerus to speak with Yochanan needs your help. He is a Roman, a centurion. But he has been kind to the people of Israel. With his own money he restored the synagogue in Capernaum. His servant, a boy, is near death, and the centurion asked us to beg you…"

Yeshua raised a hand. "Come on. We'll go to his house together."

Miryam hung back several paces, waiting as the entourage headed toward Capernaum. Then, head bowed, eyes to the ground, she followed after.

A moment later a hand grasped her arm and a gruff voice whispered, "So it's you." She stared into the scowling face of Shim'on. "What are you doing here? What do you want?" he snapped.

Miryam swallowed hard. How could she explain what she wanted? She was uncertain herself. "Just…to speak to him."

"Get out of here! Go home," Shim'on menaced. "The Rebbe doesn't need your kind following after him."

Miryam stopped in her tracks. Of course the fisherman was right. How could the righteous teacher talk with a woman like her and not be ruined?

Shim'on continued to glare over his shoulder at her as they went. His disdain held her back from following.

■■■■

Hours passed.

Joanna and Mary put Marcus' home in order. The scattered ashes from the fireplace were swept, the wine and bloodstains scoured. This was the way neighbors came and cleaned a house when someone died, when all was in readiness for the funeral visits.

Joanna washed and bandaged Marcus' arm.

Through it all, Marcus sat mute, numb. He kept watch beside Carta, willing the boy to breathe, breathe again. Listening anxiously for each thread of air, holding his own breath as he waited for the slight sound that proved Carta still lived.

What if the elders of Capernaum could not find Yeshua? The teacher often withdrew into the mountains for much-needed rest. What if he had crossed the lake or left Galilee altogether?

What if he was easily found but would not come?

For a holy man to enter the house of a non-Jew would defile him; touching a dead body would defile him.

Marcus shuddered at the image of Carta dead.

What if the thing Marcus asked was impossible?

403

The centurion challenged his despair with the things he had witnessed: Yeshua healing the child by the river. The teacher said it was faith that was important.

Faith?

Where could you find it? In the midst of unimaginable horror and your own inability to change things? Where could faith be found?

Marcus had faith in his preparation as a soldier, in his skill as a swordsman, in the obedience to discipline of the men he trained.

They were learned experiences to be drawn on in times of need.

He stared at the bronze crown of heroism without really seeing it.

What else had he experienced that he could call to mind?

Two visions radiated hope: the paralyzed man let down through the roof, and Kuza's son, Boaz.

Faith again, that would not surrender to overwhelming despair.

The confidence of the cripple's friends moved them to extraordinary lengths. Against reason and good sense they had placed their companion squarely in front of Yeshua, where he had to be regarded.

Assertive faith. Commanding faith. *Do this,* their actions shouted to Yeshua. *We know you are able.*

And Kuza, going miles away from home... miles away from his only son, Kuza left his boy's side when he might have clung to every last moment, every last breath as precious. He might have returned to a lifeless form, but he took a risk.

Assertive faith that called for action in the midst of doubt.

Outside, a distance away toward the center of Capernaum, a voice shouted, "The rebbe is coming!"

Marcus bolted upright.

A sense of *Yes* overwhelmed him. It swelled inside him the way the warmth of a furnace spills into a room, driving back the cold...driving back hopelessness.

Sprinting from the house he peered up the road a distance of one hundred yards.

A crowd was approaching. Not fifty or a hundred but a thousand. A moving mass many times wider than the highway flowed toward him. Marcus recognized the faces of the tax collector, Levi Mattityahu, Philip, Avram, and the elders of the synagogue among the throng.

And at the head of the procession, covering the distance with purposeful strides, was Yeshua.

Those who gathered at Marcus' house clapped him on the back.

Marcus, barefoot, ran to meet Yeshua.

Ten paces from the rebbe, he slowed, then stopped and saluted, bowing his head in respect as he would have done to a renowned general at the head of a legion.

"Sir?" he groped for words. What to say? How to ask?

The warm brown eyes of Yeshua caught him, held him fast, urging him to state his request without fear. The mouth was curved in a slight smile, as if he shared some secret with Marcus.

Marcus clapped his fist over his heart in the supplication of a soldier. "Sir, it's my...servant. He's lying at home paralyzed...just a lad...he has...suffered...terribly."

Yeshua came closer to Marcus. Marcus could not meet the intensity of such a searching look. He lowered his gaze to the ground. The hem of Yeshua's robe was dusty and frayed. His sandals were worn out. And yet in Him was the power and might that sword and kingdom lacked.

In a low voice Yeshua said to Marcus, "I know. Yes. I understand. I will come with you and heal him."

What? This Holy One of Israel enter the house of a Roman? The cruelty and brutality of Marcus' life flashed before him.

Marcus dropped to his knees. In the same position and with the same humility as he had accepted the crown of bravery he said, "Lord, I am not worthy to receive you. Rather, I know if you will only say the word my servant will be healed." He waited, but there was no response. The explanation then tumbled from him. "I'm also a man who understands authority. I have soldiers under me and I say to this one, 'Go!' and he goes. I say to another, 'Come!' and he comes. Or 'Do this!' And he does it."

Silence from the master. Marcus dared to raise his sight to meet Yeshua's. The teacher spoke without words as he searched the depths of Marcus' heart. It was as though he saw and understood everything. As if he had known how Marcus had grappled with his own soul and somehow he had won.

Yeshua's smile of approval shouted, *Well done. You have wrestled with the question and found the answer.*

Yeshua nodded, indicating that Marcus should get up from the dust. The rebbe said with a hint of astonishment, "Even in Israel I didn't find faith like this."

Then, turning to those who followed him, he said, "Many will come from the ends of the earth to join in the celebration in the kingdom of Heaven with Avraham, Yitz'chak and Ya'acov. You'll be surprised at who is there... and who isn't! Those who think their own righteousness is enough will not be invited!"

Did Marcus hear the rumble of distant thunder? Or was it simply the voice of Yeshua? He shook his head, trying to clear his mind.

Yeshua clasped Marcus' hand firmly "Go home. Let it be exactly the way you trusted it would be."

Marcus turned reluctantly from the sad, knowing eyes. Squaring his shoulders, he looked down the road to where a second crowd of mourners flanked the open doorway of his house. How like a tomb that dark portal had seemed a few hours before. And now...

Something had transpired. Marcus knew it. When doubt shouted from the back of his mind, he pushed it away.

Never taking his stare from the door he began to walk slowly back.

Was that movement within?

Let it be so! Marcus did not let any other thought intrude.

Yeshua issued the command. It would be so! Believe it! Walk on!

And then, in a moment of wonder unlike any Marcus had ever experienced, the boy's slim figure appeared at the door! He stood... yes!...*Carta* stood framed there for all to see. Like one who was dead, he emerged, impossibly, from his tomb! The boy smiled and waved broadly at Marcus. Not a mark was on his face. Not one bruise disfigured his pale skin.

"Master!" Carta cried in a cracking, adolescent voice as he rushed to meet Marcus. "Why is everyone here? What's happened? Are you all right?"

Marcus, weeping openly for joy, embraced him and kissed his head. "Carta! My boy! I am...yes, I'm all right. Now I am."

GEEMEL-DALET

The tang of autumn was in the air. Succoth, the Feast of Tabernacles, was near. Celebrating the fall harvests of grapes, olives, and late-ripening wheat, Succoth was known as the most joyful time of the Jewish sacred year.

And yet it was not so for Miryam, who had sunk more deeply into depression. Old Tavita worried about her continually.

Then, one day, Miryam's reprieve came in the bag of a Roman post rider from Jerusalem. He banged his fist against the gate until Tavita threw it open.

Miryam heard the old woman exclaim, "Praise be!" Then she came quickly up the stairs to present Miryam with a rolled parchment dispatch.

The address was in Barak's handwriting. Tavita knew it as well as Miryam. The servant hovered over her, waiting for her to break the seal and open it. "Well?" Perhaps the old woman believed that Miryam could not survive one more disappointment. "Is it good news?"

"Get out." Miryam's command was barely audible. "This is none of your business."

The light in Tavita's eyes dimmed. She bowed and backed away, closing the door behind her.

Miryam slit the seal with a trembling hand. She unrolled the papyrus and scanned it quickly, and cried out in joy.

My dearest love... I am in Jerusalem alone. Feast of Tabernacles. I crave your company. I am in hell without you these past weeks. Have been helpless to contact you. Trust me. I will explain everything. Have rented a room for us above the shop of the cobbler two doors on the right just inside Damascus Gate. He has been told to expect you. Wait for me there. Come at once.

Barak

Carta sipped sweetened lime juice on the balcony of Joanna's house. Marcus had brought him there for the sake of his safety. The boy would remain hidden from Vara.

"I don't remember anything unpleasant," Carta explained to Marcus and Miryam.

This was a mercy, Marcus thought. He never wanted the boy to recall what Vara had done to him.

Joanna commented, "You slept for a very long time."

Carta finished his drink. "I dreamed a lot, too." He laughed as the memory of it flooded back. "It was about you, sir," he addressed Marcus. "All about you."

"And what was he doing?" Joanna leaned forward with interest.

"Wrestling. I was lying on a riverbank watching you wrestle. I couldn't move. I tried, but I couldn't. Strange now that I think of it. You were wrestling with Yeshua of Nazareth. All night the two of you struggled beside the river."

"Yeshua is no wrestler." Marcus settled back, amused at the image.

"All the same, he was beating you. But you held on. Held on until the sky started to get light. And you said to him... 'I won't let you go until you bless me...' And then he blessed you. He said, 'I have not seen such faith in Israel.'"

Marcus blanched. Those were the exact

words Yeshua had spoken to him in the street when he healed Carta.

Joanna remarked quietly. "We Jews have a story about the Angel of the Lord who wrestled beside the river all night with our patriarch, Ya'acov. And after that night Ya'acov was renamed Israel."

"No, no. It was not an angel. It was Yeshua," Carta explained brightly. "An interesting dream. I enjoyed watching it. On and on. A hard-fought match. He made you lame, I think. Dislocated your hip. You walked away limping but quite pleased with the blessing. You yelled at me to wake up and see to Pavor's stall."

Joanna blinked in surprise at the ending. "Have you heard our story before? About Ya'acov and the angel, I mean?"

Carta shrugged. "No. But it was Yeshua, not an angel."

"Since you'll be a part of our family for a while, I'll tell you all the stories," Joanna said soothingly. "Bo will enjoy having an older cousin on hand."

Bo wandered out from his nap. He greeted Carta with a whoop and dragged him off to skip stones in the water.

Joanna poured wine for Marcus.

"He dreams our Torah," Joanna remarked in wonder. But her comment was lost on Marcus.

"It isn't safe for him to be with me anymore," Marcus explained.

"Does Vara know...that Carta didn't die?"

"I don't think so. Not yet anyway. But I can't take a chance on Vara even *seeing* Carta."

"He'll be safe here. Praetorians are not exactly welcome in the circles of Herod Antipas. And Kuza won't say anything about it. Certainly he's afraid to mention anything about Yeshua in court. As for Vara, he wouldn't dare try anything with us."

Marcus poured water into his cup, thinning the wine. "The healing of Carta will get back to him. Things like this always do. There's not much Vara doesn't know."

"He's a demon, that one."

Marcus frowned in agreement, then nodded thoughtfully. "There's another thing I wanted to talk with you about. Concerning Yeshua. I've made up my mind to tell him something." How could he put his uneasiness into words? "I'm not even certain I know what this is about, but... Barak bar Halfi is in the pay of Vara. He was with Vara when I arrived in Tiberias. He reports what he hears or sees in Nazareth concerning Yeshua's family. You see what I'm getting at?"

She shook her head and pressed her lips together. "Sorry."

"Well, listen. The chief priest, encouraged by Vara, is suspicious of Yeshua. It might be wise for Yeshua to stay away from Jerusalem awhile."

"Impossible."

"Tell him there are rumors...danger to him."

"No, Marcus. I can't tell him anything.

He's already gone to Jerusalem, to the Feast of Tabernacles."

Another thought struck Marcus. "I must go see Miryam. If she'll talk to me, that is. When she hears what Yeshua did for Carta, maybe I can convince her to go and see the rebbe herself."

■ ■ ■ ■

Marcus' thoughts were a tangle of conflicting emotions as he reined Pavor to a halt outside Miryam's house.

From anguish at the sight of Carta, Marcus had progressed...charged headlong, really... through hatred and reprisal, gnawing despair, and on to amazement and gratitude.

How he longed to share the result of his journey with Miryam!

He would force her, drag her if necessary, to see Yeshua.

He would tell her there was nothing Yeshua could not mend. No life was so broken, no future so bleak, that the rebbe from Nazareth could not soothe the hurts and heal the wounds.

Even as he pounded on the gate, some instinct warned him that Miryam was not present. There was a palpable air of desertion and a recent departure at that.

"Open the gate!" he shouted loudly enough to be heard at the lakeshore. "Miryam of Magdala! Open the gate."

The portal did in fact creak open, but the

hunched form that greeted his eyes was not Miryam. It was the aged servant, Tavita.

"What do you want?" she scolded. "Like a bull calf with your bawling."

Marcus peered around her into the garden. "I need to see Miryam," he urged. "Where is she?"

"She won't see you," Tavita returned coldly. "Go away."

"It's important! I have to speak with her."

"Listen, Roman," Tavita said, emphasizing her words with a gnarled forefinger. "You sneak in here by night and cause an uproar. Why should she want to see you if you come clamoring in daylight?"

"Let me talk to her," Marcus repeated. "I am bringing good news!"

Tavita softened a bit. "Good news? None of that here in a long time." Directing her pointed chin toward a stream of autumn leaves blowing from a sycamore fig, she considered a moment, then reached a conclusion.

"You can't see her..."

Marcus raised both hands to beg to renew the argument, but Tavita interrupted him.

"You can't see her because she's not here." Tavita indicated the spinning leaves that gusts of wind carried away toward the south.

"She's gone to Jerusalem. To the Feast of Tabernacles. Never wanted to make a pilgrimage before, so she's up to something. But gone, just the same."

Suddenly out of Marcus' thicket of confused

notions a clear path appeared, and it led toward the edge of a cliff!

"Did anyone ask her to go to the feast?" Marcus queried.

Looking sly, Tavita admitted, "She got a letter. And right after..." The crone slapped her palms together with a smack. "Just like that she's off to Jerusalem."

Barak bar Halfi!

Now it all made horrible sense.

Marcus had overheard Vara and bar Halfi plotting against Yeshua!

In his rage and desire for vengeance, Marcus somehow had thought the words applied to himself.

But it was Miryam and Yeshua of Nazareth they were planning to trap! *She'll come to me when and where I say,* Barak bragged to Vara. *Just have* him *there.*

"Old woman," Marcus said insistently to Tavita. "Your mistress is in danger. You must do two things for me without fail. Send a note to Kuza's house in Capernaum. Tell them I've gone to Jerusalem."

"And the other?"

Marcus' earnest reply came as he vaulted onto Pavor's back. "If we're wrong...if Miryam comes back here...don't let her leave until I've spoken to her."

■ ■ ■ ■

Miryam joined a band of pilgrims, two families and servants, making *Aliyah* to Jerusalem. The mood among them was cheerful as they traveled.

When at last they came to the overlook where Jerusalem glistened in the sun, exclamations of wonder gushed from them.

Zion was unveiled at their feet.

From a hill on the Emmaus road just outside the capital all of the Holy City was revealed to the travelers.

A psalm of praise, in which Miryam did not join, burst from their throats:

> *Praise the Lord!*
> *The Lord is exalted over all the nations!*
> *His glory is above the heavens!*

Even though Miryam felt cut off from her people and her God, her emotions stirred at the sight. Jerusalem reveled in the play of light and shadow. It did indeed look like the favored city of a chosen people selected by a powerful God.

Three hills met her view. Olivet hung over the city to the east. A second knoll was occupied by the lower city on the west. And central to everything else, the Temple Mount, crowned with the gleaming sanctuary of the Most High.

Walls thirty feet high surrounded three sides of the capital. On the east, where the city was bounded by a steep cliff and plunging valley, there was no need for a barrier.

The outermost partition was itself topped by towers. These were square and solid, rising another thirty feet into the sky. Ninety such bulwarks guarded the four-mile circumference of the city. Herod the Great had added other ramparts. Three had been named for Herod's brother, favorite wife, and best friend. Made of seamless stone blocks thirty feet in length at the base, they likewise spoke of permanence.

Herod's palace, sheltered behind the trio of towers, was magnificent beyond description. It contained guest rooms for a hundred visitors, and every expense had been lavished on its construction. Green lawns were bordered by legions of trees and countless artificial lakes. Rooftop cisterns also stored water. Nor was the precious liquid merely for household use. It was allowed to bubble in countless fountains and meander in garden streams.

But it was the temple that was the chief glory of Jerusalem.

A double colonnade formed of white marble pillars nearly forty feet high was only the beginning of the wonders. Nine gates were covered with silver and gold and another with Corinthian bronze. The doors, giant squares forty-five feet on a side, gleamed with precious metals.

Topping all the rest was the sanctuary itself. The face of its gate, covered with gold, measured over one hundred feet high.

Every part dazzled the eye, because whatever was not overlaid with gold and silver was made of the brightest white marble. The whole of Mount Zion resembled a snow-covered mountain topped by a gleaming treasure trove.

Surrounding the incomparable city, the hills were festooned with Succoth booths, shelters made for families to live outdoors through the week-long celebration. A haze of smoke from tens of thousands of campfires softened the autumn sunlight.

Miryam's companions worried that they would not find a good spot to camp since so many pilgrims had arrived before them. She was grateful Barak had rented a room. It was possible that they would be among a handful of visitors who actually slept in beds during the holiday.

Miryam parted from the company and entered the upper city through Damascus Gate. The street leading to the Temple Mount was packed with holiday-makers returning to their campsites from the first morning's ceremony.

She glanced up at the signs that hung above the small stores on the main street. There, as Barak had promised, was the shoemaker's stall, just across from the gate.

Would Barak be waiting for her in the room? she wondered. Strange how dead she was inside. Why was she not excited to see him?

She entered the shop. The merchant was busy with a family, selecting sandals for a trio of boys. She pretended to browse, examining footwear and replacing it on the shelf again.

Why had she bothered to come? she wondered. A few days with Barak would not solve her problem. Her unhappiness seemed an unbroken cycle. The festival would end and he would go home to Eve, leaving Miryam alone to ache for his company. Yet if she decided never to see him again, loneliness would drive her to her grave.

There was no starting over. No way to stop what was about to happen. Beginning anew was not an option for her. The fisherman who followed Yeshua had made it clear she could not approach the rebbe. He had no answers for the likes of her.

The family paid for their purchases and hustled out into the packed street.

"You need new sandals?" The shoemaker grinned at her feet.

"My brother rented a room from you?"

"Ah, yes! You're the one! Upstairs. Just up those steps. Second floor. Your brother says I should tell you he'll be back after dark. You should wait for him, he says. He says he'll bring you something to eat. Rest. You'll need to rest for the lamplighting celebration and the dancing tonight. Yes?" He stared blankly at the ceiling. "I think that's everything."

It was enough. Miryam knew she would not be going to any lamp-lighting ceremony tonight. And the only dancing she and Barak would do was in the privacy of their room.

She thanked the man and wearily climbed the steep steps.

Their lodgings were cramped but comfortable. A low table and lamp set beside the bed. There was wine, which she drank. Barak's things were piled in the corner. A tiny window revealed a view out the rear, toward the western wall of the temple. Another window opened over the street.

Miryam threw open the shutters and leaned against the sill to watch the human tide ebb and flow beneath her

There, through the gate, came the big fisherman Shim'on, Levi Mattityahu, and ten other talmidim of Yeshua following their teacher up the lane.

Without hope, she watched Yeshua pass up the street and vanish into the mob. He could heal cripples, blind men, and lepers. But he could not fix what was wrong with her soul. Hadn't Shim'on warned her to stay far from him?

And so she would.

■ ■ ■ ■

From the window of the room above the sandalmaker's shop, Miryam waited for Barak's arrival.

She decided this position afforded her the best view in the city. Rich and poor alike pushed through Damascus Gate.

The sun slipped lower in the sky, becoming a liquid, burning ball behind the haze of pilgrim fires.

A company of Roman soldiers marched ahead of the procession of Pontius Pilate, his wife, and a handful of political appointees. Miryam shuddered as she spotted the Praetorian Vara riding alongside Pilate's litter.

She covered her face with her veil and withdrew from her perch to wait until she was certain he had passed.

An hour later, announced by a fanfare trumpets and surrounded by two hundred courtiers and slaves, the litter of Herod Antipas and his mistress arrived in Jerusalem. Miryam noticed Kuza, looking dusty, disgusted, and harried as he walked amid the tetrarch's tribe of fawning sycophants.

Joanna was not with her husband. Miryam guessed she had remained behind in Galilee with Bo.

At dusk the lamps were lit and hung in shop windows up and down the street. The distant strains of music drifted pleasantly from the Temple Mount. Crowds on the lower end of Damascus Street thinned a bit as the temple festivities began. Markets were packed with strolling families purchasing supplies for the week-long stay.

Miryam resisted the urge to go out among them. What if someone recognized her? The thought of being confronted by either Vara or her brother, El'Azar, was decidedly unpleasant to her. Her lamp remained unlit. The glare from torches and bonfires illuminated the room well enough.

Hours passed, and still Barak did not come. She was hungry. The smell of braised lamb and fresh bread tantalized her senses. But here and there she noticed Roman soldiers walking two by two in the souk. What if she went out and Vara found her? What if Barak saw her with him?

Her mind played out a dozen different scenarios. None of them were pleasant. She stayed put despite her hunger. Her hands trembled at the memory of Vara in the orchard that night. How had Vara known she would be there? What had he done to make Barak tell him?

There was so much unexplained. But at last she would have the answers.

She checked the bolt. This time she would not open the door until she was certain it was Barak.

Everything would be all right once he came, she told herself. They would share a meal, talk, make love all night, and perhaps not even bother getting up in the morning.

Near midnight the celebration was only getting started. The shops remained open. She could hear the voices of shoppers through the plank floor. A cool breeze sprang up, carrying the aromas of wood smoke and cooking food.

Miryam closed the shutters and bathed in the dark. She perfumed the bed, put on a sheer cotton nightdress, then lay down.

Where was he? Didn't he want her as much as she wanted him? Why was he so late? Had he changed his mind? Had his wife come with him to the festival?

Loud conversation echoed in the street.

Young men whooped and laughed at a joke they played on one of their comrades. Miryam dozed in spite of the clamor.

Then it was quiet. The bolt on the door rattled, waking Miryam with a start.

A drunken voice crooned, "Miryam! Come on, come on! Open up."

She groped her way through the darkness to the door.

"Who is it?"

"Barak! Who else would it be?"

When she did not answer, a fist slammed against the door. "Open!" the voice demanded.

"Barak?" Was it really him? "Are you alone?"

"Alone? What do you think? Miryam, will you make me wait all night?"

Yes. It was Barak. Impatient. Eager to hold her. She threw back the bolt and swung open the door.

Barak lurched into the room, nearly knocking her down as he clung to her.

His breath was sour with wine. He was drunk. He leaned heavily against her, pushing her roughly toward the bed and pawing her clothes.

Once again the image of Vara rose up in her mind. She cried, "Barak?" She touched his face. The beard. No Roman wore a beard. It was Barak. But there were no loving caresses. No quiet words of affection. Nothing but a sort of gruff urgency as he pushed her down.

She felt sick as he touched her.

He snapped, "What's wrong with you? Stiff as a board."

She tried to talk to him, say the things she wanted to say. That she had missed him. That her life was hollow without him. That she wanted no one but him and it had always been so...

But he was in no mood to listen. Only to have her. To take her. To finish what he had been thinking about all night and then to sleep.

■ ■ ■ ■

Miryam heard Barak's bare feet padding on the floor. It was early. First light was beginning to color the sky.

"What are you doing?" she asked sleepily.

He splashed water on his face. "Got to go. Early duty in the temple today."

"Barak... I thought we could..."

He scowled defensively. "Could what?"

"Be together." She sat up on her elbow and pulled the covers back, inviting him.

He studied her body with a detached stare, the way a man who had just finished a feast might turn down a fourth helping of lamb.

"Tonight." He dried his face with a towel and slipped on his tunic.

"What's wrong with now?"

"Look," he snapped. "I told you I have things to do. Important things."

"More important than me?"

Without hesitation he replied, "You'd be surprised."

She covered herself again and reclined on the pillow. "When will I see you?"

"Tonight. Be patient. And stay here. Do as I tell you."

"I'm hungry. The shopkeeper said you were bringing food."

He cursed. "I'll have something sent to you. Don't go out. You're safe."

"What do you mean safe?"

"You know exactly what I mean." His eyes glinted fiercely. He meant Vara. Yes! He had seen Vara here in Jerusalem.

"I'm supposed to stay here all week then? Locked in this prison?"

He shrugged. "Go home if you like. If you don't want to see me."

"Oh no! Barak! That's not what I meant!"

He turned from her. "Then don't leave. I'll let you know when it's time to come out. Trust me. Now I've got to go."

He slammed the door and ran down the steps.

HEH-VAV

Marcus was days later than Miryam getting to Jerusalem. Days behind the start of the Jewish festival of Succoth. Days after tens of thousands of pilgrims stretched the seams of the Holy City, clogging the streets, crowding the Temple Mount.

Like Passover in the springtime, the autumn holy days drew a huge attendance. Marcus knew what a challenge he faced.

425

How would he ever find Miryam in the mobs?

How would he locate Yeshua to warn him of a plot?

It was late, long after sundown, when Marcus arrived at the base of the last intervening hill north of Jerusalem. The road was deserted. Everyone except the centurion had already arrived at a place of shelter for the night.

Over the rise, the sky to the south glowed, blotting out the stars.

Why was it so light? The sky could not have been any brighter if Jerusalem had been in flames.

At the top of the mount was an overlook, a vantage point where religious pilgrims caught their first glimpse of Zion. There tradition called for them to pause, to sing hymns, and to give thanks for a safe arrival.

Spurring Pavor forward, Marcus had no intention of stopping or singing. Yet despite his impatience, the panorama spread out below him made him wheel his mount sharply to a halt.

Jerusalem was surrounded by campfires! The watchfires of an encircling army hemmed in the capital!

A siege! Marcus' experience campaigning made his thoughts jump instantly to a military explanation. Had the Jews raised a rebellion? Had Pilate drawn in the legions to combat an insurrection?

Was Miryam trapped in the middle of a war?

Marcus listened for the sounds of conflict, for the grinding noise of sharpening blades, for screams of terror.

What he heard instead was music: trumpets and cymbals, pipes and singing.

And laughter.

All around Jerusalem, but especially covering the Mount of Olives on the east, the space outside the walls was planted thick with the tents of pilgrims. Outside each tent was a fire. Around each fire people danced, celebrating as if they would revel the entire night.

Commemorating the wanderings of their ancestors, Succoth was a time when city dwellers built booths on the roofs of their houses and out-of-town visitors pitched encampments.

Which made Marcus' task even more impossible.

Where in all this multiplied confusion could he possibly come across Miryam? How could he track down Yeshua?

Marcus' anxious energy evaporated. Wearily he concluded that tonight there was nothing to do except find a place to rest. Tomorrow he would use the Temple Mount as a starting point in his search.

■■■■

Finally, it was the dawn of *Hoshana Rabbah*.

The last and greatest day of Succoth, the Feast of Tabernacles.

As he had done all week. Barak rose before

the sun, intending to slip out and leave Miryam alone until after dark. When it was safe he would sneak back to her, unnoticed.

Their time together had been spent in desperate taking from one another.

She took from him, yet was never fulfilled.

He took from her with the frantic passion of a man in a hurry—too busy to see her, too disinterested to care.

When she asked him to hold her, he dismissed her irritably and went to sleep.

She knew now that their relationship was no longer a question of love, but simply a matter of holding on. There was nothing else.

Today she opened her eyes just in time to see the door close.

Would he come back to her tonight? she wondered.

He had left his belongings behind. Yes, he would come back. There would be one last attempt to find herself in his arms. One final hour in which she would pretend he loved her.

What then?

His footsteps retreated quickly down the stairs, then onto the paving stones of the street as he made his way to the morning ceremony.

Miryam had not chanced following him to see the sight for herself, but she remembered it from her childhood.

For six days a specially chosen *cohen*, a temple priest, was escorted through Jerusalem's streets, bearing a golden pitcher. Accompanied by trumpet blasts and singing, he filled the vessel from the Pool of Siloam in the oldest quarter of the Holy City. The water rose in the place where King David first made Jerusalem his capital city.

Then, with music and dancing, the *cohen* ceremoniously carried his sacred burden back to the Temple Mount. There he delivered it to the *cohen hagadol,* the high priest.

Each morning of the festival, Caiaphas received the pitcher while dressed in his ceremonial blue robe and headdress. Clasped at his shoulders was the multihued ephod, and on his chest rested the array of precious stones representing the twelve tribes. The garment's fringe of golden pomegranates and bells jingled as he walked barefoot toward the altar. There he poured the water into the basin at the altar's pedestal, symbolizing the prayers of the nation for rain.

The observance also signified the outpouring of the *Ruach HaKodesh,* the Spirit of the Most High, on His Chosen People, Israel.

While *cohanim* blew golden trumpets, the Levites sang, "Therefore with joy shall you draw water from the wells of salvation!"

For six days Miryam sat at the window and watched crowds of pilgrims calling hosannas as the golden pitcher of water was carried into the temple. She spread her breakfast on the sill and listened with wistful pleasure to distant music rising from the courtyard.

Today; the last, the seventh day, something else would be added.

Waving palm branches, a rank of men thousands deep, surrounding the sanctuary, would surge forward. These were not priests or Levites, for on this one day ordinary people were permitted to dance around the altar of sacrifice.

"*Adonai*, please save us!" they would chant. "*Adonai*, please prosper us!"

By the Feast of Tabernacles, the New Year observance, *Rosh Hashanah*, was long past. Gone for the year was the plea to be recorded in the "Book of Life."

Also over and done was Yom Kippur, the Day of Atonement, when the high priest entered the Holy of Holies. Believing Jews repented of their failings, trusting that their names would be sealed in that scroll of the Most High.

But those who came late to repentance, who had missed their earlier chance at forgiveness, were not left without hope.

On *Hoshana Rabbah*, everyone got one last and final opportunity to be reconciled with the Almighty.

> *Adonai, please save us!*
> *Adonai, please prosper us!*
> *Blessed is he who comes in*
> *the name of Adonai!*

If you believed in that sort of thing.

If you still thought that forgiveness existed anywhere for someone like you.

It was the fear of being recognized and cast out that had kept Miryam from the temple and the festivities. But this morning a longing stronger than her fears urged her to go.

She got up, washed, and braided her hair. Dressed in her finest white linen she joined the pilgrims flooding through the streets toward the temple.

■ ■ ■ ■

The Damascus Road led straight toward the south-facing entry to the great portico of the temple. Miryam was carried effortlessly along with the throng. Hemmed in, she was swept under the viaduct connecting the temple enclosure and the city. From overhead snatches of psalms drifted downward:

> *Give thanks to*
> *Adonai; for he is good,*
> *For his grace continues*
> *forever.*

It was, Miryam thought, comforting to believe that grace...the undeserved kindness of the Almighty...could never be exhausted. But she knew better. There were those who were beyond redemption...and yet, and yet...

If she could just speak to Yeshua.

The air was sharp with the chill and tangy with the wood smoke. Miryam tugged the shawl closely around her shoulders.

The mob surged like the crest of a wave racing toward shore. Up the ramp to the steps, up the steps to the portico, through the archways beneath the Hall of Meeting.

Spilling out onto the plaza known as the

Court of Gentiles, the tide of travelers widened and slowed. Miryam slipped aside from the main current into a lesser eddy of people.

Here and there sun glinted on the helmets of the temple guards. Roman soldiers were evenly spaced at all entrances.

Was Vara among them?

A family of six were near Miryam. Thinking to blend into the mass and vanish, she joined their group, matching her step stride for stride with the mother. While the father charged ahead, the mother, carrying an infant, lagged behind. A trio of wide-eyed children, frightened by the commotion, clung to her skirts.

The mother was confused. Her husband had disappeared, anxious to join the men in the inner courtyard.

Miryam spotted the entrance to the Court of Women. She would be safe there.

"It's this way," Miryam suggested to the woman.

"The children!" sighed the exasperated mother. "In such a crowd as this I could blink and lose one."

With a smile Miryam scooped up a three-year-old boy, placing him on her hip. Grateful for the help, the woman followed her.

Miryam led the way toward the sanctuary, built by Herod the Great almost fifty years before. But the Court of the Women was packed to capacity.

"No more room! No more room!" instructed a temple guard, directing women back into the Court of Gentiles.

Miryam remembered that another gate opened almost directly toward the altar. If they could climb the steps beside that portal, perhaps they would be able to see.

Squeezing through the press of bodies, Miryam forged a way for the family. They were in luck.

The sound of the shofar rang out, silencing the crowd as Miryam reached the entrance to the sacred Court of Israelites. No woman or foreigner was allowed within. But Miryam could plainly see the elevated platform of the altar where the high priest stood. All twenty-four divisions of the priesthood surrounded the altar. Behind them were tens of thousands of ordinary men holding palm branches as they waited expectantly for *Simchat Beit HaSho'evah,* the Feast of the Water Drawing.

Shepherding the family in front of her, Miryam watched as Caiaphas accepted the golden pitcher from the young priest. There was a fanfare of trumpets as Caiaphas turned toward the basin.

The child whispered to Miryam, "This means tomorrow it will rain."

Miryam nodded curtly and put a finger to her lips to silence him. The singing began as Caiaphas poured the water of Siloam into the basin at the foot of the altar.

> *Adonai, please save us!*
> *Adonai, please proper us!*
> *Blessed is he who comes in*
> *the name of Adonai!*

433

Silence. A cool wind whistled down from the pinnacles of the temple.

Miryam gasped as Yeshua came forward to the altar from the ranks of ordinary men. His steps were unhurried, solemn. He lifted his head and, with open gaze, embraced Israel gathered before him like a flock.

In a voice strong and unwavering he cried out to his people, "If anyone is thirsty, let him come to me and drink! Whoever trusts in me, as the *Tanakh* says, rivers of living water will flow from his inmost being!"

The words echoed in the porticos until the very columns of the temple shouted back affirmation of what he proclaimed.

Tears stung Miryam's eyes.

Silence. The wind. No one dared to speak.

Who was he?

What gave him the right to know about her thirst?

Caiaphas stumbled backwards and braced himself on the altar stones. Mouths of the priests opened in astonishment and anger, but there was no word or sound from the congregation.

Majestic. Contemplative. Yeshua stood before Israel like a shepherd, offering them something more.

Water to quench their worst thirst!

But where was such water? And how could he offer it to them?

The sun shone on him and, for an instant, Miryam thought his face seemed brighter than the rest. Then he took two steps back and melted into the congregation.

There followed a murmur, an awkward recovery of the rhythm of things. The trumpets blew. The music began. The dancing commenced.

The little boy on Miryam's hip declared over the din, "It will rain tomorrow."

Miryam put the child down beside his mother and wiped her tears. How could she ask Yeshua for this water? Not merely to drink and satisfy her longing, but to wash away her sins?

She took up a post beside the gate and scanned the faces of the men who danced and sang within. To find Yeshua! To speak to him! To ask him for help!

And then the ashen face of Barak appeared among the revelers. He pushed his way toward her, angry that she had come out in spite of his orders.

She raised her chin in defiance and looked away from him, pretending she had not seen him.

Then she saw something that made her turn cold inside.

On the far edge of the crowd was Vara, talking with two *cohanim*. Had he seen Miryam?

Her heart sank. She covered her head with her shawl and fled the temple grounds. She did not stop running until she reached the safety of the room.

ZAYEEN-KHET

It was the last sunset of the feast. Marcus' search had been fruitless. Several times rumors reported Yeshua was preaching in a one certain spot or other. On each occasion the rebbe had moved elsewhere before Marcus caught up with him.

He even heard Yeshua taught openly in the temple courts. The religious authorities were perplexed as to what to do about it. Apparently the priests were afraid of the throngs of pilgrims because Yeshua's popularity was increasing.

But each time the centurion's pursuit brought him back to Mount Zion, Yeshua had slipped away again.

Despite the teacher's elusiveness, Marcus knew the authorities would not wait long. Having a plot in hand, they would spring it as soon as possible.

If Marcus could just determine the exact nature of the threat.

He stayed at an inn rather than at the Antonia and conducted his searches wrapped in a cloak. Marcus wanted to avoid explaining his presence in the capital.

Surprisingly, he did not think much about Vara. Somehow, since Carta's healing, revenge was not of first importance anymore.

Tonight was likely his last opportunity to find either of those he sought. Tomorrow the holiday would end, and the travelers would disperse.

Maybe that was what the authorities were waiting for.

But if Marcus could find Yeshua in time, then the rebbe might get out of Jerusalem by mingling with the multitudes.

Of Miryam he found no trace.

Marcus' steps led him back to the Temple Mount as if the sanctuary were a beacon.

Preparations were well under way for the nightly festivities.

Four golden lamp stands towered seventy-five feet into the air. Each menorah lifted large gleaming bowls above the holy mountain. Each lamp was fed by a reservoir holding two gallons of oil. As Marcus watched, the younger *cohanim,* strapping temple workers, climbed up narrow ladders. Each had a jug of oil tied to his back, secured by a forehead strap.

After filling the menorahs, the *cohanim* again ascended to trim the lamps with fresh wicks.

At the instant the sun dipped below the western horizon there was an expectant hush.

It was the quietest moment in days.

Caiaphas, the high priest, stood on the sanctuary platform, holding cupped hands aloft.

Jewish law established that one day ended and another began when it was no longer possible to tell black thread from white by natural light.

When Caiaphas' hands dropped to his sides

a blast of rams' horn trumpets echoed from every side of the square.

With the sounding of the shofar the *cohanim* once more scrambled aloft, each bearing a torch to ignite the menorahs.

Light exploded across the Temple Mount. The darkness was not pushed aside, it vanished completely. Across Jerusalem every courtyard displayed torches and bonfires.

Singing and dancing erupted as well.

White-clad Levites of the musician order appeared with harps, cymbals, and flutes. Music flowed over the hilltop, pouring across the city like a flood of blessing.

The celebration of the Great Hosanna continued.

Waving palm branches, elderly, white-bearded men danced around the bases of the lamps.

Younger men started up an impromptu juggling of lighted torches.

Accompanied by the music and hand-clapping, the crowd burst into a hymn. Another psalm followed and another.

Hours passed. Yeshua did not appear. Perhaps he had already been warned and fled the city.

Marcus listened as the songs of praise reached an ecstatic climax:

> *Adonai is God, and He gives us*
> *light!*
> *Join in the pilgrim festival with*
> *branches*
> *All the way to the horns of the altar!*

At that moment, Yeshua appeared, seemingly from nowhere, as if he had been present the whole time.

Yeshua stood atop the flight of steps leading to the temple treasury, and his voice rang out in the night air, more piercing than the trumpet blasts. "I am the light of the world; whoever follows me will never walk in darkness but will have the light which gives life!"

Heads turned to see who had spoken.

Marcus wondered what Yeshua had meant. Indeed, who was this man who cured mortal wounds and understood hearts?

With his own eyes Marcus had seen him make the lame walk and the blind see—and then heal Carta with a word. Then Yeshua had asked his critics the question, "Which is easier? To heal the body? Or to forgive sins?"

Until now it had been natural for Marcus to exist in a physical world and never give a thought to the world of his heart. What a dark place it had been for him until he heard the teaching of the rebbe. Even love had been a tool to get what he wanted from Miryam.

Marcus was certain that a physical ailment was easier to repair than a crippled soul. To be made new required an act of will on the part of the receiver. To recognize the need for forgiveness! To ask for it! To receive it with faith and humble joy! And then, to stand up and walk! To be inwardly changed forever by the power of undeserved mercy!

That was a miracle!

This candle of understanding flickered in

the centurion's soul. And he sensed there was much more to come for him.

What was this light Yeshua promised? Was he offering an end to confusion for anyone who walked in his teaching? What would life be like if it had a comprehensible purpose, a clearly illuminated path of truth to follow?

Some of the worshippers appeared delighted to see Yeshua. Marcus heard the whispers around him. "If Messiah was to come, would he do more wonderful miracles than this man?"

Men dressed as Pharisees and others rounded on him. Their ecstatically pious expressions were instantly replaced with scowls. How dare Yeshua compare himself to the light given by *Adonai!*

Sensing trouble, Marcus started forward.

And then, in a group of Torah scholars and Pharisees not far from where Caiaphas stood, Marcus spotted Barak bar Halfi. There was nodding and pointing toward Yeshua. Then bar Halfi suddenly led a group of men away from the scene, toward one of the exits from the temple courtyard. Ten temple guards and brawny young priests.

Wherever Barak was going, Miryam could not be far away.

Marcus had to make an instant decision. He followed Barak.

An hour of circuitous walking ensued. They fought their way through the mobs of revelers heading up the ramp toward the temple. Barak was at the head of the only party moving away from the light.

Marcus trailed them at a discreet distance.

The squad halted at the base of a flight of stairs. Barak bar Halfi had a brief conference with his band. *Stay here and wait,* his gestures said.

As Marcus remained in a shadowed alcove, Barak climbed the steps and entered a room.

■ ■ ■ ■

Marcus heard a rooster crow.

It was the first sign of life in Jerusalem in hours. The last of the hardiest revelers had long since gone back to his tent. The torches of the last night of Succoth were blackened sticks, long since extinguished.

The squad of temple police and priests sprawled asleep on the steps, muffled in their cloaks against the chill. Even the lone man standing guard dozed by the balustrade, except when he stamped his feet to drive out the cold.

What was happening? What if Miryam was not in the room into which Barak had gone?

Was Marcus wasting his time?

His instincts said otherwise. He was certain Barak had led him to Miryam.

But why have sentries posted outside?

It was as if Marcus understood only half of a plot. He and the others waited for the second part to unfold.

The tramp of boots roused him.

The noise also alerted the guard, who hurriedly shook his comrades out of their slumber. As a shape loomed up, they stood to attention.

Praetorian Vara approached the temple police and *cohanim*. Marcus couldn't hear all that was said, but Vara's words reached him. "Good," Vara said. "We didn't lose him this time. He's already on his way back from the Mount of Olives. Be ready. The signal will come anytime now."

After accepting a salute, Vara turned on his heel and left.

She'll come to me where I say. Just have him *there.*

Barak bar Halfi's words to Vara replayed over and over in Marcus' head, and a dreadful certainty followed.

As gray light crept into the corners of the Holy City, there was a movement at the top of the stairs. The guards swarmed upward and rushed into the room.

A woman's piercing shriek rent the stillness. Then abruptly it was silenced.

Under his cloak Marcus gripped his sword hilt. What could he do against so many?

Barak emerged, dragging Miryam by the wrist. Her mouth was gagged. Her hair, unbound, swept from side to side as she peered frantically around for help. Barefoot and in her nightdress, Miryam was roughly shoved down the steps. Barak thrust Miryam into the hands of the guards and the priests, then turned away from the scene and left.

A diminutive man...the shopkeeper, perhaps...emerged from a ground-floor entry. Two of the guards threatened him, and he backed up quickly, slamming the door shut again.

There were priests in front, on either side, and more guards at the rear. In the center of the moving diamond, a grim-faced *cohen* and Miryam. She fought him, pulled away from him, dragging her heels.

He cuffed her across the cheek and yanked her forward again.

Along the way the *cohanim* gathered up stones and fist-sized chunks of rubble.

Follow! It was all Marcus knew to do.

■ ■ ■ ■

When Marcus exhaled, his breath hung before his face like a cloud on the climb up Mount Zion.

The marble blocks of the temple buildings were not yet warmed by the sun. The courts, so recently thronged by thousands, stood nearly deserted. Last night the scenes had been blurred and softened by the torches and the singing. Today the air, the architecture, even the day, had sharp edges to them.

What if the first time Miryam of Magdala was brought face-to-face with Yeshua it meant the death of them both?

Had Marcus somehow connected two people he cared about in a bond of tragedy?

The smoke of the first of the morning sacrifices lifted a motionless black thread into the sky.

Even from a distance Marcus recognized Yeshua. The rebbe was seated on the steps where the sun would warm his face. Around him a circle of two hundred listeners stood.

The commotion at the gate, soldiers dragging a weeping woman, made some of them back away in alarm.

Others, those dressed in the furs and brocades of well-to-do Pharisees, folded their arms across their chests. They knew what to expect. Like spectators in the arena, they wanted to be present at the kill. Smiles of excitement flickered across their faces.

Moving to his left, Marcus put a row of pillars between himself and the guards. Screened by the columns, he approached close enough to hear.

And to do what? Jump forward waving his sword and demand that she be freed? Nothing would be more conclusive of an illegal conspiracy than the presence of a traitorous centurion.

The gathering split apart, opening a corridor connecting Miryam and Yeshua. The teacher stood to receive the newcomers.

With Vara watching smugly at the side of the gathering, the *cohanim* flung Miryam into the middle of the ring, then stepped aside.

Her bare feet bloodied and stumbling, Miryam fell hard on her side. With visible effort she raised herself to her knees, then crouched there. Her hair hung down, obscuring her face, but her shoulders heaved with sobs.

"Rebbe," a priest said loudly. "This woman was caught in the act of committing adultery."

A gasp went up from the crowd.

"In our Torah," the priest continued, "it is

444

commanded that such a woman be stoned to death. What do you say about it?"

Yeshua looked at Miryam with eyes of compassion, saying nothing.

Stoned! Marcus gripped the edge of the marble column. Moving the folds of his cloak, he freed the clasp of the sword. Better that they die fighting than let her face the jagged rocks alone. It was so clear. That Miryam would be killed was incidental to the trap. If Yeshua suggested mercy, then he would be denounced as a false teacher and a lawbreaker.

But if he agreed with the sentence, then his teaching about forgiveness would be shown as a lie and his popularity would end.

The morning froze in place. No one moved or spoke. What would the teacher do? Would he sentence himself...or the woman?

Marcus saw Yeshua's head turn ever so slightly. His eyes lifted until he held Vara locked in his gaze. Marcus saw their stares meet, saw Vara's confident, arrogant smile falter.

The Praetorian dropped his eyes, mumbled something, backed away. He bumped into a priest, ducked his head, and strode briskly from the scene.

This wordless exchange took mere seconds.

What would happen? Would Yeshua see the scheme for what it was? Would he denounce the trap and call on his followers to stone the priests instead?

Yeshua bent down. With his palm he

smoothed the dust into an even surface. Then, using his finger, he wrote something.

Frustrated, the priest repeated, "What do you say, rebbe?"

A Pharisee took up the interrogation. "Sin is to be exposed and punished, according to the law! What is there to think about?"

A temple legal scholar added, "In the Torah, we find that both of them must die, the man who went to bed with the woman and..."

Another scribe hastily interrupted, "We all know what it says. We want to hear the rebbe explain his position on it."

Dusting off his hands, Yeshua stood. The front rank of the Pharisees and priests, who had pressed closer to see what he was writing, fell back a step.

"The one of you who is without sin," Yeshua said. His steady gaze moved slowly from face to face, not hurriedly, without worry or sign of anxiety. "Let him be the first to throw a stone at her."

Yeshua did not offer excuses, explanations, compromises. He did not rail at them. While his words hung in the still air, he stooped again and resumed writing in the dust.

No one else spoke. No one repeated any challenges.

A white-bearded Pharisee bowed his head and rubbed his eyes as if in prayer. Marcus saw the man look at Yeshua, then at Miryam, then up at the sun. Without a word he dropped his stone, turned, and made his way out of the circle.

A pair of Torah scholars frowned at each other. As Marcus watched, one raised his eyebrows in a question.

Replying, the other shook his head.

Both men let their weapons clatter to the pavement, then exited the crowd.

Slowly at first, in ones and twos, beginning with the oldest men present, the gathering dissolved, leaving fist-sized stones behind.

One young Pharisee, more fiery than his companions, grabbed a neighbor by the arm, trying to force him to stay. The friend angrily shook himself loose, tossed away his missile, and stalked off.

That broke any hostile will that remained.

Like ice melting in the sun, the rest of the circle flowed away from the scene, leaving Yeshua and Miryam alone.

Heaving a great sigh, Marcus slumped against the pillar.

Miryam removed the gag from her mouth. Rubbing her wrists, she glanced fearfully over her shoulder, as though expecting the mob to rush at her again.

Standing beside her, Yeshua waved his hand around the deserted courtyard. "Where are they?" he said. "Has no one condemned you?"

In a tone full of amazement Miryam said, "No man... *Lord.*"

Then, ashamed, unable to meet his steady gaze, she bowed her head again.

Marcus stared. *She really was guilty,* he thought. *And she realizes that Yeshua knows it. She's waiting for* him *to condemn her!*

"Neither do I condemn you," Yeshua said kindly. "Now go, and don't sin anymore."

He turned from her, not needing an answer.

She nodded, blinking back tears, stretching out her hand as if to call him back. As if there was something more she wanted to say.

But he walked on toward the gate of the temple, leaving her to wonder how it was she was alive.

Marcus watched her from a distance as she sat like a child on the pavement and studied clouds scudding across the sky. Their shadows seemed to pass through her like thoughts that heaven was thinking for her. The sky filled, covering the sun, blossoming with darkness. Still she did not get up.

Lightning split the sky in the east, forking many times before it struck the ground.

A plump raindrop struck her upturned face as she sat, unharmed, amid the rubble of discarded stones.

Gentle mercy!

Thunder rolled across Jerusalem.

Miryam smiled.

Marcus knew at that instant that chaos had fallen from her. Dense confusion parted and fled. Her eyes were clear, her face bright with understanding.

She spoke. "Marcus."

He stepped from behind the pillar. "I'm here."

"You knew the truth about him before I did."

"Yes."

"There is one thing more I have to do. Will you take me home now, Marcus?"

The rain began to fall. One and two drops turned into a torrent. She held out her hands, receiving the blessing.

TET-YOD

Marcus wrapped Miryam in his cloak and lifted her onto his horse. He led her toward home, walking all the way. Rain swept across the mountains in sheets.

For a day and a night and most of a second day he walked. They did not speak. He left her to her thoughts. Sometimes she slept, nodding in rhythm with the unhurried pace of the animal. But mostly her eyes were wide, her lips parted in a smile, as though she were drinking in the world for the first time.

Life. She would search its mountains and sail its rivers and inquire after the hearts of its people.

The storm broke. Light and shadow danced across the land.

Common sights seemed to pierce her soul like music.

Hills covered by night.

Candles flickering in dim houses.

Moonlight glowing in the shallow stream they crossed.

In the morning he stopped to buy bread in a village. Her head turned with pleasure at the sight of women talking together in a doorway while their children played in the garden.

Beyond the little houses along the road, she looked kindly at the shepherd who gathered a wayward lamb into his arms and carried it back to its frantic mother.

Her gaze lingered on the flight of a hawk circling above the stubble of newly harvested fields.

She stroked the bowed neck of the horse as he grazed beside her.

Other travelers passed them on the road and turned away in disgust from the soldier and the lady. Serenely, Miryam watched them go and did not hate them for judging her. Marcus knew somehow that she no longer saw her image reflected in the angry eyes of strangers.

Mercy had created a new heart within her.

■ ■ ■ ■

They arrived at the gate of her Magdala house before sunset on the second day. Miryam slid from Pavor's back.

Would she speak now?

Clutching his mud-spattered cloak around her, she said in a voice hoarse from disuse, "I can't rest until I find him. He was the only one who rightly could have thrown a stone at me...and...there's something I need to tell him, you see...and...take me on to Capernaum with you?"

Dusk was settling over the hills. Marcus was tired. "He could be anywhere."

"Will you help me, Marcus?"

He nodded, understanding. "I'll wait while you bathe and change."

A Syrian servant tended Pavor.

Tavita brought Marcus soap, water, a fresh tunic, and a tray of food. She peered at him curiously, clearly wanting to ask what had transpired in Jerusalem and how it was that he, and not another, had come back with her mistress. But months of Miryam's madness had cowed the old woman into silence. She held her tongue and went away to draw her own conclusions.

It was night when Miryam came downstairs. She carried a clay lamp in one hand and a leather pouch over her shoulder. Her skin glowed from scrubbing. Thick dark hair was braided. Though she dressed plainly in a pale-blue woolen cloak, there was no concealing her extraordinary beauty.

And now there was something more...or perhaps something less. What was missing from those wide, dark eyes? Had she finally let go of suffering as a way of life? Was it that she no longer desired her desires? Strange to see her like this, when all the things she had clung to so fiercely had floated away. Even more, she was not empty from their absence, but newly filled and changed and more beautiful for her clarity. She was, Marcus thought, like a clear glass goblet letting the color of new wine shimmer in the light.

For the first time since he met her, he felt no pain when he saw her.

Had he loved her before? Tonight he was happy for her. Maybe that was love.

"I'm ready." She smiled into his eyes.

Now it was his turn to gaze in wonder. Tears brimmed in his eyes and then in hers.

"Don't," she laughed, brushing his cheek. "I can't do this if you cry too."

He shrugged, blinked at her, and looked away, pleased somehow that she let him be a part of this...of *this!* "Let's go then."

■■■■

It was quite late that night when Marcus and Miryam reached Capernaum. A nightbird disturbed by their passing flitted amid the bare branches of the olive trees. A solitary frog croaked in the reeds.

Pavor placed each hoof carefully as if as footsore and weary as his master.

Entering the town, Marcus spotted two men that he recognized: rabbis from the synagogue. They looked askance at Miryam but responded politely to the centurion's hail. "Do you know if the Teacher is back from Jerusalem?" he inquired.

"Yes," one of them responded. "He's at supper at the home of Simon the Pharisee."

Miryam was eager to go directly there, but Marcus asked her to be patient a few minutes more.

Outside his own darkened house, Marcus

lifted Miryam down. "I'll just be a moment," he said. Removing the bridle, he turned Pavor into the pen.

The air in the house was chilly, as cold as outside. Marcus gathered his cloak closer around him and crossed in the dark to the armor rack. Removing the *corona obsidionalis* from the top of the wooden cross, he rejoined Miryam.

The home of Simon the Pharisee was not far from the synagogue but several paces nearer the lakeshore. Like its owner, it was the model of uprightness. No graceful columns, no decorative terrace, Simon's house was square and inhospitable in its appearance. The illumination coming from its interior was only what escaped from behind heavy shutters. The scraps of conversation emerging from the home were muted.

Marcus was concerned for Miryam. Why couldn't she have bright sunshine and cheery surroundings?

She must have felt his distress because she remarked, "This is right, Marcus. Don't worry." Reaching into the leather pouch, Miryam withdrew an alabaster bottle that gleamed and sparkled in a stray beam of light. Handing Marcus the now-empty pouch, Miryam walked boldly to the door and knocked.

Marcus lingered at the bottom of the steps.

It took three tries, but eventually the summons was answered by Simon's steward. As the door opened, the noise of the dinner party, talking and the clink of glasses, amplified. Lifting a lamp beside the entry, the servant recognized Miryam. "What do you want?" he asked, with no attempt at civility. The man stood squarely blocking the doorway.

Marcus could not make out Miryam's first entreaty, but the steward loudly refused her request for admission. "Go away," Marcus heard him say. "Your kind is not wanted here."

Miryam did not back down. "I must see the Teacher," she insisted. "I have something for him. Please."

She was so determined, Marcus thought, so certain that nothing would prevent her from seeing Yeshua. This time she was not running from him, but *to* him.

Tossing the cloak back from his shoulders so that the full sweep of his armor and insignia were visible, Marcus climbed the steps into the light. "This lady must be admitted," he ordered.

Stuttering and stumbling as he moved aside, the steward allowed Miryam to enter the house. Even when Marcus did not follow, the servant left the door standing open, as though afraid to offend a Roman officer by closing it in his face. Finally the steward pushed it closed from behind, without allowing himself to be seen.

Marcus crossed the road and sat on the edge of a low stone wall to watch and listen. He tugged the cloak back into place, huddling within it as the chill of weather and weariness overtook him.

Like water draining from a bath, the sounds

of conversation emanating from Simon's house dwindled and dropped to silence.

Miryam's presence had brought the banquet to a standstill.

■ ■ ■ ■

Time passed.

A gust of wind coming across the lake reached the shoreline, rustling the tree limbs. The breeze passed Simon's house, then stroked Marcus' face with a perfumed touch. Inhaling, Marcus breathed in the scent of nard, the most expensive of all fragrances, brought all the way from India. He had never known anyone who could afford it; in fact, he had only scented it on the most wealthy aristocratic ladies in Rome. What was the source of that costly aroma? How did it come to be in an insignificant, out-of-the-way place like Capernaum in Galilee?

More time passed.

Miryam of Magdala emerged from the house of Simon the Pharisee. With her, almost visible in its intensity, came the aroma of perfume. The fragrance of a garden in summer, of an orchard in blossom, overwhelmed him. She carried a lighted clay lamp in one hand. By its flicker Marcus saw she had been crying. Her hair hung loose over her shoulders.

"Are you all right?" he asked.

She tried to speak, could not, so nodded instead.

Putting out his hand, he touched her face.

It was still moist from her tears. Covering his hand with hers, she said at last, "I'm all right...like never before. I can sleep now. I'm going to Joanna's."

Frowning in thought, Marcus said, "I have something I must do...do you mind going alone?"

Miryam smiled at him. "It's just a few steps," she replied. When she removed her fingers, the priceless aroma lingered on his.

He watched after her as the lamplight faded into the distance.

■■■■

Another hour passed.

In ones and twos, Simon's guests emerged from the house. Though all spoke in low voices, there was a tone of amazement and uncertainty running through every conversation.

At last Yeshua appeared in the doorway, framed in a square of light. He told Simon good night, thanking him for the supper. As the teacher descended the steps unaccompanied, the most powerful aroma of perfume hovered around him.

Marcus called to him out of the night. "Lord...a word with you, please. Sir."

Yeshua crossed the deserted lane. Before the teacher reached him, Marcus dropped to one knee and waited.

Then the Lord stood before him. Near enough to touch. Waiting for him to speak. Marcus was filled with a sense of awe, of gratitude.

Haltingly at first, Marcus said, "I have... I have knelt before bronze gods, generals...kings of the earth. I have offered my sword and my life to them. But they never responded. They never...changed anyone. Others may demand loyalty, but you...you alone are worthy to be king!"

Lifting his hand from his side, Marcus extended the *corona obsidionalis*. "Please, Lord," he said. "Take this. I received it for bravery in battle. But you! You win victories without spears or arrows! Without fury you free captives and heal the wounded as they lie dying on the field! Take it!"

There was a long pause while the wreath somehow linked the two.

But Yeshua did not accept the gift.

He placed his palm on the centurion's brow. Warmth and peace emanated from his touch. For an instant Marcus glimpsed the star-frosted sky glistening like a diadem above Yeshua's head. The order of all things was ordained within his words!

The vision receded. A dog barked. A nightbird sang. The wind moved the branches of the trees.

"Marcus," Yeshua said with compassion, "I saw you at Idistaviso. There is no greater love than for a man to lay down his life for his friends...but my own battle is not yet done." When Marcus raised his head to question, Yeshua added, "I have another crown waiting for me in Jerusalem. And I promise you this, Marcus Longinus: you will be at my feet when I wear it...and then you will understand."

EPILOGUE

With these words the first scroll ended:

"*De profundis*... Out of the depths of despair I cried unto you, O Lord! *Ad perpetuam rei memorium...haud ignota loquor.* For the perpetual remembrance of the thing...I speak of things by no means unknown."

Here and there a letter was smudged. Tears had dropped on the ink.

Two signatures graced the bottom of the page:

MIRYAM MAGDALEN
MARCUS QUINTUS LONGINUS

Moshe Sachar looked up at the painted stars that glistened on the dome above him. How many hours had passed since he first opened this book?

How many lifetimes had come and gone since the beginning, when Miryam of Magdala came to Jerusalem: betrayed, guilty, accused, condemned, pardoned, forgiven, and changed forever by mercy?

How many weary pilgrims had knelt in the dust of the Holy City to search for the words Jesus had written with his fingertip?

What kingdoms had been forged by war and fallen into ruin since Marcus Longinus offered his crown to the gentle Carpenter of Nazareth?

Was their story just a legend? A tale so old it was merely a memory forever embedded in the stones of Jerusalem?

Moshe rested his head in his hands.

What of Jerusalem today? Did it survive? Who would tell its story?

Israel reborn! Would it perish waiting for One to come who would finally wear its crown?

There was a stirring in the alcove. Alfie Halder, carrying a candle, emerged into the hall. His shirt was untucked. His hair was mussed. He blinked at Moshe in a moment of confusion.

"Did you sleep well?" Moshe asked.

"Where are the others?" Alfie glanced around the chamber. "Are they gone?"

"There's no one here but us."

"But I heard them. Saw them," Alfie insisted.

"Just a dream, Alfie," Moshe consoled. "I've been here reading all the time you were sleeping. No one but me."

Alfie frowned and came to sit beside Moshe. "Yes. I dream a lot. Too much sometimes. Must be a dream, I guess. A very long dream. A soldier and a beautiful woman. A boy who was hurt bad. Jerusalem. Jesus. Words in the dust. Stones dropping to the ground like rain while they turned away. Finally there was a crown."

Moshe leaned forward. "Words in the dust? What words? What did they say?

Alfie lifted his face and closed his eyes, remembering. "Ten numbers and words after them. The laws. Then beside each one that was broken, he wrote a name. First just the men who were there and then... So many names. They came by themselves in the dust at his feet. So fast I couldn't read them anymore. And I thought...you know... I thought that maybe he wrote everyone's name in the dust. Everyone who ever lived and everyone who ever will live."

Moshe sat back in amazement. It made sense. "Anything else?"

"Yes. In the end he wrote one word across them all. Mercy." Inhaling deeply, Alfie asked, "Can you smell that? Nice, huh? Like orange blossoms. Moshe? Like a summer garden. Her perfume. Just a dream. Like flowers. Very nice, don't you think?"

GLOSSARY

Adonai—Lord
aliyah—pilgrimage
bema—pulpit of a synagogue
B'resheet—book of Genesis
centurion—Roman officer commanding a
  century
century—company of 100 Roman soldiers
cohen (pl. cohanim)—priest
cohort—Roman military unit containing about
  500 men
corona obsidionalis—Roman battlefield wreath
  awarded for exceptional heroism
denarius (pl. denarii)—standard Roman coin,
  made of silver
Gadol Hacohen—the High Priest
Ha'Elyon—the Most High
haftarah—a scripture portion
HaMashiach—the Messiah
Hoshana Rabbah—lit. "the great hosanna";
  the last day of the feast of Succoth
Kaddish—synagogue prayer that begins,
  "Magnified and sanctified be His Great
  Name . . ."
karkom—crocus bulbs whose flowers
  produce the spice saffron
khamseen—hot desert wind
maiestas—crime of defaming the Roman
  emperor or state
mikveh—ritual bath

Pesach—Passover

pilum—type of javelin

Praetorians—elite unit of Roman soldiers, designed to be the emperor's bodyguards

Primus Pilus—lit. First Javelin; the leading centurion of a cohort

rebbe—rabbi or teacher

Rosh Hashanah—New Year, the beginning of the ten Days of Awe

Ruach HaKodesh—the Holy Spirit

seder—Passover service including a ceremonial dinner

shammash—synagogue attendant

Shema—central tenet of Judaism: "Hear, O Israel, the Lord our God is one Lord."

sicarius (pl. sicarii)—assassin

Succoth—Feast of Tabernacles, the fall harvest festival

talmidim—followers

Tanakh—Holy Scripture

tesserarius—guard sergeant

Torah—Jewish sacred scripture; corresponds to the first five books of the Christian Bible

Yom Kippur—Day of Atonement